Dale Brown

A former US Air Force captain, Dale Brown served as a navigator from 1978 to 1986, logging thousands of hours aboard both B-52 and FB-111 bombers. Since the success of his first novel, *Flight of the Old Dog*, he has had an unbroken string of bestsellers, including *Day of the Cheetah*, *Hammerheads*, *Sky Masters*, *Night of the Hawk* (the sequel to *Flight of the Old Dog*), *Chains of Command* and, most recently, *Storming Heaven*. He lives in Nevada, where he is working on his latest novel, *Shadows of Steel*.

'Dale Brown is the best military adventure writer in the country today.'   CLIVE CUSSLER

'Clancy's got serious company.'   *New York Daily News*

'When a former pilot with years of experience in America's Strategic Air Command turns his hand to writing thrillers you can take their authenticity for granted. His writing is exceptional and the dialogue, plots and characters are first-class . . . far too good to be missed.'   *Sunday Mirror*

BY DALE BROWN

DALE BROWN

SILVER TOWER

HarperCollins*Publishers*

HarperCollins*Publishers*
77–85 Fulham Palace Road,
Hammersmith, London W6 8JB

This paperback edition 1993
3 5 7 9 8 6 4

Previously published in paperback by Grafton 1989
Reprinted twice

First published in Great Britain by
Grafton 1988

ISBN 0 586 20269 2

Set in Times

Printed in Great Britain by
Caledonian International Book Manufacturer, Glasgow

Silver Tower is dedicated to my Dad, who worked a lot of overtime to get me my first telescope that got me interested in the stars; and to my Mom, who spent a lot of long nights and early Saturday mornings ferrying me around to dozens of Science Fairs all over New York State so I could show off my telescope.

Your love and patience has paid off. See what you made me do?

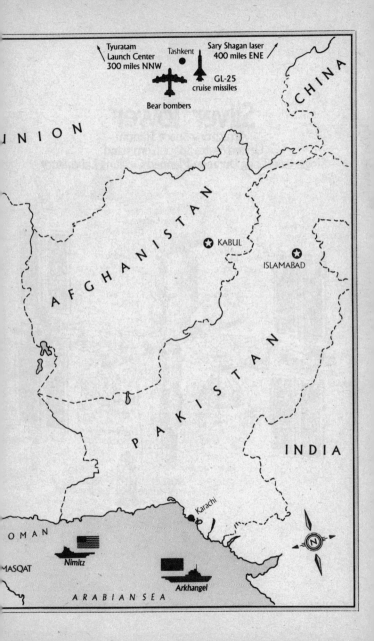

Silver Tower
Armstrong Space Station
United States Space Command
Single-Keel Long Duration Manned Orbiting Laboratory

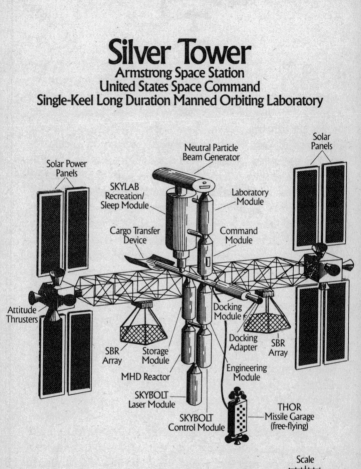

Solar Power Panels

Neutral Particle Beam Generator

Solar Panels

SKYLAB Recreation/Sleep Module

Laboratory Module

Cargo Transfer Device

Command Module

Attitude Thrusters

Docking Module

SBR Array

Storage Module

Docking Adapter

SBR Array

MHD Reactor

Engineering Module

SKYBOLT Laser Module

SKYBOLT Control Module

THOR Missile Garage (free-flying)

Scale
0   50 feet

Acknowledgements

I would like to thank several agencies, corporations and individuals for supplying information useful in the creation of this novel.

Thanks to the Defense Advanced Research Projects Agency for information on the National Aerospace Plane, the Scramjet Test Project, and the Hypersonic Technology Program; to Aerojet-General Corporation Sacramento, California, for information on the scramjet engine, space station design, and hypersonic engine designs; and to British Aerospace Corporation for information on their Horizontal Takeoff and Landing (HOTOL) technology for single-stage-to-orbit spacecraft.

The National Aeronautics and Space Administration has been of significant help in gathering information for this story, especially Mark Hess of the Public Affairs Division; also the Space Transport Division, the Advanced Space Flight Division, the Ames Research Center, and the Johnson Space Center were of immense help.

The primary source of information on vessels and weapons for both sides of the Iron Curtain has been the United States Naval Institute Military Database, Arlington, Virginia.

There are several very special individuals to whom I am especially grateful for their time and effort in helping me put this story together: For insights on the unusual problems of living and working in space, I would like to thank Loren W. Acton, senior staff scientist, Palo Alto Research Laboratory, Lockheed Missiles and Space Company. Loren was a payload specialist aboard the STS

51-F, Spacelab 2 mission, flying aboard Challenger in July 1985, and in a delightful meeting in San Francisco with members of the Association of Space Explorers USA gave me a feel for the unique stresses and unforgettable joys of travelling aboard the Space Shuttle.

For his help in gathering information on the Soviet Union's civilian and military space programmes, I would like to thank author, researcher, space expert, and good friend Dennis T. Hall, and his wife Dana. Dennis had been kind enough to take calls, send information, and answer my questions at all hours of the day, and I wish him success in his own stellar writing career.

For being there when I needed them, I would like to thank my good friends Ray and Alice Jefferson and Darrell and Susan Neufeld.

And, as always, I would like to thank Rick Horgan, senior editor at Donald I. Fine, Inc., and my wife Jean for their help and patience. Every author needs someone to bounce ideas and frustrations off, and I thank Rick and Jean for, willingly or unwillingly, being the targets. I couldn't have done it without you.
Thanks.

Dale Brown
Fair Oaks, California, 1988

1

February 1992
The Pacific Ocean

Three hundred miles east of Tokyo the aircraft carrier CV-64 USS *Constellation* rode the gentle swells of the north Pacific Ocean. She was cruising at only six knots, barely enough to maintain steerage way. The thirty-year-old, eighty-thousand-ton Kitty Hawk-class aircraft carrier was surrounded by an armada of eleven smaller support ships and other surface combatants arranged in a wide hexagon pattern.

The *Constellation* itself was buzzing with activity. Poised for battle, two F/A-18E Hornet fighter-bombers were positioned in their catapults, engines running, ready for the steam-powered push that would shoot them from zero to one hundred forty knots in three seconds. Two more F-18s on external power were parked just behind the catapult blast deflectors, ready to take their places once the first two alert birds launched. A CH-53F Super Sea Stallion III transport helicopter, its seventy-five-foot-diameter rotor slowly spinning, sat on the *Constellation's* flight deck just beside the 'island' superstructure. Another was hovering a few hundred feet from the *Constellation's* fantail, ready in a few seconds to drop on to the carrier's broad stern if ordered.

The seas behind the huge carrier were patrolled by predators of a different sort – three Los Angeles-class nuclear attack submarines that hung virtually motionless in the warm Pacific currents. Their sophisticated electronic sensors registered, catalogued, analysed and assessed each and every sound in the ocean for miles around, from the loudest clamour of propellers to the softest hiss of the smallest marine creature. Each of the sub's four torpedo tubes was loaded with long-range ASW/SOW antisubmarine missile-torpedoes, and each of the sub's vertical launch tubes was loaded with Sub-Harpoon antiship missiles.

But the man in the skipper's chair on the bridge atop the *Constellation's* superstructure did not notice any of these special additions to the *Constellation's* battle group. He was peering intently at a fifteen-inch-diameter radar scope, tracking three very large blips at its outer edge. The man looked up from the radar scope and squinted at the horizon, north between the American nuclear missile cruiser USS *Long Beach* and the tiny frigate USS *Lockwood*.

'I can just barely make them out, I think,' the president of the United States said. Two of the senior officials on the bridge glanced doubtfully at each other – no one, not even the president of the United States, could see a ship two hundred miles away.

'I think, sir,' Rear Admiral Bennett Walton said, 'that you're seeing the *Jouett*, one of our missile destroyer escorts.'

The president checked the radar again, pointing to a large blip. 'That's the *Jouett?* He looks so far away.'

'It's pretty hazy out, sir. The *Jouett* is eight miles out, but it seems farther.'

The president grunted at the scope, his expression turning pensive as the three blips moved closer to the centre of the screen. 'Who the hell are they, Admiral?'

Walton smiled. 'It's the *Kirov*, Mr President. Largest guided missile cruiser in the world. She's got the *Krasina* guided missile cruiser and the *Kresta*, an antisubmarine destroyer, with her.'

'No aircraft carrier? I would have thought the Soviets would try to match the *Constellation's* forces.'

'Sir,' Secretary of Defense Linus Edwards put in, 'they don't have enough forces to match even the *Constellation's* small battle group. It would be a waste for them to try.'

The president tried his best to ignore Edwards' bravado. The secretary of defense was an old navy sea captain who thought the US Navy ruled the seven seas. His background, the president reminded himself, clouded many of his opinions. He turned back to Walton. 'Are you worried that the *Kirov* is trailing us, even though it's over two hundred miles away?'

'Sir, the *Kirov* is about five hundred miles closer than I'd like. She packs quite a wallop, especially at only two hundred miles distant. But we're less than a thousand miles from Vladivostok, their largest Pacific naval base, so I guess we should be thankful there's only one major battleship out there shadowing us.'

He paused, glancing at a large chart of the Sea of Japan and East Asia on the bulkhead above the radar gear. 'I'm more concerned about their naval aviation forces at Vladivostok – they have the equivalent of four full naval air groups and nine heavy bomb wings out there, enough to invade Japan twice over.'

'But the *Constellation* and her escorts have enough firepower to take on anything the Soviets might throw at us,' Edwards pointed out, 'if they're reckless enough to try.'

Walton moved to another radar scope beside the main sea-mapping scope. 'Here's a display of aircraft, Mr President, within five hundred miles of us. All of them are ours or Japan's, except for this guy.' Walton pointed at a highlighted blip, again at the very edge of the scope.

'An Ilyushin IL-76G turbojet spy plane,' the admiral explained. 'It can monitor our communications, study our

13

radar emissions, map out the positions of all our ships. We also think it can monitor the progress of this morning's test.'

'How long until we start the test?' the president asked.

'We can start at any time, sir,' Linus Edwards replied, checking his watch.

'Everyone's in position,' Walton said. 'They should be running through their final prelaunch checks now. Tracking and monitoring stations and the White Sands Missile Range target area have already reported ready.'

The president nodded, then wandered out to the catwalk just outside the bridge area. Secretary Edwards and Admiral Walton followed, along with Neil McDonough, an NSC adviser, and a small knot of Marine and Secret Service guards. The president let the wind toss his thin silver hair around and inhaled deeply, breathing in the crisp salt air.

'We're finally about to do it,' he said excitedly, raising his voice over the sounds of jet turbines on the *Constellation's* seventy-four-thousand-square-foot flight deck. 'I've been waiting for this demonstration for months.'

'I have to admit,' Edwards said, 'that I feel a little uneasy about this whole thing.' He did not attempt to raise his voice over the clamour of helicopters and machinery on the flight deck seventy feet below. 'The first intercontinental missiles fired over the United States from Asia – and *we* launch them. Even with the Tridents' warheads inert, it makes me nervous.'

'Your less than enthusiastic opinion of the antiballistic missile defence system is well documented, Lee,' the president said. 'But that's one of the reasons I scheduled this test. Your opinions carry a lot of weight. If you're unhappy with the space-based defence network, others will be. If I can convince you how valuable this system is, I think I can convince others – including the Russians.'

'But a test of this magnitude?' Edwards asked. 'Six D-5

phase-three sub-launched missiles flying right through Canada and across the United States? Is a test with this much potential for mishap really necessary? An ICBM has never been flown across the pole before – '

'You mean *we've* never flown across the pole before,' the president corrected. 'We've caught the Russians firing missiles from Murmansk in Europe to their Asian ranges, and there's evidence of them shooting "ferret" missiles at Canada to test our early warning systems. We're hardly setting a precedent here.'

Edwards was about to interject something but the president continued. 'This test is vital, Lee. No matter how sophisticated a system is, people remain sceptical until they see it in action. Space Command briefs Congress almost every month on the results of their simulations, but no one believes how good the Thor kinetic-kill missile system really is. It's time to show them.' He pointed towards the horizon, where the three Russian ships were riding beyond visual range. 'Those sons-of-bitches want a show, we'll give 'em a show.'

He stepped back into the bridge and nodded to Admiral Walton. 'Let's do it.'

Walton smiled and motioned to a control panel mounted on the forward sea data console. Without hesitation the president leaned forward to the control panel and twisted a large bronze key in a triangular keyswitch. Immediately, a red light labelled 'LAUNCH' illuminated and an electric horn sounded throughout the *Constellation*.

With a thunderous roar a geyser of water erupted less than two miles away from the *Constellation*, and a huge white object rose from the sea like a bellowing whale. It blasted free of the waves, hovered about thirty feet above the water, and even seemed to slip backwards a few feet. Then, with a tremendous blast of fire, the Trident D-5/III sea-launched ballistic missile's solid-propellant motor ignited, and the missile and its ten inert warheads roared into space.

The first Trident had hardly reached full thrust when the second missile pierced the surface of the now boiling ocean. The USS *Arkansas*, the seventh and youngest of the new fleet of Ohio-class supersubmarines, began disgorging her deadly cargo at a rate of one missile every ten seconds. The stain of white hot foam stretched from the *Arkansas's* launch point towards the *Constellation*, her escorts, and the thousands of men watching the awesome spectacle.

Armstrong Space Station

'Skipper, missile launch detection.'

Brigadier General Jason Saint-Michael quickly set his coffee cup down on a Velcro mat on the bulkhead and manoeuvred himself to the main sensor operator's console. On a wide two-foot by three-foot multisensor display screen, a flashing white circle was superimposed on a polar-projection map of the northern hemisphere near Japan. A few seconds later, a short column of position readouts printed on a second screen beside the main display. The general's face seemed to take on an added intensity as he read the growing column of data.

'Three hundred miles east of Tokyo, sir,' the sensor operator read aloud. 'It's the exercise launch area all right . . .'

'All sections, stand by,' Saint-Michael said. 'Alert the station, exercise under way, red alert.' He readjusted his tiny communications earset and returned to his commander's seat – the only seat in the command module of the world's first strategic defence space station – and strapped himself in. The pedestal-mounted chair gave him a direct view of all the consoles in the space station's nerve centre.

16

He pulled out his ever-present notebook and pencil and attached the 'doodlebook' to a Velcro pad on his seat's armrest to keep it from floating off in microgravity. His fingers were already making indecipherable scratches on the paper as he barked orders to his crewmen.

'Okay, men,' he said in a deep, resonant voice, 'let's see if we can avoid letting these babies blow past us. Comm, transmit strategic warning message to Space Command, and ask them to verify that this is an exercise only.'

'Already in contact with Space Command, sir,' the communications tech reported. 'Exercise code received and authenticated.'

The general grunted in acknowledgement. 'Let's start lining 'em up.'

'SBR reports six missiles boosting,' the sensor tech reported. 'SBR is tracking . . . now confirming solid radar lock on all six missiles.' SBR was the acronym for space-based radar, two huge, football-field-sized, phased-array radar antennas installed on the station. Because of microgravity, the normal size limitations of a radar antenna did not apply in space; therefore, Armstrong Station's SBR was dozens of times larger and hundreds of times more powerful than most moveable earth-based radars. The SBR could scan over a thousand miles in all directions from the station, detecting any object more than two metres in size in space, in earth's atmosphere and on earth itself. Although SBR stood for space-based radar, the acronym also referred to a wide range of sensors aboard the space station used to detect and track objects in space – radar, infrared, optical, Doppler, magnetic anomaly, radio, radiation, and laser.

Saint-Michael's four technicians worked quickly, speaking rarely and only in clipped, unemotional, well-rehearsed phrases. They had practised hard for this very important test, and they knew the eyes of the world were on them.

17

'How does our orbit look?' Saint-Michael asked.

'We should be in position to intercept throughout the boost and midcourse phases,' a tech replied. Armstrong Station was in a seven-hundred- by one-hundred-mile elliptical polar orbit, roughly centred near the north pole. Because the northernmost part of the orbit was farther from earth, the station spent two and a half of its three hour orbit over the pole, allowing it to scan longer for attacking north-launched missiles.

'Missiles are above the atmosphere,' the tech at the master multisensor console reported. 'Approaching one hundred miles altitude.'

'Thor missiles ready for launch,' another tech reported. The general nodded once again. The SLBM-29A Thor missiles were Armstrong Station's antiballistic weapons. Resembling long metal cigars, the cylindrical missiles were simple but effective. Ten of them were loaded into a circular free-flying carrier-ejector 'garage' that was attached to Armstrong Station's long main structural keel by a steel tether. The missile garage was equipped with thrusters that would allow it to point its business end towards the attacking ICBMs in response to remote slaving commands from the space station's sensors.

'All six ICBMs are approximately two minutes from burnout,' the main sensor tech reported. 'Approaching max firing range.'

'Prepare to launch missiles,' Saint-Michael ordered. 'First three missiles on full automatic intercept during ICBM boost. Fourth missile on SBR intercept mode only in midcourse intercept. Program fifth Thor for blind-launch intercept. Program sixth Thor missile for full manual track in midcourse phase – Chief Jefferson will perform the intercept. Program the remaining intercept missiles for full automatic in case any get away.' The missile tech's fingers flew over his controls.

'SLBMs approaching optimum range.'

Saint-Michael turned to the chief sensor technician, Space Command Chief Master Sergeant Jake Jefferson. 'Ready, Jake?' Jefferson, a finger lightly resting on a large steering trackball on his console, nodded.

The general flipped his communications earset to stationwide intercom. 'Attention on the station. Stand by for missile launch.' He sat back and laced his fingers. 'Launch commit all Thor interceptors.'

A single switch was activated. 'Launch commit.'

The SBR tracking computer had been feeding tracking information to the Thor ejector, pointing the ten missiles towards the six sea-launched ballistic missiles flying at thousands of miles an hour through space. Three of the Thor interceptor missiles had also been receiving precise guidance information from the SBR sensors, so their onboard sensors already knew where to look for the SLBMs. These three missiles, with super-accurate data being constantly fed to them, waited in the ejector for their computer-directed launch command.

Of the other seven Thor missiles, two were launched immediately after Saint-Michael issued the launch commit signal. The first of these two missiles was directed entirely by Armstrong Station's powerful SBR and other sensors, simulating a failure of the Thor's on-board trackers. The second missile, simulating a failure of all tracking data uplink signals from Armstrong Station, relied solely on its on-board radar and infrared sensors for the intercept.

Despite the technician-induced failures, however, the two Thor missiles performed flawlessly. Each Thor missile had a two-stage solid propellant motor capable of ten thousand pounds of thrust, which instantly accelerated the four-thousand-pound missiles to fifteen thousand miles per hour in a few seconds. Shortly after their motors fired, a one-hundred-foot-diameter steel mesh web unfolded from the Thor missile's body, effectively increasing the missile's kill radius.

The first two interceptor missiles did not need the webbing to neutralize their targets. The space station's SBR sensors detonated the one-thousand-pound high-explosive flak warhead on the first Thor missile a split second before the mesh hit the ballistic missile's upper stage, instantly shredding the SLBM's protective warhead shroud, destroying the sensitive inertial guidance electronics, and sending the entire upper stage spinning off into space. The second Thor missile, directed by the radar seeker head on the missile itself, made a direct hit on the SLBM upper stage moments after third-stage burnout, completely destroying the ballistic missile.

'Two hits confirmed,' a tech reported aboard the space station, and a cheer went up among the crew. Saint-Michael gripped the armrests on his commander's chair and allowed himself a faint smile.

That was enough for Jefferson. He took a deep breath and hit the launch button on his manual control console, ejecting the Thor missile that was to be manually guided.

'Thor six away,' he announced.

A split-second later, Armstrong Station's intercept computers decided that the two lead ballistic missiles were in proper range, and the first two fully automatic Thor missiles were ejected from the launcher garage by blasts of supercompressed nitrogen gas.

'Thors one and two away.'

Saint-Michael nodded at Jefferson. 'You're right on so far, Jake. Show those guys down there what a spacer can do.'

Taking his cues from the SBR-directed interceptors, Jefferson punched the command keys that ignited his missile's solid-fuel motors and unfurled the one-hundred-foot steel snare. His computer monitor showed the sensor image of the trailing sixth sea-launched ballistic missile, and a circle cursor represented the sensor image of the Thor missile as it sped away from Armstrong Station.

'Gently, carefully, Jefferson pressed the enable switch on the side of the tracking console with his right middle finger and rested his right thumb on the trackball. As long as he depressed the enable button, any movements of the trackball would trigger tiny vernier thrusters on his Thor missile's body, which would slide the interceptor missile in any direction to align it with its target. Jefferson's job was to keep the SLBM roughly in the centre of the circle all the way to impact.

'Direct hit on Trident number one,' a tech reported. 'Thor two is ten seconds to impact. Thor three is launched . . .'

'Three out of six hits,' Saint-Michael said. 'Good, but not good enough . . .'

'Good proximity hit on Trident two,' came another report. 'Four out of six destroyed . . .'

'Excellent,' the general was saying, 'excellent – '

'Clean miss on Trident three!' the tech suddenly shouted. 'No snare, no proximity detonation.'

Saint-Michael felt a nervous tingling in his fingers that caused him to concentrate even harder. 'Auto launch commit on Thor number seven,' he snapped. But the technician had anticipated his command and the missile was already speeding out of its chute.

Jefferson was having problems of his own as Saint-Michael leaned over his shoulder.

'It's like tryin' to thread a needle with two baseball gloves on,' Jefferson muttered. He risked glancing up from his tracking monitor at the missile-status indicators. 'I've used up three-quarters of the vernier thruster fuel. This is turning into a tail chase . . .'

'Easy, Chief,' the general said. 'You got it wired. Relax.' He was also talking to himself.

'Tridents three and six approaching MIRV separation . . .'

Saint-Michael sat back and looked nervously at the

back of Jefferson's sweaty right hand. The two remaining SLBMs were almost ready to MIRV – each of the missile's ten individual reentry warheads was soon going to separate from the carrier bus. If they did, it would be almost impossible to knock down the small warheads.

Jefferson's thumb barely touched the trackball's surface as he attempted to nudge the interceptor towards the ballistic missile bus. The sensor image of the SLBM was becoming more and more erratic. Jefferson's thumb quivered slightly as he fought for control.

'You got it, Jake. Easy, easy . . .'

'It's gonna miss,' Jefferson said through clenched teeth. 'Launch another interceptor, Skipper. Fast. It's gonna – '

Jefferson's console instruments froze. The chief master sergeant didn't notice the frozen readouts . . . he was totally absorbed in trying to merge the two sensor images even though he no longer had control.

'You *got* it,' Saint-Michael said as he read the frozen numbers. 'Twenty-five-foot snare on the webbing and a snare detonation. Good shooting, Chief.' Jefferson nodded thanks and pulled his hand away from the sweat-moistened trackball.

'MIRV separation on Trident three,' a tech reported. 'Thor seven is . . .' He paused, studying the computer analysis of the sensor inputs. 'It looks as if Thor seven snared all but one of the MIRVs just after MIRV separation,' he said. 'I'm tracking one single warhead. Track appears a little wobbly, but I think it'll reenter the atmosphere intact.'

'Will it impact in the White Sands range?' the general asked.

After an excruciatingly long pause during which Saint-Michael was about to send another Thor in a long tail-chase after the rogue warhead, the tech responded. 'Affirmative, Skipper. Well within the range, but at least five miles outside the target cluster on the range. Clean miss.'

'Okay . . . Well, we didn't kill it but we nicked it enough to send it off course. And we got fifty-nine of sixty warheads . . .'

'Ninety-eight point three per cent effective,' Colonel Wayne Marks, deputy commander for engineering, added, slapping the technicians' shoulders in congratulations. 'Pretty good county fair shooting, I'd say.'

Saint-Michael retrieved his coffee cup. 'Unless you're under that one remaining warhead,' he said.

USS *Constellation*

'Very well,' Rear Admiral Bennett Walton said. He returned the phone labelled 'CIC,' combat information centre, to its cradle and looked over at the president.

'Sir, Cheyenne Mountain reports one Mark 21C dummy reentry vehicle impacting at the White Sands Missile Test Range.'

The president felt his face flush with excitement. He turned and smiled at the secretary of defense. 'One warhead? Just one?'

'That's it, sir,' Walton said. 'And that one warhead was diverted off course and missed its intended impact point by eight nautical miles. If the warhead had been active, the fireball would not have extended to the target. Communications say Armstrong's after-action report is being received in CIC.'

The president shook hands all around, then sat back in the carrier commander's seat and sipped coffee.

'Damn, I think we've got something here . . .'

The Kremlin, USSR

Through swirling gusts of snow that fell outside the triple-paned windows, the Soviet Union's Minister of Defence Sergei Leonidovich Czilikov had difficulty seeing even as far as the frozen Moscow River and the new Varsauskoje Highway that spanned its southern and northern banks. He watched policemen trying to direct traffic around a minor collision in the middle of Bakovka Avenue east of the new Kremlin Administrative Centre. Another long, severe winter was coming.

Czilikov turned away from the icy scene outside, but things were equally as depressing and cold inside. Seated around a long oblong oak table in the cavernous office were the members of the Kollegiya, the Soviet main military council. The Kollegiya included three deputy ministers of defence, a KGB general, the commanders of the five branches of the Soviet military, and five generals representing various support and reserve elements of the military. Fifteen men, six in business suits with medals and ribbons, the rest in military uniforms, and not one of them, least of all Czilikov, under the age of sixty. All but one, the relatively young KGB chief, Lichizev, were Heroes of the Soviet Union.

They were surrounded by aides and secretaries in hard metal folding chairs arranged along the century-old tapestries covering the walls of the room. Two elite Kremlin guards, each armed with AKSU sub-machine guns, flanked each heavy oak door leading into the chamber.

Everyone in the large, cold room looked on edge. Czilikov knew what each of them was expecting. As he moved to the unoccupied head of the conference table, the hubbub of noise died abruptly away.

'We must attack,' Czilikov said. The faces of the fourteen men remained stony, grim. Mindless cattle, Czilikov thought to himself. The new general secretary had such a firm stranglehold on these formerly powerful soldiers, Heroes of the Soviet Union, that most were afraid even to look up from the table. The spirit of *glasnost* in general secretary Mikhail Gorbachev's regime had been squashed.

'Intelligence reports are conclusive, *tovarishchi*,' Czilikov declared. 'Nearly all of the pro-Khomeini factions have been defeated by the moderates, and the pro-Western government is consolidating control of both the people and the military. The Alientar government in Iran has promised a return to pre-Khomeini wealth and prosperity for its people – funded by the Americans, of course. The KGB predicts that the Iranians will agree to the reopening of air and naval bases and listening posts in Iran in exchange for generous financial assistance. Which means that arms sales to Iran from the West, which were nothing more than secretive trickles, may soon flow like vodka.'

Czilikov fixed each of them with an imperious stare. Despite his age, his eyes danced with the same fire as when he was a young tank commander rolling triumphantly across Poland in World War II. 'The old efforts to consolidate the Transcaucasus under our rule by kindling this wasting, bloody war between Iran and Iraq have failed. Our former leader, more concerned with his television image than the needs of the future world Communist state, failed to anticipate that religious fanaticism can be a powerful, sustaining force – particularly in Iran. Our lack of success in supporting the Hussein regime in Iraq has seriously hurt our prestige. The result is that we are in danger of losing all our influence in the whole Middle East.'

'Could this really be so, Comrade Marshal?' Deputy Minister of Defence and Chief of Ground Forces General Yegenly Ilanovsky asked. 'Surely the hatred that the

Iranians have for the Americans can't be erased overnight? Thousands were killed in the American bombing raids on Tehran and Kharg Island just a few years ago.'

'Raids which the Iranians themselves foolishly invited by attacking American shipping in the Gulf and staging that Christmas terrorist attack on Washington,' Admiral Chercherovin, commander in chief of the navy, said. 'They seem to have an instinct for self-destruction.'

'Which may play into our hands nicely,' Lichizev, the KGB representative, put in. 'As for how the Iranians feel about the Americans at the moment, my agents in Iran report a distinct softening in attitude. Public memory can sometimes be conveniently short, and official memory can be adjusted. The CIA has given vital military support to the puppet regime of the Ayatollah Falah Alientar. They have helped crush his enemies very effectively, much as they did when the Shah Pavelirili Rezneveh was in power, before they got an attack of democratic conscience . . .'

'It is obvious that past transgressions have been forgotten,' Czilikov summed up. 'And if the United States and Iran sign a friendship and cooperation agreement, the Iran-Iraq war will be over within days. Iraq will not fire on an American vessel, and the skies over Iran will be nearly impenetrable if American planes are allowed to land there. We will be as powerless as we were in Egypt twenty years ago.'

The Kollegiya became silent. The next question hung over the group like a poised guillotine blade, but no one was going to ask. Czilikov's gaze swept over the grey-haired men at the table, but he met few direct glances.

They were waiting for their orders, Czilikov decided. Well, give them the order . . .

'Operation Feather has been approved by the Politburo,' Czilikov finally said. 'The plan for the occupation and control of Iran and the Persian Gulf. Swift execution is essential. The United States must be prevented from entering the Persian Gulf with a major naval air force. We don't want a repeat of their flagging operation of five years ago. We must take tactical command of the Persian Gulf theatre before Iran formally asks the United States for assistance. Ayatollah Larijani has established a government-in-exile in Syria and has been persuaded to help us. He will announce that it was the pro-West members of Alientar's party who precipitated the war with Iraq. He will denounce the war as an American plot to divide the Islamic brotherhood. He will call for a holy war against Alientar's puppet regime.'

Czilikov paused, letting his carefully chosen words sink in. 'Then he will announce an alliance with President Hussein at-Takriti of Iraq to unite the two warring nations under a new flag, creating the Islamic Republic of Persia.'

Czilikov returned to his seat and motioned to First Deputy Minister of Defence Sergei Khromeyev, chief of the General Staff of the Armed Forces. Khromeyev stepped before a wide flat-lens computer screen set up in a corner of the room.

'The tentative scenario has been approved by the Politburo,' Khromeyev began. 'The ultimate objective of Operation Feather is to consolidate the Persian Gulf region under complete political and military control of our Soviet Communist party. The party, through the defence council, has ordered the Stavka to accomplish the objectives set out in these orders.'

Khromeyev referred to a folder on the long conference table as a detailed computer-generated map of the Persian Gulf appeared on the screen. 'A small but dramatic Iranian attack against one of our destroyers in the Persian Gulf will precipitate our defensive containment response. The attack will be preplanned by GRU and KGB agents in place in Iran, and will use Iranian Silkworm antiship missiles fired from Bandar-Abbas near the Strait of Hormuz.

'We already have an entire carrier task force in place. The Kievclass *Leonid V. Brezhnev* aircraft carrier is stationed in the Persian Gulf. The *Brezhnev* battle group is nearly unopposed – the Americans, I'm glad to say, still refuse to put one of their carriers in the gulf out of fear of reprisal. The *Brezhnev* has six cruisers, ten destroyers, and ten support vessels. When the destroyer *Sovremennyy* is attacked, the battle group will attack the Iranian military ports of Abadan, Bandar-Abbas, and Bushehr. The group will be reinforced by Tu-95 and Tu-121B naval bombers from our ports in South Yemen. Control of Bandar-Abbas will give us control of the Straits of Hormuz, the major chokepoint, as you well know, of the entire Persian Gulf. The southern *Teatr Voennykh Deistvii* will occupy Tehran, with assistance from three divisions from Afghanistan, which will control the eastern border. Southern TVD, Caspian flotilla, and Iraqi forces will capture the western frontier.'

Czilikov noticed a few nervous faces in the Kollegiya. They were not, it seemed, itching for battle. They would follow orders, but this was a far more ambitious operation than they had expected.

Khromeyev pushed on. 'Syrian and Iraqi forces will contain any American military reaction from Turkey, and the *Brezhnev* carrier battle group in the Persian Gulf will close off the air and sea approaches to the Persian Gulf, the Gulf of Oman and the Arabian Sea.'

Czilikov stood and faced the Kollegiya. The computer map had frozen with the scene of red sickles and hammers spread from Syria to Pakistan.

'In one week we will occupy Iran,' Czilikov said. 'A coup will reinstate the Islamic regime of Larijani, which will, as mentioned, unify Iran under the Islamic Republic of Persia. We will retain both political and military control of the region and prevent the United States from ever regaining a strong foothold in the Persian Gulf.'

There was a low rumble of voices. Czilikov sat, folded his hands before him on the table, waiting for the rumble to subside. A few short years ago such a bold plan would have provoked vigorous, angry protests. No longer. Already the men surrounding Czilikov began to quiet. The members of the Kollegiya were either too dumbfounded or afraid or both to speak out. Czilikov let his words linger for a few moments, then said, 'Your comments, *tovarishchi*.'

'It's a brilliant plan, Comrade Marshal,' Ilanovsky said enthusiastically. 'A swift, crushing pincer that will grab the entire region away from the US.'

'I assure you the navy stands ready, gentlemen,' Admiral Chercherovin added. 'The *Brezhnev* battle group can easily control the region, and our naval aviation forces from South Yemen and Vietnam will intercept all American rapid deployment air forces.'

Each of the commanders of the armed forces, in turn, weighed in with their enthusiasm and support for Czilikov's invasion plan. But such overwhelming support didn't especially hearten the Minister of Defence. Intimidated military commanders tended to make unreliable decisions. He was about to make some comment about his staff's excessive enthusiasm when he noted a quiet but animated discussion between Deputy Minister Alexi Ivanovich Rhomerdunov, commander in chief of aerospace forces, and one of his staff members. The staffer was all but being pushed back into his seat by Rhomerdunov, who had to be at least thirty years older than his enthusiastic aide.

'Is there a problem, Comrade Rhomerdunov?'

All heads swivelled in the direction of the seventy-year-old head of air defence forces. Rhomerdunov straightened in his seat, stabbing an angry glare in his aide's direction. 'No, Comrade Minister.'

Czilikov nodded and was about to issue his orders to

the Kollegiya when Rhomerdunov cleared his throat. 'Excuse me, Comrade Minister' – he again looked apprehensively in the aide's direction – 'perhaps there are some important points to be made about this Iranian offensive.'

The members of the Kollegiya froze and stared at Rhomerdunov, as if he had just badly insulted the minister of defence. Czilikov said nothing. Then, without further prompting, Rhomerdunov's aide stood and straightened to attention. The officer was tall, lean, powerfully built. Ukrainian, obviously, judging by his wide shoulders, flat nose, and square jaw, Czilikov decided. He hit on the man's name as he began to speak.

'Sir, I am – '

'I know who you are, General Lieutenant Aviatsii Govorov. As the Soviet Union's first space shuttle cosmonaut and a Hero of the Soviet Union you're known to us all.' Czilikov ground a fist into his palm in barely restrained anger. 'Your contributions to the scientific and military excellence of our country forgives many . . . transgressions. Since you have seen fit to grant yourself permission to speak before the Kollegiya, please proceed. I'm sure everyone wants to hear from the new commander of the space-defence command.'

'My apologies, sir,' which was as far as Govorov's apology went. Most officers below the rank of three-star general would be a mass of jelly speaking in front of Kollegiya, even without committing a major breach of protocol. But it didn't seem to affect young Govorov.

'Well, *proceed*, General Lieutenant.'

Govorov stayed at attention. 'It is my opinion, Comrade Minister, that this mission to attack Iran will ultimately fail.'

Rhomerdunov straightened in his seat and looked straight ahead, as if steeling himself for the executioner. All eyes in the room moved from Rhomerdunov's granite face to the surprised Marshal Czilikov.

'I've heard,' Czilikov said, 'that subtlety is not exactly your style. I see it is true.' He looked to Rhomerdunov, who kept staring straight ahead. Well, Czilikov thought, it seemed the old war horse Rhomerdunov wasn't afraid to challenge the party, even if it was indirectly through his deputy Govorov.

As for Govorov, he took Czilikov's silence as a cue to continue. 'The Americans have a device, Comrade Minister, that is not only capable of warning of any impending invasion but also of directing American and NATO counterforces. This device, sir, is the Armstrong Space Station – '

'The space station? Their military station? It's only been in orbit for a few months – '

'Yes, and it is fully operational,' Govorov said. 'As we all know, sir, the Americans have successfully completed their first operational test of their illegal Thor space-based interceptor missile. Although the test was less than perfect – '

'*That* is an overstatement, Govorov,' Khromeyev put in. 'The Americans called it an operational test, but it was carefully staged to ensure optimal results. In spite of their choreography, our intelligence reported several clear misses with the Thor missile. It is an obvious propaganda ploy – '

'Our intelligence puts the effectiveness of the Thor missile at no better than eighty-three per cent,' Govorov agreed, 'which my staff feels is no better than fifty per cent in an actual wartime scenario. But, sir, the Thor missile is not at issue. My staff is more concerned with the system of advanced sensors now in use, especially the phased-array, space-based radar aboard the space station Armstrong. It has a far greater capability than we first estimated. We believe, sir, that the space-based radar can track and identify objects on land, sea, and in the air from ranges in *excess* of sixteen hundred kilometres.'

31

A clamour of voices erupted in the conference chamber. Czilikov's voice boomed out above them all. 'Sixteen hundred kilometres? That's impossible. No radar can do that.'

'No earth-bound radar, sir. But a radar mounted in space has no size or geographical limitations. It's limited only by the power available to it – and the space station has enough solar-energy capability to power the whole Kremlin.'

'You are trying to tell us,' Deputy Minister Ilanovsky said, 'that a single space station can monitor all movement of military equipment involved in Operation Feather? Thousands of vehicles spread out over millions of cubic miles of space in mountainous terrain and in bad weather? That is preposterous – '

'It may sound so,' Govorov said to the commander of the army, 'but our estimates confirm it.'

'I say that whether this radar can do all of these things is still immaterial,' Deputy Minister Marasimov, the commander of Strategic Rocket Forces, said. 'The station is in polar earth orbit. It does not permanently position itself over the Middle East. It can only provide short-term glimpses of the region a few times each day. Which would make it impractical as a warning and control station.'

Govorov hesitated for a moment. 'That's true, but – '

'This expensive toy has no more capability than an ordinary reconnaissance satellite,' Marasimov went on, smiling benignly at young Govorov. 'What you have said about the Armstrong's radar is true . . . if the radar is in operation when it passes over the area, if it works properly, if its operators and interpreters correctly analyse the images, and if they can get the information to regional commanders in time to be of some use. By my count that's four pretty damn big ifs.'

Marasimov nodded to Czilikov. 'I believe our young

colleague has presented some very . . . interesting information, but I also believe that the radar on the American space station would be no obstacle to the success of Feather.'

Govorov looked amazed. 'Excuse me, Comrade Minister, but – '

'Thank you, General Lieutenant Govorov,' Czilikov said, dismissing him. 'I will expect detailed briefings on each command order of battle for Operation Feather in two weeks.'

Govorov sank back into his metal folding chair as Czilikov continued issuing his orders. He struggled to remain poker-faced, his eyes narrowed into angry slits as a few of the deputy ministers and marshals cast amused glances his way.

They can't believe now, Govorov told himself. But they will. The American space station won't just be talked, or wished, away.

Edinburgh, Scotland

From the northernmost cannon mounts known as the Argyle Battery of Edinburgh Castle, the view of the New Town section of Edinburgh was breathtaking. Far below the craggy heights of the ancient castle, which seemed to grow out of the rock like a gnarled oak, the snow-covered Princes Street Gardens stretched from St Cuthbert's Church to Waverley Station to the east and far, far down the Lothian Valley to the North Sea. Beyond Princes Street Gardens, the modern shops, hotels and homes of New Edinburgh – 'new' in this instance meaning the part of town that was only two hundred and forty years old, as opposed to the rest, which was over twelve hundred – bustled with activity despite the cold winds and occasional snowfalls.

There were a few die-hard tourists visiting this imposing stone castle overlooking Edinburgh, but for the most part the site was deserted except for the warders and members of the Castle Guard. Only a few hardy, well-dressed individuals stood by to watch as the Royal Scots Dragoon Guard made their way to the Mill's Mount gun platform for the one o'clock signal.

'The townspeople, merchants and sailors of Edinburgh have set their timepieces to the one o'clock gun ever since the time of Napoleon Bonaparte,' a tour guide was saying. His thick Scottish brogue, dulled by the chill winds swirling around the top of the castle, made him difficult to understand, but the man who stood a few feet to his left, dressed in a grey trenchcoat, wool-brimmed hat, leather gloves and sunglasses, was not really listening. 'It is even said that Saint Christopher, the patron saint of travellers, stops by Edinburgh every day to check the spin of the earth and moon with the gun so sailors won't get lost.'

'Why do they fire the gun at one o'clock?' a man with a slight Middle Eastern accent asked. He had been waiting there for some time, and was now standing right up near the chain and stanchions that kept visitors away from the small fifty-five-millimetre howitzer. 'It seems a strange hour. Why not signal at noon?'

Now the man in sunglasses was interested, but not in the tour guide's reply – being a native of Scotland, he'd already guessed the answer.

'Ye forget, sir,' the tour guide replied, his lips forming a sly smile, 'you're in Scotland. Having to fire only one shot per day, rather than twelve, appeals to a Scotsman's sense of economy.'

The foreigner gave a short laugh and the tour guide went on with his well-rehearsed script. The Scots, the man with the sunglasses observed, seemed as fond of

34

making fun of themselves as they were of the English and Irish.

Presently the guards entered the chained-off area, and at the direction of the officer in charge, fired one economical round to the north over the New Town. By force of habit the man in sunglasses checked his watch – the timing was perfect. The Scots were nothing if not both thrifty and punctual.

The tourists quickly retreated out of the numbing wind that blew in from the glacial bay called the Firth of Forth; even the Dragoon Guards' pace seemed to quicken as they marched off the Argyle Battery back to the massive group of two-hundred-year-old buildings called the New Barracks.

The man with the slight Middle Eastern accent turned away from the Mills' Mount Battery as if reluctantly relinquishing the sting of the icy winds on his face and walked down the cobblestone concourse towards the Portcullis Gate. He almost walked right into the man in the sunglasses. 'Excuse me.' His voice was even colder than the chill Scottish winds.

The man in the sunglasses began in French. '*Pardonnez-moi, Monsieur le Président* Alientar.'

'McDonough?'

'Yes, Mr President.'

'I was afraid you were not going to come. I thought your government was going to change its mind again.'

'We can talk over here, sir,' McDonough said, letting Alientar's shot glance off him unanswered. He led him past the former cart sheds turned souvenir shops and down a narrow alley to the Back Parade between the Butts Battery and the building marked 'Governor's Residence.' They then turned left across to a cobblestone halfmoon carriageway to an entrance in the rear of the governor's residence.

'We are going in *here?*' President Alientar asked.

'The English and Scottish governments were kind enough to offer us a secure place to talk,' McDonough said. They walked up the stone-and-tiled portico of the rear of the building and were immediately met by a member of the Royal Scots Dragoon Guard in a black cold-weather uniform. No kilts, dirks or ceremonial basket-hilt broad-swords here – the guard had a very mean, modern-looking Heckler and Koch MP5a3 assault submachine gun at port arms. He checked McDonough's ID, compared it against a separate roster, motioned them inside.

A man dressed in household whites but clearly a member of the Dragoon Guard – the bulge of a Special Air Services Browning high-power automatic pistol was visible under his tunic – led the two foreigners through the outer galley and kitchen area, through the well-appointed dining room and large sitting room and into a smaller office area. He eyed them both suspiciously, then left without saying a word.

'Not very friendly . . .'

'He probably feels this meeting of foreigners demeans the surroundings,' McDonough said, and motioned Alientar to a leather-covered seat. A few moments later the guard returned with a tray of tea and scones.

'*M'omercia*,' McDonough said in Gaelic. 'My thanks.' The guardsman gave McDonough a piercing look, obviously feeling that the foreigner was making fun of him by speaking the ancient Scottish tongue. He left with a loud thud of the heavy oak door.

'No doubt my presence is a particular irritant,' Alientar said. He eyed McDonough as he removed his hat, coat, and gloves. 'What is it you do, Mr McDonough?'

'I'm an assistant to the president of the United States. I'm assigned to the National Security Council but I report directly to the president.'

'Are you a military man?'

'Retired – United States Air Force. I was an air attaché to Tehran before the revolution.'

'A spy, then.'

'No, an *air attaché*. I was liaison between the Iranian and US air forces.'

'You would deny it in any case,' Alientar said blandly. McDonough took a deep breath, surprised at how steady his hands were as he poured the tea.

'I am distressed that the president did not send one of his *senior* advisers to this meeting,' Alientar said. 'I would have expected at least a cabinet-level officer, or the vice-president.' He looked casually around the office, as if trying to decide whether or not to continue. 'This troubles me – troubles me deeply. I question the sincerity of your government if they can't at least send someone of ministerial or ambassadorial rank – '

McDonough thought how a few years back Bud McFarland said almost the same thing to second-rank Iranians when he had come to Tehran to sell arms for hostages. Full-circle . . . 'My apologies if we've offended you,' McDonough said. He had been expecting this. 'But the president requested this meeting in anticipation of a more formal state visit by you to Washington at the earliest opportunity. He asked me to talk with you, hear you out, and transmit your messages to him.'

Alientar shrugged. 'Very well, but I *am* disappointed. And to have this meeting in Scotland? In the dead of winter? A poor choice.'

'Excuse me, *sir*, but this was by far the most secure place for this meeting. True, it's not recommended that you stray too close to these Royal Scots dragoons. Too many Scottish seamen in the Royal Navy have lost their lives in the Persian Gulf because of your predecessor's attacks on British escort vessels in recent months. But almost any other site would be far more dangerous.'

37

McDonough paused for a moment, then went on. 'Internal disputes in your own Revolutionary Guard make it no longer safe for you to be in your own palace in Tehran. Half the Muslim nations have shunned you or are afraid to show you any friendship, and the other half wants you dead. Even France, where you've stayed for the past month, is close to deporting you because of the terrorist attacks you provoke by being there. You were let into Great Britain only after personal assurances from my president that secrecy would be maintained. All in all, I'd say we are lucky that this meeting is being held in the office of the governor of Scotland rather than in some jungle hut in South America – '

'I resent the implication that I am some sort of banana republic tyrant come begging before a third-rank American bureaucrat. I am the president of the Islamic Republic of Iran. I am the political and religious leader of fifteen million Muslim soldiers of God who would gladly die for Allah, and myself. Please do not insult me.'

McDonough shrugged, thought to himself that this Iranian was even touchier than he'd expected.

'I apologize for my remarks – '

'I would hear the apology from the president himself.'

'I'm afraid that's impossible.'

'*Why* impossible?'

McDonough sighed. 'Sir, in this election year it would be ill-advised for any American politician to be seen with you. This meeting alone carries significant risk . . . But the president does feel it's urgent to open a dialogue with you. I happen to be the best-qualified person in the administration to talk to you about your present situation.'

'You are also . . . how do you say it . . . *deniable?* A secretary of state must answer to the people and to Congress. A junior aide in some back-room office in the White House can easily be hidden from public view.'

McDonough smiled in spite of himself. 'You know your American politics, *Monsieur le Président.*'

This small bit of flattery went a long way, helped Alientar to save some face. 'Continue, Mr McDonough. You are impertinent but I believe we can still talk business.'

McDonough nodded. 'Well, in this case business simply involves an exchange of information. The president wants to know how you view the situation in your country.'

'That is all?' Alientar let out a short laugh. 'I dare say your point of view is more informed than mine at this point.' He turned away and stared out one of the tall columnar windows of the Governor's House. 'They thought the Ayatollah Khomeini was Jesus Christ resurrected,' Alientar said finally. 'The damned outcast socialists, the bored students, the poor starving fundamentalist Muslims – it was as if they all wanted to re-create the New Testament, with Ruhollah Khomeini as Jesus and the Shah as Pilate. There were secret police and atrocities on both sides, but Iran was a flower in the desert in the days of the Shah. Khomeini was supposed to make it better, and I believe that he could have made Iran prosperous under Islam. But he began to believe the things they were saying about him. He waged war on whoever the priests and elders told him were threatening his ascent to glory. He slaughtered thousands of the Shah's men, the only Iranians who knew how to run a government. He strangled the life out of the foreign oil companies. He made war on the Israelis, the French, the Americans, the British and then the Iraqis. He ordered the slaughter of ten thousand children in one month by sending them, unarmed, against Iraqi tanks – and he rejoiced afterwards. The power, it simply drove him mad.'

Alientar paused for a moment, then continued. 'He spent millions on educating the young *mullahs* overseas. We were taught diplomacy, defence, finance, every facet

39

of government; then when we returned, he tossed us aside in favour of the religious fanatics. Many of us were made military field commanders – many of us died in Iraqi bombing raids or at the hands of the Khomeini's Revolutionary Guard.'

'But not you. Your military successes led you back to Tehran.'

Alientar looked surprised. 'Yes. I led a successful guerrilla attack against some isolated Iraqi headquarters. My squad of old men and children had been abandoned by our Revolutionary Guard regulars; we were cornered like rats and we fought like rats and somehow were victorious. We captured some useless desert territory and a few Soviet tanks. They made me a hero and suddenly I found myself with access to the inner circle of power.'

'Where you began to build the groundwork for a more moderate government,' McDonough added.

Alientar looked at him. 'I cannot tell if you are baiting me or if that is what you really believe. Never mind . . . I was a lackey in the so-called Islamic Revolutionary Council. I kissed the feet of the psychotic fundamentalist warmongers like everyone else. But I discovered that I was not the only one who wanted a more moderate, more profitable Islamic government. A group of us arranged for arms to be secretly shipped from several countries, including the United States, and only a fraction of those weapons ever found their way into the hands of the Iranian army or the Revolutionary Guard. The rest were stored in secret caches in Iran and Pakistan and Saudi Arabia, waiting.

'It was a bad day, back in 1986, when our operation was revealed during your infamous Iran-Contra scandal. We went underground when our activities were made public, survived the internal investigations, and became stronger. The Revolutionary Guard may be the flower of the Ayatollah's chivalry, but they are just as corrupt as

40

anyone. They kept their tongues silent for a little gold –
no, hear me out, McDonough,' he said as McDonough
seemed about to interrupt. 'You asked for information;
you need background to understand it . . . When Khomeini finally became too ill to function, Larijani, Khomeini's chosen successor, inherited a sinking ship. Even the
support of the Soviet Union could not save him when we
decided to take over – '

'Yes, my government is impressed with your ability to
consolidate the rival factions in your country,'
McDonough said. 'Your progress has been encouraging.
We know, of course, that there are still fundamentalist
religious leaders and Revolutionary Guard commanders
who claim you don't represent them, but their numbers
seem to be dwindling. The president is optimistic.'

Alientar stood and began to pace the tiny office,
absently studying the books on the floor-to-ceiling book-
shelves lining the walls. He stopped and opened a concealed panel above a small letter desk, revealing a very
well stocked liquor cabinet with rows of shining crystal
snifters and gracefully fluted decanters.

'I learned much in the West. I learned about single-
malt Scotch whisky' – he poured himself a shot and
returned to the high-backed leather seat – 'and I learned
about the rivalry between the East and West. I think I
learned what motivates the Russians – fear of powerful
neighbours, losing control of territories, having insecure
borders, not having access to warm-water ports. And I
believe I learned what motivates the West – worrying
where the next tank of gas will come from, fear of losing
markets, losing investment opportunities, losing control
of the Soviets. There is a saying in the Middle East . . .
there is no difference between Russian money and American money, but with the Russian money comes Russian
troops, and with American money comes Exxon and
Holiday Inn.

'Iran is tearing itself apart, Mr McDonough,' Alientar said matter-of-factly, as if casually describing the weather outside. 'I have two choices. I can allow my country to be dismembered like a wounded hare set on by a pack of wolves, or I can align with a keeper to save us from self-destruction. I prefer the latter. I would like our keeper to be the United States of America.'

McDonough nodded, his face showing no expression.

Alientar went on, 'If promised money, arms, and assistance from the West, I will pledge to withdraw from this Soviet-inspired war with Iraq, retreat back to our prewar boundaries and open negotiations with President Hussein of Iraq to normalize relations. If I manage to keep myself alive in the process, I will authorize an exchange of ambassadors between our countries, allow foreign oil companies access to petroleum deposits and eventually try to return Iran to its prerevolution status while retaining a moderate Muslim society and government . . . It would also be in our interest to arrange that docking rights be granted to American naval vessels and aircraft, and to reestablish an American military presence in Iran. I believe the wolf with the sharpest teeth ready to swallow us is the Soviet Union, which would like nothing better than to have direct access to the Arabian Sea and the Persian Gulf and control of the Strait of Hormuz. It would be of incredible strategic value to them.' He looked squarely at McDonough. 'Or to the United States.'

'Our immediate priority,' McDonough said, 'is a stable, neutral and genuinely moderate regime in Iran. Naval bases and listening posts may come later.'

Alientar nodded, but his expression showed scepticism. 'Of course. So what will you tell the president?'

'Tell him? Well, I believe I'll tell him that President Alientar has promised the world. Again. I'll offer the opinion that you are in no position to deliver anything, that you can't even guarantee your own safe return to Iran.'

The Iranian nearly threw the glass of whisky to the floor. 'You are an insulting – '

'I'll also tell him that the factions inside Iran that engineered the terrorist attacks in Washington, DC, still exist and still influence your actions – the evidence is in your self-imposed exile. I'll also tell him that you don't have the power to stop the on-going Revolutionary Guard speedboat attacks on neutral shipping in the Persian Gulf. *And* that any substantive deal with you would be a waste of time.'

Alientar appeared ready to go for McDonough's throat.

'*However*, sir, the president disagrees with my view in this matter. He will ask me what you have offered, and I will say that you have offered to form a stable, moderate Muslim government friendly to the West; that you have offered naval bases and air strips; that you generally feel that the United States is the lesser of two evils and you can better profit by us than by the Russians. I'll tell him about your supposed concern for the strategic balance in the region but also make clear that above all you are looking out for number one.'

Alientar kept seated, trying to decipher McDonough's words.

'Will that supply the requisite amount of humility and defiance, Mr President?'

Alientar managed a smile: a bright man, this McDonough . . . 'You are indeed insolent, McDonough, just like the rest of your kinsmen in Scotland. But you have another very annoying attribute – you seem to know what you are talking about. You are a man I can deal with – for now.'

'That's real good, Mr President, because until there's a noticeable and positive shift in the political climate in Iran, I will be your only contact with the American

43

government . . . For now, I've been authorized to deliver to you the following message: The United States views the evolving political scene in the Republic of Iran as a necessary and vital precursor to future stability in the region. Such stability is without question of major importance to the United States. Outside intervention of any kind would be seen as a destabilizing influence on this politically sensitive area, and we would view such outside actions as a potential threat to the security of the United States and her allies.' McDonough took a deep breath, needing more breath for this diplomatic jargon with its weight of hot air, which was not especially his style . . . 'Therefore, the United States will take such actions as it deems necessary to protect our interests in Iran, the Persian Gulf, the Gulf of Oman and the Arabian Sea region to prevent such destabilizing influences. We ask for the full cooperation of the government of President Falah Alientar in any future conflicts where our two governments might be at risk.'

Alientar tossed down the rest of the Scotch. 'Your president has just written himself a blank cheque, drawn on *our* account.'

'It's a matter of public record that the president supports you and your government. I'd suggest that you nourish his support. There are others besides myself who'll be pushing him to have nothing to do with your government until we have some assurances that you won't become an embarrassment.'

'And what would you have me do, Mr McDonough? You've already told me that my promises mean nothing to you.'

'Free elections, open negotiations, end actions against neutral or unaligned shipping in the Persian Gulf . . .'

'You think it is so easy,' Alientar said. 'Just stop the fighting. Lay down your weapons; come out and shake hands, eh?'

'Could be.'

'Perhaps you are more naïve than I thought, McDonough. From the time when I took control of the government my weapons have been my survival. If I lay them down . . . I will be destroyed, from without as well as within.'

'Your internal fight will be your own. Washington won't interfere. This president feels differently than past presidents – to him political unrest, even civil war, is another turn of the wheel of social evolution. Only when outside governments try to influence or intervene is action dictated.'

Alientar stood and retrieved his coat. 'What assurances do I have, McDonough, that your government will act to protect Iran from foreign interference?'

'None. But you understand the workings of the American government better than most in the Middle East. The president wants to strengthen ties with Iran and keep Soviet influence in the region to a minimum. In an election year like this, *open* commitments to you will be few if any. But if we're pushed to protect our interests in the Persian Gulf, we will act. You can take that one to the bank, sir. And you know about banks, they're the ones with stuff that makes the world go round.'

2

The crack of the bat reverberated through the stadium like a shot from a high-powered rifle. It was one of those unmistakable, instantly recognizable sounds – a good, solid, snapping *thwack* that even those who didn't follow baseball knew meant 'home run.' The left fielder did not even bother looking up for the ball, merely hung his head in disbelief, spat on the turf and punched a fist into his glove as he watched four men orbit the bases and stomp on home plate. Twenty thousand fans in the Oakland-Alameda County Coliseum groaned as Reggie Jackson, manager of the Oakland A's, headed for the mound to give the pitcher the hook and put in the fourth A's reliever of the game.

'It's about time Jackson took that guy out,' veteran battleship commander Captain Matthew Page, age fifty, said, his face a deep crimson. 'Three innings, five earned runs. Great. Just great.' He took a gulp of beer.

His wife shook her head at him. 'Matt, your blood pressure . . .'

'My blood pressure would be a damn sight better if Jackson would learn how to tell when a reliever is starting to miss the strike zone. Kelly has a split-finger, a curve, and a slider. In the sixth inning he came out and pitched ninety per cent split-fingers. His one slider went straight in the dirt. The man was in *trouble*. In the seventh he shook his right arm before he went into his motion and everyone was surprised when he walked two guys and

46

allowed two base hits. Now Wade Boggs . . . God, isn't that guy ever going to retire? . . . Nails a half-assed curve for a grand slam. I would've had a guy warming up in the bullpen the minute I saw – '

Captain Page's daughter, Ann, reached over to her right and picked up the wall phone in the US Navy's officers' Coliseum skybox and handed the receiver to her father.

'What's this?'

'It's for you.' The other navy commanders and their families in the skybox strained to listen. 'It's Reggie Jackson. He wants you to be quiet and stop annoying your family.'

Captain Page's ears reddened beneath his sandy salt-and-pepper hair.

'You're right about his blood pressure, Mother,' Ann said, tweaking one of the battleship commander's ears. 'He looks like he's ready to pop any second.'

Amanda Page couldn't suppress a smile.

'Very damn funny, missy,' Page said, but he allowed a smile through the gruffness. He leaned over his daughter. 'Big deal, Spaceman – oh, I'm sorry, Space*person*. Well, you're not so fancy your old man can't still pop you one.'

Ann held up her fists in mock-defence as the other navy men cheered her on. As the action on the field resumed, however, her father ruled himself the winner and ordered Ann to get him another beer.

On her way back from the skybox wet bar, sixteen-ounce beer in hand, Ann caught a glimpse of her mother gloomily leaning on the concourse railing.

'Mom? Everything okay?'

'Of course, sure, dear,' Amanda Page said, the tone of her voice denying the words.

Ann moved closer to her mother, who was staring out beyond the Coliseum Auditorium and across to San Francisco Bay and the hazy San Francisco skyline. Ann followed her gaze. One of the hundreds of towers, cranes, buildings, and other structures along the waterfront, Ann knew, was the massive grey steel superstructure of the USS *California*, secured at the Oakland-Alameda Naval Station. The fifty-eight-thousand-ton Iowa-class nuclear-powered battleship was the main escort ship in the fifteen-ship carrier battle group of the USS *Nimitz*, which would pass under the Golden Gate Bridge in four days to begin an eight-month cruise to the Indian Ocean.

Ann touched her mother's arm. 'You still have three days with him . . .'

Amanda shook her head. 'He's already gone, Ann. He's been gone for a week now.'

She turned to her daughter. 'Can't you see it? You've been home for a week now. He may be on terra firma but his mind, his heart, has been on the bridge of the *California* for days. That skybox is the ship's wardroom. Officers' country. He's listening to the game on Armed Forces Radio or on the TV rebroadcast from Managua, surrounded by his senior officers.' She managed a strained laugh. 'I don't know why it should bother me so. After all, I've been a navy wife for twenty-one years. This is your father's twelfth cruise. It's just . . . well, all that news about Iran, the counterrevolution business, the Persian Gulf – '

'Dad isn't going to the Persian Gulf, he's going to the Philippines.'

'I don't think so,' Amanda said quietly. 'I overheard a conversation last week. I think they might be sending the *Nimitz* to the Persian Gulf.'

'If all these rumours were true, Mom, the Persian Gulf would be clogged with US ships. You can't make yourself crazy over Officers' Wives Club gossip.'

'That's not it.' She paused, looking for the words. 'It's just that . . . it's different this time. It's not only your father leaving . . . it's you, too . . .'

'Me? Mom, I haven't been home in eleven years. You've been by yourself – '

'For too damn long, for too damn long. But that's not the problem. You've been away but at least I've known where you were – Harvard, MIT, Stanford, Houston. I knew if something . . . happened to your father that you'd be back and we'd be together no matter how far away you were.' She turned back to the railing. 'I can look out there and see your father's ship and I know that he's surrounded and protected by the best men and the best equipment in the world. But when I think of where *you're* going and the risks you'll be taking, well, it's hard for me even to comprehend it. I don't think I've ever felt this scared before. I admit it . . .'

Ann didn't have an answer, and now it was Amanda trying to reassure her daughter, which she did by giving her a quick hug.

'I'm sorry, Mom. I guess I've been so wrapped up in this thing, so preoccupied with my research that I never thought about how it would affect you.'

Amanda shook her head. 'Nor should you. You're like your father. He's said how sorry he is to be leaving me alone hundreds of times but it would take the guns of all his battleships to keep him from going. I admire you both so much; I wish I had more of your drive . . . I wish there was more time for the three of us to be together. Years pass quicker than any of us realize, you know. It's easy to take things for granted – not to mention feel sorry for myself. I'm sorry . . .'

Ann held her mother close, then lifted the cup of beer she was holding in her hands. 'The captain will be getting powerfully parched,' she said.

Her mother gave her a knowing smile. 'I heard some more Officers' Wives Club gossip,' she said as they walked past two young boys selling Oakland A's pennants. 'About that space station, Silver Tower . . . and how the

Russians hate it. *And* how vulnerable it is. But I suppose I'm being an alarmist about that, too?'

Ann was about to reply but stopped abruptly. What could she say that would really help? As a diversion, a welcome one, she pointed to a man with a portable video camera standing in front of the officers in the skybox. She guided her mother back to the box, where they took their seats at either side of Captain Page.

'Smile,' the cameraman said. 'You're on Diamond Vision!'

The family surrounded by the other men and their families waved at the camera. As they did, Ann glanced at the huge scoreboard in centre field: Her father's image was flashed, displaying his gold-trimmed hat with the words 'DLGN-36 USS CALIFORNIA' on the peak and his Oakland A's T-shirt. A caption under his picture on the full-colour scoreboard screen read 'Captain Matt Page, Commander, USS *California*.' Ann's picture was on the screen too: 'Dr Ann Page, Mission Specialist, Space Shuttle *Enterprise*,' the legend underneath it read. A ripple of applause came from the crowd.

'We're famous, babe!' Matt Page said to his wife, hugging her close. Amanda Page looked at her daughter, forced a smile, waving with restraint into the camera.

It turned out the only possible way to stay clear of the dozens of sailors tramping in and out of the bridge of the USS *California* was to stand behind the captain's high-backed seat, which was what Ann Page found herself doing one week after the baseball game. On the bridge was sheer bedlam: volleys of shouted orders, ringing phones, and a hodgepodge of engine and equipment sounds.

Through it all, Ann noticed, Captain Page was very much in control. No comparison to the overaged boy at the ballgame.

It was actually exhilarating to watch. He seemed to know just when a man would be in arm's reach or earshot when he needed him. The phone mystically stopped ringing when he needed to use it. His coffee mug never grew cold or was less than half full – in spite of the activity, a steward would somehow make his way to the captain's chair to refill the short, stubby mug labelled 'The Boss of the Boat,' and of course it never dared slide down a table or spill one drop on to the boss' plywood-starched khakis.

'Are you sure it's okay for me to be here?' Ann asked at a relatively quiet moment. Her father waved his coffee mug around the bridge.

'Of course it is.' He turned to a young officer. 'Dammit, Cogley, out of the way, if you please. I'm trying to talk to my daughter . . . No, I'm glad you wanted to come aboard. Your mother, as you know, doesn't feel right coming on board before a cruise. She never has, not in all our years of marriage. Not once. She stays on the dock until the ship passes under the Golden Gate or wherever, but she never comes on board.'

'Yes, I know.' Half her response was blocked out by a thick clipboard of papers that Cogley had thrust between her and the captain, every sheet of which Page impatiently initialled at the corner.

'Okay, now weigh anchor, Cogley . . . I'm sorry, Ann. No, your mother doesn't seem to like it on board the *California*.'

Ann tried to tell him he must know why, but a horn blaring from just outside the bridge drowned out her words, followed by 'All ashore, all guests ashore.'

'I've got to go, Dad,' Ann said, but he didn't hear, his attention elsewhere. She followed the outstretched arm of a grey-and-blue-uniformed Marine escort and headed for the exit.

She had just reached the top of the steel ladder that led

51

down to the main deck when she felt a hand on her shoulder, turned and found her father standing in front of her.

'You weren't going to leave without saying good-bye, were you?'

'I didn't know if I'd get a chance, and I really think I'm in the way.'

The harried petty officer, Cogley, came up to the captain with still another clipboard. 'Excuse me, sir – '

'Cogley, dammit, shove off with that stuff. Tell the officer of the deck to stand by until I'm ready.' Cogley hurried off.

'You're convincing me,' Ann said, 'that that guy's name is "Cogley Dammit" or "Dammit Cogley."'

'I know, I know . . .' Matthew Page steered his daughter away from the head of the stairway. 'Listen, honey, I wanted you to come with me on board so we could have a little chat – '

'About what?'

'About you. Your shuttle flight.' He paused. 'I still can't believe it. My daughter, a shuttle astronaut – '

'*C'mon*, Dad . . .'

'No, now wait a minute. I'm not going to get all gushy over you. I just want to – '

'Yes?'

'Ann, I've heard things. There's real concern about your mission, about this Skybolt laser you're working on.'

'I really can't talk too much about Skybolt, Dad. Not even to you. You can understand – '

'I know, I know, but dammit, you know I've never been too happy about your decision to fly to this space command station. The dangers are – '

'Keep 'em barefoot and pregnant?'

'Ann, honey, you're not listening.'

'I'm sorry, that was a cheap shot, I know you don't go

52

for that male chauvinist stuff. But, face it, if you were talking to a son . . .'

'I'd still be damned worried. This space station project of yours is dangerous. Things are happening, weird things. I just wish you'd – '

'Stay on the ground? Safe from the action. Away from my *work*.' Ann shook her head. 'Whatever you say, you still think it's okay for men to go off and face whatever's out there, but not women – '

He looked at her. 'Could be, honey. I guess I am a bit old-fashioned.'

'You're a damn sight better than most, but you have tended to put Mom and me on a pedestal. We're not china dolls. We won't break. I'm a scientist. Mom is your wife. We're both pretty tough. No kidding.'

Her father shrugged, knew she was right even if he couldn't buy all of it.

'And Dad, I know about the dangers. We get briefings, too.'

The loudspeaker gave another warning for visitors to clear the ship. Ann took her father's hands.

'I'll be thinking of you up there,' he said. 'And I still wish you weren't going.'

'And I wish you weren't going on this cruise . . . to the Persian Gulf.' The mention of the *California's* classified destination startled him.

'How . . .?'

'It doesn't matter,' she said quickly. 'But you have about as much chance of keeping me from going on the *Enterprise* as I have of dragging you off your ship . . . Now' – she stood on tiptoes and kissed her father on the cheek – 'have a safe cruise and hurry home.'

He straightened, hugged her. 'And success and a safe trip to you, Ann.'

The Marine escort guided her to the wide covered main gangplank on the *California's* starboard gunwale. A small

53

knot of reporters was waiting for her when she stepped off the platform on to the dock but she ignored them and quickly found her mother standing near the raised officers' wives' railed greeting area.

'He'll be all right,' Ann said quietly. Her mother's eyes never left the bridge as the USS *California* began slowly to slide away from its mooring towards the Golden Gate.

June 1992
Vandenburg Air Force Base, California

'*Lift off. We have lift off of the Space Shuttle Challenger, STS Mission 511. It has cleared the tower . . .*'

The Challenger's *pilot ran his fingers down the Space Shuttle Main Engine, the SSME status readouts on his computer monitor.* '*All main engines look good . . .*'

The young woman beside him acknowledged with a nod. No NASA simulator could ever fully prepare a person for the feeling of a space shuttle at liftoff. Noise. Incredible, ear-splitting, thundering noise. Vibration enough to feel intestines shake . . .

As the stowed service arm and gantry slid from view out the forward windscreens, Ann Page could even see a few seagulls scurry from the fiery behemoth as it lifted upward. The sight of the petrified sea gulls made her smile despite the adrenalin coursing through her, tightening her muscles, constricting her throat.

'*Instituting roll manoeuvre . . . roll manoeuvre complete,* Challenger, *you look beautiful . . .*'

On hearing the last report from Ground Control, Ann reached up through the gradually building 'g' forces to the upper left of her left forward instrument panel and flicked the ADI attitude switch to LVLH. '*ADI attitude switch to local vertical, local horizontal,*' *she announced over interphone. Her pilot in the right seat nodded and did the same on his panel.*

'Thank you, Dr Page,' the pilot said over interphone, and suddenly the pilot looked young – very young. Like a guy she had known in high school.

Ann watched the mach meter on her main instrument panel while at the same time checking her number-one cathode ray tube computer monitor and panel C2, the computer control panel and manual main engine controls. The engine control sequence for launch and ascent was controlled by computer, but she was obliged to be ready for any malfunction right up to complete engine failure. If that happened, it would be up to her and her pilot to control the engines manually and set up her shuttle for an RTLS – Return to Launch Site abort. As she watched her instruments she kept in mind her training – think 'abort, abort' until five minutes into the flight, after that think 'orbit, orbit.'

Forty seconds after takeoff the shuttle exceeded the speed of sound, and Ann saw the main engines throttle back automatically to sixty-five per cent.

'Control, this is Challenger. Main engines at sixty-five per cent. Confirm.'

'Challenger, we confirm SSMEs at six-five per cent, right on the mark.'

They were approaching a critical phase of flight when all aerodynamic forces affecting the shuttle – thrust, drag, gravity, and lift – were exerting equal pressure on the ship all at once. It was 'max Q.' The main engines were throttled back to avoid tearing the shuttle apart as it reached, then exceeded max Q. The shuttle's computers would control the delicate transition as the huge craft sliced its way skyward.

A few moments later Ann could see the pilot give a sigh of relief as the main engines began to throttle up under strict computer control.

'Control, this is Challenger. Max Q. Main engines moving to one hundred per cent.'

'Copy that, Challenger. *Max Q. Max Q. Max Q . . .'*

A blinding flash of light, a sensation of warmth, a feeling of weightlessness . . . 'Max Q., max Q . . .'

Ann was suddenly awake, waves of pain lancing through her abdomen. The rumpled sheets felt like damp mummy's shrouds, strangling her. She fought back the pain and kicked the sheets free.

'A damned nightmare,' she said half-aloud, her breath coming in gasps. After months of briefings, simulators, studying, she had finally had a *Challenger* nightmare.

Exhausted, drained, she rolled across the bed and glanced at her watch on the nightstand. Two A.M. That made the eighth time in five hours she had been forced awake by butterflies invading her stomach and her dreams. Butterflies? Those things were dive-bombers, nuclear explosions, earthquakes. Forget it, sleep was impossible.

They had warned her about *Challenger* nightmares, everyone from mission commanders to local food-service people – nearly everyone even remotely involved with the rejuvenated space shuttle programme seemed to get one. But she figured it was even worse for her . . . a civilian mission specialist with very little flight-deck training. Well, even though she had two hours until her alarm would go off, she crawled out of bed and into the bathroom. Trying to sleep would only prolong the punishment.

Feeling as drained as if she had run a marathon, Ann stripped off her nightshirt and panties and stood in front of the mirror in the glare of the bathroom's single light bulb. Her doomed attempts to wrestle a few hours' sleep had left her, she noted, with light brown circles under her dark green eyes . . . 'Too bad they don't wear helmets in space any more, at least the visor would hide this,' she told the unappetizing mirror image. In fact, little she saw in a mirror ever pleased her. People said she was always her worst critic, but still . . . She frowned at the too-round green eyes, the straight auburn hair, the unremarkable breasts, the too-skinny legs . . . although the ankles were good. (But great ankles never got a girl a date.) All right, she wasn't bad, but nothing to write home about either. A seven. Maybe a seven and a half . . .?

Besides, a body was not something to show off – it had always been something to work on, to operate. She had exercised hard all through high school and college, not because it was the thing to do but because she wanted to excel at one thing – running. She had trained her body to perform well in track and field events, not to win beauty contests. She even had a few trophies on display at her parents' house. The result of her efforts were a healthy if less than spectacular body, a daily running habit – and dates too few and far between. Who was it who said you couldn't be too thin or too rich? Half-right, whoever it was . . .

She unwrapped clear plastic from a drinking glass, filled it with lukewarm tap water and took a sip. She could feel the liquid go down, then seem to solidify in an acid lump in her throat. Wouldn't go down and it wouldn't come up. Great way to start the day. Strange, she hadn't thought about high school or college or her social life in months. Even the shuttle pilot who'd popped into her dream had been a long-forgotten high school boyfriend. On a day like today she'd better be thinking of something else.

She took her time after her shower, drying herself and combing her long red hair, and still found herself with an hour to go before her planned wake-up time – two whole hours before her taxi was due.

She dressed in thin cotton long underwear, cotton gym socks, and her powder blue NASA flight suit. She put up her hair in her trademark ponytail, redid it twice to kill time. It didn't help. Still an hour and forty minutes until the taxi was to arrive. Nothing on TV at three in the morning.

Once again her stomach started to gnaw at her . . . To hell with waiting for the taxi. She slipped on her black flying boots, left the room key on the bed, turned out the lights and closed the door behind her.

In the lobby of the Vanderburg Air Force Base Visiting Officers' Quarters, she had to cough twice to get the clerk's attention. 'Can you call the base taxi and get me a ride to the Shuttle Flight Center?'

The clerk stared at her shuttle crewmember flight suit and did a double take – even with one-a-month shuttle launches from Vandenburg, a shuttle crewperson was an unusual sight. 'Transportation is swamped on a launch day,' the clerk said. 'The Shuttle Flight Center will pick you up – '

'At four A.M. I want . . . I have to go out there now.'

The clerk caught the hesitation in Ann's voice, and her expression changed from bored to irritated. 'I'll check.'

As the clerk dialled a desk phone Ann wandered through the lobby and over to a wide, floor-to-ceiling window facing the Pacific Ocean. Washed clean by the night air and lingering Santa Ana winds, the predawn sky glistened with hundreds of stars. A tiny sliver of moon was about to dip a horn into the cold water, and the big bright planet Jupiter sparkled brilliantly.

'Miss?' The clerk had to raise her voice to get Ann's attention. 'Transportation says they can't get out earlier than four-thirty.'

'Never mind,' Ann said, heading for the door. 'I'll walk.'

'Walk? To the Shuttle Center? That's ten miles . . .' But Ann was already out the door . . .

Ten blocks later she had left the main base behind. Ahead were miles and miles of emptiness – abandoned thirty-year-old wooden barracks, parking lots, crumbling buildings and athletics fields giving way to occasional sand dunes and grassy meadows.

As the bright glow of civilization behind her melted away, the feeling was electric, and she found her pace quickening. The ocean breeze was like an amphetamine. To the west the stars appeared so bright and near they seemed to cast a reflection off the gentle ocean waves. To the east the first faint outlines of the San Rafael Mountains could just barely be made out.

She found herself now in a gentle, easy jog . . . the butterflies, the nightmare, even the grouchy desk clerk, all seemed part of some happy conspiracy to make her experience this rush, this mysterious communion with earth and sky. Her boots crunched on hard sand, and her cheeks stung from the cold breeze as she stepped up her pace, the chill air seeming to flow into her veins and through her whole body.

This was her place, all right. Free. Open. The thought of being cooped up, strapped in, locked in place seemed scary, repugnant.

She had reached the top of the small rise, and abruptly found herself a few hundred yards from a tall fence illuminated every fifty yards by powerful searchlights. A concrete guard shack blocked the road in front of her. Air force security guards with rifles and dogs patrolled the fence; the dogs were barking, straining against their leashes, their super-sensitive noses picking up the intruder.

Three miles beyond the twelve-foot-high fence stood a massive structure, brilliantly illuminated and clearly visible in spite of its distance. It looked like a skyscraper sitting in the middle of nowhere. A few hundred yards from the building was a squat, ungainly shape dwarfed by the skyscraper, surrounded by open-skeleton towers on two sides and also illuminated by large banks of super-powered spotlights. She was looking at the ultimate, the rebuilt space shuttle *Enterprise*. And the skyscraper-like building to the right of it – the one she had first seen when she had come over the rise – was the new Vandenburg Vehicle Assembly Building. There was movement of the men near the front gate and the concrete guard shack but it didn't register in her mind. Her attention was all on the ungainly, squat machine sitting on top of a tall concrete pedestal in the distance.

From a distance it looked so small. She had seen many shuttles, of course. She had been in *Enterprise* numerous times on dry-run rehearsals, emergency egress training, orientation walkarounds. From up close at the shuttle's base or on the access tower the thing looked huge. She had never felt confined or claustrophobic around the shuttle – until now. From this vantage point it looked like a toy model.

And she was going to strap herself in that toy and let someone ignite four million pounds of propellants and rocket fuel under her, blasting her at twenty-five times the speed of sound hundreds of miles into the sky. Was she crazy?

Even crazier was that she had had to *work* to get aboard that thing. She had to apply, be interviewed, beg, plead, cajole just to be considered. After that there had been months of waiting, then six months of training, study, simulators, tests, exercises, presentations – all so she could live hundreds of miles above the earth's surface, breathing recirculated air, eating irradiated food, drinking chemically produced water and coping with microgravity.

She was so caught up in conflicting emotions that she didn't notice the air force security police jeep drive up alongside her. It was the heavy breathing of a huge Doberman pinscher that pulled her back.

'This is a restricted area,' one patrolman said as he approached, shining a flashlight into Ann's face, his M-16 automatic rifle at port arms. 'Identification. Now.'

She absently reached into a right thigh flight-suit pocket to retrieve her ID card. It wasn't until she had unzipped that the guard recognized her.

'Dr Page?' He took the ID card from her, scanned it, handed it back. 'Saw your picture in the paper. You're going on this morning's flight . . .'

'Yes, right,' she said, hoping she sounded more official than she felt.

The guard handed the dog to an airman beside him, looped the rifle back on to his right shoulder. 'You shouldn't be out here alone . . .' He stopped and looked at her. 'Everything okay?'

'Yes. I was just a little impatient to get to the pad so I decided to walk . . .'

'From the main base?'

'I . . . I ended up jogging. It felt good, peaceful . . .'

'Yeah, I guess it would,' he said. 'I'd probably do something like that if I was going to ride that candle . . . I'd want to take one last look at ol' Mother Earth before leavin' . . . Well, I'll have to take you to the Shuttle Flight Center, Dr Page. You can't be walking around out here by yourself. I'm surprised someone didn't pick you up when you left the main base.'

She scarcely heard him, had withdrawn into her thoughts again. What was it that was bothering her? Was it fear of death? She had never confronted death before. Even in shuttle training, even through all the briefings and classes, she had never thought about dying. Besides, that was a no-no, everybody knew that.

She let herself be led to the jeep, rode with the security guard commander, nodding absently at his comments.

No, damn it, she wasn't afraid to die. She knew it was possible, knew it could happen any moment without any warning. But, to coin a cliché, it went with the territory, and it was a territory she badly wanted.

As her attention drifted back to the security guard, she

heard him saying he'd always wanted to go up on the shuttle but didn't have any specialized degree beyond an AB. Besides he was only an enlisted man, the officers copped the girls and the assignments.

'The girls, I don't know,' she said. 'But all you need is a technical degree and you can be any rank. Doesn't matter. Hey, I don't have any rank. I'm a civilian. They need technical degrees and volunteers willing to dedicate themselves to the programme. Back in the seventies and eighties they wanted experienced flyers and senior officers. Now, they need crewmembers for a whole range of jobs . . .'

Ann realized she sounded like a NASA recruiter. Was she really as enthusiastic as she sounded? Was it really so simple? Right now she needed to believe that this flight into space was at once routine and a chance of a lifetime. That's the only way she'd get through this thing.

As the jeep pulled up in front of a low steel-and-concrete building, the Vandenburg Shuttle Flight Center, she took a final look overhead. The ebony sky was brightening to azure blue, closing off the vastness that would soon enclose her.

Space Shuttle *Enterprise*

Three hours later the crew of the Space Shuttle *Enterprise* stepped into the elevator in the service tower and rode it to the orbiter entry level. They walked across the service arm and into the 'white room,' where white-suited, surgical-masked technicians used vacuum cleaners to remove any bits of dirt and gravel off their boots and uniforms that could accumulate in the crew compartment during microgravity flight. Then, one at a time, they walked towards the circular side hatch into the shuttle.

When it was her turn, Ann stopped and shook hands with one of the techs.

'Thanks,' she said quietly. They shook on it. No more words were necessary.

Originally, *Enterprise* had been built for landing tests. In 1977 it had been released off the back of a modified Boeing 747 carrier plane to test its ability to glide to a landing with no power. It was never intended that *Enterprise* ever be launched into space.

The *Challenger* accident in 1986 had changed that. It had been far less expensive to refit *Enterprise* for space flight than to build a new orbiter, so the refitting process began late in 1987. *Enterprise* inherited much of the new 1980s technology in space shuttle design. The first difference was obvious as Ann stepped towards the entrance hatch – the absence of the thermal protection system's insulation tiles. Instead, the shuttle used a smooth fabric blanket made of carbon-carbon – lighter, stronger and less expensive than the silica tiles on *Columbia* and *Atlantis*. Earlier, only the shuttle's nosecap and wing leading edges had the extreme high-heat protection of carbon-carbon alloys – now the entire surface had it. Whereas the old exterior had looked rough and scaly, like a lizard's skin, the new exterior was pure white, smooth and glassy.

Ann was helped through the entry hatch and into the middeck area of *Enterprise's* crew compartment, where she looked down at the storage compartments, personal hygiene station, and airlock hatch. 'Weird,' she said, 'I'm standing on the wall, like Spider Woman.'

Captain Marty Schultz, the *Enterprise's* payload specialist, was just stepping up the ladder to the upper flight deck. 'Wait till you get into orbit on Silver Tower,' he said. 'Walls, ceiling, up, down – all gone. Silver Tower is another world.'

She crawled up the ladder behind Schultz, who was

now standing beside three seats on the flight deck, and looking high 'above' herself, saw Air Force Colonel Jerrod Will, the mission commander, and Marine Colonel Richard Sontag, the *Enterprise's* pilot, in their seats. They looked 'down' as she crawled into the flight deck and pulled herself up.

'Crawl across the seats and take the right side,' Shultz said. She manoeuvred herself across the flight deck and on to the right-hand mission-specialist seat. A technician walking on marked areas on the payload control panel in the back of the flight deck helped her strap in and handed her a 'Snoopy's hat' communications headset, which looked like an old college football helmet with wide ear cups.

'Your portable oxygen system is on your right here,' the tech told her as Ann strapped herself in. He talked her through a preflight of the portable oxygen system, POS, and her comm panel while Schultz and Kevin Baker, the grey-haired designer of Silver Tower Thor interceptor missile system, crawled into their seats. Ann felt more normal after she was strapped in, but the sight of technicians standing sideways on the walls while she was seated facing up was still disorienting.

'I can see why some people get airsick on the ground,' Baker said.

Marty Schultz gave the older man a reassuring look. 'As I just told Ann, once they close the hatch we're in a new world. The first time I rode the shuttle the transition from earth-normal to space-normal was really bizarre. I felt like I was sitting on my back two hundred feet above ground.'

Ann could feel her toes grip the front of her seat as Schultz went on. 'But you get over it. Now I look forward to the switch. Everything's a lot freer in microgravity, including your imagination.'

Colonel Sontag glanced over his shoulder at the three

mission specialists. 'All strapped in back there?' he asked over interphone. All three said they were.

Sontag gave them a thumbs-up. A moment later: '*Enterprise*, this is Vandenburg Launch Control, radio check on a/g channel two. Over.'

Colonel Will: 'Good morning, Control. Loud and clear, channel two.' The radio check was repeated several times on a variety of frequencies.

'*Enterprise*, we are T-minus eight-zero minutes, mark. Launch advisory check.'

Over Will's right shoulder Ann could see a large red light marked 'ABORT' snap on, grow dim, blink off. 'Abort check OK, out.'

Minutes later a white-clad technician flashed one last thumbs-up through the entryway access, then ducked below, and the heavy main entrance hatch closed with a *thump*.

'*Enterprise*, side hatch secure.'

'Roger, copy,' Sontag said. 'Crew, cabin pressurization coming up. Pressure on your ears.' Commander Will flipped switches, and Ann could feel her ears pop as the cabin pressure was increased to check for leaks or an unsecured hatch.

'Control, this is *Enterprise*. Cabin pressure normal, one-six point seven psi. Over.'

'Roger, *Enterprise*. Out.'

'Ann, you're cleared for power on your payload monitoring panel,' the pilot, Sontag, said. 'Check out your baby back there and report any problems when your check is completed.'

'Roger.' Ann flipped a guarded switch marked 'PL MON ONE' and watched as the instrument panel to her right came to life. Except for a few miscellaneous supplies, the Skybolt laser she had developed was *Enterprise's* only cargo on this trip, and it was her job to check the systems on the forty-thousand-pound laser module to be sure there was no damage that might cause contamination or a hazard during launch.

The exhaustive check of the laser module's five separate sections took longer than she had expected. Finally she reported back. 'Payload monitor power off, Colonel. Check complete. Everything's in the green. Ready for launch.'

'Control, this is *Enterprise*. Ready to resume countdown. Over,' Sontag reported.

Colonel Will, with six years flying space shuttles, turned to the computer keyboard, punched in 'SPEC 99 PRO' and the computer monitor on Sontag's side changed from a blank screen to a pictorial representation of the *Enterprise's* launch trajectory. Will checked the display. In case of a malfunction of all three of the general navigation computers, the GNCs, he would fly the *Enterprise* manually into orbit using the computer display as a road map. He keyed his microphone. 'Control, this is *Enterprise*. Flight plan loaded and checked. Over.'

The checklists ran faster and faster. From T-minus twenty minutes to T-minus five minutes, Will and Sontag worked furiously. Their main job was to start the three auxiliary power units, the APUs, which supplied hydraulic power to *Enterprise*. During launch the APUs would make sure the *Enterprise's* aerodynamic surfaces were in their streamlined launch position; during landing or during an emergency the APUs would supply hydraulic power to the surfaces to allow the shuttle to be flown like a conventional aeroplane.

After T-minus five minutes Will and Sontag could do little but watch the computers on *Enterprise* and acknowledge status checks from Vandenburg Launch Control.

'T-minus two minutes,' Launch Control reported. 'H-two and O-two tanks pressurized, *Enterprise*. You are go for launch. Over.'

'Copy, Control. We're go for launch.' Sontag looked over his shoulder once more at Page, Schultz and Baker.

'Here we go . . .'

'Put the pedal to the metal, Colonel,' Schultz said and immediately regretted it. Pretty callow stuff, he told himself. The others indulged him by ignoring it. Ann settled herself as far as possible in her seat and pulled her seat straps tight as she could stand it. The air felt electric – not stuffy or humid but super-charged with power. Far below she could feel the rumble of another piece of equipment – the solid rocket booster's ignition APUS. The thought of six million pounds of thrust about to be let loose made her eyes shut tight.

'T-minus ten seconds . . . nine . . . eight . . .'

She nearly jumped out of her seat as she felt a gentle touch on her left hand.

'Relax.'

It was Marty Schultz, nodding. 'It'll be fine, relax.'

She took a deep breath, feeling as if it was the first she'd taken in hours.

'. . . Six . . . five . . . four . . . ignition sequence start . . . main engine one ignition . . . two ignition . . . three ignition . . .' Sontag wasn't talking over the interphone – he was screaming out loud across the cockpit: '. . . Manifold pressure good all three engines . . . three in the green . . .'

One hundred feet behind Ann, the three main engines were cranking out one-and-a-quarter million pounds of thrust, but almost no noise or vibration could be felt. Ann did feel a *twang*, the sway of the orbiter towards the external tank as the main engines moved towards full thrust, but even that wasn't too noticeable.

She knew from endless simulation what came next. She could just make out the ABORT line on the front instrument panel. It hadn't come on, thank God. When the orbiter realigned itself after the *twang* it meant –

67

It felt as if a freight train had just rumbled out of nowhere right beside her – from near-quiet to ear-splitting sound – as the solid rocket booster ignited. She couldn't help letting out a gasp as the solid rocket boosters, the SRBs, exploded into action. In three seconds the thrust beneath her had been multiplied by a factor of five; now the fury of over six million pounds of thrust was alive, and *Enterprise* had not yet even left earth.

Suddenly a huge hand pressed against her chest, causing her to involuntarily expel air in a grunt. Stars clouded her vision, but she could see the launch service tower drop from view.

Airborne.

'*Enterprise*, you have cleared the tower. Engines look good.' Ann was surprised to see Will and Sontag reaching up to their forward instrument panels; she tried to raise her hand against the 'g' forces, found they were light but building. Soon even lifting one hand took effort.

'Control, this is *Enterprise*. Main engines at sixty-five per cent. Over.'

'Roger, *Enterprise*. Standing by for max Q.'

Ann clutched the armrests of her seat. Here came one of the most critical moments of the launch – the moment when all the dynamic pressures affecting the shuttle were –

'Max Q, Control. Main engines one hundred per cent.'

'Roger, people. Very pretty launch. Spectacular. Out.'

'Coming up on SRB burnout, Control.'

The solid rocket boosters burned out and were jettisoned precisely on schedule, under computer control. *Enterprise* was now several hundred miles west of Mexico on its southern pole-to-pole trajectory. The SRB motor casings, each floating to earth under three one-hundred-fifteen-foot-diameter parachutes, would be retrieved over the Pacific Ocean.

Enterprise's ride was somewhat different from other

shuttle flights. First, *Enterprise* was following an eccentric elliptical polar orbit instead of a circular equatorial orbit. And second, *Enterprise* was climbing to an altitude of five thousand miles so that it could rendezvous with Silver Tower as it travelled in high orbit. Because of fuel limitations, previous shuttle flights had been limited to a maximum altitude of about seven hundred miles above earth.

It was several hours before Will finally announced: 'Welcome to space, crew. OMS burn is complete. We are in orbit.' Relief washed across everyone's face.

'We're within a few miles of Silver Tower's orbit,' Sontag reported over interphone. 'We saved ourselves a few hundred pounds of fuel on that burn, so we have a small safety margin. I'm estimating linkup with Silver Tower in two hours – it's about fifteen thousand miles ahead of us, but we're gaining . . . Marty, you're clear to open the cargo bay doors. After that you'll all be cleared to unstrap to begin system checkouts. Kevin, check the middeck for any damage or anything out of place.'

Schultz and Baker acknowledged Sontag's call and began to unstrap. Ann looked on as Schultz's straps began to float around his vacated seat before he resecured them.

'Remember,' Schultz said, 'even though you're weightless up here in orbit, your body still has mass that you need to overcome, which means stopping yourself after you get moving.'

'So I noticed,' Baker mumbled after he'd unstrapped and promptly collided head-first with the ceiling.

Schultz watched as Baker manoeuvred himself around and floated out of sight down the ladder to the middeck level of the crew compartment.

'Now to get those cargo bay doors,' Schultz said. With Ann floating beside him, he made his way to the aft flight deck instrument panel. Ann looked out the windows facing into the cargo bay but it was too dark to make out any detail.

'Panel R13 has the door controls,' Schultz was saying. Over interphone he said, 'Check power levels for cargo bay doors, Colonel Sontag.'

Sontag checked the power distribution panel near his right elbow. 'Switches set.' Next he checked a bank of three ammeters, switching the monitor controls through each of the fuel cells to check their output. 'Power's on-line, Marty.'

'Rog.' To Ann, Schultz said, 'Okay. Electrical power runs the hydraulic motors that operate the doors. There are also electrical backups, plus the doors can be opened and closed by the remote manipulator arms and even with an emergency space walk if necessary. The radiators deploy after the doors are fully open.' Then over interphone Schultz reported: 'Doors coming open.'

'Clear to open,' Colonel Will said.

Schultz activated the controls. Instantly the payload bay was bathed in a brilliant blue-white light that reflected off the aluminium insulation covering the Skybolt laser module. The space shuttle *Enterprise* was flying upside down in relation to the earth's surface, so *Enterprise's* sky was the earth – and Ann was seeing this 'sky' for the first time. 'My God . . .'

The *Enterprise* was just crossing the dawn-line between Hawaii and Australia. It looked like a relief map being lighted from the side – each island in Micronesia, it seemed, was visible in stark detail. They could recognize the Solomons, the Samoas, even the New Hebrides Islands. There were a few puffs of clouds but otherwise it was like looking at a meticulously rendered painting of the whole South Pacific.

'Ann?'

'It's . . . beautiful . . . so *immaculate* . . .' She said quietly. Schultz nodded. 'I never stop being awed by it myself. If that sight doesn't move you, you belong in a basket.' He turned to the interphone. 'Bay doors open. Radiators deployed. No damage so far as I can see on the radiators.'

'Copy,' Sontag said. Will double-checked his readouts with Mission Control through a direct UHF radio and data-link originating in a station antenna farm at Yarra Yarra in western Australia.

'Mission Control confirms clear for orbit and rendezvous with Armstrong.'

It was some two hours later when Ann peered out the forward windscreens into the grey-black void, but all she could see were a few stars too bright to be obscured by the brilliance of earth. 'Colonel Sontag, you must have X-ray vision if you can see that station out there.'

'It's still very faint,' he said, 'but it's there. Mostly it looks like another star.'

She shook her head. 'I'm going back to the aft console.' The pilots nodded and continued scanning their instruments.

Marty Schultz had deployed the shuttle's remote manipulator arm and had scanned space for a few minutes with the arm's closed-circuit camera at high magnification, but it wasn't until *Enterprise* was ten miles away from the station that he spotted it.

'It looks like a toy, like a Tinker Toy, from here,' Ann said.

'When they first launched it they treated it like one,' Schultz told her. 'People, some people, called it a boondoggle, big waste of money that could better be spent carpeting the Pentagon hallways. A lot of us were afraid it would end up like Skylab – a blaze in the sky and a crash to earth.'

Kevin Baker, still trying to get his balance in this world of microgravity, manoeuvred beside Page and Schultz at the aft crew station, saying, 'I remember that too well, and the argument over who owned the space station. The US taxpayer spent billions launching it and a conglomerate of scientists, some of them not even from the US, managed to put a clamp on any military research aboard it. You would have thought the station was a broken-down tenement building the way they talked about it. The Silver Sausage . . . the space suppository . . . remember?'

Ann nodded, straining for a better view of the station. 'But this Brigadier General Saint-Michael apparently did a good job changing people's minds.'

'That he did,' Schultz said, 'and everyone's taken the station very seriously since. That toy, Ann, weighs in at about five hundred *tons*. What you see is the product of twenty shuttle sorties over four years, plus another dozen unmanned supply rockets. Thirty billion dollars' worth. The world's most expensive condo, you might say . . .'

As *Enterprise* drew closer to the station more details could be seen, and on the screen Ann pointed to a tiny dot just below the station.

'Is that your Thor system?' Ann asked Baker.

'Sure is, twenty nonnuclear interceptor rockets, a laser decoy discriminator and a radar detector and tracker. The Thor is our first antiballistic missile defence system in thirty years. Simple, low cost, *and* effective – if I do say so myself . . .'

Attention was soon diverted to the TV screen, filling with the image of the station, and the crew was ordered back to their seats for docking. Schultz stowed the camera and remote manipulator arm back into its cradle in the cargo bay and shut down the aft console. 'Crew ready for docking,' he reported.

Within a mile of the station the digital autopilot had reduced *Enterprise's* forward speed to one thousand feet per minute. A thin laser beam from the space station lanced out towards *Enterprise*, towards the two sensors on the forward and rear ends of the cargo bay. The forward sensor was a large lens that focused the laser alignment beam on to the aft sensor. The digital autopilot would make tiny corrections to the shuttle's course whenever the laser beam drifted off the aft sensor, in this way aligning *Enterprise* with the docking tunnel on Silver Tower.

With near-magical precision the computers controlling the *Enterprise's* reaction-control system thrusters positioned the docking adapter in the cargo bay within a few feet of Silver Tower's docking tunnel, which was then manoeuvred over the adapter, and the two docking rings locked and sealed into place. Next an open-latticework support beam was extended and locked into cleats in *Enterprise's* cargo bay. The support beam strengthened the union between the two spacecraft, effectively making them one unit. Finally the connecting tunnel between the docking module and *Enterprise's* docking adapter was pressurized to two atmospheres and checked.

'Adapter leak check is good, Armstrong,' Colonel Sontag reported to the docking officers on Silver Tower. 'Docking complete. Over.'

'Checked over here, *Enterprise*,' from the docking officer aboard Silver Tower. 'Welcome aboard. You're clear for crew transfer.'

'Roger. Thanks.' On interphone Sontag announced, 'Docking complete, crew. End of the line.' Ann, Baker and Schultz sent up congratulations to *Enterprise's* commander and pilot, but Colonel Will waved them off.

'The autopilot did most of it, and frankly it was a lousy job. I could've got us right on the mark.' Will then directed shutdown of most of *Enterprise's* systems and began preparation for transfer to the station, with Sontag and the rest of the crew moving downstairs to the transfer area on the middeck.

Colonel Will pressurized the airlock and air space, and he and Sontag checked the pressure readouts. 'Sixteen psi in both areas,' Will said, undogged the first hatch leading to the airlock, then rechecked a second pressure gauge for the airlock itself. Satisfied, he opened the heavy steel door to the airlock.

'See you,' he said, checked a POS mask and rebreather in the airlock and strapped on the face mask. Sontag closed the airlock chamber door and sealed it tight, and Will checked the pressurization gauge leading from the airlock to the transfer tunnel, then undogged the upper airlock hatch. There was a slight hiss of equalizing air but no sign of leaks or damage.

'Welcome aboard, Colonel Will,' a voice said above him. Will looked up through the transfer tunnel to see a youngish Space Command airman smiling down at him.

Will unstrapped his face mask and glared at the technician. 'You're supposed to wait until I open my airlock hatch, John.'

'I was right behind you, sir,' Airman John Montgomery told him. 'Believe me, Colonel, I'm not going to let myself get sucked into your cargo bay.'

'One day that's going to happen.' Will turned and unlocked the airlock hatch leading to *Enterprise's* crew compartment. He wasn't smiling. 'Clear for transfer, crew.'

One by one the crew of *Enterprise* floated up and out of the airlock and into Silver Tower's spacious docking-control module. Sontag, the last one leaving *Enterprise*, latched and double-checked each hatch behind himself; *Enterprise* would now be sealed up and apart from the station.

Armstrong Space Station

It was a long thirty-foot journey along the four-foot-diameter transfer tunnel. The crew members were met at

74

the other end by technicians who helped them through and gave them sneakers with stiff Velcro 'hooks' on the soles.

A man with gold braid on his lapel stepped forward. 'Welcome to Silver Tower. I'm Colonel Jim Walker, vice-commander and deputy commander for operations around here.' He shook hands with the newcomers, Ann and Baker. 'I hope these pirates gave you a good ride.'

Walker was another one of the so-called typical space-soldiers Ann had met in the Space Command, which was responsible for all space-based defence. He looked young for his rank, thin but not too tall, with a nearly bald head. His manner and appearance suggested quiet intelligence, not the old-fashioned domineering military presence – a scientist or engineer instead of a soldier. Most of the members of Space Command, drawn from the ranks of the military's scientific elite, were like that. In college they might have been labelled 'computer weenies' – on Silver Tower they were commanders, leaders, innovators. To Ann he said, 'I'm looking forward to working with you on your project.'

'Thanks to you I have a project to work on. I've heard it was you who applied the pressure to finally get the Skybolt project approved.'

'Thanks, but General Saint-Michael is the mover and shaker around here. He was the one who set things going.'

'Is General Saint-Michael – ?'

'You'll be meeting him soon. He's been occupied most of the day with repairs on our main data-link transmitter.'

'I hope it's not serious,' Baker said.

'No, but it needed the general's direct attention. He's like that. Nothing's too big or too small.' The deputy commander led Ann and Baker through the small docking module and then through an overhead hatch. At first it seemed all the eight main pressurized modules on Silver Tower were the same small size as the docking-tunnel connector or at most a larger version of the spartan working interior of the space shuttle. When Ann entered the first module, she found out she was wrong.

It was spacious and well lit. Two senior officers and four technicians hovered in front of control panels, sipping coffee and exchanging reports. Green plants and flowers – natural carbon-dioxide scrubbers – sat Velcroed to pedestals around the module.

'This is the command module,' Colonel Walker said as the group floated up through the small connector into the module. 'All communications, earth surveillance and station operations are conducted here. The general's work area is over there.' General Saint-Michael's work area, Ann noticed, was different from everyone else's in at least one respect – it had a chair. The men who served under the general were expected to stand, anchored to the deck by their Velcro sneakers or attached to variable-height work platforms. Fuzzy Velcro loops were everywhere – on the ceilings, walls, floors, even on instrument panels.

Baker pointed to the module's 'ceiling.' 'Instrument panels on the ceiling, Colonel? Why?'

Walker turned to Baker. 'Tell me, Mr Baker – which is the ceiling? Is that the ceiling . . .?'

Walker detached himself from the Velcro 'floor' and floated up to the ceiling, hovering a foot above Ann's head. He anchored his feet to Velcro footholds moulded into the 'side' instrument panels. 'Or is this the wall? In space, and *especially* on Silver Tower, conventional up and down don't exist – they mean something else. If we create a module with five hundred square feet of earth-conventional floor space, we can in effect triple that amount by mounting some instrument panels on the ceiling. The cost of building materials is cut by more than half. A few years ago we had a new technician on board who got so confused about which way was up – literally – he got real sick. This was back when Silver Tower wasn't any more than two tin cans. He'd got up a few hours earlier than anyone else and was walking on the walls for two hours before realizing that the floor was down there. We've now made a yellow-coloured Velcro loop carpet for the "floor" to end the confusion. Anyway, we keep monitoring and auxiliary controls up here. Someone using them keeps out of the way of people using the conventional control panels and we double or triple our work space. It all takes some getting used to but after a few days you'll be swinging around the cabin like you were born here.'

Walker detached himself from the ceiling, floated back to the deck and motioned to a group of two technicians and an officer manning a large, multiscreened unit that looked like an air traffic controller's console. 'The SBR, space-based radar, operators are there. They scan preprogrammed areas of the Soviet Union and other countries for any missile-launch activity as we fly over them. The radars on Silver Tower can direct and track any object larger than three thousand pounds at almost any altitude – even on the ground or below the surface of the water. We also can tie in with geosynchronous infrared satellites for missile-launch detection. Right now the SBR is tied into Dr Baker's Thor missile garage tethered beneath the station. Eventually we'll be in direct control with and control of hundreds of Thor missile garages in earth orbit, directing the strategic missile defence of the whole damn northern hemisphere.'

He turned to Ann. 'Your laser system is what's got us really excited. If you're correct in your prediction that a one-minute laser barrage will have the power to destroy hundreds of missiles, we may have the ability to neutralize the whole Soviet nuclear arsenal.'

'*If* it works, Colonel,' Ann said. 'The problems we need to overcome are still pretty huge . . . For now, I'd put my money on the Thor missiles.'

77

Walker accepted that with a shrug, then led the way to the next module, which was like the command module except a bit less organized. Again, four technicians manned the module, two of them positioned in front of large banks of equipment.

'This is the experimentation module,' Walker said. 'Personnel and equipment are moved in and out of this area on a weekly basis. Some weeks it's bacteria – others it's transformers or superconductive circuits. All of the equipment bays are temporary – we can remodel this entire module in half a day. Dr Baker, this will be your office.'

'Great, it's bigger than my lab at Los Alamos.'

Walker led them through the side hatch into a long glass-lined connecting tunnel. 'This leads to the second parallel column of modules. We've built each of these connecting tunnels with thick Plexiglas so that it can double as a sort of observation deck. This view is . . . well, see for yourself.'

The view was breathtaking. The entire space station was spread out before them, a science fiction movie come to life.

Far below them the centre open-framed keel stretched far out into space, almost out of sight. Nearly a thousand feet long and a hundred feet square, the keel held large silverized fuel tanks, mounting and equipment housings for a variety of antennas, and miles of pipes and tubes snaking throughout. Beneath the keel were mounted the huge curved space-based, phased-array radars, their foot-ball-field-sized electromagnetic eyes continuously scanning planet earth beneath them. At the very ends of the keel were two solar-energy collectors, each twice as large as the radars – massive, delicate, incredibly thin-looking sheets of glass aimed at the sun.

'On earth those collectors would weigh eighty tons apiece,' Walker said. 'Up here, of course, nothing. We

78

use a tiny, fifty-horsepower electric motor to keep them pointed at the sun. They supply enough power for two stations. While the station is in sunlight they provide direct energy. We also use them to recharge a bank of lithium-hydroxide batteries for emergency use and to break down waste water to produce hydrogen and oxygen for our fuel cells and station thrusters.'

'Is that what you'll use to power Ann's laser?' Baker asked him.

'Unfortunately, no,' Ann answered for him. 'We need ten times more collectors for just one burst. We'll use a small nuclear MHD reactor to power the laser.'

Baker pointed towards the very ends of the keel. 'The station thrusters are also out there on the keel?'

'Right,' Walker said. 'Five small hydrogen rocket engines on each end of the keel. They fire automatically about two dozen times a day to correct the station's altitude, attitude, alignment and orbit. They're also used to move the station if necessary.'

'And you get the fuel for that from water?'

'Right again. We use electrolysis chambers powered by the sun to crack waste water into hydrogen and oxygen gas that's collected and stored in those tanks out there. We bring up a shuttle full of water about once every two months, and we also get water from the fuel cells, where we recombine hydrogen and oxygen to produce electrical power and water. In an emergency a full complement of twenty crewmen can survive up here for six months without resupply.'

They continued through the thick Plexiglass tunnel to the next module. Ann and Baker found themselves in an immense structure many times larger than the command module and laboratory modules they'd just left.

'This is a complete Skylab module, the first component of the original NASA space station launched two years ago,' Walker explained. 'This segment of the station was first lofted before full-scale Shuttle flights resumed. As you can see, it's as large as the third stage of a Saturn booster, sizable enough for the experimentation we were doing originally, but certainly not now.

'When full-capacity Shuttle flights resumed, we built the rest of Silver Tower using cargo bay-sized modules. We now use the Skylab section for living and recreation quarters. For those purposes, there's more than enough room.'

'That must be your gymnasium over there,' Baker said, pointing to one area of the module.

'Uh huh, everything today's astronaut needs to keep his body fit,' Walker said, accenting his voice like a carny pitch-man. 'Treadmills and Soloflex weight – you shall forgive the expression – machines here, exercise bicycles over there. At the other end a videotape and audio tape library, computers, television . . . We get two hundred channels from all over the world.'

Baker examined one of the 'weight' machines. 'Clever,' he said. 'Using thick rubber bands to create resistance. Obviously a typical weight machine won't work up here.' He studied the treadmill. 'How does this work?'

'Same as a regular one except you strap on this bungee cord belt first. You can adjust the tension of the bungee cords to increase the resistance. The skipper – General Saint-Michael – practically lives on the treadmill. No one can keep up with him and he's forty-three years old.'

They made their way to the sleep module, a series of small chambers that looked like curtain-covered horizontal telephone booths arranged like two-tiered bunkbeds. Each end of the module had two very large rooms, bathrooms.

Walker peeled back the sides of a sleeping bag in the chamber. 'You can adjust the elasticity of the sleeping bag covers. We've learned by now that crew sleep better if they feel at least a little of the sensation of gravity.

Sleeping while floating around weightless isn't all that comfortable. We've begun using those zero "g" vacuum showers like the Russians have, but they can be a real pain. By the way, the sleep module – actually the whole station – is coed. No separate facilities. We haven't had too many women on Silver Tower . . .'

Ann wondered what it would be like bunking with a dozen men. They'd probably feel more uncomfortable than she would. A battleship commander's daughter, she'd grown up seeing men being men. She also *liked* men, too often more than they returned the favour . . .

The group moved down to the next hatch; this one double-sealed and leading up to another docking module like the one connected to the command module. According to Walker this docking area was better suited for transferring supplies and fuel from a shuttle or an unmanned cargo vehicle. He motioned to the lower hatch. 'That leads to the storage and supply module, and below that is the MHD reactor. MHD, as Ann can tell you, Dr Baker, stands for magnetohydrodynamics – a way of producing massive amounts of electromotive force in a very compact unit. We'll cut across here to engineering.'

Engineering was much like the command centre. 'It's really the computer centre,' Walker told them. 'The kitchen – uh, galley – is located here as well.' He continued on, pointing to a hatch at one end of the computer module. 'There is your office, Ann – the control module for your laser, Skybolt. Nobody's been in it except when it was connected and tied into the rest of the station last month.'

They opened the hatches and entered the module – or tried to. Unlike all the other pressurized modules, the Skybolt control-and-experimentation centre was choked with equipment, wiring, pipes, conduit and control consoles, with a lone work space tucked in a far corner.

'Wh – where do I work?' Ann said. 'I mean, where's my lab, my instruments, test gear? It's – '

'It's all there,' Walker said, trying to sound upbeat. 'But it's been compacted to fit into this one module. Your control console is over there, plus a few other panels on the ceiling.' He understated, Ann thought. The main control consoles were on the module's ceiling, surrounded by built-in handholds and footrests. She forced a smile in Colonel Walker's direction, but she was getting dizzy just looking at the overhead console.

'Welcome to Silver Tower.'

3

June 1992
Defense Intelligence Agency, Virginia

'All right, Mr Collins,' George Sahl, deputy director of operations of the Defense Intelligence Agency, said. 'You've got my attention – and apparently the attention of your section chief.' He looked warily at Preston Barnes, in charge of the KH-14 Block Three digital photo imagery satellite. 'Spill it.'

Jackson Collins, associate photo analyst under Barnes, cleared his throat and stepped up to Sahl. 'Yes, sir. The Russians are going to invade Iran.'

Barnes closed his eyes and muttered a 'Collins-you-idiot' to himself and not audible to the others, he hoped. Collins noticed the deputy director's shoulders slumping. Before Sahl could say anything Barnes turned angrily towards his young photo interpreter. 'Collins, didn't you ever learn how to give a proper report – ?'

'Easy, Preston,' Sahl said, raising a hand to silence his division chief. 'I've scanned your report and your analysis, Mr Collins. Now I want you to *tell* me. Briefly, please.'

'Yes, sir . . . The military buildup around the southern TVD Headquarters at Tashkent is inconsistent with either a fall offensive in Afghanistan or the army's seasonal manoeuvres scheduled for this month. The offensive – '

'What offensive?' Barnes said.

'A CIA report circulated through the division last month about a suspected, unusually large-scale Russian push into Afghanistan sometime this fall.'

Barnes shook his head. 'This CIA calls every resupply

mission to Afghanistan an offensive. Overland routes into the central highland have been cut off recently by bad weather and the Afghan government has all but folded its tents. Naturally the Russians have had to step up supply flights.'

'But, sir, not with as many as six Condors . . . Those photos showed hangars large enough for An-124s –'

'Condors?' Sahl didn't like to hear that. 'Where did you see *Condors* in the southern military district?'

'It's . . . an educated guess, sir. Those large temporary hangars I mentioned in the report are large enough to accommodate Condors –'

'*Or* any other Soviet aircraft flying,' Barnes said. Collins looked away – he'd never expected to have to fight off his section chief.

'What else?' Sahl prompted him. 'Your report mentioned the rail units. You counted forty per cent more activity in the Tashkent yards. What about that?'

'Yes, sir, the actual count is up thirty-seven per cent from activity this same time last year, also several weeks prior to manoeuvres, and up twenty-four per cent from the Soviets' last real large-scale offensive into Afghanistan two years ago, when they put down the Qandahar uprising. And that had been the largest Soviet offensive since their invasion of Czechoslovakia. Whatever they're planning now, it'll be larger than either of those –'

'Collins,' Barnes said quickly, 'you can't make conclusions like that based simply on the number of rail cars in a switching yard. There could be dozens of reasons why there were more cars there . . . Look –' and he softened his voice – 'these reports can set a lot of things in motion. Things that cost a lot of money and a lot of effort by a lot of people. Dangerous things. They get a lot of attention. If we're wrong and we send all these men and machines off on a wild goose chase . . .'

Collins' face hardened. He dropped two eleven-by-fourteen black-and-white photographs on Sahl's desk. 'You can't ignore *this*, Mr Sahl,' he said, pointing a finger at the first photo. Sahl studied it.

'What . . .?'

'It's a computer-enhanced KH-14 image of one side of one of the large two-acre hangars at Nikolai Zhukovsky Military Airfield at Tashkent.' Sahl peered at the highly magnified photo. Trailing behind the hangar was, he saw, a fuzzy, rectangular object. Almost no firm detail, though. He studied the photo for a moment longer, looked up at Collins. 'It's a scrub photo.'

'Sir, it is a photo of a GL-25 missile launcher. There are – '

'Collins, it's a scrub photo,' Sahl repeated. 'Magnification, contrast, grain, background – it's not worth piss for analysis. It's a scrub photo.'

'*Sir*, I counted seventy of this same weird-looking rail car in Tashkent. All of them surrounded by guards, all of them bracketed by security rail cars. I understand no certain judgement can be made on the basis of this photo, but an *educated* guess can easily be made – it's a GL-25 long-range cruise missile launcher, mounted on an allterrain carrier. Here, look – two missile canisters, the control centre – '

'It looks like a concrete container to me,' Barnes said. 'Or a gravel container. There's nothing unusual about it.'

'The KH-14 wasn't properly stabilized,' Collins said, 'but you can still make out the – '

'Collins, you can't make out that kind of detail on a scrub photo,' Barnes snapped.

'I can. I did, sir.'

'If you look at a photo – *any* photo – long enough,' Sahl said quietly, 'you'll likely see what you want to see. That's why we have parameters for how much a photo can be enlarged or cropped.'

'Then I'd like to request another overflight by the KH-14,' Collins said. 'We need more photos of those rail cars.'

'All right, all right,' Sahl said. 'I agree. I can start the request for some air time on KH-14 for Tashkent, but I'm not sure if they'll approve it.'

'Sir, I realize you suspect this is just another junior photo interpreter trying to score points, but it's not. I really believe there's something going on. Something big.'

Sahl tried to hide a wry smile, took one more look at the photos, then tossed them on the desk. 'You mentioned Iran. Tell me, Collins, how could six invisible Condor transports and seventy alleged GL-25 mobile missile launchers in Tashkent lead you to the assumption that this is all part of an Iranian invasion group?'

Collins hesitated. Too late to retreat now, buddy, he told himself. 'It wasn't just the missiles or the transports, sir. It's the buildup of Russian ships in the Persian Gulf and the *Brezhnev* carrier battle group that sneaked into the Gulf last month. It was that unsuccessful counterrevolution in Iran that CIA said was sponsored and financed by the Russians. It's – '

'It's also bull, Collins,' Barnes cut in. 'Your job isn't to come up with a wild hypothesis based on second- and third-hand information. Your job is to take KH-14 imagery and describe it. Period.'

'I thought my job was analysis. This is important, I know it. And I know it's urgent enough to require special attention – '

'Are you sure it's not you who wants the special attention?' Barnes said, fixing him with a drop-dead stare.

Sahl raised a hand.

'That's enough for now, Preston. I believe Collins is one hundred per cent sincere. Give him that.' He turned to the photo interpreter. 'Hot dogs come by the gross around here, Mr Collins. Plenty of people want to make the splash, but they do it knowing that they don't have to take the heat – the *real* heat – if they're wrong. Are you willing to take the heat?'

His question hung in the air for a moment, a long moment; then Sahl said, 'Why don't we try a little experiment? I'm going to put your name on this report. I'll clear it for the director's review and put it on his desk with a recommendation based on your findings that we follow up on this with another series of KH-14 overflights. If there's any heat from the director's staff, you take it. Sound good?'

Collins looked frozen in place . . . It's not a KH-14 Block Three analysis, he thought, or a Satellite Photo Recce section report – it's *my* report. A Jackson Collins report. Okay, damn it, I asked for it . . . 'Yes, sir – with one request. That I be given another week to make the presentation my way.'

Sahl glanced at Barnes. 'What's wrong with this?' and glanced at the thick report on his desk.

'It's a standard section report, sir. As it stands it doesn't convince anyone of the seriousness developing at Tashkent. I mean, it didn't convince *you!*'

'And whose fault is that?' Barnes said.

'It's mine, sir. I'd like a chance to fix it.'

Sahl was impressed. This wasn't what you'd expect from a youngster. 'I'm putting it on the director's staff-meeting agenda for Friday,' he said. 'This is Tuesday. You have until Friday morning to redo the report and refine your presentation. If you can't do it by then, forget it. This division doesn't operate on your personal time-table or mine or anybody's.'

No hesitation this time from Collins. 'Thank you, sir. I'll be ready.'

He hoped.

It was 6:30 in the morning. Ann activated a powerful fan built into the shower floor below her that sucked away the water blobs that were moving up her back, arms and legs. She swept a few persistent blobs from the shower walls, took off the plastic eye protectors, opened the stall and reached for a towel. A wide mirror mounted on the wall caught her reflection, and as she had done three weeks before in the visiting officers' quarters back in Vandenburg she stopped to take stock. Space was *murder* on a woman. Even though daily exercise had kept her face naturally lean, fluids and fat cells had redistributed themselves, giving her a slightly Oriental look, which contrasted with a noticeable increase in height – microgravity had awarded her three extra inches – and a loss in body weight of about six pounds.

Well, maybe as usual she was too hard on herself, but she certainly didn't feel too desirable at the moment, although normal female desires were intact. Part of it, she knew, was that her work on Skybolt had gone forward in fits and starts, with more problems to overcome than she'd anticipated. Any time her work was not going well her self-image took a hit. She knew it was irrational to link her desirability as a woman with her progress in the laboratory, but she couldn't separate the two . . . She had been using her intelligence and professional acumen to win acceptance for so long.

Telling herself to cut it out, she promptly ignored her own injunction, wondering what the station's commander, Brigadier General Jason Saint-Michael, thought of her work so far. A strange man, Saint-Michael. Difficult to get a fix on. Considering what Colonel Walker had told her about the general's sponsorship of her project, she had expected a warm welcome from him. But their first meeting the day after she arrived had been a very perfunctory affair indeed. When the conversation turned briefly to the laser, he had shown little enthusiasm. It seemed he was preoccupied with something else and not really listening to what she had said.

As she pulled on a fresh, powder-blue flight suit and set off for the station's galley, she mentally reviewed what else she'd learned about Saint-Michael in the short time she'd been here. Most of her information had come from the talkative engineering chief, Wayne Marks. The way Marks told it, Saint-Michael was a legend in Space Command – what some called a 'fast burner.' After graduating at the top of his pilot class he'd made captain easily and become an Air Training Command instructor pilot. From ATC it was on to Air Command and staff college at Maxwell Air Force Base, Alabama, where he wrote a paper laying out fundamentals of what would later be called the United States Space Command, an organization that would control America's space-based defensive armaments.

Saint-Michael's paper somehow found its way to the desk of the president who liked what he read, and Saint-Michael, at age thirty-two, found himself with a general's star and stewardship of the nascent Space Command – an organization that at the time existed only on paper. How Saint-Michael was able to build up Space Command to its present level was never precisely clear to anyone outside the inner circle of power, but it was said that the general, by sheer charismatic force, had eventually been able to make converts out of his strongest adversaries. It seemed he had that sort of effect on people.

At least that was Marks's version. For her part Ann, feeling a bit let down, she admitted, by her nonreception, had failed to discern any special magnetism, animal or otherwise, in the man. He was efficient, no question, in complete command of the myriad operations aboard

Silver Tower. But there was also a remoteness about him, a detached air edging on imperiousness that tended to leave her cold. If indeed he was a fast burner, he hadn't turned any of his heat her way . . .

She moved through the cargo docking area and across to the connecting tunnel leading to the primary docking module. As usual she stopped and admired the spectacular view of Silver Tower orbiting above planet earth. The most eerie sight was space itself – a deep pure, haunting blackness that was remarkable for its uniformity, its lack of gradation. As a child growing up in Massachusetts she had always felt insignificant somehow, watching an approaching thunderstorm darken the landscape. During the summers she had often camped in the Maine woods, where it had been so dark she literally hadn't been able to see her hand in front of her face. But space was a million times more so. The darkness was *total*, absolute, shrinking, swallowing everything in it. Space somehow seemed like a living thing, like two giant hands cupped together around the tiny station, cutting out all air and light . . .

It took less than a minute for Ann to reach the galley and begin the delicate task of making coffee: put 'coffee bag' into an insulated drinking cup, snap lid on, watch as hot water is injected in cup. By the numbers, like so much else around here.

'One for me, too, please,' a deep voice called out behind her. She turned and saw Jason Saint-Michael floating through the hatch.

'Good morning, General,' Ann said. As she placed a coffee bag into another cup, she watched the powerfully built officer plant his feet on a Velcro pad six feet away and stand with arms crossed.

'I take mine black,' he said.

She nodded and reached for the first cup of coffee,

which had just finished. She tossed the cup over to Saint-Michael, noticing with satisfaction that it sailed directly into his hand. 'You're really becoming a pro at this.'

'Fixing coffee isn't exactly high-tech, General.'

'How's the space-sickness?'

She looked at him. *Why the sudden interest in her?* 'All right. I still feel the "leans" when I move upside-down but the nausea is going away.'

'It takes some people longer to adapt.' He seemed to study her for a long moment, then asked: 'And how's life on the station going?'

'Life? As opposed to work?'

'I guess that's what I mean. I know there have been some problems getting the laser ready for the first beam test, but maybe you're worrying too much. You stay off by yourself when you're not working on Skybolt . . .'

'Does that worry you?'

'It does, frankly. You don't have to be a shrink to realize that someone who stays by herself so much may be having trouble coping. Problems like that get exaggerated in space. Up here we're all our brother's keeper . . .'

Ann took a sip of coffee (actually 'sipping' with a strawlike drink tube on the cup was very difficult) and squinted as the liquid stung her throat. 'I'm sure you're right but I don't think I'm a candidate for special treatment – '

'Anyone hassling you, bothering you in any way?' he persisted. 'I know being the only female on the station can be a little awkward – '

'*You* know what it's like?' She smiled when she said it.

'Well, I'm guessing it's a little like being the only general officer on this station.' He didn't return the smile. The lady seemed pretty damn defensive . . . 'I can't exactly be "one of the boys" around here, but I can't afford to alienate anyone, either. I walk a tightrope, which I *imagine* you have to do, too . . . Look, I'm just

91

trying to help. Sorry if I'm out of line.' He watched her for a moment. 'You don't much like it up here, do you?'

'What I like doesn't matter. I also don't want any special treatment, okay, General? I have a job to do – and that's what matters . . .'

An awkward silence, then: 'You're really very attractive, you know.'

She just looked at him, started to say something, then set down her coffee cup on the Velcro counter. 'General, if you really knew what it's like to be the only female on this station, you wouldn't have just said that.' She pushed off the floor, floated past him out through the galley hatch.

He watched her receding form, shook his head. Way to go, Jason. You really can be an ass.

'Attention on the station, two minutes . . . mark. Report by station when secure for test.'

Ann took one last sip of water from the squeeze bottle, then stuck it on a Velcro strip on the ceiling. On earth she might have squirted the rest of the water down her shirt to help battle the heat and perspiration, but in space such a luxury was impossible. The Skybolt control module was oppressively warm, stifling; the equipment air conditioning and cooling fans may have been keeping her instruments comfortable, but the module's lone occupant felt as though she was in a sauna.

She sat at her tiny control station completely surrounded by equipment. The only illumination came from the twelve-inch computer monitor in front of her. A narrow corridor, too narrow for two people to pass by each other, led from her station to the sealed module hatch and connecting tunnel. The air had the faint smell of ozone, electrified air and sweat.

But soon after beginning work on Silver Tower, Ann had learned to ignore such things. She had no room to work in because she had four times more equipment than any other scientist or any other project ever had before. Today all the hard work and sacrifice . . . if that's what it had been – was about to pay off. Or so she hoped . . .

'Skybolt is ready, Control,' she reported. 'System is on full automatic.'

'Copy, Skybolt,' Saint-Michael said over interphone. 'Good luck.'

'Thank you, sir. Thirty seconds.'

She made one last systems check. Her master computer would make a three-second self-test of the superconducting circuits, micro-processors and relays under its control. The results of the self-test flashed on her screen: all systems go.

It was working, Ann thought. It was working perfectly.

'It's not working.'

Chief Master Sergeant Jake Jefferson pointed to his large two-foot by three-foot rectangular display screen, representing the one-thousand-mile scan range of Silver Tower's huge space-based, phased-array radar. He had electronically squelched out all objects detected by the SBR that were less than five hundred pounds, all ground returns and all previously identified objects; even so, the screen was filled with blips. Each blip had a code assigned to it by Silver Tower's surveillance computer. On the margins of the rectangular screen, data on the object's flight path and orbit were displayed. Any object within fifty miles of Silver Tower's orbit was highlighted. The tech pointed to the nearest such object on the screen.

'There it is, Skipper.' Saint-Michael manoeuvred himself around to the screen and anchored himself on the Velcro carpeting.

It was an Agena-Three cargo spacecraft, one of the small fleet of unmanned modules used to resupply the American and European space platforms. This one had been fitted with detection-and-analysis equipment as well as sensors to record laser hits made against it. The Skybolt computer had already been programmed to consider this Agena 'hostile.' For the next three hours the Agena would follow a track similar to the track a Soviet ICBM would follow from launch to impact in the United States.

'Altitude?'

'Five hundred on the nose.' Jefferson pointed to the object's flight data readout, which had just appeared. 'We should be picking up its identification beacon any sec – '

An extra three lines of data printed themselves just under the flight data block, identifying the newcomer as an Agena-Three unmanned spacecraft launched from Vandenburg and belonging to the United States Space Command. The information remained on the screen for three seconds, then disappeared as the computer squelched off the identified.

'Bring it back,' Saint-Michael said. Jefferson punched two buttons on his keyboard, rolled a cursor over to the spot where the blip had been and pushed a button. The Agena's blip and data block returned.

'Skybolt hasn't keyed on it yet?' Saint-Michael asked.

'Negative.'

'Maybe it squelched it out.'

'Skybolt doesn't squelch out any targets,' Colonel Walker reminded Saint-Michael. 'It's supposed to track and evaluate everything detected by the SBR. If it's considered hostile, it's supposed to act.'

'Maybe Skybolt wasn't reprogrammed to consider it a hostile,' a technician, Sean Kelly, said.

'Or maybe Skybolt is screwing up,' Saint-Michael said. Jefferson nodded in agreement, then keyed his interphone mike.

'Skybolt, this is Control . . .'

Saint-Michael grasped his shoulder. 'Don't, Jake. Let's see what Skybolt does.'

'Go ahead, Control,' Ann replied.

Jefferson looked at Saint-Michael, then at Walker. Walker shrugged, silently deferring to his commanding officer. 'Disregard,' Jefferson said, and clicked off his mike.

The group watched as the Agena spacecraft marched across the screen. The SBR tracked it easily.

'Still nothing?' Saint-Michael asked.

'Not yet,' Jefferson said. 'Target on course. Thirty seconds to midcourse transition . . .'

Suddenly the station's warning horn blared, crowed three times; then a high-pitched computer-synthesized voice announced: 'Attention on the station. Tracking hostile contact. Tracking hostile contact.'

'About thirty seconds late, but it finally found it,' Walker said.

'Skybolt transmitting warning message to Falcon Space Command headquarters, sir,' the communications officer reported. A pause, then: 'Falcon acknowledges.'

'So we have a machine fighting our battles for us,' Saint-Michael muttered. 'Damn thing even makes radio calls.'

'Attention on the station' – the computerized voice. 'Impact prediction on hostile contact. Impact prediction on hostile contact.'

'It's finally figured out what's going on,' Saint-Michael said. 'Well, let's see how well it reacts.'

'Coming up on midcourse transition,' Jefferson reported. 'Thirty seconds to simulated warhead-bus separation.'

The Agena would not actually release any warheads, but the spacecraft's orbit had been sequenced like a real ICBM to monitor Skybolt's performance. The goal was to destroy the ICBM as early as possible, either in its very vulnerable boost phase or at the latest at the apogee – the ICBM bus's highest altitude in its ballistic flight path.

Once past apogee the target would become increasingly difficult to hit.

'Skybolt had better damn hurry,' Walker said. 'The thing will MIRV any second . . .'

Abruptly every light aboard Silver Tower dimmed. The station's backup power systems snapped on. Warning horns blared.

'MHD reactor activated,' someone in the command module called out.

'Skybolt's not tracking the Agena,' Jefferson reported. He checked his instruments, squinting in the sudden gloom of the command module. 'Still not tracking . . .'

The rest of his sentence was lost in a deafening blast. It was as if a huge bolt of lightning had just burst directly beneath them. The entire command module felt warm, and flesh crawled.

'*Laser firing!*' Jefferson shouted. 'Firing again . . . again . . . still firing . . .!'

Walker grasped a handhold – although the station did not move, the sudden burst of energy surging through the station made it feel as if the whole five-hundred-ton facility was cartwheeling. 'Skybolt's still not tracking the target,' he shouted. 'It's firing, but not at the Agena.'

Saint-Michael swung round to another technician near the connecting hatch to the research module. 'Any hits, Bayles?'

The tech shook his head. 'Clean misses. Sensors not recording any energy levels at all.'

'Damn. Discharge inhibit,' Saint-Michael ordered. Immediately, the crackle of electricity and the sound of lightning ceased. Slowly the cabin lights returned to normal.

Saint-Michael put a finger on his mike button, expecting the next call . . .

'Control, this is Skybolt,' Ann said over the interphone.

'The laser's being inhibited in your section. Check your controls.'

'I ordered the stop,' Saint-Michael said.

'Why?'

'Because it wasn't hitting anything.'

Silence. Saint-Michael watched his crewmen slowly relaxing from the tumult of Skybolt's first bursts and the multiple alarms it had set off. 'Station check,' he said, forcibly trying to control his own accelerated breathing.

'Skybolt is ready for another series,' Ann reported.

'Agena target is well past MIRV transition,' Technician Kelly said. 'It'll go out of range in sixty seconds.'

'Let's wait until the second orbit, Ann,' Saint-Michael said. The techs in the command module showed they agreed with the decision by wiping sweat from foreheads and reaching for water bottles.

'But, sir – '

'The target is almost out of SBR range. You'll get another chance soon.'

.A long pause, then: 'I'm clearing off, Control.' Walker looked over at his commander and smiled.

'She didn't sound happy,' Walker said.

'I'm not celebrating, either. God, I didn't know that thing made so much racket. Did we sustain any damage from the power drop?'

Walker checked with the four techs in the command module. 'No damage, sir. I didn't expect that drop either, but it makes sense. The MHD reactor needs a big jolt to get started.'

'But not from the main station batteries,' Wayne Marks put in. 'Skybolt's battery is charged from the solar arrays, but it's supposed to cut off before MHD ignition.'

'Can the voltage spike suppressors handle it?'

'I don't see why not. I'll check everything out before the next test series.'

Saint-Michael nodded and manoeuvred over to the

Agena-monitoring panel. 'I really would've been happier if the laser had hit its target . . .'

At which point Ann entered the command centre and without a word to either Saint-Michael or Walker, reached across Jefferson's shoulder and punched up the target-sensor summary on his console.

'Where's the hit summary?' She scrolled through the timed readouts, then turned on Jefferson. 'I said, where are the hit records?'

'That's it, Ann,' Saint-Michael said. 'Skybolt didn't hit the target.'

'What the hell do you mean?'

'I mean, it didn't hit. Skybolt never even tracked the target. It spotted it thirty seconds after it appeared on the SBR, but it never locked on.'

'But it *fired*. Thirty pulses, seventy-five millisecond bursts, one hundred kilowatts on the *dot*.'

'Ann . . .'

'Skybolt can't fire unless it's tracking a target. It announced detection. It projected the flight path. It computed the track and fired . . .'

'But it never locked on,' Walker insisted. 'The skipper inhibited discharge when he was told Skybolt wasn't tracking and that no hits were detected. That's a proper precaution, you've got to admit.'

Ann punched a few more pages on the computer screen, finally convinced herself they were right. 'I don't understand. Everything checked out. The laser worked perfectly . . .' She turned to Saint-Michael. 'Well, we'll try it again in forty minutes. We'll nail it for sure this time.'

Saint-Michael nodded. 'But I'll keep the beam inhibit on until we see that Skybolt has locked on to the target.'

'*That's* really not necessary, sir.'

'Ann, I can't allow that laser to fire into space indiscriminately. I don't know where it went. It could be a hazard – '

'A seventy-five-millisecond burst of only one hundred kilowatts is no hazard.'

'At close range it could be. There's obviously a glitch somewhere. Skybolt is getting an erroneous tracking signal and firing when it shouldn't. For all we know we may have hit someone's satellite.'

Ann looked deflated, said nothing.

'And that power surge was completely unexpected,' Saint-Michael added.

'Power surge?'

'You didn't notice it?' Walker said. Ann shook her head. 'It dimmed all the lights and almost took out all station power. The backups kept the main power from dumping.'

'But Skybolt has its own batteries. It doesn't draw on station power at all . . .'

'Well, in this case it did.'

'That's impossible . . .'

'Ann,' Saint-Michael said. 'What we've been saying is the truth. Skybolt didn't track the target until nearly thirty seconds after it appeared on radar. It never locked on to the target. It drew off station power to activate the MHD reactor, it fired without locking on to anything and it failed to hit the target. Period.' He ignored her high dudgeon. 'I'll allow a second test firing, but only after engineering confirms that our suppressors and power backups can handle another surge. If they can't assure me that this station's equipment won't suffer any damage, the tests are over until the problem is corrected. If we go ahead with the test, I'll maintain a command-beam discharge-inhibit until I see a positive target lock-on. If I don't see a lock-on to the designated target, the test is over.'

'General!'

'All clear, Dr Page?' Saint-Michael accented each word.

Drop dead. '*Clear*, sir.' She slid past Saint-Michael and Walker and headed back to the Skybolt control module, the two officers watching her half-glide, half-jump through the connecting hatch.

'She's been working sixteen, twenty hours a day on that thing,' Walker said. 'I'd be pissed, too, if my pride and joy had just flunked out.'

Saint-Michael was noncommittal. 'Get me a report on the power situation and the crew's technical opinion on a second test firing. Also check out the Agena and the SBR. Maybe . . . maybe the problem's not with Skybolt.'

Walker nodded.

'And you handle the command inhibit.'

'Where will you be?'

Saint-Michael watched the hatch leading to the connecting tunnel close. 'In the Skybolt module. Pipe all communications down there.' Without waiting for Walker's response Saint-Michael headed towards the connecting hatch.

It was a tight squeeze but a few moments later Saint-Michael had wedged himself into the narrow walkway down the middle of the Skybolt control module.

He clicked his wireless microphone on. 'Control, this is Alpha Status of the backup power systems.'

'Sir, this is Marks. Backups are fully functional. No apparent damage. They're doing what they're supposed to do.'

'How much time until the Agena comes back around?'

'Estimating fifty minutes, sir.'

Saint-Michael looked at Ann, who was busy pulling a relay box from an electronics cabinet and inspecting the settings on a long row of circuit boards. 'You've a go for another shot, Ann.'

She pretended not to hear and slapped the box back into its slot, snapped the latches shut, manoeuvred towards Saint-Michael to another relay box and nearly jammed Saint-Michael in the ribs as she removed it. 'Excuse me, sir.'

'Listen, Page, you had better get that damned chip off your shoulder. It's too much baggage for this station – '

Ann ripped a twelve-inch-square circuit board out of the relay box with an angry yank. 'Yes, *sir*. I'm sorry, sir.' She avoided his stare and went back to her work space to find a replacement circuit board.

'You know this test will fail, too, don't you?' Saint-Michael said.

Ann turned on him. 'Thanks for the vote of confidence, General. But that's all right. I knew that's how you felt right from the beginning. You never wanted this project – '

'You have got things screwed up . . .' He shook his head. 'How did you ever get picked for this project? Sure as hell not for your glorious personality.'

She plugged the new circuit board into its slot. 'I'm *here*, sir, because this is *my* project. If you don't think it'll work, if you think it's all a waste of time, that's your prerogative – '

'I didn't feel that way at first. I guess it's your wonderful attitude that jams my gears – '

'My attitude has nothing to do with this project or your gears . . .'

'Has everything to do with it.'

She ignored that and moved back to her work station, punching buttons on the keyboard hard enough to rattle the desk.

'"*My*" laser, "*my*" module, "*my*" project. This isn't *your* anything,' he said.

'I designed it . . .'

'Did you build it? Did you fly it up here? Did you hook it up by yourself? Are you going to test it yourself? Now that there's a glitch in it, I suppose you think you're going to fix it yourself. It won't tie into the SBR, it won't isolate

101

from the station's batteries, it won't lock on, it won't hit what it's supposed to hit. But Ms Super Scientist is going to fix it in fifty minutes by *herself*, and by God she's going to have a successful second firing or else.'

Ann stared at the computer screen, her lips tight.

Saint-Michael was on a roll. 'Far be it from you to ask for help from any of us lowly military people. Your laser won't tie in with the SBR? Well, we happen to have three SBR experts on board this station but you haven't consulted any of them. You have a tracking problem? We have Kevin Baker, a thirty-year veteran in space-tracking hardware and software on board, but you haven't talked to him . . . Let me make some wild guesses here. You also haven't asked one single person, on this station or on the ground, for help. You're not in contact with anyone at your lab in Boston or your corporation in California. No one on this station knows anything about your systems. As a matter of fact, I'll bet I'm the only person on this station who's ever been inside this module since it's been activated. How am I doing?'

Ann's fingers stopped tapping on the keyboard. She looked up from her work-desk at Saint-Michael, shrugged, kept quiet.

'Ann, this is a tremendous project. The first space-based antiballistic missile laser. Two hundred megawatts of energy. Capable of destroying a hundred missiles a minute, maybe more. It's a fantastic device. And it works – the laser works exactly as advertised. You've done a tremendous job.'

'I hear a "but" coming.'

'You're right,' the general said, smiling in spite of himself. 'But . . . no one person can be an expert on everything. You designed the Skybolt module to "snap together" with Silver Tower. It's a technological marvel that the thing works at all. But there's a problem, and you're stuck – '

'I am not "*stuck*".'

'Then why did you replace that relay circuit board?'

She narrowed her eyes, then picked up the circuit board she had removed from the electronics rack. 'This? It's a tracking interface channel multiplexer board. It controls the logic channels between the SBR and the laser-mirror aiming unit . . .'

'But you said in Control that everything checked out OK. And your last-second self-test, which repeated out in the command module, said everything was ready. Now, how did you know which board to replace?'

Her eyes lost some of their anger, refused to meet his. 'I'm . . . I'm trying certain critical circuits. One might be . . . be fused or shorted – '

'Or maybe you happen to have a spare of that particular board. Maybe you felt the need to try something, anything, before the next Agena pass. After that, you have at least twenty-four hours to hunt for the real problem before the next pass.'

She stared at her workbench.

'Let me make a suggestion. If you agree, I'll pass along a request from you to meet with Colonel Marks, Kevin Baker, Chief Jefferson and Technician Moyer just before the shift change. I'll tell them you'd like to talk with them about the beam test and Skybolt's interfacing problem.'

He glanced over his shoulder towards the command module. 'I can almost guarantee that those guys will be tickled to get their hands on Skybolt. You'll get help out your ears. It couldn't hurt.'

She looked up from her workbench. 'You really do want to help?'

He touched her lightly on the shoulder. 'We *all* want to help. And it's nothing personal, so don't get all crazy on me. We're involved in the success of this wonder device of yours, too. Hell, I might even get another star if it works . . . promotion by association, you might say.'

She allowed a smile, then typed in a command on her keyboard and went to her microphone. 'Control, this is Skybolt.'

'Go ahead.'

'Second Skybolt beam test is postponed for a systems check. Skybolt is in stand-by. MHD is deactivated.'

'Copy and confirmed.'

She looked at Saint-Michael. '*I'll* ask the others to meet with me, General. I guess it's about time we got acquainted.'

Three days later the space station's crew gathered in the command module to hear an announcement from Saint-Michael. As was his habit, the general got straight to the point. 'We're moving Silver Tower,' he said.

'Moving?' Colonel Marks said, clearly upset. 'Where? I haven't heard anything about this . . .'

'You have some special feeling for this particular orbit, Wayne?'

'It's just . . . unexpected, Skipper.'

'Space Command and the Pentagon have brought a few items of interest to my attention that I think we can help out with. For the first time since Thor was first deployed on this station, Armstrong Station has a chance to act less like an orbiting laboratory and more like a tactical fighting unit. The primary objective of the move is reconnaissance. We have the most sophisticated space-based radars in the world on this station, but right now they're only used to scan empty sky above Russian missile silos and scan for aircraft flying over the pole. We've become little else but a redundancy, and I think we should be doing more.'

Heads nodded. Ann knew that what Saint-Michael was saying was right. Silver Tower tended to be thought of solely as the perfect place to conduct weapons experiments for the Strategic Defense Initiative Organization.

The Skybolt project was only one of several being conducted on board the station – others included Kevin Baker's Thor experiment, and experiments on superconductor technology and space-based miniaturization. Silver Tower usually had as many civilians on board as military men, and the station's docking ports were always occupied.

'So what's the job?' Colonel Walker asked. 'Who are we going to spy on?'

Saint-Michael brought out a chart that he had been keeping beside his work station and Velcroed it to an instrument panel. It was a Mercator projection map of the globe with a wavy line drawn through it. The uppermost crest of the line passed over Iran; the lower part of the line passed between Chile and New Zealand over the south Pacific Ocean.

'I propose moving Armstrong Station to a seven-hundred by one-hundred-mile elliptical orbit. Three-hour orbit; two hours and ten minutes over Africa and lower Asia. One-and-a-half hours within direct scanning range of Iran. And I want it in the very same track on each orbit.'

There was a low rumble of voices as the crew of Silver Tower studied the chart. It was Colonel Marks who spoke up again.

'On the same track? You mean – pass over the exact same points on the earth on each orbit?'

'Exactly.'

'That sounds serious, General,' Walker said.

Saint-Michael nodded. 'It is. I've received an . . . observation, I suppose is the best word . . . about a surprisingly large military buildup in the Soviet's southern military district. The observation hasn't alarmed many in the Pentagon because the buildup coincides in some degree with an announced Soviet military exercise and a suspected fall resupply push into Afghanistan. Even so, there are a few who believe something far more extreme may be happening . . . something like an invasion of Iran.'

Again there was a low rumble among the crew. Saint-Michael quieted them down, then went on. 'The idea of an invasion of Iran may sound far-fetched, but to me, at least, it makes sense. Iran is in a state of transition. Its people are deeply divided between the old Khomeini Islamic fundamentalists and those who genuinely want to reestablish ties with the West. The prolonged war with Iraq has weakened the country's defences. The point is, Iran is ripe for the picking.'

'So what are we supposed to do, General?' Kevin Baker asked. Baker looked ten years younger than his actual age of sixty-five as he stood in a nylon athletic warm-up suit, fresh out of the vacuum-shower after sixteen hours in space working on the station's Thor I garage. 'What are the orders from Washington?'

'I'm not talking about orders from Washington. This idea is mine. As I think you know, I have a good deal of discretionary authority when it comes to the operation of this station. I use it to avoid waste, accelerate research and development and make this station the most effective military unit of its kind. At least that's what I try to do. But it's been my feeling that Armstrong's great potential has been going to waste. We spend more energy on systems to defend ourselves than we do on providing a necessary strategic warning or tracking capability for Space Command. Now we have an opportunity to provide that capability, so I need input from you. Let's hear it.'

'It'll eat up tons of fuel,' Marks put in. He made a fast mental calculation. 'It'll mean sideslipping the station . . . at about nine hundred miles every hour.'

'So?'

'So!' Saint-Michael had to work to hide a wry smile – he had just activated Marks' mental microprocessors . . .

'Sir, it takes three hundred pounds of liquid hydrogen and oxygen a week for station-attitude adjustments – which equates to approximately three hundred miles' worth of movement. You're proposing to move the station nine hundred miles laterally an hour. That's an extra nine hundred pounds of propellant *an hour*. That's' – a slight pause – 'twenty-one thousand, six hundred pounds of fuel *per day*. One-third of a shuttle cargo flight full of fuel – one-fourth of an Agena-Three vessel . . .'

'If the proposal is approved,' Saint-Michael said, 'there'll be a two-per-week resupply sortie. An Agena-Three unmanned cargo module can supply us with four days' worth of fuel.'

'Why an elliptical orbit, General?' Walker asked. 'An elliptical orbit only gives you a look once a day at most. An equatorial orbit will give you a look several times a day.'

'I did some wagging on the computer,' Saint-Michael said. 'A one-hundred-and-fifty-nautical-mile equatorial orbit will place us over two thousand miles from the recon target area. That's the space-based radar's extreme range limit. I believe it'll be worth the extra fuel to set up an elliptical orbit, especially if it's adjusted for earth rotation – an equatorial orbit can't be adjusted.'

Saint-Michael stepped back to his chart, pointing towards the rectangle marking the recon target area. 'It'll be dicey,' he said quietly. 'Even without the threat of a Soviet invasion of Iran or a US–USSR confrontation, we'll be orbiting over the worst possible place on earth. We'll be flying almost directly over the Soviet Union's primary antisatellite unit at Tyuratam, and the Sary Shegan Missile Test Centre on Lake Baikash, where the Soviets supposedly have an active antisatellite and anti-ballistic missile laser – '

'Not "supposedly," General,' Ann put in. 'A laser powerful enough to blind satellites definitely has been in operation there for twenty years. The intelligence reports are underestimates. The Russians have a functional anti-satellite laser system at Sary Shegan, maybe powerful enough to damage this station.'

'There's little chance of that, Dr Page,' Jefferson said. 'This station is heavily armoured. After all, that's why it's called Silver Tower. The titanium-silver armour is stronger than – '

'Jake, the nickname is sort of outdated,' Walker interrupted. 'Only the original pressurized modules have the armouring, not the add-on centre beam, radar arrays, fuel tanks or solar arrays.'

'Right,' Ann said, 'that laser at Sary Shegan could slice through every unprotected device like butter.'

There was a moment of silence, then Saint-Michael turned to Colonel Marks. 'Wayne, could the electrolysis unit handle seven extra thousand gallons of water per day?'

'Easy,' Marks said. 'The unit was designed for a station twice the size of Silver Tower.' The electrolysis unit, powered by the huge solar arrays, converted Silver Tower's fuel – plain seawater – into hydrogen and oxygen gas. Radiators, perpetually facing away from the sun towards the minus-three-hundred-degree coldness of space, then condensed the gases into liquids for storage, or pumps simply sent the gases into the station's four positioning engines to adjust the station's orbit and attitude. One unmanned Agena-Three supply tanker carrying sixty thousand pounds of water from earth would be enough for satellite, shuttle, and hypersonic plane refuelling and full station operation for a month.

'General, will moving the station interfere with any further Skybolt tests?' Ann asked. 'I'll be ready for another free beam-test in three days. If things go well I'll be ready for another Agena-Three live-fire target test in a week.'

Saint-Michael paused. 'Sorry, Ann, but I have to recommend to Space Command that the Skybolt test be postponed for now. We'd be sure to catch hell for firing the laser so close to the Soviet Union's ICBM fields.'

'General,' she said quietly, too quietly, 'we all worked *very* hard to advance this project ahead of schedule after the first partial-power test failed. In my opinion, sir, a successful Skybolt test should claim higher priority than an unsolicited recon mission.'

'Your comment is noted, and now – '

'Then I have your assurance, General, that my objection will be given equal weight with your own arguments when you make your proposal to Space Command.'

'As commander of this station I'm obliged to include recommendations and advice from all members of my crew. I am *not*, however, required to give assurances to *anyone*.' He turned to Colonel Marks. 'Wayne, I'd like you to double-check my figures on the proposed orbit and fuel calculations. Colonel Walker, get together with Wayne and set up a rough resupply schedule system using both shuttle and Agenas.' He took a deep breath. 'Dr Page, please outline the delays in your programme and any potential problems caused by the delays.'

He scanned the faces around him. 'I want the data ready for encryption and transmission by tomorrow morning. I'll propose the station repositioning for three days from now.' He looked directly at Ann, who didn't blink.

'That's all.' The group filed out, a few talking briefly with Saint-Michael before leaving. Ann made sure she was the last to talk with him.

'This plan comes as quite a surprise, General. I thought we had made a commitment to the Skybolt project.'

'That hasn't changed, Ann. I'm not cancelling Skybolt. But Armstrong Station is an operational military base, a tactical unit first and foremost. I've been supplied with information about a situation that could develop into a direct threat against the US. I've studied the available information and I've formulated a response for consideration and approval by headquarters – '

'But what about – ?'

'Ann, you can believe me or not, but I'm telling you I will not cancel Skybolt.'

Okay, okay, she thought. Better not press him any further. In fact, better try to cool it. She had to live with these guys. And, when you thought about it, her future was in Saint-Michael's hands . . .

4

USS *California*

'Dammit, Cogley,' Captain Matthew Page said, 'I don't want copies of *Nimitz's* transcript of the satellite messages. It takes an extra half-hour for them to relay the messages to us and for Comm to type them out nice and pretty. Half of Asia could get blown up in a half-hour. We've got our own FLEETSAT terminal; I want copies of the transmission from that.' Cogley nodded and turned but Page grabbed his arm. 'Cogley, give me those messages you have. It's better than nothing. Tell Comm I want updates every half-hour.'

Cogley scurried away and returned a few moments later to fill Page's coffee cup. 'Thanks. Now tell Comm to start earning their salaries or I'll keel-haul them.' Cogley disappeared.

Page took a sip of coffee, looked skyward. 'See that, Ann?' he said, half-aloud. 'I call him other things besides "Dammit Cogley."'

It was the first time he had thought of his daughter since leaving Oakland, and the realization hurt him. My daughter, the astronaut. She had been on the evening news half a dozen times and in the newspapers constantly. A laser expert. Smarter, more famous, better paid and certainly better looking than her old man.

He felt a lurch from an errant wave and his eyes quickly scanned the digital inertial sea-motion gauges and the computerized compensating equipment on the master bridge-console. All functioning normally. The Arabian

111

Sea could be a wild place sometimes – even without the interference of other people's navies.

At least Ann didn't have to deal with twelve-foot waves, he thought. They didn't have waves in space. He remembered reading about a 'solar wind' powerful enough to move huge space stations, and micrometeorites that could slice through steel. It sounded much more dangerous than the sea.

He had always wanted to ask his daughter about things like the solar wind and micrometeorites but just never did. Funny – whenever he saw his daughter, he never thought of asking her about lasers, or space, or physics. She was a world-class scientist, one of the nation's best. She could probably write a book about the solar wind. But whenever he saw her, she was his daughter – nothing more, nothing less, nothing else.

You're an old idiot, Page told himself. You've never let her know how proud you are of her, how happy you are about her success. You see her maybe twice a year and then it's always 'get me a beer' or 'help your mother' or 'when are you going to come down to earth – joke – and crank out some grandkids?'

He went out on to the catwalk and took in the clean, crisp salt breeze and the sounds of waves crashing against the bow of his eleven-thousand-ton guided-missile cruiser. Off in the distance he could just make out the massive outline of the *Nimitz* as it launched another pair of F/A-18D fighters on a night patrol. The *California* was positioned as the 'goalkeeper,' the largest and most powerful ship cruising except for the main carrier in the battle group. The *California's* eight anti-aircraft guided-missile launchers, two 127-millimetre guns, eight Harpoon antiship missile launchers, four 324-millimetre nuclear torpedo tubes and eight ASROC antisubmarine missile launchers were the last layer of protection for the ninety-one-thousand-ton carrier and her thirty-six hundred crewmembers.

Dammit, he thought, why feel guilty about speaking your mind? Deep down he couldn't help feeling that Ann had no business being on a space station or flying in a contraption like the Space Shuttle. Both were dangerous enough without the Russians screaming about them being a threat. And what was wrong with asking for a few grandchildren? Ann was an only child. It would be nice to have a few rug rats around after the navy dry-docked him in a few years.

Chief Petty Officer Cogley ran up to him now and held out a computer printout. 'Message traffic from the Persian Gulf, sir.'

'I'm not asking too much, right, Cogley? But no. She's gotta go off and play spaceman. Big deal.'

'Your daughter, sir?'

'What? What about my daughter?' Page snapped himself back to the deck of the *California* and Cogley wisely decided not to pursue whatever the captain had been muttering about.

'Three point ships from the *Brezhnev* battle group heading south for the Strait of Hormuz,' Cogley read. 'Space Command thinks they're exiting the Gulf for an early force rotation. The carrier *Brezhnev* herself is hanging back for now. We'll be able to wave bye-bye to them as they exit the Gulf of Oman.'

For a brief instant Captain Page's mind registered the words 'Space Command,' but he didn't make the connection and assumed Cogley was referring to the air force . . . They're all the same, aren't they? he liked to say. 'Thanks, Cogley. Keep the reports coming.'

Dark clouds raced across the skies, but Captain Page looked up and stared at the sky as if his daughter Ann could look back down at him.

'Well, daughter, for once I'm damn glad you're tucked away up there . . .'

For the third time that hour General-Lieutenant Alesander Govorov rested a hand near a clear plastic-covered control panel on the master control board. He was careful to double check that the plastic cover was still in place, but he could not prevent his hand from moving towards the three switches recessed beneath the cover. Slowly, almost reverently, he tapped the plastic above the switches and imagined the results.

Switch one: Activation of an electromechanical interlock that absolutely committed a launch and attack on the target selected by the tracking computer. Even if an explosion or massive power failure cut power to the entire launch complex, the Gorgon missile's internal circuitry could still successfully process an attack on the target. Activation of the switch would also set off several warning alarms through the antisatellite missile-launch complex and would automatically transmit warning messages to the Space Centre headquarters at Baikenour, to the Kremlin, and to several alternative command and control centres throughout the Soviet Union.

Switch two: Fully automatic launch preparation. Final inertial guidance corrections, final target processing, opening of the missile silo's twin steel muzzle shutters, retraction of all service ports, arms, and umbilicals, and preparation of the twin one-thousand-decalitre chemical reagent vessels for the turbo-powered cold-launch mixing process.

Switch three: Launch commit. The four underground turbopumps would force-mix a sodium carbonate slurry with nitric acid in a large steel vessel under the silo, yielding huge volumes of nitrogen gas in seconds. The reaction vessel would store and compress the gas until the pressure reached one million kilopascals, then force the neutral gas into the silo. The gas would spit the twenty-thousand-kilogram Gorgon missile nearly twenty metres above the silo, where the missile's exhaust gases would not scorch or damage the silo on first-stage motor ignition. In less than fifteen minutes another missile would be hauled in place and made ready for launch.

Govorov could almost see the numbers on the computer monitor displaying the results. A long first-stage burn as the SAS-10 missile ploughed through the thick atmosphere. A high-impulse second stage to accelerate the missile to orbital speed. A third-stage orbit-correcting burn, followed by steering burns and thruster course corrections.

Then, close in. Acceleration to nearly three times the speed of sound – but there would be no sonic booms: the missile would be hundreds of miles above the atmosphere in space by then. Random manoeuvres, some as much as forty degrees off, all with the Gorgon tracking system locked in. Then impact, explosion, destruction. The SAS-10 carried a one-thousand-kilogram high explosive flak warhead. Small by any ballistic-weapon standard but devastating to an orbiting target. Without the firmness of the earth to cushion or protect it, destruction would be total.

Good-bye, American Space Command Brigadier General Jason Saint-Michael. Good-bye, Space Station Armstrong. The pieces of your station will create hundreds of new shooting stars every night for weeks.

But the plastic cover remained over the three master-launch control keys, and the numbers on the computer monitors showed exactly as they had been showing for a month – Space Station Armstrong safely in its orbit, set up to watch Minister of Defence Czilikov's folly in Iran a total of sixteen hours a day, telling the world about the big mistake the new leadership of the Soviet Union was about to make.

Govorov turned to the chief duty officer in the Gorgon launch control and monitoring centre. 'Status of the target, Lieutenant Colonel Gulaev?'

'Unchanged, sir. Station Armstrong is thirty-one minutes ten seconds from apogee. Speed and track, unchanged. We can set our chronometers by it.' He turned to face his superior officer. 'They are not merely goading us, are they, Comrade General? They know about Feather?'

Govorov was slightly taken aback by the question involving the Iran operation. Not by the fact that Gulaev, Govorov's youngest but by far most intelligent duty commander, had discovered Feather – he was exposed to as much message traffic and strategic operational briefings as Govorov himself, and he was a bright kid. But Gulaev, the grandson of one of the Soviet Union's most highly decorated World War II flying aces, had done what few in the Kollegiya had done: he'd pieced together the inner workings of Feather and *then* tied the movements and capabilities of the Americans' most sophisticated and secret military device into the classified Soviet military operation. Gulaev was thinking several steps ahead of most of the military high command.

'You seem to know a good deal about Armstrong,' Govorov said, 'and you are talking too much about Feather. I would strongly advise you to keep your thoughts to yourself – or better yet, do not have such thoughts.'

Gulaev looked grave, but Govorov managed an encouraging smile. 'No, the Americans can't know about Feather. The operation is too ambitious even for the Americans to imagine.'

Gulaev nodded, but his inquisitive face was stony as he turned back to his duties. His question bothered Govorov. The Americans, he was certain, were using the powerful space-based radar on Armstrong Space Station to maintain the longest possible surveillance on the region. Why? Certainly not to watch a few ships in the Persian Gulf.

Always believe the worst and hope for the best – at least that was what he had preached to Gulaev and the other young officers in his command. Time to get off your mindless high horse, Hero of the Soviet Union Govorov. Think like your young officers: *The Americans knew or have guessed the invasion plans. Armstrong Station has detected vast numbers of weapons, numbers inconsistent with a simple exercise or with any resupply efforts into Afghanistan. In response they have moved the station into an orbit with the apogee, the highest point of the orbit, directed over the Soviet-Iran border. Moreover they have placed the station in a higher elliptical orbit, which allows them to scan the Iran-Persian Gulf area longer and places them a bit further away from any Soviet antisatellite weapons. They are expending tremendous amounts of fuel and energy to ensure that the station passes over the same exact points on the globe on every orbit . . .*

'Lieutenant Colonel Gulaev.'

Gulaev got up from his chair and was quickly beside Govorov. 'Sir?'

Govorov put a hand on his shoulder, 'Never be afraid to question everything and everyone, Lieutenant Colonel. I know it's not wise to question those in authority, but in my command I demand it. It's old fools like me that will drag our country down.'

'No, General-Lieutenant, you – '

Govorov raised a hand. 'You were right, as usually is the case. We have to operate under the assumption that the Americans have discovered or at least suspect our plans in the Persian Gulf and Iran and have repositioned the space station to maintain an early warning and surveillance watch on the area. If our intelligence is correct, the station's space-based radar will be able to direct forces to engage our invasion forces on several fronts at once. Comments, Lieutenant Colonel?'

The reply came surprisingly quickly. 'It's imperative that we destroy the space station Armstrong, sir.'

'Except the Kollegiya has not authorized such an attack,' Govorov said. 'We're not at war with America. Feather is an operation to occupy Iran, take control of the Persian Gulf and prevent the reintroduction of superior American forces in the region. We are *not* trying to start a new Patriotic War – '

'Then I believe, sir, that Feather will fail. Can we, can *you*, sir, allow that to happen?'

Govorov winced inwardly, nodded towards his office. Gulaev set his headset down on the master console and followed him. Govorov motioned for Gulaev to close the door as he sat behind his desk in the tiny office.

'You've evidently interpreted my invitation to speak your mind a bit more broadly than I intended,' Govorov said. 'Space Defence Command personnel are interviewed frequently by the KGB, and remarks like "Feather will fail" are bound to be remembered by some eavesdroppers, ready and willing to exploit them to advantage. Please, exercise more caution in the future. You're a damn fine officer; I wouldn't want to lose you to some three-man radio outpost in Siberia – or worse.'

As he spoke, Govorov was reminded of his own highly impolitic remarks before the Kollegiya. Maybe he wasn't the one to be giving this lecture. But then again, who better to preach than a sinner who had suffered for the same sins in the past?

Gulaev appeared chastened.

'You are right, of course,' Govorov said. 'Feather will hardly be a surprise to anyone if the space-based radar is as effective as I believe it is.' He paused long enough for Gulaev to think he had been dismissed. Then: 'Lieutenant Colonel Gulaev, I'd like your estimate of the effectiveness of the SAS-10 Gorgon missile system against the space station Armstrong.'

Gulaev paused a moment then answered firmly. 'Ineffective, sir. At most we can attack the station with six Gorgon missiles. Armstrong has ten Thor missiles it can use against them.'

'But the effectiveness of the Thor missile system was reported at only fifty per cent,' Govorov said, testing his subordinate.

'Sir, as you know the GRU and KGB adjusted the results of the Americans' live-fire test to approximate effectiveness under less than ideal conditions. The facts are that the Americans used seven Thor missiles and destroyed fifty-nine ICBM warheads. That's an eighty-five per cent effectiveness rate. No matter how extensively the test was staged, sir, the fact remains that the American space station successfully intercepted six missiles – Trident missiles, which are more elusive targets than Gorgons. The Thor missile tracked and killed an individual *warhead* – a much smaller target than a Gorgon. And, sir, although the present groundspeed of the station is slower, the station at apogee is at the extreme altitude length of the Gorgon. Which means that the Gorgon couldn't tail-chase the station in its orbit but would have to fly directly at it and attack before its fuel supply was exhausted. That would make it a virtual stationary target for the Thor missile.'

Govorov hated to consider the obvious implications of that . . . All the plans, all the misgivings, all the perceived deficiencies of the Space Defence Command's major weapon system that Govorov had been aware of all these years – young Gulaev had just articulated them in one breath.

'And your alternative?' Govorov asked in a monotone that denied what he was feeling inside. 'Come on, Nikolai Gulaev. I know you are going to say it . . .'

'Elektron?' Gulaev said matter-of-factly.

Without a word or expression Govorov picked up the telephone on his desk and punched an office extension. 'Operations? General Govorov here. Find an immediate replacement for Lieutenant Colonel Gulaev on the console duty desk, effective immediately and until further notice. No reason . . . by my authority . . . Yes, I also need a clerk to get some orders cut for me . . . Yes, he's fine . . . get him in here immediately.' And he hung up.

'Lieutenant Colonel, you have just said the magic word.' Under the bewildered gaze of the young officer he stood, walked over to a steel locker in a far corner of the office and pushed it aside, revealing a wall safe. In a few moments he was holding a red-covered notebook, which he promptly dropped into Gulaev's hands.

'Elektron is right. And it is now your project. Yours alone. That document outlines all the procedures necessary to implement the deployment of two Elektron spacecraft with specialized weapons. I – '

Gulaev could not help but interrupt. 'What sort of weapons?'

'Patience. I will draft special orders authorizing you to implement those instructions. You are released from all duties except those outlined in that folder. The folder is classified top secret. Absolutely no one is authorized access to the information in it below the office of first deputy minister. Understood?'

Govorov didn't wait for a reply. 'Collect your special orders from my office in one hour. I will expect daily reports from you on your progress. Report to your station on the main console until your replacement arrives.'

Gulaev snapped to attention and hurried out.

As he did, Govorov glanced at the old-fashioned analogue clock on the wall. How fitting that the most technologically advanced organization in the Soviet Union used a round sweep-head clock to tell time. Govorov hated the clock. It reminded him of what the Aerospace Forces of the Soviet Union – all of the armed forces of the Soviet Union, for that matter – were like. Some were still no further advanced than that fifty-year-old clock. And some dinosaurs would prefer they were back in the days when that clock was made, when the Soviet Union was one of the most devastated, mistrusted, divided, oligarchical and bankrupt countries on earth. Then a weak and demoralized Russian military followed Joseph Stalin, the ruthless, power-obsessed dictator, into verbal ruin. Now another weak and demoralized military was about to follow another power-hungry head of state into a certain clash with the most powerful nation on earth. This time, though, Govorov was determined to turn aside certain failure . . .

Gulaev was right. It was Govorov's responsibility, his duty to do everything he could to forestall a Soviet defeat in Iran and the Persian Gulf and anywhere else. Gulaev now had the responsibility for activating the secret plan for the destruction of Armstrong Station – Govorov's job would be to convince the minister of defence to hold off Feather until the secret operation could be set in motion.

Govorov ordered his plane immediately fuelled and ready for departure in an hour. By then Gulaev would have his orders and Govorov would be off to Moscow to try to convince the Kollegiya to avoid suicide and face facts. He would much rather be going up against the enemy. Dinosaurs were hard to kill . . .

Armstrong Space Station

As Ann Page had predicted, her report on the potential Skybolt project delays caused by moving the space station into a geosynchronous orbit over the Middle East had negligible effect on Space Command. Saint-Michael had got the green light, and for the past several days the space station's crewmembers had worked overtime gathering information and staying on alert for a Soviet response. *A Soviet response*. Put that way, it sounded so neat and tidy, so impersonal and even reasonable, Ann thought. Like playing a game of chess. She imagined just how devastating a Soviet 'response' might be and felt a chill. She was actually glad she had her work to concentrate on. She'd have been a nervous wreck, standing in the command module and watching the display screen read out possible threats.

Kevin Baker put aside another relay circuit board and sat down beside her on a small workbench in the cluttered Skybolt module.

Ann looked at him. 'I was thinking about how unreal a lot of this is. What might be happening down below. The fact that we're even up here in space at all . . .'

Baker nodded. 'I know what you mean. I think of all the years I spent in labs . . . not quite like this but, you know, filled with the same clutter. And no one giving much of a damn. And now suddenly I seem to be at the centre of everything that's important, but the feeling is pretty much the same. Solve the problem, devise solutions, check out hypotheses – '

'And what's your favourite? Hypothesis, that is . . . How can we get this laser of ours to do what it's supposed to do?'

Kevin noted the word 'ours' and was pleased. 'Well,' he said, looking at the maze of wires and circuit relays in front of him, 'why don't we start with this left GCS-B data relay? What do you have connected to it? Looks like platinum.'

'It is platinum. That's the MHD master superconductor relay. I call it the toaster.'

'Not a bad name for it. This is the first superconducting

relay I've seen that's smaller than the size of a cement truck. So where's the automatic test centre?'

Ann motioned to the ceiling and Baker let out a low groan. Working on the ceiling might have been old hat for her, but his station laboratory had been a virtual re-creation of his earth-bound laboratory, where computers never floated to the ceiling. Shaking his head, he lifted towards the ceiling, anchored himself on Velcro-covered footpads and punched instructions into the test computer. The renewed frustration in his voice echoed throughout the Skybolt module.

'What is *this*?' gesturing to sixteen long rows of numbers.

'It's a linkage of all the relative program sequence codes of the relay circuitry. There are sixty-four displays of each two hundred fifty-six bit word. You need to cross-check each display with – '

'Wait a minute. That's over sixteen thousand data bits . . .'

'For the *left* MHD relay circuitry data bus,' Ann continued. 'There's another check of the right data bus and the main driver.'

'God, how can we check all this? It'll take days. Maybe weeks.'

'I haven't run through the whole check,' she told him. 'The toaster has run perfectly for two years. I've got three hundred other components that I'd suspect before the toaster, so it gets a lower priority. I'll check it later.'

Baker seemed not to hear her as he twisted off four Camlock fasteners on the tiny self-test console, lifted the front panel clear and peered inside. 'Good, at least you have standard connectors in this thing. I'll rig up a fibre-optic network line from Skybolt to my lab. I can plug my computer right into this console and have it check all the data registers for us. It'll do the check in a few minutes and give us the answer in English, not in this hexadecimal gobbledegook. You'll be able to monitor your toaster continually after this.'

'That's great, Kevin. How soon can you get it set up?'

'A few hours for the network line and connections, and a few more to write the program to compute and cross-check the checksums.'

Ann nodded, looked at the self-test console. 'Do you really think the problem is in there?'

'Don't know a lot about superconducting relays. In fact, I know damn little about most of the other toys you have in here. But your self-tests aren't telling you what the problem is. We've gone over most everything else except this thing. I'd say the problem has to be here.' He detached himself from the ceiling and glided back to the deck.

For the first time in days, Ann allowed herself to hope that the problem would actually be resolved – providing, of course, that no new and unanticipated glitches loused it up . . .

Moscow, USSR

'Are you crazy, General Govorov?' First Deputy Minister of Defence Khromeyev asked in a low, biting tone. Both Govorov and Deputy Minister of Defence Rhomerdunov, commander in chief of the Soviet Aerospace Forces, stood at attention in Khromeyev's spacious office just outside Minister of Defence Czilikov's conference chamber. Govorov had caged his eyes forward, unblinking, but Rhomerdunov's eyes followed Khromeyev's nervous pacing. The two senior officers had once spent eighteen straight days together in a muddy foxhole in Mukacevo near Budapest during the last weeks of the Great Patriotic

War forty-eight years earlier, and there was little Khromeyev could say or do that could really frighten Rhomerdunov. The chief of the general staff finally waved both Rhomerdunov and Govorov to chairs.

'Sergei,' Rhomerdunov urged, 'listen to what General Govorov has to say – '

'We've heard it before, Alexi,' Khromeyev said. 'Your cosmonaut has already made quite a name for himself in the Kremlin, thanks to his rather undisciplined speech before the Kollegiya. Now he wants to speak with the minister of defence *again* about postponing Operation Feather.' Khromeyev stared at both Rhomerdunov and Govorov for long, tense moments. 'What the hell is going on, Govorov? Is this some sort of power play? A challenge to your superior? A move for attention? Minister of Defence Czilikov spoke with Marshal Lichizev. The GRU knows of no such super-radar on board the American space station Armstrong. They acknowledge that the sensor capabilities of the station are indeed advanced, but not advanced enough to track hundreds of land, air and sea vessels for millions of cubic kilometres – let alone direct the defences of the American rapid deployment force in the region.'

Khromeyev abruptly moderated his voice. 'The minister of defence appreciates your concern and attention to detail, General Govorov. But he has conducted his own surveys of members of the Kollegiya and of the scientific community and decided that the space station Armstrong is not a threat to the success or failure of Feather. Your comments have been duly noted but – '

Govorov could no longer take it. 'Excuse me, sir, but it isn't necessary to address me like an overzealous child. I'm willing to stake my professional career on what I say. If Feather is to succeed, if this country is ever to be secure, the space station Armstrong has got to be destroyed or at least crippled.'

125

'That's enough . . . Rhomerdunov,' Khromeyev said, now ignoring Govorov, 'I can't allow this insubordinate officer of yours to see the minister of defence. He'll have all our heads, and he'll be right. I suggest, Alexi, that you explain the chain of command to General Lieutenant Govorov. Have him review the oath he took, especially the part about unquestioningly carrying out the requirements of all military regulations and orders of commanders and superiors. He seems to have a deficient memory in that area. Explain to him that if we were not approaching a period of great need he would be relieved of his position. Be sure that he understands that the Kollegiya is not here for his personal aggrandizement. Dismissed, damn it.'

Rhomerdunov could barely wait until he was back into his staff car. 'Govorov, your career may have ended five minutes ago. Aerospace Forces won't be heavily involved with Feather – the minute things calm down you'll be relieved of duty and reassigned – '

'*No.*'

'Very brave of you, Alesander. Brave to the last. Your big mouth has destroyed you, just as I warned you it would.'

'And I tell you, Deputy Minister, that this has not ended. I remember my oath of allegiance very well. I swore to protect my country and my people to the last drop of blood in my body. I'm *trying* to do that.' As the dark Mercedes sedan swung on to the heavily crowded Volokolamskoje Highway northwest towards Moskovskij International Airport, Govorov turned intently to his superior officer.

'I need authorization, sir,' he said in a low voice. 'One launch. In twenty days. Aboard the Elektron . . .'

Rhomerdunov's face drained. 'Elektron . . .? Govorov, you *are* a fool.' He shook his head, speaking almost to himself, as if the young officer was no longer in the car. 'I was wrong to try to support your ideas . . . You're letting your obsession cloud your common sense.'

'You know damn well that's not true, sir. What I'm saying is a fact . . . The power of Armstrong Station, the danger our forces will face because of it – all true. Feather will be crushed or at least helplessly stalled in the mountains or the Arabian Sea. A stalemate for Feather is just as bad as a defeat. It is a defeat . . . please, hear me out . . . The Space Defence Command has the ability to stop Armstrong Station from becoming the pivotal unit in the American defence. Three Elektron spaceplanes armed with Scimitar hypervelocity projectile missiles – '

'Scimitar? What the hell are those? I've never heard of them.'

'Code-named *Bavinash*. Low-cost, so-called throwaway missiles developed in secret by my people. They are little more than long bottles of gas with a molybdenum-uranium armour-piercing nose and a rocket engine. An Elektron can carry ten of them on a rotary launcher in the cargo hold. They're laser-guided from Elektron and they fly at nearly a kilometre a second to their target. They – '

'You have a weapon designed for the Elektron space-plane? But the Elektron is a cargo ship, a damn space taxi. Whatever possessed you to develop an offensive weapon for it? In *secret*, no less . . .'

Govorov allowed a smile. 'It was an American idea, actually. When I first flew the Elektron five years ago the Americans were convinced it was a Soviet space fighter plane. Ordinarily I wouldn't have paid any attention to such blatant anti-Soviet propaganda ploys – at the time the Americans were trying to discredit *our* shuttle pro-gramme to mask their own shuttle failures. But the idea intrigued me, and I did some research to discover the exact plans for the so-called Soviet space fighter-plane. I was shocked to learn there were *no* such plans. So when I was chosen to head the Space Defence Command I began a secret programme to develop a twenty-first-century space force that would be superior . . .'

Rhomerdunov was speechless, not able to take in what he was hearing. But as the Mercedes swung on to the specially constructed off-ramp from the Volokolamskoje Highway, he turned to Govorov, shaking his head.

'These so-called *Bavinash* missiles . . . are they . . . ready for use?'

'Within twenty days, sir.' Govorov felt his face flush with excitement, realizing that Rhomerdunov was at least listening to him. 'I have already given orders . . . Two Elektron spaceplanes will be readied at Tyuratam for launch in three weeks. Each will be fitted with ten Scimitar missiles – more than sufficient to destroy the American space station. As long as it exists our own survival is only a matter of time – '

'*You have already given the orders?*'

Govorov checked himself. Now, with Rhomerdunov interested in the project, this was the time for fence mending. He didn't want his superior thinking him a loose cannon.

'I have briefed my staff on the project, yes. But, of course, it waits for your approval. I have not ordered any attacks on Armstrong, per your orders and the orders of the Kollegiya. But I felt that, under my limited authority, at least the groundwork should be laid for preparation of the Elektron, should my observations on the capabilities of Armstrong's space-based radar be true . . .'

The Mercedes slowed and stopped at a guard house on the outskirts of Moscow Airport. Papers were exchanged and a quick search of the car was conducted by an army sergeant accompanied by a Rottweiler guard dog. Rhomerdunov, distracted by what he'd heard, did not protest when the massive black-and-tan animal was allowed to sniff the interior of the car for explosives. A few moments later the car was speeding towards the separate VIP terminal where Rhomerdunov's jet was waiting.

Inside the terminal's waiting room Rhomerdunov finally spoke to Govorov: 'I've been ordered to Tashkent, to supervise the southern TVD air defences in case retaliatory strikes into the Soviet Union occur during Feather. Otherwise I would go with you back to Tyuratam to inspect this . . . this so-called secret space force you've developed. Bear this in mind, General Govorov. Normally I would consider all you have said and done as the ultimate in insubordination and abuse of power. The secret development of a weapon, regardless of its necessity, its use, or the intentions of its developer, is a treasonable offence. If the information about this Scimitar missile or the arming of Elektron spaceplanes leaks out and is discovered by the Politburo or the general staff, you may find yourself in Lubylanka Prison for a very long stay.'

Govorov kept quiet, and it was then that Rhomerdunov decided to trust the young officer. There were really only two choices: ignore Govorov and quietly remove him as a threat to Rhomerdunov's authority, or believe in him and his convictions and back him. If Govorov had shown any hesitation or uncertainty, Rhomerdunov would have let the matter die then and there. But with his steely blue eyes convincingly steady, Govorov looked, spoke and acted like a man firmly committed to his beliefs. And just because those beliefs were hugely upsetting didn't make them wrong. It would have been easier to believe Govorov was carried away by his *idée fixe*. But if he was crazy, he was the most intelligent and well-organized psychopath in history . . .

'We must take steps, Govorov, to be sure that the development of this Scimitar missile, the arming of Elektron spaceplanes and the formation of a space-borne attack unit have been *thoroughly* documented. These programmes must become authorized as revived projects of the Aerospace Forces and the Space Defence Command, not as the clandestine and illegal activities of a renegade.'

Govorov's attention was on the word *we*, and he had to struggle to resist the urge to break out into an unmilitary cheer. Deputy First Minister of Defence Rhomerdunov had just identified himself with the plans. There was still hope . . .

'We'll discuss this further, Alesander.'

Govorov nodded, noticing that boarding preparations were being completed. An air force *Starshiy Serzhant* came up now to Rhomerdunov and reported that his plane was ready for boarding. Govorov picked up Rhomerdunov's briefcase and carried it to the boarding ramp outside an Antonov An-72 military transport jet.

'Sir,' Govorov handed the briefcase to a crewmember but looked directly at Rhomerdunov. 'About my ongoing preparations . . .?'

'They are to continue. Quietly. I will contact you when it's possible. Be prepared to fully brief myself and the Kollegiya on the project.' He paused as a few officers stepped behind him: 'And be prepared to dismantle it. Both with equal speed.'

Govorov saluted, and Rhomerdunov stepped on to the escalator and disappeared from sight.

Armstrong Space Station

'It's ready.'

Kevin Baker and Ann Page floated next to Baker's master laboratory-computer console, looking expectantly at a 'READY' message on the terminal screen. Baker manoeuvred himself down to the console near a microphone but then stopped short and motioned to Ann.

'Be my guest.'

Ann slipped down to the microphone. 'Toaster checksum.' Her words were typed across the computer monitor screen, and immediately a message flashed across the screen: 'TOASTER. CHECKSUM READY.'

'Run,' Ann said.

Instantly a chart was drawn on the screen showing a graphic presentation of the sixteen-thousand memory locations available in the Skybolt superconducting circuit relay. The screen asked, 'WOULD YOU LIKE A TEST RESULT PRINTOUT?'

'Yes,' Ann told it.

Another prompt requested, 'READY TO START.'

Ann said, 'Start,' and immediately several columns were filled with figures representing the memory location being examined by the computer.

'I can't believe you put this together in just eight hours,' Ann said to Baker. 'I couldn't have done it in eight weeks.'

'It's just knowing how to use the resources that are available,' Baker said. That and fifty years' experience as a computer engineer, he thought to himself. He ought to be able to pull a rabbit out of his hat once in a while. She was the geniusy one, but there was still room for operations guys too . . .

Slowly, the numbers began to change as each memory location in the electronic relay was examined, its data-correct checksum value computed, the memory location analysed and the resident checksum value computed. If the two checksum values were different, it would indicate a problem in that particular memory location. The circuit controlling that memory location could then be checked for malfunctions, which would lead to the solution of the Skybolt laser's tracking and power-supply problems.

Baker glanced at his watch. 'Eighty seconds to check one register. Sixty-four registers . . . about an hour and a

131

half for the left MHD superconducting relay. That's a lot longer than I expected.'

'Considering it would normally take one of us about five minutes to check each register, I'd say that's pretty good.'

'Yes, well, did you find anything else while I was programming the computer? Something we maybe overlooked?'

'I wish I had. No, everything else checked out. You were right. I think the problem is in one of the "toasters." Why are the solutions in the last place you – '

Suddenly, a shrill Klaxon alarm echoed throughout the station. The horn blared three times; then a computer-synthesized voice announced, 'Missile launch detection. Missile launch detection.'

Ann detached herself from her Velcro anchor pad and shot for the hatch to the connecting tunnel between the experimentation module and the command centre. She was through the portal in an instant.

To her surprise very little had changed in the command centre. Colonel Walker was peering at the monitor that Sergeant Jefferson had been assigned; everyone else was closely monitoring his own instruments.

'Coming through, Ann.' It was General Saint-Michael pushing past her. He caught hold of his commander's chair, manoeuvred around it and strapped in. She noticed that he was wearing a damp flight suit, as if he had hurriedly jumped out of the shower after hearing the alarm. He put on his communications earset and she quickly readjusted hers as Baker moved beside her just inside the command-module hatch.

'Missile launch detection, infrared telescopic scan and confirmed by SBR,' Jefferson reported. 'In the vicinity of Bandar-e Lengeh in Iran.'

'Silkworm?'

'Not yet confirmed, sir . . . wait, now confirmed, General SBR tracking three Silkworm-F subsonic missiles heading two-six-one, velocity one-seven-zero knots groundspeed and accelerating.'

'Target?'

There was an uncomfortable pause. Then: 'Looks like three Soviet battleships in the Strait of Hormuz . . .'

'Transmit tactical warning message to all forces in the region. Continue tracking. Any aircraft up?'

'Soviet airborne from the *Brezhnev*, sir. An Antonov Ru-18 carrier recon plane . . . SBR now reports total of five missiles in flight from Bandar-e Lengeh.'

'Any of ours up?'

'We've got one RC-787B AWACS plane over Saudi Arabia,' another tech reported. 'No confirmation of missile launch from him.'

'Status of missiles?'

'On course for the destroyers, speed now three-one-zero and accelerating . . . Sir, aircraft launching from the *Brezhnev*. Two highspeed aircraft . . .'

'The alert fighters,' Walker said. 'Any chance of those fighters chasing down the Worms?'

'Range from fighters to destroyers, one hundred twenty nautical miles. Range from missiles to ships . . . mark . . . forty nautical miles. Groundspeed of missiles now four hundred knots. Approximately six minutes to impact. Fighters now approaching five hundred knots groundspeed and accelerating rapidly.'

'No chance they'll catch up,' Walker said. 'They'll arrive just in time to see the Worms hit those ships.'

'They might be able to get the Silkworms with a long-range-missile shot,' Saint-Michael said. 'How much longer do we have on this orbit?'

'We go out of effective SBR scanning position in fifteen minutes.'

'Then let's get set up for regional displays of the area.

Get everybody in here, Jim. We're going to need tactical SBR scanning recordings of the whole area. A lot of people are going to be asking us what we saw – I want multisensor descriptions of everything within range. Status of those Silkworms?'

'Impact in five minutes. Fighters both at eleven hundred knots and steady. ETA six minutes.'

Saint-Michael shook his head. 'Those Russian pilots are going to have to be very, very good to tag those Worms,' he said, then it dawned on him – the irony of the situation. Here they were in a way rooting for the damn Russians – the bad guys. He guessed it was because the missile attack seemed unprovoked. Except was it really unprovoked, or was it just meant to seem that way . . .?

USS *California*

'The *space station* saw the missile launch?' Captain Matthew Page asked as a sheet of computer paper was handed to him. His chest heaved slightly – he had sprinted the entire way from his stateroom to the USS *California's* combat information centre when the news of the attack had been received.

'That's what they say, sir,' the operations officer told him. 'About two minutes ago. They're tracking five Silkworm-F missiles launched from Bandar-e Lengeh, a military base about eighty miles southwest of Bandar-Abbas in southern Iran. Target is reported to be three Soviet destroyers approaching the Strait of Hormuz. The Soviets have launched two Su-27B fighters from the carrier *Brezhnev* and are pursuing.'

Page studied the large wall-size computer-generated tactical display, which integrated all of the information pouring into the *California* from all sources to give a near-real-time map of all that was going on around them. The

134

symbols representing the vessels in the Persian Gulf itself were unmoving, marked with Xs to show that their positions were estimates only. Only the icons representing images from the *California's* radar were marked with blinking asterisks, indicating real-time positions.

'The information on this board is old,' Page said irritably. 'Can't we hook into whatever this space station is using?'

'Checking, sir.'

Page studied the board. 'The *Brezhnev* was over a hundred fifty miles from the strait. It'll be a miracle if those fighters can get those destroyers in time.'

A warbling tone echoed in CIC, and the operations officer picked up a black security phone. He immediately handed it to Page, who listened intently for a few moments. '*California* acknowledges. Out.'

He turned to the operations officer, 'Mr Meserve, put the boat at general quarters.'

'Aye, sir.' Meserve picked up another telephone. 'Bridge, ops. Sound general quarters.' A few moments later the *California* was reverberating with a series of loud electronic bells and the blaring announcement: 'General quarters. General quarters. All hands man your battle stations.'

Meserve stayed on the phone for another two minutes. 'All stations report manned and ready, Skipper.'

'Very well.' Page again picked up the red phone, the direct communications line to the *Nimitz*. 'Sir, the *California* is at battle stations.' He replaced the red phone in its cradle and picked up a shipwide intercom microphone.

'All hands, this is the captain. There is an attack in progress against three Soviet destroyers in the Strait of Hormuz, about seven hundred miles west-northwest of our position. The attack is coming from Iran and is apparently unprovoked. Two Soviet fighters are airborne heading for the strait, so Admiral Clancy aboard *Nimitz*

135

has ordered the battle group to general quarters. The group is not in any present danger, but stay on your toes. Out.'

Page replaced the microphone just as Chief Petty Officer Cogley came up to him with a steel helmet, flotation jacket and antiflash red-lens goggles. 'Thanks, Cogley. I'll be on the bridge in a few minutes.'

'Skipper. Data link established with the space station.'

Page turned towards the large tactical screen just as it transformed itself: the range of the display shimmered and changed from a five-hundred-mile circular display – the extreme range of the limited radar data received from the ships in the *Nimitz* battle group – to a thousand-mile-high resolution square display. Now, instead of only open ocean to look at, the screen showed several bodies of water and the political boundaries of a dozen countries. Each blip on the screen, aircraft as well as ship, was labelled and identified with a real-time flashing indicator. In less than a minute Page was able to read and assimilate the entire tactical situation in the Persian Gulf.

'Amazing,' Page said.

'Armstrong says the data link will last only a few more minutes, Skipper.'

'Armstrong?' Suddenly, Page understood what the tiny voice inside his head had been saying. '*Armstrong*. The space station. My daughter is on that thing. What the hell is she doing over the goddamned Persian Gulf?'

No one replied. Captain Page wiped his forehead and realized the stuffy, ozone-smelling walls of CIC were starting to close in on him.

'Meserve, get me a printout chart of the last possible tactical display before Armstrong stops transmitting and bring it to the bridge.'

'Aye, sir.'

Page bulled through the corridors and stairways of the *California*, swearing loud enough for anyone nearby to hear. 'That damned daughter of mine . . . I *knew* she had no business on that damn orbiting bull's-eye. I *knew* it . . .'

The number of personnel on the bridge had doubled since Page had left it. The helmsman and signalman now had partners beside them, the Marine guards were doubled, two damage-control seamen were rechecking fire extinguishers, and lookouts with StarLite night-vision binoculars were stationed on the catwalks scanning the horizon. Page eased into his swivel seat.

He picked up a microphone. 'CIC, bridge. Status?'

'Bridge, CIC. Silkworm missiles are thirty seconds from impact . . . sir, Russian fighters launching missiles.'

'Give me a running narrative on the action.'

'Aye, sir. Now showing only one Silkworm missile in flight . . . Russian fighters still twenty miles from Soviet vessels . . . not showing any Silkworm missiles in flight . . . fighter images merging with ships . . . carrier *Brezhnev* launching aircraft. Now four high-speed aircraft leaving the *Brezhnev* moving northeast at three-zero-zero knots and accelerating . . . Slow-moving aircraft leaving the *Brezhnev*. Silver Tower says they're rotorcraft.'

'Silver what?'

'Sorry, Armstrong Space Station. "Silver Tower" is a nickname for the station's antilaser coating – '

Page's voice boomed out over the bridge. '*Antilaser coating . . .?*'

'Armstrong reports only one minute of scanning time available, sir . . . first two Soviet jet aircraft turning northbound past the destroyers . . . no speed being registered by any of the three vessels. They appear to be dead in the water . . . losing the real-time signal from Armstrong, sir. We'll get you the latest area chart immediately.'

'What about that air force AWACS? Can we tie into their data transmissions?'

'I'll try, Skipper.'

Page tossed the microphone down on its hook. *Antilaser coating? Goddamn*, she never said she'd be a target for damned *lasers* . . .

Armstrong Space Station

'Picking up emergency locator beacons from the area of those Soviet vessels, General,' Jefferson reported. 'A few distress calls.'

The command module was unusually silent. No one could speak except in muted, clipped voices. They had all witnessed, first-hand, the beginning of what appeared to be a major confrontation between Iran and the Soviet Union.

Silver Tower was now on the short one-hour portion of its three-hour orbit, hurtling towards perigee, its closest approach to earth, only eighty miles above the edge of the atmosphere. This part of the orbit was a busy time for the crew, especially now. Along with the normal house-keeping functions of running the huge station – power collection and storage while on the 'day' side of the orbit, systems maintenance, and inspections – the massive amounts of data collected by the crew had to be stored and prepared for dissemination, and then the proper preparations made in Silver Tower's numerous sensor banks for the next two-hour pass over the conflict area.

What made the job even more pressured was the constant stream of calls to General Saint-Michael, asking for a description of exactly what had happened in the Persian Gulf.

'Negative,' Saint-Michael said into his earset. 'Sir, I'm sorry, but I have my orders. My amended orders are to transmit my stored data to the Joint Chiefs directly . . . No, we don't have the time to retransmit it to Sixth Fleet

138

or Seventh Fleet Headquarters. We'll have just enough time to beam it out once before we have to start setting up for the next orbit over the area . . . Yes, Admiral, it was the *California* that requested the data link . . . the *Nimitz* listened in but it was the *California* that asked . . . Yes, sir, they must have data from shortly after the Silkworm launch was detected. They may have even seen the impact themselves . . .'

Saint-Michael rubbed the painful throbbing in his left temple. At a slight tap on his shoulder, he opened his eyes and saw Ann moving beside his seat with a cup of coffee.

'You look like you can use – '

Saint-Michael shook his head and tapped his earset. 'I'm on the scrambled satellite link. Admiral Walton.'

Ann nodded, listening in as Saint-Michael took the cup of coffee and continued speaking into the microphone.

'I'm sorry, sir? Yes, we can use the data link itself for voice as well as SBR data transmissions. It's a frequency-agile scrambled micro-wave transmission. It's not completely jam-proof or completely secure, but it's real-time voice and data at the same time, and I think that's what you want . . . What? It was working fine with the *California*, Admiral . . .'

'The *California?*' Ann said. 'Where? Where is he?'

Saint-Michael held up a hand. 'Yes, Admiral. I think the *Nimitz* should get the data, but *California* seemed to be better set up to receive it. That's your primary battle management ship, she has better satellite arrays and combat-control displays . . . No, we'll beam it to anyone who's set up to receive it . . . Yes, sir . . .'

'How's my father? Was he . . . in the fight?'

'Dammit, Ann . . . no, Admiral. Stand by one.' Saint-Michael turned to her. 'The *Nimitz* battle group was seven hundred miles away in the Arabian Sea when the attack started. Now please, be quiet.' He turned back to his earset and continued his conversation.

Colonel Walker interrupted Saint-Michael's transmission with the 'CALL' function of the interstation communications system. 'Ten minutes, General.'

'Gotta go, Admiral. We're ten minutes from horizon passage . . . Thank you, sir. Armstrong out.' Saint-Michael immediately switched to stationwide intercom. 'Attention on the station. Message from the Joint Chiefs, transmitted through US Navy Commander in Chief Pacific Forces. Well done. That goes double for me. But now we get to do it all over again – ten minutes to horizon crossing, stand by for target area.'

The Kremlin, USSR

'It . . . is . . . impossible . . .'

Marshal of the Soviet Union Sergei Czilikov read the dispatch slowly, his gnarled fingers digging deeply into the paper. He dismissed the messenger with a wave of his hand. First Deputy Minister Khromeyev stepped towards the minister of defence's desk, and Czilikov handed the message to him.

'A communication between space station Armstrong and the commander in chief of Pacific Forces in Pearl Harbor, Hawaii,' Khromeyev muttered, reading the message, 'discussing the transmission of real-time, space-based radar data to ships of the Seventh Fleet detachment in the Arabian Sea.'

'Govorov . . . the space station Armstrong . . . is it possible?' Czilikov asked. 'That station is sixteen hundred kilometres in space, travelling twenty-eight thousand kilometres an hour. Is it really possible that it can report on the position of all combat vehicles in that region?'

'This message says nothing of the sort, Comrade Minister. We've had satellites that can transmit real-time imagery for a decade. The technology is rather commonplace. Watching a few ships in the Persian Gulf from space is child's play and has been for years.'

'But the attack was detected so quickly . . .'

'Three hours? Sir, in these days a child in a sailboat on the Persian Gulf can report an attack to the world in three hours. I still have not seen any evidence of the Americans' vaunted high-technology space-tracking system.'

Czilikov nodded slowly. 'Very well, Comrade Khromeyev. I will go along with your assessment. Feather will continue as planned. Were there any serious casualties aboard the *Sovremennyy*?'

'No casualties, sir. An unexpectedly high number of injuries but none serious. The *Sovremennyy* was hit by three missiles and suffered extreme damage, much more than planned. In addition, the patrol vessel *Buchara* was hit by a fourth Silkworm missile. Several injuries, heavy damage, but she's still under her own power. However, sir, there are unexpected bonuses. As unfortunate as the injuries are, it should serve to fuel outrage and help win support for the operation. This is no longer an "unfortunate incident" – it is a major act of aggression. There also can be no charge of a contrived attack . . .'

'No, but I wish it weren't through our own ineptness that it was so.' Czilikov paused, thinking. 'Strategically, we're in good shape. The *Brezhnev* is still in grave danger from land-based attack, but Chercherovin assures me the carrier and her escorts in the gulf can take control of the skies until Bandar-Abbas, Tehran, Tabriz, and Hamadan airfields in Iran are taken by Rhomerdunov and Ilanovsky. Once the air force and army control those four fields, they will be able to sufficiently seal off the skies for Chercherovin to move more ships into the gulf.'

'And the American, French and British ships in the gulf? What of them?'

'They are already overwhelmed. We outnumber them two to one. Once the *Brezhnev* controls the skies over the region, the Western ships in the gulf will be impotent.'

Khromeyev nodded. 'Stationing the *Brezhnev* in the gulf was a master stroke, the tactical advantage we now have there far outweighs the dangers we faced moving it past the Strait of Hormuz. Who would have thought the Americans would allow us such free access into the gulf? At the very least, I expected them to match our forces – even that was never fully accomplished.'

'And that will be the Americans' greatest mistake,' Czilikov said. 'They wanted to play power politics in the Persian Gulf without supporting their policies. Soon they will pay the price . . .'

Armstrong Space Station

The master SBR display now only showed the three-hundred-mile area surrounding the Strait of Hormuz, but even so it took Jake Jefferson and two other technicians to process the volume of data being collected.

'The *Brezhnev* is within one hundred miles of Bandar-e Lengeh,' Jefferson reported. 'Numerous aircraft in the area.'

'Those Russians sure are getting ballsy with that carrier,' Walker said, studying the display. 'Only one ship, a Krivak-class frigate, between it and Bandar-Abbas. If the Iranians decide to shoot again, the carrier will make one inviting target.'

'Aircraft launching from the *Brezhnev*, sir,' Jefferson reported again. 'Fast moving, not rotorcraft.'

'I still can't figure the Iranians shooting at those ships,'

Kevin Baker said. 'Did it look like those Soviet ships were threatening them, about to go into Iranian waters?'

His question got him no answer. Saint-Michael was intently scribbling in a notebook, Ann stayed near him.

'Where is the *California?*' she asked.

'Still about six hundred miles away from the Strait of Hormuz,' Saint-Michael said distractedly. 'The *Nimitz* will probably move a few hundred miles closer, within flying range of its fighters, and wait there.' He looked at her. 'I'd say your father's safe, don't worry.'

'Safe? I wish I could believe that.' She looked at the master SBR display. 'How come we can't see the *Nimitz* and the *California* on the screen?'

The general was now ignoring her, so Walker took it up: 'The Joint Chiefs asked us to zoom in on the Strait of Hormuz. They want a detailed look at where that Soviet carrier *Brezhnev* is going and what she's going to do.'

'But the *Nimitz's* battle group . . .?'

'Still under surveillance. The SBR still scans the area for a thousand miles around the target area, and that includes the Arabian Sea and the *Nimitz*. The results of its scans are still recorded – we just don't display the whole area. There's just too much data to digest, and we can't keep both shifts going 'round the clock.'

'But how can you tell if something's happening near the *Nimitz?*'

'The system is programmed to alert us if the SBR detects a threat near our own ships. An alarm will go off and the display will change to scan – '

'Rotorcraft recovering on the *Brezhnev*, sir,' a tech cut in. '*Brezhnev* turning northwest into the wind again.'

Walker motioned to Ann. 'Why don't you check those monitors there? You can use them to plot out the *California's* position.'

Ann thanked him with her eyes and moved over to the unoccupied computer monitor. She studied the display, noting with fascination that it identified the type of vehicle, its location, its speed and its probable destination and time of arrival. It was identifying trucks, boats and planes of all sizes, even barges and light aeroplanes – it even had a line of data on a contact labelled 'MARINE MAMMAL.'

There was nothing on the screen mentioning the *Nimitz* or *California*, so she used an arrow key on a small keyboard to scroll through several pages of SBR contact-data reports. The list was very long, and she worked the arrow key faster and faster –

'Ann, hold it.' Saint-Michael suddenly appeared beside her. 'Scroll forward again. Did you see a blinking data line a second ago?'

'Yes, I think so.' She scrolled forward, wondering what she could be looking for.

'Faster, Ann.' The general finally nudged her aside and pounded the arrow key, finally stopping at a data block that blinked on and off about once every two seconds. He touched his earset controls.

'Full SBR master display.'

Walker turned towards his commanding officer. 'Sir, that will spoil the data transmissions for the area. *Nimitz* and JCS are only formatted for a three-hundred-mile dis – '

'I want full SBR display, Jim. Right *now*. Those Soviet fighters that launched a few minutes ago from the *Brezhnev* – they went inland. And fast.'

He made his way back to his command chair and strapped himself in just as the large master SBR display shimmered and transformed itself back to its large-scale diagram of the entire target region. Several blocks on the display were blinking – areas in northern and northeastern Iran, southern Iran and Afghanistan. The dot representing the *Brezhnev* was also blinking furiously.

'Get on 'em, dammit,' Saint-Michael ordered.

The response was immediate. 'Fast-moving fighter aircraft, origin *Brezhnev*, four hundred seventy knots, one thousand feet above the ground. Sixty miles south of Shiraz.'

'Four high-speed, low-altitude aircraft heading south, origin estimated as Lyaki on the Caspian Sea, one hundred forty miles north of Tehran.'

'*Brezhnev* launching . . . Two high-speed aircraft heading north-northwest along the Iranian coast – '

'The *California* is on channel six, General,' Walker cut in. Saint-Michael punched a button on his communications panel.

'*California*, this is Armstrong Alpha. We've detected several high-speed Soviet aircraft overflying Iran. Several from Lyaki heading for Tehran and Tabriz, several from the *Brezhnev* heading north towards Shiraz and Esfahan. It sure looks like an invasion force.'

Commander Meserve aboard the *California* turned pale in the unearthly blue glow of the *California's* combat information centre, then whirled towards the intercom.

'Attention all hands. Condition yellow. Repeat, condition yellow. Captain to CIC.' He turned again to the headset that linked him with the orbiting space station. 'We're blind down here, Armstrong. We've lost the real-time display. Can you assist?'

'You need to reconfigure your display for one-thousand-mile scan range,' Saint-Michael told him. 'We're only programmed to transmit either the full-scan picture or the three-hundred-mile scan of the strait.'

Captain Matthew Page was sweating in his life jacket as he trotted back into CIC. 'Report, Commander.'

'Armstrong reports several aircraft from the Soviet Union and from the carrier *Brezhnev* entering Iranian airspace. Says it looks like an invasion force.'

'A *what?*' Meserve held out the headset to Page.

'Armstrong, this is Captain Page. General, what the *hell* is going on?'

Saint-Michael keyed his earset. 'It's confirmed, Captain. Six high-speed aircraft heading towards Tabriz, six towards Tehran, six towards Esfahan and six for Bandar-Abbas. We're also showing eight large, slow-moving aircraft at low altitude heading for Tehran. SBR hasn't identified them yet but I think they're probably troop transports or heavy bombers. Take your pick – it spells trouble.'

The eight men in CIC looked to Page for orders. After a few moments he pulled the headset's microphone to his lips. 'How much longer do you have on this orbit, General?'

'One hour of reliable real-time data. After that another half hour of less precise position-only data until we drop below the horizon. It'll take another hour after that to resume coverage – '

'Can't you slow yourself down, sort of hover over the area? Buy more time?'

Saint-Michael rolled his eyes in exasperation and glanced at Ann. 'Haven't you ever explained this to your father?' He returned to the laser communications link. 'Captain, just take my word for it. We can't *hover* anywhere.'

'Stand by, Armstrong.' Commander Meserve had pushed the red telephone into Page's hands. 'Page here.'

'Matt, this is Admiral Clancy. The group is on yellow alert. Repeat, yellow alert.'

'Aye, sir. We went to yellow as soon as we got the word from the space station.'

'Very well. Stand by to manoeuvre. We'll be launching Hawkeye radar planes, four escorts and two patrol birds. Are you still in contact with the space station?'

'Affirmative. We've lost the real-time display but we

146

have voice contact. We'll be reestablishing data link with Armstrong momentarily.'

'It looks like you're it, then, Matt. We've lost the real-time display and we have no voice contact. Maintain contact with Armstrong Station by the best possible means and report any significant developments to us pronto. Advise them that we'll be launching aircraft and request maximum SBR coverage. Over.'

'Aye, aye, sir. Out.' Page replaced the red phone and returned to the headset. 'General, aircraft will be launching from the *Nimitz* shortly. Can you keep those planes under surveillance until we get our equipment reconfigured? We're still blind down here.'

'Affirmative, we'll give you voice narrative until you get your tactical screen reprogrammed.' Saint-Michael turned to Jefferson and spoke through the wireless intercom. 'Jake, you're on channel six. Give the *California* verbal advisories on any aircraft or vessels near the carrier group or near the aircraft it'll be launching. Get Kelly to help the Squids on the *California* to get their display reformatted.'

'Yes, sir.' Jefferson positioned himself in front of the master SBR screen and readjusted his headset as he studied the screen. '*California*, this is your controller on board Armstrong Station. Fifty-seven more minutes until we're out of optimal SBR range. How copy?'

Page nodded to his senior radioman in charge of the *California's* combat-information electronics system. 'Loud and clear, Armstrong.'

As Jefferson issued his report the crew of Silver Tower watched the Soviet attack rapidly intensify.

'More aircraft launching from *Brezhnev*,' a tech reported. 'Several aircraft over Tabriz and Tehran. ETA for large Soviet jet aircraft from Baku Military Airfield is five minutes.' Ann and Kevin Baker could only stand by as the SBR technician reported wave after wave of aircraft swarming over Iran. Through it all, Sergeant Jefferson continued his calm, steady litany in a low, unwavering voice.

'Looks like an execution,' from Colonel Walker. 'We've picked up the first emergency reports from Iran. The word is the Soviets are attacking with *chemical weapons*.'

The Kremlin, USSR

The battle staff members, chaired by Minister of Defence Czilikov himself, had met every hour on the hour since the first Silkworm missile was launched by exiled Iranian Revolutionary Guardsmen and Soviet agents. First Deputy Minister of Defence Marshal Khromeyev conducted the latest hourly operations briefing.

'The first sorties from the *Brezhnev* have already returned,' he began. 'All aircraft report complete success. No opposition all the way to their targets and only minimal on their return route. Latest casualties and losses are one Sukhoi-27 fighter bomber from the *Brezhnev* shot down by Iranian anti-aircraft artillery while exiting hostile territory; one Tupolev-26 bomber from the Seventy-Fifth Naval Aviation Bombardment Squad at Lyaki lost over Tabriz in Northern Iran, all four crewmembers lost . . .'

'That's *all?*' Czilikov said. 'Out of nearly a hundred aircraft over Iran in eight hours only two were lost?'

'Yes, sir, I would like to mention the actions of the men of the Second Rescue Operations Force aboard the *Brezhnev*. When the Sukhoi was reported downed the men of the Second ROF volunteered to attempt a rescue of the downed airman. Two Mil-14 helicopters from Second ROF were dispatched along with a single Yakovlev-38 vertical-takeoff-and-landing aircraft for support cover. After destroying an Iranian gunboat near the crash site, the Second ROF rescued the Sukhoi fighter pilot and all three aircraft safely returned to the *Brezhnev*. The Sukhoi pilot immediately volunteered for another sortie. I request that the men of Second ROF be awarded the Order of Lenin for heroism.'

'So ordered,' Czilikov said. 'In less than half a day the forces under Admiral Chercherovin have crushed all opposition from Iranian land, air and sea forces. The skies over Iran, Iraq and the Persian Gulf belong to *us*.' He turned to Chercherovin. 'And what about the Americans in the area? What has their reaction been?'

'Negligible, Comrade Minister. The four American vessels in the Persian Gulf have taken our warning and stayed away from the *Brezhnev* – as a matter of fact, they've kept their distance even when the *Brezhnev* and her escorts moved to launch or recover aircraft. In response, all aircraft involved in Feather have stayed a minimum of one hundred sixty kilometres from all American ships, as you ordered. The Americans are not stupid – they know they're significantly outnumbered in the gulf. They won't risk destruction for Iran.'

'And the American carrier fleet in the Arabian Sea?'

'Absolutely no response, sir, except to launch a few medium-range reconnaissance aircraft near Iran's southern shore to monitor our invasion. Admiral Ynoliev of the *Brezhnev* had allotted ten Sukhoi fighters to counter any actions made by the *Nimitz*, but none was necessary. The *Brezhnev* remains at the very edge of the *Nimitz's* effective combat radius. The American carrier will have to move several hundred kilometres closer to the Gulf of Oman to be able to strike at the *Brezhnev*, but if it does it will expose itself to counterattack by the *Brezhnev's* escorts. The exact distance between the *Brezhnev* and the *Nimitz* is, I feel, significant, Comrade Minister. The Americans are telling us they're aware *and* concerned about our operation but for now will not interfere. The reality of the situation is obvious to anyone – neither the *Nimitz* nor the Persian Gulf flotilla is in a strong enough position to strike.'

Czilikov, as much as his aged face would allow, managed an almost childlike smile. 'The great American navy, confined like a spoiled brat in a crib.'

'Perhaps we put too much emphasis on the disposition of the American surface forces, sir,' Deputy Minister of Defence Marshal Yesimov, the commander in chief of the Soviet Air Force, said. 'It is the heavy and medium bombers of the American air forces in Turkey and Diego Garcia that are our chief concern. Those bombers will undoubtedly be allowed use of Saudi Arabian bases as staging areas. The *Brezhnev's* planes cannot counter enemy land-based aircraft from Turkey and Saudi Arabia *and* carrier aircraft from the *Nimitz* all at once, no matter how skilled their pilots are.'

Noting something less than pleasure on the face of Admiral Chercherovin, Yesimov hurried to put his remarks in context. 'My comments are, of course, not meant to reflect on Admiral Chercherovin's brilliant execution of phase one of Operation Feather. What I'm concerned about is phase two. Our use of chemical weapons to neutralize the Iranian surface-to-air missile batteries was, I feel, an . . . unfortunate miscalculation. We've been able to land only a small regiment of paratroopers in Tabriz, Esfahan and Shiraz – the chemical residues are still too dangerous for any more than a small neutralization force. The defences surrounding Tehran were stronger than we had anticipated and the battle for Tehran Airport hasn't yet been resolved. Also, Bandar-Abbas was too heavily damaged to land transports at its airfield – our carrier-based fighter-bombers were, unfortunately, a bit too enthusiastic.'

Commander of the Red Army Ilanovsky cleared his throat several times and added, 'Marshal Yesimov is correct, sir. Although we have made remarkable headway, our gains are still not consolidated . . .'

'We must push forward,' Czilikov said in a deep, rumbling voice. 'The speed of our false Iranian attack has frozen the Americans. They may have had plans to reestablish ties with the present Iranian government but the distrust, *distaste*, most Americans feel towards all Muslims is still there – and that has worked to our advantage. We've not even received an official protest from the US government.'

Czilikov turned to the army commander in chief. 'Marshal Ilanovsky, Tehran and Bandar-Abbas must be subdued immediately. We must take control of the Strait of Hormuz for our resupply ships to enter, and the central command and control centres of the Iranian military must be neutralized. You have explained the dangers and difficulties associated with conducting military operations in the chemical anti-exposure suits and hermetic equipment, but we can't wait for another twenty-four hours to consolidate our advances. At least a full division must advance on both Bandar-Abbas and Tehran within six hours.'

'*Six hours?* With full hermetic equipment? That is impossible,' Ilanovsky said abruptly.

'We have the transport resources,' Marshal Yesimov put in. 'I can land a division within an hour of notification that your shock troops have secured the airfield at Bandar-Abbas and made sufficient repairs – '

'Another raid on Mehrabad Airport in Tehran from the *Brezhnev* should crush all opposition,' Chercherovin said. 'Doshan Tappeh Airfield in Tehran can be used as an alternative; a squad of shock troops has already occupied that airport, although they hold it by a shoestring. The Antonov-124 may not be able to land at Doshan Tappeh, but a smaller Antonov-72 or -74 should be able to land there.'

151

'And Bandar-Abbas?' Ilanovsky asked, trying to calm his anger at being upstaged by the others in the general staff. 'What happens after my shock troops are put in place? They're elite soldiers, not engineers. Who will repair the runway?'

'Combat Engineers from the *Brezhnev* will be landed in Bandar-Abbas to make repairs,' Chercherovin replied easily, bathing in the satisfied smile of approval from Minister of Defence Czilikov. 'Equipment can be airlifted from the *Brezhnev* easily – provided your soldiers can secure the coastline.'

'One company of Seventh Shock Force can control the whole damned town,' Ilanovsky told him. 'Bring your ditch-diggers to repair the damage *your* pilots caused – my men will protect them.'

'Then we're decided,' Czilikov said, shooting a stern look at both generals. 'The *Brezhnev* will be responsible for repairs to the airfield at Bandar-Abbas and for a second heavy strike on Tehran. The air force will provide air support and a second bomber strike. Communications will be maintained so that the transports are airborne and over Tehran and Bandar-Abbas when the respective airfields are secure. Those two divisions will be in Tehran and Bandar-Abbas within six hours.'

'Meanwhile, sir,' First Deputy Minister Khromeyev picked it up, 'a full division of hand-picked Iraqi infantry led by *Glavnyi Marshal* Valeriy Belikov, the commander of the Southern *Teatr Voennykh Deistvii* will once and for all take and hold Abadan and Khorramshahr along the Iran–Iraq border, making it possible for Soviet vessels to safely dock at Al-Basrah in Iraq. With their country surrounded on all sides, the leaders of Alientar's government will have no choice but to surrender.'

Czilikov scanned his battle staff. 'This is the culmination of a thirty-year plan, comrades. The actions we take in the next seventy-two hours will decide the conflict –

even, perhaps, the future of Soviet history. If we can subdue Iran and cause a new pro-Soviet revolution to occur in the Middle East, it will signal a new era of Soviet power and influence. Who knows how far we can go . . .'

It was a grandiose thought, more political than was usual for Czilikov. Why, Czilikov asked himself, had it been necessary to go against his own grain and invoke the future like some bombastic commissar? Maybe because the feeling of ultimate victory, somehow, wasn't there yet. Yes . . . they'd made spectacular advances, demoralized the battle-weary Iranians, caught the United States napping and unprepared to take action. But it was as if they were clinging to the pinnacle of success by a hangnail rather than standing firmly on top of it.

His generals had followed along blindly, Czilikov reminded himself. There had been no long discussion, no arguments, no turmoil, no extended planning sessions. They were fighting this war not so much because they believed in its objectives as because they believed that they would be exiled or disposed of if they refused. That was why he felt the need to remind them of their duty. Real soldiers, real Russian warriors wouldn't need such a reminder – but the general staff never behaved like real Russian warriors. Czilikov thought he saw a spark in them during the meeting, when they had argued about their forces' respective capabilities, but the arguments had quickly died away. True Russian warriors? Where the hell were they? Not here . . .

That is, except for one. There was one . . .

'We'll meet again at precisely zero-three-hundred hours,' First Deputy Minister Khromeyev said to the battle staff. 'The final plans for the thrust into Bandar-Abbas and Tehran will be ready for presentation and ultimate approval by the minister of defence.' Khromeyev turned to Czilikov again. *'Tovarishch Chayzeyaen,*

153

pazhalosta?' Czilikov shook his head, still lost in thought. Cattle. Mindless cattle . . .

'Dismissed. *Pastayach*.' The battle staff members shuffled to their feet and began to file out, but as the large outer doors of the conference room swung open the retreating generals and admirals abruptly stopped. Czilikov noticed it and followed Khromeyev's gaze out through the doorway.

There, standing at attention, was General Govorov. An aide stood alongside him, carrying a small pile of computer printouts. Govorov wore a dark grey military space suit that he himself had designed for the 'new breed' of Soviet soldier. His boots were high-polished, his utility uniform was immaculate – overall, there was something in his bearing that suggested limitless self-confidence.

Khromeyev looked as if he were about to explode. 'Govorov, I warned you to – '

'Comrade Minister,' Govorov said to Czilikov, interrupting Khromeyev, 'I must speak with you.'

Khromeyev's face flushed. 'Get out before I have you – '

'Come,' Khromeyev heard behind him. Czilikov was on his feet, motioning to Govorov.

'But Comrade Minister . . .' Khromeyev protested.

'You may go, Khromeyev. Be sure the plans are ready for me by zero-three-hundred hours.' A final look from Czilikov sent the stunned chief of the general staff hurrying out of the door.

Govorov moved quickly into the conference room and stood in front of Czilikov, feeling less sure of himself than his little performance had, he hoped, indicated. His aide carried the sheaf of computer printouts as if it was dinner on a silver tray.

'Sit down, General Govorov,' Czilikov said, a smile slowly forming on his lips. 'We need to talk.'

Govorov sat, reminding himself what steel was behind that smile.

5

'Attention on the station. Shipwide message broadcast for all personnel.'

Saint-Michael shifted restlessly in his seat. Colonel Walker was at his post near the master SBR display with Jefferson, continuing to reprogram the space-based radar unit for its next pass over the Persian Gulf conflict area. The command module was crowded with all of Silver Tower's crewmembers, including the two civilian scientists and Will and Sontag of the space shuttle *Enterprise*, now docked on one of the space station's shuttle-docking bays on a resupply mission.

'Armstrong, this is *Nimitz*. How copy?'

Saint-Michael checked the communications setting on his panel. 'Loud and clear, *Nimitz*. Armstrong standing by.'

'Armstrong, this is Secretary of Defense Edwards. I am in the White House with the Joint Chiefs, the chairman of the National Security Council, the House and Senate majority and minority leaders, and the chairman of the House and Senate Foreign Affairs committees. The president and the vice-president are on their way, but they directed me to start this transmission in case they hadn't arrived when your orbit brought you near North America.'

The transmission was clear but the voice was barely recognizable. A computer, synchronized with the US Navy's atomic clock in Fort Collins, Colorado, scrambled and descrambled the laser-beam transmission five times a second, and the resultant secure transmission wavered like an old-style short-wave radio.

'The president has directed me to inform you of his decision concerning the Soviet attack on Iran,' Edwards went on. 'He's decided to intervene in the conflict to prevent further Soviet advances into Iran and the Persian Gulf region.'

Ann Page felt her face flush and her fingertips grow numb as she listened. Her *father* was down there, in the *Nimitz*'s battle group – probably, she guessed, the spearhead of the American opposing force . . .

'The president, in consultation with our allies and with Congress, has ordered that steps be taken by all available forces to halt any further Soviet acts of aggression in the region. To this end he has appointed Rear Admiral Clancy, commander of the *Nimitz* carrier battle group, as overall theatre commander of Allied forces. He has taken direct command of all service forces effective immediately . . . However, Brigadier General Saint-Michael, as commander of Armstrong Space Station, has superbly demonstrated the special value of his installation. Therefore, by order of the president, Jason F. Saint-Michael is hereby promoted to the rank of Space Command Lieutenant General and is of this moment deputy commander of Allied forces in the Persian Gulf region.'

In spite of the serious circumstances, a ripple of applause and a few muted cheers broke out among the crew. Saint-Michael remained stone-faced, and the congratulations quickly petered out – this was definitely not the time nor place for applause. And Ann in particular was upset about her father being in the eye of the coming storm . . .

'Your assignment, General Saint-Michael, is to direct offensive forces and position defensive forces in support of US operations in the Persian Gulf region. You are to use all means at your disposal to warn Allied forces of attack or potential threats against them, to direct offensive forces safely to their targets and to provide Allied forces with as much reconnaissance data as necessary to carry out the objectives of their missions. The president and everyone in this room here have full confidence in you. Good luck.'

A moment after the circuit went dead, Saint-Michael opened the interstation address system.

'Attention, a plan has already been devised and briefed to me by the Joint Chiefs to ward off any more Soviet attacks into Iran. That plan will now be implemented. Our job is to see that it's successful. Our other task, if not already obvious, is to survive to continue our assigned duty. I don't need to tell everyone here that Armstrong Station is a prime target for attack.

'We have weapons to defend ourselves with: the ten Thor antiballistic-missile interceptors we control are now committed to use for station self-defence. A second Thor garage is being sent to us. But our prime defence is nothing more exotic than watchfulness and preparation . . . Effective immediately this station is on twenty-four-hour yellow alert. The station will be on red alert over the Persian Gulf horizon if hostilities of any sort are taking place on earth or in space. I'll review duty items to be performed while under yellow alert.

'Crewmembers will carry a portable oxygen system at all times with the mask around the neck. Personnel off duty or sleeping will wear the mask at all times. The oxygen supply will not be allowed to drop below three-quarters full at any time. A fire watch will be posted in all modules, and all modules will be sealed. A verbal cross check of connecting tunnel atmospheric security will be made to the fire watch before moving among modules. Two off-duty personnel will be assigned spacesuit duty in two twelve-hour shifts. Their duty will be to rescue injured personnel in case of catastrophic damage. They will prepare rescue balls and the lifeboat for station personnel. The spacesuit duty roster will be announced immediately by Colonel Walker . . .'

He paused, looked at Ann, who shifted uncomfortably until he went on, 'I want to hear from any research personnel who feels that the new dangers involved are unacceptable. In the next few days you will undoubtedly be exposed to significant risks – risks that you couldn't have anticipated when you signed on. Neither I nor anyone in Space Command will hold it against any of you if you decide against continued duty aboard Silver Tower during these hostilities. You may return to earth aboard *Enterprise* when she departs tomorrow. Thank you. This station is on yellow alert.'

Ann had drawn fire watch for the galley-computer control module, but she returned to the command module after retrieving her portable oxygen system. Saint-Michael was just ending another laser-transmitted message with earth when she approached him.

'Congratulations on your promotion,' she said, her smile somewhat forced.

He nodded, figuring silence was the best tactic with her.

'I caught that look when you made the announcement about leaving the station.'

'Well, the announcement applied to you as much as anyone and – '

'I'll tell you right now, General, I'm not leaving.'

'Look, Ann, two Pages involved in this thing could be one too many. Maybe you shouldn't reject the option out of hand. At least think about it.'

Ann thought he was also telling her that her leaving would be doing him a favour . . . It wasn't at all what she'd expected . . .

'Okay,' she said quietly. 'I'll think about it.' She

lingered for a moment then turned and made her way to the connecting tunnel.

At the hatch Kevin Baker, on fire watch in the command module, checked the atmospheric pressure of the connecting tunnel. 'Pressure's good,' he said.

Ann double-checked the gauge and nodded. They had rehearsed red alert procedures dozens of times, but it felt very different doing them for real. 'Checks. Clear to open.'

'What were you talking about with the general?' Baker asked before he undogged the hatch. 'Are you on your way home?'

'I don't want to be, but . . .' She shook her head. 'You know, I just can't figure the man out.'

'What do you mean?'

'It's just that . . . hey, listen, don't mind me. I guess I've got a lot on my mind.'

'No problem,' Baker said as he activated the interlocks, then opened the hatch. 'By the way . . . here.' He pressed a sheet of folded computer paper into her hand.

'What's this?'

'The results of the MHD superconductor relay circuit tests. Better get going; they're checking everyone in.'

It took her a few moments to double-check the atmospheric integrity of the computer-centre galley, enter the module, seal it off and report in with Colonel Walker that all hatches were sealed. They'd been waiting for her. Next they checked and double-checked the integrity of each module and each hatch all over the massive installation. They had just finished the checklist when Sergeant Jefferson announced, 'Five minutes to horizon crossing. Stand by.'

What to do now but listen, watch and wait for the next twelve hours? Ann fixed herself a cup of coffee and unfolded the printout of the computer-driven MHD superconductor relay circuit test. She let the long paper

159

strip unroll itself in an undulating stream across the galley and scanned the long rows and columns of numbers, reading off the computer's analysis of the thousands of –

And *there it was*. On the left MHD control-circuit relay, three quarters of the way through the test strip – it would have taken at least thirty hours to find it if the check had been done by hand – one of the sixteen thousand 256-bit data words did not agree with its error-trapping checksum. Kevin Baker's computer, programmed with all of the MHD relay's error readouts, even pinpointed the fault's exact location –

'Attention on the station. Horizon crossing – mark. Stand by for target area. The station is on red alert. Out.'

Ann quickly scanned the rest of the printout. No other faults. She depressed the intercom button. 'Colonel Walker, request permission to enter the Skybolt module.'

A pause, then: 'Sorry, no. We wouldn't have fire coverage in the computer module with you in Skybolt.'

'It would only be for a moment – '

'We're on *red alert*, Ann.' It was now a very annoyed Lieutenant General Saint-Michael talking into the intercom. 'We're two minutes from moving directly into the sights of six Soviet Gorgon antisatellite missiles. We're already in the sights of a two-hundred-megawatt Soviet antisatellite laser site. The time for tinkering with Skybolt has passed. Maintain your post.'

The line snapped dead. She could feel the stares, hear the imagined whispered comments directed at her through the walls.

Well, *damn* him. The man had put her in her place by embarrassing her. Above and beyond . . . For a moment there, back in the command module, she'd actually thought he . . . Cool it, you're one of the crew, lady, nothing more, for *sure* nothing more . . .

'SBR contact on aircraft transponders,' Jefferson

reported. 'Identification positive and confirmed. Four-ship F-18 patrol from the *Nimitz*.'

Another tech announced, 'Sir, voice and data link reestablished with the *California*.'

USS *California*

'Skipper, the space station is back.'

Captain Page acknowledged and put a few last sentences in his personal ship's log before snapping the ledger closed. 'Right on time.' He fixed the headset and keyed the microphone.

'Armstrong, this is the USS *California*. How copy? Over.'

'Loud and clear, *California*,' said General Saint-Michael. 'Are you receiving our data transmissions?'

Page glanced over at Meserve, who nodded. 'Digital imagery coming in clear as a bell, Skipper.'

'Affirmative, General. Congratulations on your promotion. When we get back, sir, you're buying the bar.'

'A deal.'

'Advisory for those patrol planes,' Colonel Walker cut into the ship-to-orbit link. 'Several fast patrol boats operating at their twelve o'clock, seventy nautical miles. Could be those new Iranian hydrofoils or the small corvettes they took out of mothballs. If they're corvettes they have naval Hawk-Four surface-to-air missiles that might give the Hornets trouble.'

'Copy, Armstrong. We'll divert the Hornets around them. No telling who the Iranians might decide to shoot at right now.'

'New contacts,' Sergeant Jefferson reported. 'Low altitude jet aircraft heading south along the west shore of the Caspian Sea. No definite number yet.'

'Copy that, *California*?' Saint-Michael asked.

Meserve and Page were peering over the shoulders of the three radiomen who manned the data display unit of CIC's control console. The operators were switching the displays back and forth, trying to keep up with the volume of data being received. Finally Page punched the mike button in frustration.

'Armstrong, we can't keep up with that thousand-mile display. We're going to cut ours back down to three hundred miles. Keep us advised of activity outside the three-hundred-mile radius of the Strait of Hormuz. We'll concentrate our surveillance in the area where the *Nimitz*'s planes will be operating.'

Saint-Michael said over a closed interphone, 'He must think I have a hundred people up here to watch the screens. He's got twice the people I have but he's only watching one-tenth of the area.'

'I think I understand his situation,' Walker said. 'SBR is decades ahead of the *California*'s technology. It's like trying to get a drink of water from a fire hose.'

Saint-Michael shrugged and keyed the microphone. 'Roger, *California*. Understand.'

'We've got a count on those newcomer Soviet planes,' Jefferson said. His rising, excited voice made Saint-Michael swivel around to face him. 'Total of twelve aircraft. Four slow-moving planes were joined with two flights of fast-moving planes. The group is turning slightly southeast, Skipper. I *think* they're heading for Tehran – '

'Aircraft launching from the *Brezhnev*, sir,' a tech reported. 'Two high-speed aircraft heading east-northeast.'

Saint-Michael hit the mike button. '*California*, this is Armstrong. Fighters from *Brezhnev* heading your way.'

The reply was immediate and, to no one's surprise, as excited as Jefferson's. 'We got 'em, Armstrong.'

'Be advised – twelve Soviet aircraft heading south from Lyaki, suspected target Tehran. No positive ID; it could

162

either be another Backfire bomber strike force or a four-ship Condor troop transport formation with eight fighter escorts. Or both. Whatever, it looks like a major production.'

'Armstrong, this is *Nimitz*.' Even through the scrambler interference Admiral Clancy's rasping voice could easily be identified. 'Copy all. Your execution code is Sierra Tango November one-zero.'

Saint-Michael had been anticipating that. 'Armstrong copies Sierra Tango November one-zero. Out.' He switched to stationwide intercom. 'Attention on the station. Voice communications blackout is in effect. And repeat – this station is on red alert.'

To Walker, Jefferson and the three sensor technicians, Saint-Michael said, 'All right, listen up. We've just received an execution order directing the interception of that Soviet attack force apparently heading for Tehran. We'll maintain surveillance over the whole region, but if it gets too much to watch we'll keep on the northern attack group and let Clancy and the *California* watch the southern attack group – '

'New aircraft, sir . . . eight high-speed aircraft east-bound from . . . it looks like eastern Turkey.'

'Right on the mark,' Saint-Michael said. 'That's Tango November, the F-15E Rapid Deployment Force alert birds from Kigzi Airbase in Turkey. We should have eight more F-15s ready for launch at Kigzi; I want them airborne with their tanker as soon as possible. Talk to the second group on channel eight. Remember, no voice. I want vectors for the first group of F-15s over data-link channel nine to bring them around behind that group of Soviet heavies and their escorts.'

'It will be my pleasure, Skipper,' Sergeant Jefferson said, turning towards his screens.

'Picking up two more eastbound planes,' a tech

reported. 'High speed, low altitude . . .' A hint of surprise was apparent in his voice. 'It's an . . . intermittent return.'

'Our aces in the hole,' Saint-Michael said. 'Those are the F-19 *Nighthawk* stealth bombers from Kigzi – even the SBR is having trouble maintaining a solid track on them. They'll be on data-link channel ten. If anyone gets near them or if they get fired on, warn them – but I'm betting nobody will.' Also hoping . . .

'Tango November flight closing within one hundred nautical miles of those Soviet formations,' Jefferson broke in. 'The Soviet strike formations still on course, now approaching Bandar-e Anzali on the south shore of the Caspian.'

Saint-Michael turned to Sergeant Jefferson. 'Jake, transmit code Foxtrot Bravo on channel nine. Get an acknowledgement by each flight lead.'

Jefferson interrupted his digitized vectoring instructions and tapped out the simple instruction-code, prefix and two-letter command. The code would be picked up on the heads-up display on each F-15 Eagle fighter. Each pilot would then check in with their formation leaders, who would then relay a reply via satellite communications system back to Armstrong Station.

'All elements of Tango November acknowledge your Foxtrot Bravo command, Skipper.'

'Range?'

'Eighty miles and closing fast. Those two separate low-altitude aircraft are passing south of the Soviet formation. It looks like they're going to beat the Soviet strike formation in Tehran.'

General Saint-Michael settled nervously back into his seat. *Looks like* . . . Sure . . .

It took only ten minutes for the eight advanced F-15E Eagle fighter-bombers to cover the eighty miles between them and the huge Soviet formation. The Russian pilots

164

were cautious – occasionally a pair of Su-27s would peel off from the formation, reverse course and scan the sky behind the formation to search for pursuers. Electronic eyes scanned for radar signals that might attack from surface-to-air missile sites, but the formation was safe from any Iranian defences; Iran had all but used up its resources in its long struggle with Iraq, and the Russian planes knew it.

Undeserved, though, was the threat from American bushwhackers. With Silver Tower as their 'eyes', the F-15 weapons-system operators, WSOs, did not need to use their position-disclosing air-to-air radars to track the Soviet aircraft ahead, and when the Soviet fighters would backtrack to search behind their formation, Armstrong Station directed the Eagles away from the Flankers and then back together again once the danger of discovery was past.

Just as the latest pair of prowling Flankers had returned to their place in the twelve-ship formation, the Eagles made their move.

In full afterburner, consuming over sixteen hundred pounds of fuel per minute, Major Alan Fourier, the Eagle formation leader, took his eight fighters screaming towards the Soviet attack formation at twice the speed of sound. In less than two minutes they had eaten up the remaining fifteen miles between the two formations. As they drew within five miles the group split – four Eagles, led by Air Force Captain Jeff Cook, took the high-patrol Soviet aircraft, and Fourier took four Eagles down to the lower ones. By the time they caught up to the Russian planes their fuel supply was half-exhausted, but their tactic had its desired effect.

Fourier's group of four F-15s passed fifty feet below the first Soviet formation, flying over nine hundred miles an hour faster than the large Soviet aircraft. The Americans stayed in a mallard-like V formation, flying so close that they almost looked like one large aircraft. Fourier made mental notes as they made their fast observation pass . . . The Soviet formation had broken into two separate cells; the lower cell consisted of four Sukhoi-27 Flanker air-superiority fighters and two supersonic Tupolev-26 Backfire bombers.

'Look at all the stuff on those Flankers,' Fourier's WSO said as he hurriedly made notes in a logbook. 'Wing-tip missile, one underwing missile each side, one underwing bomb each side, one long-range fuel tank under the belly. Major league bomb-booms.'

'Heavy,' Fourier said, taking a deep breath. His WPO was typing all the information into his satellite transceiver unit. 'You'd better be getting all this out.'

'Sent, repeated twice, awaiting acknowledgement,' the WSO told him. 'It looked like one full rack of six hundred pounders each under each wing of those Backfires.'

'Like you said: major league.' Fourier keyed his microphone switch for the first time since takeoff: 'Tango November flight two, this is lead. Did you blow the whistle?'

'Lead, this is flight two lead. That's a rog. Acknowledgement already received. We've got four Flankers and two Condor tanker-transports up here.'

'Copy, flight two lead. We've got four Flankers with bombs and two Backfires with bombs down here.'

'Acknowledgement coming over the SATCOM,' Fourier's WSO reported over interphone. 'Message received says, "Bravo November." '

Fourier's grip tightened on the stick and throttle. He did not need the tiny codebook he carried on his kneeboard to decode that message.

'Tango November flights one and two, check in with last message received. Red Lead has Bravo November.'

'Two.'

'Three.'

'Four,' came the short, jabbing replies from his own flight.

'Blue Lead has Bravo November.'

'Two.'

'Three.'

'Four.'

Fourier adjusted his oxygen mask, took a deep breath. 'Send the reply,' Fourier told his back-seater.

Fourier heard a few keytaps, then: 'Acknowledgement received.'

The veteran F-15 pilot checked his heads-up display. The laser-derived threat-display projected on to his windscreen showed every aircraft around him, American and Russian, in detail – without one electron of energy coming from any of the American aircraft.

Up until now this had been just another routine fly-by patrol. Missions like this, shadowing Russian, Iranian, Syrian and Iraqi planes over the Persian Gulf and Saudi Arabia, was a common practice. Even playing 'chicken' or 'tag' with Soviet naval aviation Backfire bombers went on all the time.

But now the game turned dead-serious. Fourier felt sweat trickle down the back of his neck, felt the tension take over his body. His next command to his attack group – world wars had started over less . . .

'Tango November flights, execute Bravo November . . . now.'

The entire fly-by, the sending and receiving of all coded messages and the coordination to implement the order transmitted by Armstrong Station – all took a little over thirty seconds. In that time they had sped ahead of the startled Soviet aircraft by nearly ten miles.

On Fourier's order the two groups of four F-15 Eagles executed a hard left turn at ninety degrees of bank, pulling nearly seven 'g's as each pilot applied back-stick pressure. At the same time they decreased their throttles back from max afterburner to military power to avoid overstressing their fighters. They continued the hard turn until they were two hundred seventy degrees to the left of their original heading.

When the two groups rolled out of the turn they found the Russian planes dead ahead of them, less than eight miles away.

'Fox One,' Fourier said – and the skies were suddenly on fire.

Disorganized, with aircraft all around them in the pitch-black skies over Iran, the Russian pilots were forced to do the wrong thing: stay on their original heading. The four Backfire bombers accelerated and started a descent towards the protective radar clutter of the Elburz Mountains of northern Iran, but with escorts and wingmen all around them the huge bombers never strayed from their southeasterly course. The Flanker fighter-bombers followed the Backfire bombers down but dutifully stayed with the bombers in tight formation.

The Condor transport pilots, feeling safe with four of the Soviet's most advanced fighters surrounding them, took no evasive action. Two of the Condor's escorts accelerated to give chase to the undetected intruders, but their new and untried Kalskaya-651AG pulse-Doppler attack radars lost track of the American fighters when they went into their hard turns, and the two Flankers had begun to return to their formations. All twelve Soviet pilots felt safe from attack when the intruders disappeared . . . their threat-detectors and electronic countermeasures equipment never gave any indication that the intruders had activated any airborne search or missile-guidance radars.

But with Silver Tower's space-based radar tracking both the American and Soviet aircraft, no airborne radars were needed. As soon as the eight F-15s were rolled out and heading directly broadside to the Soviets they launched their radar-guided AAM-155C Viper missiles, and with each Eagle launching six Viper missiles, the sky was suddenly filled with death-dealing fire.

The Viper missiles took their initial guidance vectors from the data-link between the Eagles and Armstrong Station, which helped to point the missiles towards their targets – no threatening radar signals that could have given the position of the Eagles away were transmitted. Once stabilized in flight, the Viper's own on-board terminal-guidance radars automatically switched on and started to seek targets on their own.

The two Sukhoi-27 Flanker fighters that had given chase were the only ones able to spot the missile launches and take evasive action in time, and the Viper missiles chasing them exploded harmlessly after their propellant was exhausted. One of the Backfire bombers had accidentally released a cloud of chaff as the bomber's defensive-systems officer activated his countermeasures equipment, and a Viper missile locked on to the radar-reflective tinsel and steered away a bare half-second before ploughing into the bomber's left engine.

But those were the only three out of twelve Soviet aircraft to survive. Forty-five Viper air-to-air missiles found targets that night, sending two and a half million pounds of Soviet machines, and men, crashing into the northern Iranian mountains.

Fourier and his seven attacking Eagles did not wait to check on the outcome of their assault; immediately after launching their Viper missiles they accelerated at max afterburner once again, climbed and turned westward for home. Each had kept two Viper missiles on wingtip pylons ready to launch in case of pursuit.

But there was no pursuit. The two remaining Su-27 Flankers circled the area over the Elburz Mountains for a short time as the Russian emergency frequency was filled with the sounds of air-crew locator-beacons bleeping and buzzing, activated automatically on ejection or on impact with the ground. They copied a few calls for help and a few position coordinates of downed pilots or aircraft for possible rescue, then climbed out of the dark Iranian mountains and headed north for safer territory. The one remaining Backfire bomber decided to follow its escorts home instead of risk a lone penetration run towards Tehran.

'Tango November flight, post-release and station checks.' Fourier stripped off his oxygen mask as he received acknowledgements and bingo fuel-updates from his wingmen. He felt wrung out. He looked at the weapons-control and flight-director on his heads-up display with a sense of awe, and some mistrust. It was damned effective, this Armstrong Space Station. He'd always thought of the station in abstract terms, as an idea waiting to be made real, to have a real impact – He'd learned better this night . . .

Still, a fighter pilot liked his fights in the raw . . . radar against radar, missile against missile, gun against gun, pilot against pilot. This SBR, in a way, was too many legs up. But the Russians would be sure to make that same estimate . . . and even surer to do something about it. Question was . . . when, how?

'Pyekatah Raz, pyekatah Raz, tah gruppa trety Aviatsii,' came the heavily garbled and barely readable radio call. *'Atvyet syeychas zhe.* Infantry one, this is Aviation Group Three. Answer immediately.'

The young Russian radioman of the Seventy-First Shock Troops quickly logged the time and frequency on which he had heard the call, picked up his microphone and replied, 'I read you, Aviation Group Three. This is Seventy-First Shock Fire Base Seven. Proceed.'

'Roger, Fire Base Seven. We are en route to your

location for peripheral bombing strike. Requesting discrete forward combat controller frequency and vectors. Over.'

'Copy, Group Three. You are weak and barely readable. This is the incorrect frequency. Repeat, incorrect frequency. I require authentication before assigning a combat controller.'

'Roger, Fire Base Seven. Understand. That is the standard procedure. Standing by to authenticate.'

'I'm unable to give you an authentication,' the radioman said. 'Stand by.' The young Russian infantryman stood up, went to the door of the administration office turned radio room of Tehran's Mehrabad International Airport, and waved down a senior *starshiy praporshchik*.

He returned to the radio. 'Stand by for authentication, Group Three.'

'Roger, Fire Base Seven.' A pause, then: 'Fire Base Seven, can you give us the weather and tactical condition there?'

The radioman checked for his senior warrant officer, who was being bombarded by requests from senior officers as he tried to make his way to the radio room.

'Fire Base Seven. Reply, *pazhalosta*.'

The infantryman made one last check; the warrant officer was still being intercepted by officers who wanted something done *now*. It was improper procedure to give any information on the radio without authentication, but this was a special headquarters-only frequency, and these flyboys were Russians, and the *starshiy praporshchik* was taking forever, and all they wanted was the weather . . .

'Fire Base Seven, do you read? Please reply. Over.'

The infantryman went back to his seat. 'Group Three, this is Fire Base Seven. I read you. I do not have the latest weather, but the temperature is cold and there are no clouds. Runway two-nine is open. Winds are variable from the west at ten kilometres per hour. We are under sporadic mortar and small-arms fire from outside the airport boundaries, but the SPETNAZ Special Forces and the Seventy-First have secured the airport and the town of Mehrabad. You will probably attack the town of Akbarabad east-northeast of the airport. That's where most of the mortar attacks are – '

'*Spakaystvey*,' came a shout from behind. The radioman turned to see an enraged senior warrant officer descending on him. 'Who are you talking to? Who?'

'Aviation Group Three . . .' The radioman let go the microphone like a child dropping a stolen cookie. 'He called in requesting a combat strike controller – '

'Did you authenticate?'

'No, sir, I called you immediately.'

'Then what were you giving him?'

'The weather. He asked for the weather and the tactical conditions here. There's nothing classified about the weather – '

'You idiot, we're in blackout conditions. The enemy can home-in on these radio transmissions and locate our headquarters here – '

'But they spoke perfect Russian . . .'

'*That* is your proof?' The warrant officer switched to broken English. 'Am I now *Amirikanskiy* when since I speak English?' The warrant officer grabbed the microphone. 'I think this is the medium bomber force from Lyaki. Whoever they are, I hope they won't report this major breach of radio security. We'll all be shot if they do.' He keyed the microphone. 'Aviation Group Three. Are you prepared to authenticate?'

A slight pause, then: '*Da, pyekatah syedmoy.*' The two infantrymen looked at each other in relief.

'Proceed, Group Three.'

Another slight pause, then in crisp, clear English they heard, 'Authenticate my ass, jerkoffs.'

The warrant officer stared at the young infantryman

long enough to see the man's face drain of all colour, then lunged at the large red button on the portable communications console and activated the emergency attack-alert signal.

The horn had only echoed through the airport grounds for ten seconds when the first bombs hit.

The two F/A-19C supersonic NightHawk stealth bombers raced across Tehran-Mehrabad International Airport at six hundred knots and barely one hundred feet above ground. The six Soviet SA-13 Gopher motorized surface-to-air missile batteries surrounding the airport saw nothing but faint radar echoes until the two bombers were less than ten miles from the airport, and by the time the missiles were ready to fire, the NightHawk's eight thousand-pound, laser-guided, runway-cratering smart bombs and antipersonnel bomblets were already falling.

The two NightHawk fighter bombers did not survive the killing battlefield air defences the Soviet army had established around Tehran Airport, but before the NightHawks were destroyed by gunfire from a battery of three ZSU-23/A radar-guided anti-aircraft artillery weapons, they had reduced the peripheral defences and central command and control units to rubble.

The hundred Soviet army troops that survived the bombing had to face an even worse threat than a surprise American stealth bomber attack: the sight of hundreds of vehicles of all descriptions slowly moving, unopposed, down Makhsus Road from Akbarabad and Tehran towards the airport. The pop-pop-pop of gunfire and the cries of blood-anger from the advancing Muslim hordes could be heard for miles.

Armstrong Space Station

'Attention on the station. We're passing under target-area horizon. Stand by for recon data transmission and reconfiguration. This station is on yellow alert.'

173

The command-module people relaxed, rubbing aching muscles and tired eyes – all but Saint-Michael, who watched the last transmitted picture of the northern Iran area, a hand cupped to his earset. The display was already twenty minutes old but he watched it as intently as ever, especially the IFF transponder images of the F-15E Eagle strike force, designated Tango November, and the last images of the two F/A-19C NightHawk bombers over Tehran.

A few moments later Colonel Walker manoeuvred over to him. 'Message from Kigzi Airbase, General. Tango November flight is checking in. All eight of them.'

Saint-Michael nodded. 'That's great news. We should be getting their report in – '

He stopped. Walker obviously had more.

'Tango Sierra flight . . . ?'

'The navy intercepted a broadcast in the clear from Tehran. Two American fighter bombers shot down over Mehrabad Airport.'

Saint-Michael brought his hand down hard on the arm of his commander's chair.

'That Russian radio message also reported the destruction of Seventy-First Shock Troops Headquarters at Tehran Airport,' Walker quickly added. 'Thirty-eight dead or injured. Last report was that the airport was being overrun by Iranian militiamen.'

Saint-Michael rubbed his throbbing temple. 'I'd hate to be a Russian ground-pounder in Tehran right about now.'

Walker handed Saint-Michael a printout. 'I saved the best for last, General. The navy also sent along an intercepted radio message from a Russian rescue patrol in the Elburz Mountains. They're describing debris scattered across five hundred square miles of mountains. At least seven fires out of control in the area from aircraft-crash debris.'

Saint-Michael nodded, but his mind was still on the

four men of the downed NightHawk fighter-bombers. 'After twenty-one years in the service, Jim, that was the first time men under my command have died. Goddamn, and I'm sitting up here out of it – '

'Then this is also your first major battle victory,' Walker said. 'Ten American aircraft have destroyed at least seven Soviet aircraft, including a Soviet transport and supersonic bombers, plus they've knocked out a major occupation force headquarters and allowed local forces to retake a major airfield from hostile forces. Losses to our own have been low – two advanced aircraft, four men. Losses to the enemy . . . well, this battle could have been pivotal, sir. That's not a bad day's work, no matter where you sit.'

Saint-Michael stared at Walker. 'Thanks, but if this is what victory feels like, I'm glad I haven't had a taste of it before this.' The general's eyes flitted back to the SBR display and the frozen images of the NightHawk bombers.

The Kremlin, USSR

'Is it war, Comrade Minister?' Deputy Minister of Defence Khromeyev asked in a low voice.

Minister of Defence Czilikov was almost too angry to reply. 'They must pay. For every drop of our blood shed in Iran, for every gram of our steel lost in those Iranian mountains, the Americans must pay, and they will . . .'

Czilikov stared at the computer-generated wall map of the Persian Gulf region. He stood and walked slowly towards it as if it depicted some gruesome atrocity. Indeed, for him it did. 'Nine planes destroyed; three hundred and thirty men dead or injured in the north. Sixty dead or injured in Tehran, sixty captured. *All in four hours . . .*'

'They came out of nowhere,' Admiral Chercherovin said. 'The American fighters attacked without warning.

Somehow they approached the formations in the north and south without revealing their presence, and launched missiles from long range without radar guidance. The aircrews say they never received any advanced warning. *None*. And it was three hours before sunrise . . .'

'They were overconfident,' General Ilanovsky said between clenched teeth. 'Cocky. Their incompetence caused the loss of one hundred and twenty of my best soldiers. . .'

'It's *you* who are the incompetent,' Chercherovin said, jabbing a finger at the commander in chief of ground forces. 'You had over a hundred SPETNAZ troops at Mehrabad Airport, supposedly the elite of our army, and yet you couldn't hold off a bunch of undisciplined militiamen.'

'*Enough*,' Czilikov said. 'You will stop this stupid bickering.' His ice-blue gaze took in the faces of the Kollegiya. 'The pride of the Soviet Union. Heroes, all. Am I to bring this gaggle of children before the general secretary when the Stavka Council of War meets in two hours? Are we going to point fingers and accuse each other and argue like old women? We'll all be shot, and we'll deserve it.'

He gestured to the wall-sized computer screen. 'I want an answer. I want an answer to what we've suffered today.' Czilikov turned to the newest addition to the group. 'General Govorov. Your opinion?'

Govorov stood. 'Sir, there can be only one answer to how our forces were attacked so successfully: the space station Armstrong.'

'*Armstrong?*' General Lichizev of the KGB shook his head. 'I told you, Govorov, it's impossible – '

Czilikov turned again to Govorov. 'Continue.'

'Sir, as I've indicated before the radar aboard Space Station Armstrong has the power to track both American and Russian aircraft. It's a relatively simple matter for the

176

Americans to position their aircraft for attack, using data transmissions from Armstrong. The American aircraft would not need to use their radars to find our planes. Nor would conventional radar be needed for bombing raids, cruise missile attacks, or submarine attacks . . .'

'Then it's obvious . . . the space station must be destroyed.' Czilikov bit off each word.

'I agree,' Govorov said quickly, earning no points for that gratuity with Czilikov. Still, the message wasn't lost on the minister of defence: Govorov had been right, Feather had to fail as long as Armstrong Station was in orbit.

General Marasimov, commander of the Strategic Rocket Forces, spoke up now. 'An attack with the Gorgon antisatellite missiles – '

'Will also fail,' Govorov said. 'Armstrong is very well protected. The station's Thor missiles used for antiballistic missile defence are even more capable against the clumsy Gorgon missile. The Gorgons, however, can be used as a prelude to the main attack force . . .'

'The main attack force?' Czilikov said.

Govorov glanced at his superior, Marshal Rhomerdunov, who nodded. Now. Now was the moment if there ever was one . . .

'Comrade Minister,' Rhomerdunov began, and all heads turned to him, 'a plan . . . I have a plan to deal specifically with the threat of a heavily armed and protected orbiting platform. A plan to lift the Soviet Aerospace Forces into the next century.' Govorov was careful not to show any reaction to Rhomerdunov's plagiarism . . . 'A plan, sir, previously approved by the Kollegiya, to arm the Elektron spaceplane with specially designed missiles. They – '

'*Missiles?*' Czilikov said. 'Missiles on a one-man spaceplane? What are these missiles? I wasn't informed – '

'The plan was approved years ago by the Kollegiya,

sir,' Rhomerdunov said uneasily. 'The implementation was not begun until recently.' Czilikov appeared ready to continue his questioning but held back, and Rhomerdunov, encouraged, quickly pressed on. 'A group of these Elektron space fighter-planes led by General Govorov will be sent to destroy this Space Station Armstrong.'

Instead of the expected murmur of voices, there was silence, finally broken by Czilikov. 'Everything that General Govorov has predicted has unfortunately come true. The American space station is indeed more powerful than we had imagined. They have, it seems, the capability of transmitting space-based radar data from the station to a variety of users – ships, ground installations, headquarters, even aircraft. They are also able to vector attack aircraft so as to avoid danger of counterattack. The time has indeed come: Armstrong Space Station must be destroyed.'

Czilikov turned to Rhomerdunov. 'That will be your assignment. It will be carried out immediately. I will inform the Stavka.' And to Govorov, 'You will lead the attackers.'

'Sir, it may still take several days, perhaps weeks, to prepare the Elektron spaceplanes for launch from Tyuratam. It will take time to mate the spaceplanes with their SL-16 Krypkei boosters. The Elektron spaceplanes are not part of the standing strategic defence force – '

'They are now,' Czilikov said. 'I authorize a minimum of two fully armed Elektron spaceplanes on 'round-the-clock alert at Tyuratam spaceport.' He returned to his seat at the head of the oblong conference table. 'But we can't wait weeks or even days to begin our counteroffensive. Our advances have been stalled. The Americans are getting stronger and we are getting weaker. I want a plan to retake the offensive, to recoup our losses and advance Operation Feather to success. The Stavka and Politburo demand nothing less than complete victory, and I'm with them.'

'The major threats to us in Iran and the Persian Gulf remain, sir,' Admiral Chercherovin said. 'They are the American carrier task force in the Arabian Sea and the land-based Rapid Deployment Force bombers and long-range fighters in eastern Turkey.'

'Saudi Arabia hasn't yet allowed American offensive aircraft to use its bases,' Marshal Yesimov of the Air Force put in, 'but the Americans may convince them. Qatar and Kuwait may also let American ships or planes use their bases. Certainly, the Iranians will agree to anything the Americans want if they are assured protection . . .'

'Then swift, decisive action must be taken,' Czilikov said. 'General Govorov, once more, *all* efforts must be made to knock out this Space Station Armstrong, and *now* . . . All our other actions may be pointless unless Armstrong is neutralized.'

'I understand, sir,' Govorov said. 'And perhaps all of our objectives can be accomplished at once – '

'How?'

Govorov fought showing even a hint of a smile. 'The space station is formidable when it is protecting others from attack, but I feel it may not be so if it is forced to protect *itself*.'

'But you have said that the Elektron spaceplanes will not be ready for such an attack,' Khromeyev said. 'And Marshal Rhomerdunov has said that the Gorgon anti-satellite missiles are ineffectual against such a facility.'

'That is my estimation as well. But meanwhile, there is another weapon we have not considered that may prove effective in convincing the Americans of the seriousness of moving their space station within striking distance of the Soviet Union. I refer to the laser at our Sary Shegan facility. Intelligence reports only a portion of the American space station is covered with reflective antilaser coating. Sustained bursts from our laser might do very considerable damage . . .'

Czilikov's eyes brightened. 'I want a full report on how soon the laser can be activated; I want it on my desk in an hour.' He turned to Admiral Chercherovin. 'You must regain control of the region. And fast.'

He waved off any further discussion. They all had his message – produce or else.

6

Saint-Michael entered the engineering module, where he found Ann. They stood together in the cramped compartment, exchanging polite nods.

'I think this may be a good time to talk,' Saint-Michael finally said.

Ann pretended not to hear him as she pulled a refrigeration coil from the food storage unit and began adjusting the temperature setting.

'Ann . . .' Saint-Michael grabbed the coil from her and replaced it in the unit. 'Ann, I want you to leave on *Enterprise*. In four hours.'

She turned and faced him. 'So now you're *ordering* me to go? What happened to my options?'

'If you want to call it an order, then it's an order.'

She looked at him, weighing an answer, then sighed softly. 'What gives, General? I mean, what the hell is this all about? I can repair Skybolt. I've found the problem. Only a few more days up here and I'll have the thing licked. But you're all fired up to see me leave without accomplishing what I came here to do. My *job*, for God's sake . . .'

'Ann,' he finally said, '*I* want you back on earth.' He paused for a moment, then added, 'Safe.' His eyes narrowed with anger and frustration, but it wasn't anger at her – it was more at himself. 'Dammit Ann, do I really have to spell it out for you?' He paused, waiting for her

181

to understand and respond. 'All right, what I'm *trying* to say is – '

'Attention on the station,' came the sudden blaring of the stationwide loudspeaker address system. 'Emergency condition one. The station is on red alert.' Then, on the stationwide earset address system: 'General Saint-Michael, this is Walker. Satellite relay message from the *Nimitz*. They are under attack.'

'I'll be right there.' He turned, stopped, and lightly touched her shoulder. 'Safe from *this*, Ann.' Then he was off to the connecting tunnel, leaving Ann with very mixed feelings . . .

Saint-Michael, back in the command module, ordered: 'Report.'

'An Air Force 767B AWACS picked up a small flight of six fast-moving low-altitude jet aircraft over Iran,' Walker said, not taking his eyes off the master SBR status screen. 'The AWACS was chased away by Su-27s from the *Brezhnev*, so we don't have details. They can't tell where the aircraft's origin was, but they say they're moving too fast and too low for Silkworm missiles. They think they're Soviet Su-24 Fencer tactical bombers launching from one of the Soviet navy's Caspian Sea bases. They're heading south at five hundred knots, right for the *Nimitz* battle group.'

'How long until we cross the target horizon?'

'Still forty minutes. Could have been launched just after we crossed under the target horizon. They timed it perfectly. Looks like the *Nimitz* is stage-centre, sir . . .'

Over Southern Iran, One Hundred Fifty Miles North of the USS *Nimitz*

'Tally, Tally, Tally! Lead's got 'em at eleven o'clock!'

The commander of the lead F-14E Tomcat Plus, J. B.

Andrews, tightened his grip on the throttle as his weapons systems officer called out the report. He had been staring intently at the rolling, rock-covered hills rushing under the nose of his fighter as he and five other hunters from the aircraft carrier USS *Nimitz* slashed across southern Iran, prowling for attacking cruise missiles.

Andrews and his fellow 'airhogs' were knifing through thick air only a thousand feet above the Iranian desert, and the Tomcats were protesting every minute of it. The fighters performed much better at a high altitude, where their 'lifting body' fuselages and big computer-controlled variable-sweep wings met little resistance. Down below, the aircraft picked up every tiny wind shift, every thermal and every dust devil, creating such violent turbulence that the formation had to spread out farther and farther apart to avoid collision. Everything depended on the lead aviator's eyes – if the leader hit the ground, the rest would surely follow.

'Vectors, Chili,' Andrews called out.

The backseat WSO checked the display of his enhanced digital AWG-9 attack radar. 'Left ten. Altitude looks good. I'm locked on . . . fifty miles now.'

'Pirate flight, lead is locked on to bogeys, coming left.'

'Two's locked on.'

'Three's locked on.'

'Four is no-joy.'

'Five no-joy.'

'Six is . . . stand by. Locked on.'

'We launch at twenty, Pirates. If you're not locked on, get ready to turn tight and bob till you drop.' To conserve fuel and maximize performance, each Tomcat had taken off with only two AIM-120RC AMRAAM missiles aboard. Even so, after travelling at max afterburner for nearly twenty minutes, the fighters were fast approaching their safe fuel-turnaround point. It was essential that they launch their AIM-120RCs in the next few minutes.

'Forty miles. Still locked on.'

'Four is locked on.'

'Five?'

'Negetron. Five is boppin.'

'Thirty miles.'

A faint high-pitched tone activated in the lead WSO's helmet. 'Good tone. Ready.'

'Rog. Count me down.'

'Twenty-five . . . twenty-four . . . twenty-three . . .'

Andrews suddenly felt that inner calm that always preceded engagement. He wasn't thinking anymore. Reflexes had taken over. Reflexes honed in a hundred aerial manoeuvres over four continents. Besides, this intercept should be no big sweat. Though cruise missiles were deadly against ships, they were sitting ducks for fighters. They couldn't manoeuvre or shoot back. The Tomcat's advanced digital attack radar made it possible for Andrews to attack from as far away as fifty miles, but twenty was optimal for –

'Pirate flight. Bandits. Two o'clock high!'

Andrews risked a quick glance to his right, caught the glint of sunlight. Four Su-27 Flanker carrier-based fighters were diving out of the sun.

'Two, three, four – stay on the cruise missiles. Four and five – engage.'

'Twenty miles. Good tone . . .'

Andrews saw the target and radar lock-on symbols merge and the word LAUNCH flash at the bottom of the HUD, his heads-up display. Fighting off a massive wave of turbulence that shuddered through his Tomcat, he slid his gloved right thumb to the launch button. Suddenly, the target and radar symbols disappeared from the HUD and the word 'LAUNCH' at the bottom was replaced with the word 'FIRE' in the centre of the display.

He pressed the LAUNCH button. Nothing.

'Chili, check your switches. Negative launch.'

No reply.

'Chili!'

Andrews strained against his harness straps and turned to look behind him, recoiling instantly at the searing blast of heat that hit him full in the face and the grisly sight of half-charred, flaming flesh that had been his WSO. That had not been turbulence he felt a moment ago. His Tomcat had taken a missile right up the tailpipe.

The formation leader turned forward just in time to see two Sukhoi-27 fighter-bombers zip past his nose less than two hundred yards away. He yanked his stick left and up to pursue, but his Tomcat continued to loll sluggishly to the right and down. The HUD was blank. Most of the lights and gauges on his instrument panel were dark or at zero. He made sure the throttle was at military power – yes, he could still feel what he thought was thrust from his twin Pratt and Whitney turbofan engines. He began to get some stick response so he tried to reacquire visually the two Soviet fighters while he waited for his plane to recover . . . he hoped . . .

He kept one hand on the stick and the other on the throttle, believing his crippled fighter was giving chase right up to the moment it slammed into a hillside just outside the town of Humedan on Iran's southern coast. never had a chance even to consider reaching for the tion handles.

USS *California*

'Bridge, this is Combat. ASM contact, zero-eight-zero degrees relative, sixty nautical miles, less than one hundred feet above water.'

Matthew Page reacted instantly to the report of the oncoming cruise missiles. 'Helm, left twenty degrees, heading two-six-zero. Conn, advise *Nimitz* of contacts. Combat, are any Tomcats giving chase?'

'No friendly fighters showing. Six Soviet fighters heading north-west back towards the *Brezhnev*.'

He hadn't expected that the missiles would be escorted by fighters. It looked like everything might depend on his fire-power. 'Combat, launch commit all Standard missiles.'

'Launch commit, aye – ' The controller barely had time to finish his acknowledge when the roar of missile-motor ignition filled the air.

Fully automatic, the *California*'s fore-and-aft Mark 26 dual-rail missile launchers had stood like tin soldiers at attention, pointing straight up. At launch command, two SM2-ER Standard surface-to-air missiles slid from the magazine racks below deck up into each of the launchers' rails, and the launchers swivelled right and down until the missiles seemed to be pointing directly horizontal. There was a slight pause, then a burst of flame followed by a cloud of smoke that covered the bow and stern of the *California*. The launchers swivelled to vertical once again, ready for a reloading.

'Four Standards away.'

'My course is two-six-zero, sir,' the helmsman reported.

'Very well. Ready the starboard Phalanx guns and both 127-millimetre guns. Combat, where are those cruise missiles?'

'Showing heavy uplink jamming from something, possibly Soviet airborne jammers . . . Wait, now showing two cruise missiles in flight, sir. Bearing zero-seven-zero, twenty miles, course one-six-zero true.'

'Helm, hard to port, left forty degrees, launch commit all Standards and the forward one-twenty-seven. Comm, signal *Nimitz* to begin evasive action to starboard. Move.'

The USS *California* heeled sharply to starboard as it began a hard left turn, the deck tilting far enough so that only a few feet of free-board remained. The deck made one small pitch to port when the ship completed its emergency turn as its computerized stabilizers fought to haul the eleven-thousand-ton vessel upright. A split second after the deck levelled itself, the fire, smoke, and noise returned. Four Standard missiles immediately leapt from their rails and arched towards the grey horizon, quickly speeding away from view.

'Four Standards away, sir. Forward one-twenty-seven ready. All Phalanx stations report ready.'

'Commit the aft one-twenty-seven.'

'Aye, sir . . . *Nimitz* reports launching aircraft but can't manoeuvre to starboard. They report their Phalanx systems operational.'

Page's oaths were drowned out by the booming of the *California*'s two five-inch, dual-purpose cannons. Alternating with computer-controlled precision, the two cannons fired one radar-guided three-hundred-pound flak shell every two seconds, the *California* seeming to jump sideways at each ear-shattering report.

'Status! Where are those damn – ?' Page's next words caught in his throat as he stared, transfixed, out the starboard side of the bridge at an apparition that was coming ever closer.

Like a flaming spear driving right for the heart of *California*, it appeared to be flying slowly, almost its short cruciform wings and long cigar-sh[...] blackened and burning. It trailed a long line of th[...] smoke, and it seemed to wobble up and down unst[...] Yet it kept coming . . .

'Hard starboard, flank speed,' Page ordered. The helmsman spun the wheel but his reply was drowned out by the long, whining staccato of the starboard Phalanx Close-In Weapon System, a radar-guided twenty-millimetre Vulcan multibarrelled machine gun used as a last-resort defence against antiship missiles. Page watched smoke issue from the Phalanx muzzle and then an answering puff of fire from the already flaming airborne spear, followed by a deafening roar . . .

Just before Captain Matthew Page died, he thought of his wife Amanda, her eyes the same sky-blue as the cloudless canopy over his head. He smiled as the darkness descended on him.

Armstrong Space Station

Ann bypassed the safety procedures and cross checks as she hurried to the command module. Crewmembers turned towards her as she approached Saint-Michael.

'Still no word,' the general told her. 'The frigate *Oliver Hazard Perry* is alongside the *California* now.'

'What did they say? What happened?'

'Our ships were attacked by six Soviet medium bombers,' Jim Walker said. 'The bombers had Su-27 fighters from the *Brezhnev* escorting them and carried Kelt antiship missiles. Apparently the Su-27s managed to down six of our Tomcats, which were pursuing. The *California* and the other escorts sent four of the bombers into the gulf, but the others got their missiles off. Two of the missiles hit the *California* broadside – '

'At least it wasn't nuclear,' Saint-Michael said quickly, not looking at Ann 'The *California* radioed a distress call and the *Oliver Hazard Perry* got to her within minutes. We'll know better what the *California*'s situation is when they put out the fires.'

'How long . . . until we can restart surveillance on the area?' Ann asked, trying not to show what she was feeling.

Saint-Michael wanted to hold her at least, but for the time being they both had their roles to play . . . 'Twenty minutes,' he said in answer to her question. He wished he could say more, reassure her . . . but that would be phony as well as embarrassing. Looking at her, though, seeing what she must be going through in her worry about her father, he could only admire her and feel for her. A considerable lady, hell . . . a terrific woman . . .

Tyuratam, USSR

It was a big surprise for the junior airmen and their supervisors to see General Lieutenant Alesander Govorov, the commander of Space Defence, out early that morning inspecting the area. Accompanied by the newly promoted Colonel Nikolai Gulaev, Govorov entered the vehicle assembly building of Glowing Star, Tyuratam's antisatellite launch site, and came up behind *Starshiy Praporshchik* Igor Cacreyatov, who happened to be sitting with his feet on his desk, sipping coffee laced with a bit of East German schnapps. The big senior warrant officer stared idly out the window watching the work out on launch pad two.

'Work seems to proceed slower than usual, Airman Anokhin,' Cacreyatov said over his shoulder. 'I'll postpone the inspection of launch pad two until tomorrow, but it had better be done then or I will crack some heads.'

Gulaev glanced at Govorov, half expected to see the Space Defence commander pull out his 7.62-millimetre Tokarav TT-33 automatic pistol and blow poor Cacreyatov away, but to Gulaev's surprise Govorov's face showed a wide smile as he picked up the tiny two hundred fifty millilitre schnapps bottle, ran his nose over the mouth and nodded his approval at the scent.

Without turning around, the senior warrant officer said, 'I can tell without looking, Anokhin, that you have something in your hand that will cost you a month of kitchen duty and a week's pay if you so much as think about stealing or drinking.'

'I think not, Comrade.'

Cacreyatov got to his feet in a flurry of arms and legs and stood at attention, eyes straight ahead, chest heaving.

'I think I've found the reason why my Elektron project is delayed, Colonel Gulaev,' Govorov said. The thin smile stayed on his lips as he dropped the tiny bottle of schnapps on to the cold concrete floor. Cacreyatov's reflex was to try to reach out and grab it, but he wisely kept at attention.

'The instant that bottle hit the floor, Cacreyatov, you were no longer a *starshiy praporshchik*.' Govorov was no longer smiling. 'What lower rank you sink to – or whether your military career comes to a sudden end – depends on your answers now and your actions in the next forty-eight hours.' He let the words sink in, then: 'Now, Colonel Gulaev has reported to me that the second Elektron has been sitting beside that SL-16 booster for three days. When he inquires about its status, he gets no reply. You will give *me* a reply, Cacreyatov, and you will give it to me *now*.'

The freshly demoted senior warrant officer said he had no excuse, sir –

'Wrong answer, Cacreyatov,' and Cacreyatov could almost see five thousand rubles a year fly out of his pocket. 'This is not a damned military academy. When I ask a question I expect a real answer. So once again – what is the reason for the delay?'

'Sir, I . . . was unclear about the procedures dealing with the Elektron. My men are not allowed to work near the Elektrons without direct supervision from Colonel Gulaev's special personnel.'

'Do Colonel Gulaev's men prohibit any contact with the Elektron?'

'No, sir . . .'

'Is access limited in any section of the Elektron?'

'Well, the cargo area is sealed, and some components in the cockpit are removed or sealed – '

'Per my instructions,' Govorov told him. 'Does this limited access to the cargo bay or those security-sealed cockpit components explain the delays?'

Cacreyatov kept his mouth shut.

'No? Then it seems you've lied to me. Why the hell is that SL-16 not ready for launch?'

'Sir, replacement parts were not ordered in time. They have just been installed, but the crews haven't – '

'Who didn't order the parts in time?'

Cacreyatov closed his eyes, bracing for the execution. 'Sir, I failed to order the third-stage pressure-test fittings in time for the final mating. The tests are being completed this morning. When the tests are finished I will make the final inspection. The second SL-16 will be ready for launch in forty-eight hours.'

Govorov nodded at the veteran maintenance officer. 'Now understand this. For the good of my command I should bring you up on charges for having liquor in this building, but I can't spare the time to court-martial you. You *will* lose, however, one pay grade for every hour over forty-eight that both of those SL-16s are delayed from launch readiness. You will lose another pay grade for every launch countdown hold attributable to you. If you run out of pay grades you will spend a year at hard labour for each hold. And don't push your technicians too hard to make up for your own laziness, Cacreyatov – they might decide to get sick, and then where will you be?' He did not need to spell it out. The message was received.

'I take responsibility for Cacreyatov's incompetence, sir,' Gulaev said as he and Govorov headed for the exits. 'If I'd supervised his section more closely I might have spotted his laziness earlier – '

'Call it a hard lesson learned, Nikolai. No commander

191

should operate from a chair. You were thorough in your inquiries, but you never went personally to inspect the progress on the ships.' He glanced at his deputy. 'Get Elektron number two manned and ready to fly in two days. That's the way to redeem yourself. And good luck, Nikolai . . . More depends on you than you can imagine.'

'Yes, sir . . . By the way, sir, Colonel Voloshin, the pilot for Elektron Two, has already reported to Glowing Star. I've thoroughly examined his fitness reports and evaluations and find them to be excellent.'

'Good . . .' Govorov's voice trailed off as he caught sight of Elektron One, mounted on top of an SK-16-A booster three miles away. The three-stage solid- and liquid-propellant rocket, similar to the long-abandoned American Saturn-V booster, was well over two hundred and twenty feet tall and weighed nearly two hundred and fifty tons. It carried four 'strap-on' solid propellant boosters on its lower stage to lift its payload to the required one-thousand-mile orbit around earth.

'I want to go up to the Elektron,' Govorov said, as he got into the waiting staff car. 'Arrange it, please.'

'Yes, sir,' Gulaev said. He was on the Zil limousine's carphone in an instant, and a few minutes later they were riding the service elevator to the SL-16's capsule.

Unlike the booster, the Elektron spaceplane was painted a dull grey, a colour designed to help stabilize its temperature once in space. It was fifty feet long and thirty feet wide from wingtip to wingtip. Its nose, wing leading edges and underside were all covered with protective silica tiles. The aft end of the spaceplane was round and fit perfectly into the thirty-foot-diameter third stage of the SL-16 booster. Forward of the mating area the spaceplane's fuselage flattened into smooth, gracefully flowing lines, making it somewhat resemble a manta ray. The cockpit was a small bump on the upper side. The bump continued down the Elektron's spine to form the small ten-ton-capacity cargo bay and main-engine housing, then flared gently into a dorsal atmospheric stabilizer.

Technicians accompanying Govorov and Gulaev set up safety barriers and attachments to the Elektron as Govorov inspected every square inch of the spaceplane's surface. 'Looks good,' he said as he checked the last of the tiles. 'They did a tremendous job.'

'The tiles are reinspected twice a day, sir,' Gulaev said. 'That will continue right until liftoff.'

The technicians finally unlatched the hatch on the upper side of the cockpit. As if he travelled in a spaceplane every day of his life, Govorov knocked gravel from his boots, grabbed a boarding bar mounted just above the hatch and climbed into the cockpit.

Cacreyatov, Gulaev, the two technicians – for a brief moment all of them faded from Govorov's mind as he slid into the seat of the Elektron spaceplane – no, he told himself, the space *fighter* . . .

Its cockpit was futuristic, featuring advanced digital instrumentation, a wide laser-projection heads-up display and a digital computer-controlled weapons monitor panel. Three redundant microprocessors handled all on-board functions, but almost everything from orbital insertion to reentry and landing could be accomplished manually or by remote control with ground controllers. The cockpit was large enough for the cosmonaut inside to swivel around and operate a second set of controls mounted behind him, and a docking port on the Elektron's belly allowed easy docking to *Mir*, the Soviet Union's orbiting module. That was essential: on its planned seek-and-destroy missions the Elektron would most likely need refuelling before a safe landing could be attempted.

'Excellent . . .' Govorov said in a half-whisper. He examined the weapons control panel and the switches mounted on the multifunction control stick, satisfying himself that the positioning was correct for a gravity-free environment. Up in space with the normal sense of up and down suspended, a pilot could not rely on muscular cues to tell him in a split-second's time what switches to pull. So it was necessary to realign all the switches in the spaceplane cockpit to conform to a functional hierarchy.

Gulaev looked on, thinking that he would not want to exchange places with his commander and pilot this strange craft. There was something ominous about the spaceplane's dark interior. It had never struck him so before, but now . . . He broke from his reverie and checked his watch. 'Excuse me, General. We must report back to the command post.'

Govorov nodded, still running his hands over the controls. A few moments later he grabbed the entry bar above the hatch and pulled himself out of the cockpit.

'Yes,' Govorov said, 'yes . . .' – and patted the exterior of this flying marvel, or was *caressed* a better word . . . ?

Armstrong Space Station

'Attention on the station. Target horizon crossing. Situation is red alert.'

Ann was at her station in the engineering module when the latest announcement came over the speakers. Until a few minutes ago she had been trying to make up her mind about leaving Silver Tower. It had been one of the hardest decisions of her life, and what made it worse was knowing that Skybolt was literally just a hairsbreadth away from operational effectiveness. If she could only do just one more test . . . But there seemed no chance for that now. Things down below were happening too fast. Even she had to recognize priorities. Besides, the argument Jason . . . *Saint-Michael* . . . had made about there maybe being too many Pages involved in this thing was beginning to

194

sink in. She really hated not knowing what kind of shape her father was in, or even if he –

She'd made her decision. Go. She'd have another crack at Skybolt, maybe before too long, and meanwhile she wasn't doing a hell of a lot here. She *would* miss the stubborn general, though. It felt strange to admit that, stranger still that it was true . . . They'd hardly done anything but go at each other since she'd come on board. But now she felt she knew the reason for it, at least part of it. They were two of a kind, she and Saint-Michael. Both driven. Both territorial, possessive. Both unsure how to connect on an emotional level. Had he been trying to make contact with her all along and she'd been too dumb, or stubborn, to recognize it? Was their interrupted exchange before the attack on the *Nimitz* carrier group leading up to something? Thinking on it now, she believed so and wanted to kick herself. Great going, Page. You've done it again. This is a man to appreciate, for God's sake. And he *is* a man . . . like someone else she cared about on the *California* . . . She could hear the broadcasts and conversations about the stricken USS *California* but fought back the impulse to leave her station again and rush to the command module. She wriggled uncomfortably in the 'g' suit she'd put on in preparation for leaving Silver Tower aboard the shuttle *Enterprise* and tried not to think dreary thoughts.

In the command module the engineering chief, Colonel Marks, asked Saint-Michael: 'Are we going to attack their carrier, General?'

Saint-Michael shook his head. 'My orders are to protect Iran from Soviet invasion, not to destroy the *Brezhnev*. It seems we've made a hard but fair trade – the *California* for those Soviet transports and fighters we jumped over Tehran. If the Russians back off now this whole thing just may blow over – '

'Aircraft launching from the *Brezhnev*,' Sergeant Jake Jefferson broke in. 'High speed. Heading west.'

'*Westbound?*'

'Yes sir. *Nimitz* launching aircraft in response. Also heading west.' Jefferson turned to Saint-Michael. 'Looks like no one's going to back off today, General . . .'

Saint-Michael activated his communications panel, checked the scrambler/descrambler and keyed the microphone. '*Nimitz*, this is Armstrong. Come in.'

'Clancy here, Jas. Go ahead.'

'We picked up those Flankers heading west, Admiral. Are your aircraft pursuing?'

'Affirmative. The Air Force has an E-767B AWACS orbiting east of Riyadh. It asked for protection from those Flankers until it can get some F-15 reinforcements from Kigzi Airbase. The 767B will be returning back under friendly Rapier SAM cover until our F-15s catch up to them.'

'Copy. We've got the whole area covered. Are you receiving our data transmissions okay?'

'So far. The *Ticonderoga* is relaying SBR surveillance data to us. It's a bastardized way of doing it, but with *California* out of commission we don't – '

The transmission halted in a loud, piercing squeal that caused everyone listening in to rip their earsets away from their heads.

'What the hell . . . ?'

Just as Saint-Michael called out for a damage report a tremendous lurch threw everyone on Silver Tower towards the Velcro-covered floor. Technicians yelled out in pain – no one could stop himself as bodies slammed to the deck. It was as though they were ragdolls hurled to the floor by an angry child. The module seemed to be spinning in several directions all at once.

General Saint-Michael, the only one secured in place, set his communications panel to stationwide address.

'Attention on the station. Collision warning. Damage report on loudspeaker. *Enterprise*, clear for emergency disconnect. This station is on red alert.' He unfastened his safety belt and tried to rise out of his seat but found he was held fast.

Gravity! For the first time Silver Tower had been exposed to it. Whatever caused it, the station would soon tear itself apart if the huge forces did not stop.

With great effort Saint-Michael managed to overcome the unexpectedly severe 'g' forces and haul himself out of the commander's seat. It felt as if he was riding a fast express elevator from the first to the eighth floor. . .the gravity had a terrific pull after weeks of microgravity.

Walker, Jefferson and the other techs were slowly overcoming the sudden gravity surge and struggling to their feet. Saint-Michael made his way to the station's attitude-control panel.

'Check out Davis and Montgomery,' Saint-Michael told Walker, before turning to the panel.

The two techs were wincing with pain on the deck. 'One broken leg,' Walker reported after examining Davis. He checked the other tech. 'A possible broken rib, maybe internal injuries.'

'And there's a fire on the number three fuel-containment vessel.' Saint-Michael hit keys on a keypad, twisted one of them, then punched a button. 'I've jettisoned the vessel.'

The sudden gravity now began to subside. Saint-Michael and the others could hear the loud bangs and hisses as Silver Tower's ten banks of powerful thrusters began to reestablish the station's normal orbit and attitude. A few more moments and all but a barely discernible amount of gravity was gone.

'What the hell *happened?*'

'The containment vessels on the right keel below,' the

197

general said, scanning the computer monitors. 'The explosion started the station spinning.' He picked up his earset. 'The damn squeal in the earsets is gone.' He replaced his earset on his left ear but used the microphone and the loudspeaker system once again:

'Attention on the station. There has been an explosion of one of our fuel cells. Normal microgravity will be returning shortly. Report by loudspeaker to Colonel Walker any – '

The lights in the command module dimmed nearly to black. A control panel sputtered and smoked in a cloud of sparks. The air in the module suddenly felt hot, like a sauna.

Saint-Michael immediately put on his POS face mask and told his crew to do the same. 'Off-duty personnel report to the lifeboat,' he ordered. The lifeboat was a nonmanoeuvrable pod fitted with life-support systems.

As Walker began checking each man's face mask connections and POS settings, Saint-Michael plugged his earset communications cord into the microphone jack in his own face mask. 'All personnel report by module.'

'Sergeant Bayles in the lifeboat, Skipper. I've got Moyer, Yemana, Kelly and the engineering techs with me. Everyone's okay. Sleep and rec modules evacuated, checked and sealed. I'm in a spacesuit and ready to assist in personal transport.'

Kevin Baker, still at his post monitoring the command module, fumbled with his POS mask but finally reported. 'Baker here, sir. I'm okay. I can see Ann through the connecting tunnel. She looks okay, too. The main connecting tunnel outside the command module has depressurized – looks like *Enterprise* has emergency-disconnected. Repeat, main connecting tunnel to the shuttle is *not* secure.'

'Page here. Engineering is secure. I'm on POS.'

Saint-Michael looked over at Walker, who was standing over a space-suited crewman. 'What's the problem, Jim?'

'Looks like Sergeant Wallis's intercom is out, Skipper.'

Saint-Michael threw his notebook towards Walker – it actually arced a bit in the tiny amount of gravity still lingering instead of floating in the usual straight line. 'Pass a message to him with that. Tell him to start deploying the rescue balls, then have him help Davis and Montgomery into the lifeboat and switch places with Bayles. Have him fix his intercom in the lifeboat. Sergeant Bayles, come up here to the command module.'

Wallis acknowledged Walker's hastily scribbled note with a thumbs-up and started to unpack the station's rescue balls – large man-sized sealable plastic and canvas bags. In an emergency a crewmember could seal himself inside a rescue ball and pressurize it with his portable oxygen system. The ball could then be transported by a space-suited crewman from a depressurized or contaminated module to the lifeboat, another safe pressurized module or the space shuttle or other rescue vessels. Wallis had a rescue ball open and Velcroed near each person in the command module by the time Bayles had made his way to the command module, and then helped the two injured crewmen towards the hatch to the connecting tunnel.

'Station integrity check, all sections,' Saint-Michael ordered by loudspeaker. 'Atmosphere checks okay everywhere on the station except for main transfer tunnel and docking bay. No contamination, just a heat build-up . . .'

'General, I think I see the problem,' Wallis reported. He was holding the stationwide address-system microphone to his helmet glass and screaming at the top of his lungs, but his voice sounded as if his head were inside a tin bucket. 'I'm in the connecting tunnel between the research and sleep modules. I can see the keel. The radiators look as though they've been ripped apart by a

'. . . a giant lawn mower. Almost nothing – ' And then only a muffled scream.

'Wallis? Christ, what – ?'

At that instant the lights dimmed again in the command module. Control panels flickered, then returned to normal. The computer monitors began to fill with error and warning messages. The air in the module became stagnant, near unbearable.

'Skipper . . .'

'Wallis? You all right?'

'I'm . . . okay. We got tagged by some kind of laser beam, sir. I *saw* the damned thing. It hit the keel, then passed over the pressurized modules. There's sparks flying out of the keel . . . I think it might be one of the SBR antennas – '

'Can you make it to the lifeboat?'

'I think so . . . Sir, it's the number-one SRB antenna for sure. The antenna looks chewed up and the control box is sparking – '

'All right, good job. Now get to the lifeboat and have someone look you over. Baker, Page, report to the lifeboat. Ann, you'll have to use the connector between Skybolt and the storage module. Do a double-check before you open the hatches, all of you. Now move.'

Saint-Michael turned to Walker, who was checking the status and control panel with Jefferson. 'Checks, General. We've lost the number-one SBR antenna.'

'How about the system?'

'The other antenna wasn't touched,' Jefferson said. 'It's working. I can reprogram it, okay. It may not have quite the resolution or power but I think we'll still be on-line.'

'Any other faults?'

'We may have lost a thruster,' Walker said and moved quickly from panel to panel, scrolling through the seemingly endless lists of error messages on the screens. 'The number-one negative-Y thruster is showing zero chamber

200

pressure. The number-two thruster is firing full-time now to compensate. We're sucking fuel pretty bad.'

'And with a lost fuel cell, we'll be in trouble – fast. I'll need endurance figures as soon as possible.'

'Yes, sir,' Walker said, giving the general a worried look. 'Skipper, could it be the laser at Sary Shegan? Is it possible . . . ?'

'Possible? It happened, Jim. They hit us with their chemical laser. The pressurized modules survived because of the silver armour, but we all know the systems mounted on the keel are vulnerable – '

'We're back on the horn with the *Nimitz*, General,' Jefferson reported.

Saint-Michael returned to his seat and strapped in. '*Nimitz*, this is Armstrong. How copy?'

'Weak but readable, Armstrong,' a radio operator replied. 'Stand by for Admiral Clancy.'

'Sir,' Walker cut in, 'I've got *Enterprise* on the VHF. They're asking for instructions.'

'Good. Tell them to stay at least five hundred yards from the station and be ready to retrieve the lifeboat. Also tell them to keep their open cargo-bay pointed away from earth in case that damn laser fires at us again.'

'Rog.'

'Armstrong, this is Clancy. What the hell happened up there?'

'We were attacked, Admiral. I've got half the crew in the lifeboat. Three injuries, two may be serious. Possible serious damage to our attitude-control system. One ruptured fuel tank, other collateral damage. Our SBR still shows operation. We're going to try to make repairs.'

'What attacked you, Jas?'

'We figure it was our friends at Sary Shegan. I'll get back to you when we have a full damage assessment.'

'Okay, Jas . . . Listen, Jas, I'm afraid I've got some very bad news . . .'

Saint-Michael held his breath. He had an idea what was coming.

'It's the *California* . . . so far we count six hundred men dead . . . Matt Page didn't make it.'

Saint-Michael didn't reply for a moment, then clicked the microphone back on. 'I'll let his daughter know, Admiral. Thanks for getting us word.'

'He was hell on wheels, Jas. Did a great job. The men loved him, and that's no BS. Tell her.'

'Yes, sir. I will. Armstrong out.'

Saint-Michael scanned the command module. Of the other crewmembers only Walker seemed to have heard. He looked at the general and shook his head. Saint-Michael told himself to put Captain Page's death out of his mind for now. Somehow he'd deal with it, with Ann . . . later. Right now he had this station to command. He looked to his right and saw Jefferson giving his master SBR console an affectionate pat.

'Good news, Chief?'

'Yes, sir, SBR is back on-line. Only a slightly narrower scan area – maybe a hundred miles less, plus a bit reduced resolution.'

'That news might be academic if we take a few more hits from that laser . . .'

Jefferson nodded and turned back to his screens, trying to assimilate the mountains of data that had been received in the short time since the SBR became operational. Less than two minutes later he called out another report.

'Several slow-moving jet aircraft over Tehran, General. Swarms of them. Extensive fighter coverage.'

'God, the Russians must be taking Tehran,' Walker said, looking at the display. 'Three Condor transports already on the ground at Mehrabad Airport. Could be as many as six hundred troops. The Iraqis have almost reached Abadan, too.'

Saint-Michael tried to assess possible implications. He

had just finished calling Bayles and Moyer forward to help with the data transmissions and analysis when the *Nimitz* broke radio silence once again.

'Looks like the shit has hit the fan for real, Jason,' Admiral Clancy was saying. 'A coordinated attack. Fighters from the *Brezhnev* have chased away all the Hawkeye surveillance planes that we'd sent up to patrol the area. They're mounting another air attack on Tehran, and Iraqi forces are moving across the border towards Abadan. The Soviets have got the whole northern gulf sewn up tight.'

Bad news, no question, Saint-Michael thought. Tehran was important, of course, but there was one place that was even more critical now. He keyed his microphone, 'Looks bad over Tehran and Abadan, Admiral. But those guys have left themselves a little too open over Bandar-Abbas, do you agree?'

'On the nose, Jas. That's where we push. I'm going to need your help on this one. Maybe even use that trump card we talked about. How much time left on your orbit?'

'Sixty minutes.'

'Should be enough. Just hope whatever the hell hit you doesn't take a curtain call.'

'Copy, Admiral. Armstrong out.' Saint-Michael turned and stared wordlessly at the master SBR monitor for a long moment.

Walker couldn't take the silence. 'Skipper, what's up?'

'Clancy's going to start an offensive . . .'

'An offensive? With what? Where? The Russians are overrunning Iran from all points.'

Saint-Michael looked at Walker. 'We're going to play some sky-poker,' he said. 'Just hope our bluff works.'

From the moment Jason Saint-Michael appeared at the hatch to the sausage-shaped crew-rescue lifeboat, Ann *knew*. She could read it in his face. She'd been expecting it . . .

'Ann, I . . . I'm sorry . . .'

She leaned back against a compartment. 'He's gone?' She knew, but it needed to be said so that she could begin to feel it, to really know it . . .

Saint-Michael moved to her, took hold of her. 'Admiral Clancy told me a few minutes ago. He said to tell you what a fine officer your father was, that the men – '

She nodded at him, tears running down her cheeks, pushing him away and clutching at him all at the same time.

He pulled her to him, held her as she let out her grief. They stood together that way for who knows how long, sharing the intimacy of each other in a way neither could have managed minutes before.

Finally, Saint-Michael gently drew away from her, began to move towards the hatch. He turned around once, paused. 'He did a job, Ann . . . manoeuvred the *California* right in front of the missiles. If they'd got by, thousands would have been killed aboard the *Nimitz*. The whole group would have been forced to retreat . . . I know it's no help now, but I want you to know . . .'

She nodded. 'Thanks, I know. He even used to say it was how he wanted to go. But it doesn't make it any easier . . .'

'Nothing ever does,' he said, and exited the hatch, leaving her alone with her grief.

7

July 1992
Over the Persian Gulf, One Hundred Kilometres
South of the *Brezhnev*

It appeared simple. Ridiculously simple.

The Soviet Su-27 Flanker pilot from the *Brezhnev* couldn't help smiling. After all the talk about how autonomous American fighter pilots were, how innovative, how creatively unpredictable – here they were, ten American F-15 Eagle fighters, driving directly into the hands of their enemies.

The Soviet aircraft carrier *Brezhnev* had spotted the Eagle attack formation three hundred kilometres away and had scrambled ten advanced Sukhoi-27 fighters to intercept, with ten more of the air-to-tower missile-equipped fighters to follow. There were only three places from which an American counterattack on the *Brezhnev* could have come: Kigzi Airbase in Turkey, Riyadh in Saudi Arabia, and the Gulf of Oman, where the *Nimitz* was located. All of those areas had been bottled up tight by the *Brezhnev*'s planes and ships. An attack group would have to circumnavigate the Iraqi and Soviet forces in the west, the *Brezhnev* and her escorts in the Persian Gulf and the destroyers and battleships in the Strait of Hormuz if they had any hope of attacking the Soviet army and navy positions in Tehran and Tabriz. It was a move of desperation.

The closing rate between the two opposing fighter groups was well over two thousand kilometres an hour, which also favoured the Soviet defenders. The F-15s from

Riyadh had already been flying for nearly an hour and were probably overloaded with weapons and fuel. The Su-27s, virtually identical to the single-seat version of the American F-15, had just launched from the *Brezhnev* minutes ago and were loaded with AA-11 aspect-to-air missiles, not fuel. The F-15s would have no time to dogfight. They would try, as their current flight profile suggested, to blow past the Su-27s, get as close as possible to the *Brezhnev* and launch their missiles. Desperation. Sheer desperation . . .

'Group One leader, this is Control. Hostile contact bearing two-six-zero, range seven-five kilometres. Acknowledge when locked on.'

The lead Flanker pilot thumbed his microphone switch. 'I understand, Control. Intruders are locked on radar, seventy kilometres and descending slowly. Requesting final authority to attack.'

'Request approved, Group One.' He then switched to English to invoke the universal fighter pilot's credo: 'Good luck. Good hunting.'

The lead Flanker pilot felt a rush of adrenaline. Invoked in English, the fighter's credo always seemed to hone his instincts.

'Group One, sixty kilometres. Final arming check – now.'

'Red Flight checks.'

'Gold Flight checks.'

'Group One, lock and ready in file.' The lead pilot pressed his target-designate switch until the radar-tracking cursor had switched to the lead American plane. A high-pitched four-beep sequence and a flashing green light on his arming panel told him his ADC-1054W attack radar was locked on. Perfect. No manoeuvring, no jamming . . .

Fifty kilometres. 'Group One . . . launch!'

It was an exhilarating sight. In complete unison, twenty

AA-11 advanced long-range radar-guided missiles filled the sky, speeding to their targets. The missile-attack aspect was ideal. The American F-15s were in a slightly steeper dive, trying to make it to the relative safety of the Persian Gulf's choppy waters, where they figured they would be lost in radar clutter. But in fact they were exposing more of themselves to the missiles' powerful on-board terminal homing radars.

The lead Flanker pilot made one quick check of his formation, then checked his radar for possible survivors – and saw the impossible.

The American F-15s were still on radar. All twenty AA-11 missiles had *missed*.

And then he saw why: the F-15s, which had been at fifteen hundred metres altitude when the Flankers launched their missiles, were now at five thousand metres. The American planes had somehow managed to climb nearly four thousand metres in ten seconds. Even an AA-11 missile, which could turn at well over seven 'g's, couldn't keep up with a climb-rate like that at such close range.

The leader of *Brezhnev* Fighter Group One yanked his Su-27 Flanker fighter into a hard climbing turn to pursue, but he knew without checking his radar that the move was pointless. He had to steel himself to key his microphone.

'Control, this is Group One leader. All targets are still . . . still airborne and have manoeuvred above us. Last read-out showed them at five thousand metres and climbing. Turning to intercept.'

'Group One, this is Control,' came the scratchy message from the air combat controllers aboard the *Brezhnev*. 'We have intruders at your five o'clock, altitude five thousand metres, range forty kilometres, air speed six-four-three kilometres per hour. Turn right heading zero-two-zero, initial vector for intercept.'

'Group One copies all.'

'Group One, state your bingo.'

The Group One leader checked his fuel gauges, feeling his cheeks and ears redden. He could easily imagine the words being said about him right now on the bridge of the *Brezhnev* – he had been too cocky, too sure of himself, taking the long- to medium-range shot without bothering to move in closer. It had to be some sort of electronic jamming or deception that made the American F-15s appear to be lower than the Su-27s. No aircraft could climb four thousand metres in ten seconds.

To make matters worse he was now in a tail-chase with the American fighters – and with no airborne defenders between them and the *Brezhnev* . . .

'Group One shows two-zero minutes to bingo.' Even the fuel situation had got worse. The Americans were still on emergency fuel, he was sure – especially after that crazy manoeuvre – but now the odds were no longer in the defenders' favour.

'Group One, Alert Group Two is preparing for launch. We will recover your group at bingo minus five. Acknowledge.'

'Group One copies.' They had fifteen minutes now to chase down the Americans, or Group Two – the youngsters aboard the *Brezhnev* – would launch and go for the intercept. The sheer embarrassment of *that* was almost unthinkable.

Not checking to see if Red Flight had managed to keep up with him as he sped eastward towards the evading American fighters, the leader of *Brezhnev* Group One put his Sukhoi-27 Flanker in a max afterburner climb and searched frantically on wide-scan radar for the intruders. He had even less time than he'd first thought: if the F-15s carried Harpoon antiship missiles they could attack from as far away as sixty kilometres, perhaps more at high altitude . . .

There. 'Control, Group One leader has the intruders.

Twelve o'clock, thirty-six kilometres and high. Beginning intercept. Group One, check in.'

'This is Red Flight. We are at your six o'clock, one mile. Couldn't keep up with that turn, Viktor. Joining on your right wing.'

'Copy. Gold Flight, take the high patrol. Red Flight will pursue and close.'

The closure rate sucked his breath – the F-15s were cruising, straight and level, at only five hundred kilometres per hour. The Flankers were speeding towards them at nearly three times that velocity. The lead Flanker locked on to four of the ten intruders; his fire-control system would now attack four separate aircraft at once –

Suddenly one of the intruder aircraft heeled sharply over to the left and descended, rapidly.

'Red Five, one intruder peeling left and down at your eleven o'clock. Follow him. He's yours.'

'Red Five has him locked on. Pursuing.'

The distance had decreased rapidly to less than twenty kilometres when the leader noticed the formation of American F-15s making a shallow left turn. 'Intruders are evading left. Red Flight, echelon right for pursuit.'

'Two.'

'Three.'

'Four.'

The leader took a quick glance to his right as he continued his shallow left turn behind the American F-15s. The four Su-27s with him were in perfect alignment, turning canopy-to-belly instead of in extended wingtip-to-wingtip to help maintain a solid radar lock-on.

The formation had drifted nearly ninety degrees away from the *Brezhnev* carrier battle group when the Group One leader heard: 'Group One, Group Two is airborne. Joining on you for intercept.'

'Copy, Control. We are pursuing intruders. Red Flight, lock and ready in file.'

'Two.'

'Three.'

'F –'

'Group One lead, this is Red Five. I have a visual on the intruder: it's *not* a fighter. Repeat: *it is not a fighter.*'

The Flanker tried to absorb this, then shouted out: 'Red Five, destroy it. Red Flight, launch . . .'

Again the leader's windscreen filled with white streaks as the AA-11 missiles sped after their quarry. They launched at less than eighteen kilometres – no aircraft in the world could possibly evade an AA-11 missile at that range . . .

But when the leader looked at his radar screen again, only three of the nine intruder aircraft were missing. Worse, the intruders were now far to the left – had moved nearly perpendicular to the flight path of the AA-11 missiles in literally the blink of an eye.

'Control, three attackers destroyed. Red Flight, follow me in close to the survivors. Red Flight, what did you see?'

'They're *drones*. A Himlord remote-piloted vehicle. The one I saw was damaged, spinning out of control . . .'

'Drones.' So that was it. The Flanker leader didn't know exactly what Himlord stood for, but he knew what they were – extremely powerful, highly manoeuvrable unmanned reconnaissance drones. Which was why they could outturn an AA-11 missile: the Himlords were designed for such extreme manoeuvres . . . He had seen films of Himlords pulling giant 'g's in all flight regimes. The NATO countries and their allies used Himlords for battlefield reconnaissance, but it was obvious that these were intended here as diversions . . .

. . . Or decoys . . . ?

'Lead, Red Three has a visual on the hostile.'

A quick scan . . . and there it was. Even at four kilometres he could see it easily. It was huge, with a long pointed nose, a set of canards on its forward fuselage, very large main wings with winglets on the tips, and a set of dorsal and ventral stabilizers. Its large turbojet engine released a puff of black smoke every few seconds. Amazingly, the six drones flew in almost perfect formation, staying abreast of each other in spite of each sharp turn and change in airspeed.

'Control, this is Group One lead. We are pursuing drones . . .'

'Group One, this is Group Two lead. We are at your six o'clock at thirty kilometres. Do you want us on a low patrol? Over.'

'Group Two, negative. Return to base immediately. We've been decoyed away. We have twenty fighters chasing a few goddamn drones. Group One, break off attack. Control, this is Group One. Returning to base immediately.'

The radio was filled with static. He was at extreme radio range, and the Himlord drones obviously carried small broad-band jammers as well.

The Group One leader ripped off his oxygen mask in frustration. They had spent nearly an hour, dozens of missiles and thousands of gallons of precious fuel chasing nearly worthless drones. What was the real target . . . ?

A few minutes later, with the American Himlord drones far behind them and still heading for the western shores of the Persian Gulf, Group One's leader finally regained contact with the aircraft carrier *Brezhnev*.

'Control, this is Group One. We are one hundred kilometres out. Request approach clearance.'

'Group One, approach clearance *only* granted. Repeat, approach clearance only is granted. Aircraft launching at this time.'

A few moments later he heard the reason. 'Green Four, this is Control. Hostile airborne contact bearing zero-four-five range, range one hundred kilometres at your twelve o'clock.'

'Copy, Control,' the Green Four leader acknowledged. 'Picking up J-band height-finders near reference F-one-oh-two Delta and Lima.'

F-102 – that was Bandar-Abbas and Bandar-e Lengeh, the two Iranian military bases at the Strait of Hormuz. Green Four was a flight of five Yakovlev-38 vertical takeoff and landing fighters from the *Brezhnev*, all at least twenty-five years old. No match for any weapons on shore with J-band height-finders armed with high-performance surface-to-air missiles. The Su-27s would have a tough time against them, let alone the aged Yak-38s.

But hostile missile sites at Bandar-Abbas? The Iranian sites had been destroyed long ago, way back at the start of hostilites. The whole area had been contained. Who . . . ?

Armstrong Space Station

'They're turning back towards the carrier, Skipper.'

General Saint-Michael swivelled his seat around and quickly scanned the master SBR display. He nodded at Chief Jefferson.

'Good job, Jake. Do you have enough fuel to recover those Himlords?'

'I don't think so, but then again, I've never flown a drone before. I think we'll be dropping through the horizon before I can recover them anyway. After that they'll be on automatic pilot until they flame out.'

'Try to get them as close to that Bahraini data-relay ship as you can. They should be able to recover them.'

Jefferson carefully transmitted new flight commands to the six remaining Himlords in flight. 'Those things are amazing. I'd swear I could turn a ninety-degree corner with one if I wanted, even with this bastardized remote-control relay setup. I would've loved to see the faces on those Su-27 pilots when I had those Himlords climbing at ten "g"s right after missile launch.'

Saint-Michael looked around the command module, shaking his head. The short time in gravity had brought every piece of dirt, every liquid ball, every lost pencil and scrap of paper out of known hiding places and into everything. Yemana and Page had come out of the lifeboat and were running hand-held vacuum cleaners over everything, their POS masks resting beneath their chins, ready at a moment's notice to be put back on.

Three injuries, one serious. A crippled station, leaking fuel, extensive damage. Even though Silver Tower had just participated in a major diversion a thousand miles away, the station was not fully capable. Not by a long shot. In fact, it was barely holding on to strategic function.

'That's about as cocky as we can afford to get, Chief,' Saint-Michael said. 'We managed to sucker half the *Brezhnev*'s air-to-air assets away from Bandar-Abbas – now I hope the air force and navy can do the rest.'

The assault had begun just as the *Brezhnev*'s Su-27 Flanker Group Two had catapulted off the deck to help in the abortive pursuit of the High Manoeuvrability Long Range Reconnaissance Drone (Himlord) aircraft. Ten of the *Nimitz*'s Sikorsky SH-60T SeaHawk transport helicopters had been loaded with ten US Marines in full combat gear, and two CH-53E heavy-lift choppers had been loaded with two British Rapier-tracked surface-to-air batteries apiece. The choppers hedge-hopped over the rugged southern Iran coastline as far as possible from the Soviet cruisers in the Strait of Hormuz, and dropped on to the wrecked airstrip at Bandar-Abbas. With a force of elite navy SEALS blazing a path, the Marines took Bandar-Abbas in a fierce but short battle. By the time Group Two had reached the confused and disorganized

Fighter Group One, the Marines had secured Bandar-Abbas airfield and, with a few Iranian regulars coming down from the rugged coastal mountains, had managed to secure the skies over the Strait of Hormuz.

Right behind the Marines, under air cover of the *Nimitz*, ten C-130 Hercules transports had reinforced the Marine unit at Bandar-Abbas with three hundred US Army Rapid Deployment Force troops from Diego Garcia in the Indian Ocean. Another sixty Marines had retaken Bandar-e Lengeh, the major Iranian naval missile base overseeing the strait, and fifty RDF troops had soon reinforced that stronghold and established another anti-air battery there.

On balance, a pretty good day.

Moscow, USSR

Minister of Defence Czilikov refused – or was unable – to look directly at his assembled battle staff as First Deputy Minister of Defence Khromeyev rose to give the daily briefing on Operation Feather, this time before the entire Stavka. Czilikov could *feel* the eyes of the Soviet general secretary bearing down on him as, area by area, the situation in Iran and the Persian Gulf was described.

'The region has been roughly divided in half, along the fifty-four-degree east longitude line,' Khromeyev reported in a flat voice. 'The Americans control the Strait of Hormuz, the Gulf of Oman, and all Iranian territory east of Yazd in central Iran.' The general secretary's eyes now darted towards Czilikov as he heard the news about the strait, the essential choke-point for the whole region. 'Our forces control the Persian Gulf north of Bahrain, as well as every major Iranian city except for Bandar-Abbas along the strait. Our flag flies from the Mediterranean Sea to China – '

'Never mind the grandiose symbolism, Marshal Khromeyev,' the general secretary said. 'Such flowery speech doesn't hide our badly worsening position.' He swivelled towards Czilikov.

'I don't want your dog-and-pony show, Marshal Czilikov. I want *details*. The *Brezhnev* is no longer east of Qatar – it is almost as far north as Kuwait. Yet we no longer control the Strait of Hormuz. *Why?*'

'The Americans have mined the deep-water channel between Iran and Qatar in the gulf, General Secretary – '

'Then destroy those mines. Retake the channel. We have the firepower, don't we?'

'We don't have the resources, sir,' Admiral Chercherovin put in. 'The Americans control the skies during daytime. A squadron of B-52 bombers from Diego Garcia can sow mines for ten thousand square kilometres in one pass. We can sweep perhaps half that area at night, but the bombers return with more mines – '

'You are saying we do not control the airspace over the Persian Gulf?'

'Not . . . entirely, sir. We can protect the *Brezhnev* and her escorts with our forward units at Al-Basrah and Abadan, but the fighters from the *Brezhnev* have only a seven-hundred-kilometre combat radius. That places them near Bandar-Abbas, where the Americans and Iranians have deployed surface-to-air missile sites, fighters and bombers to defend the strait. Shipborne fighters, which must expend almost half their fuel just to get to a fight, are no match for ground-based fighters . . .'

The general secretary ran a hand across the top of his bald head in exasperation. 'You are talking *riddles*, Admiral. The *Brezhnev* was in a position to defend our forces at Bandar-Abbas. How could we have lost our advantage?'

'The *Brezhnev*'s resources were stretched to the limit, sir,' Czilikov said, figuring he'd better say something fast.

'The *Brezhnev* carried forty-five tactical fighter aircraft. Ten were used as escorts for the raids on Mehrabad and ten were airborne in support of the attacks on Abadan. Ten were launched to pursue what we thought were American F-15s attacking from Saudi Arabia. When the American drones evaded the first patrol, all the *Brezhnev*'s fighters except five reserve alert aircraft were sent after the drones. This left nothing to assist the shock troops at Bandar-Abbas except our old Yak-38 VTOL fighter-bombers, and they were no match for the British Rapier and American Patriot surface-to-air missile sites the Marines brought with them. Five hundred American Marines and two hundred Iranian soldiers landed ashore in three hours. There really was nothing we could do – '

'But what about our ground-based long-range bombers?' the general secretary pressed him. 'Certainly we could have attacked those positions with something besides fighters from the *Brezhnev*? Those Yak-38s should have been escorting the bombers, not attacking.'

'A bomber attack was considered and rejected. If a bomber attack had been attempted immediately when the American Marines attacked Bandar-Abbas, a smaller-scale bomber force might have succeeded. But the area was secured by the Marines in only three hours. It would take one full Tupolev-26 squadron, perhaps two, or a full Tupolev-146 bomber squadron to uproot the American Marines now. Also, the Americans are moving at least one full squadron of F-15 fighters to Bandar-Abbas – they control the skies of the southern gulf.'

'Then *attack*. Use an entire squadron. Whatever is necessary to retake Bandar-Abbas – '

'With twenty supersonic bombers?' Czilikov interrupted. 'Not only would our losses be heavy, but the Americans might think the launch represented a possible threat to the *Nimitz* carrier battle group or to the American airbase in Saudi Arabia. They might counter with considerable force, even threaten to use nuclear weapons against our forces – '

'I don't believe that,' the general secretary said. 'They're not crazy. They couldn't hope to control such a drastic escalation . . .'

'If they lost the *Nimitz* carrier group, sir, their only tactical response to avoid losing their foothold in the region would be an all-out attack. From our point of view, it's a huge risk to take. We have no conclusive evidence that the Americans would *not* attack with nuclear weapons. Remember Kennedy at the Bay of Pigs? And ever since, they've refused to say what they *wouldn't* do.'

'Rationalizations for doing nothing, Czilikov. The Politburo is already demanding an explanation, and we've got to give them one. The Americans are threatening to mobilize for a general war. We've lost the element of surprise. There is even a rumour that the Americans have captured a member of the KGB who participated in the initial attack on our own vessels in the Persian Gulf – '

'That is impossible,' Marshal Lichizev, the commander of the KGB, said. 'All of our operatives are accounted for. It's an obvious bluff.'

'No matter. Denials do no good.' The general secretary looked at each of the Stavka members seated in front of him. 'Feather had to be a swift, decisive, massive blow to occupy and dominate the region. It had to be a coordinated, precision strike at the major strategic choke-points. Instead, we're caught on unsteady, indefensible ground. Rather than a swift victory, I'm left with a damn stalemate. *Worse* than a stalemate: our clumsy lies are exposed, naked before the entire world. The great bear with its nose caught in the mousetrap . . .

'*Heroes* of the Soviet Union.' The general secretary's voice was laced with irony. 'In eight hours I go before the Politburo and tell them how I plan to proceed. As I see it we have three possible options: retreat in disgrace, hold

217

our unsteady and embarrassing position, or attack.' He turned again to Czilikov. 'Do you have an answer, Marshal Czilikov? Is Operation Feather a failure? Do we turn and run? Will I be the first leader of the Soviet Union to order a retreat in the face of vastly inferior forces?'

'What you want, I cannot give you – '

'What? What did you say?'

'You don't want recommendations, Comrade General Secretary. You want to dictate. I will not be dictated to, nor will I be insulted.'

The general secretary leaned towards Czilikov and in a low voice said, 'Be careful what you say, old man.'

'Sir, you can insult the title of Hero of the Soviet Union if you like, but you cannot ignore its implications. Nor can you ignore the consequences if your senior military staff should resign or retire during an operation of the magnitude of Feather . . .' Czilikov's face was flushed as he spoke.

The general secretary looked around the conference table. All faces were turned towards him.

'What do you see, comrade?' Czilikov went on, encouraged by the silence. 'Are you perhaps trying to compute how many would follow if I leave or am removed?'

'I am always computing that, Marshal Czilikov.' It was an uneasy reply.

'Comrade, I am your ally,' Czilikov said, his voice more conciliatory. 'I believe in Operation Feather. But it's a military operation, not a political one. Occupation and control of the Transcaucasus and Persia can only be brought about with the use of military force. And it cannot happen instantly. The advances we have made in the past twenty-four hours are, I believe, nearly miraculous. Our forces have taken control of over a million square kilometres of territory in mere hours. Our objective is close at hand. But we *cannot* proceed rashly, or all our efforts will be for nothing.'

The general secretary paused, knowing he was, at the moment, outmanoeuvred and not knowing precisely what to do about it. 'Well, then, Czilikov, I put it to you. I have a meeting in eight hours. What is the new *military* plan?'

Czilikov nearly preened. He had, it seemed, made the general secretary back off. 'The forces in Iraq, Iran and the Persian Gulf must stay in place. It is absolutely essential. They must be able to defend themselves against any attack or intrusion, but without increasing their ranks.'

'No reinforcements?' the general secretary said. 'If we stop hostilities, isn't that the time to enhance our forces?'

'Not immediately . . . sir. We must *appear* as if we are prepared to pull out of the area, to release our newly acquired territory. We must not, of course, retreat or give away an inch of ground.'

'So we are reverting to a defensive war? I don't understand, Czilikov. If we stand still we will eventually be pushed back – if not by the Americans then by world opinion and its condemnation. Or by both.'

'We will be fighting a defensive war on one front *only*,' Czilikov said, and turned towards Marshal Rhomerdunov, the commander of aerospace forces. His old foxhole compatriot allowed a reassuring smile.

'On an entirely different front,' Czilikov went on, 'we will take command. And, sir, when that happens we will win much, much more than Persia and Transcaucasus . . .'

Tyuratam, USSR

He tried to be patient and gentle in his lovemaking, but he was too keyed up, too mindful of what the next day might bring. Alesander Govorov resisted his young wife's

219

spirited foreplay and took her quickly – almost savagely. She strove to match his intensity, to counter with a frenzy of her own, but she couldn't fake her orgasm fast enough. He withdrew from her, wrapped his powerful arms around her chest as he lay behind her on his left side, then kissed the back of her neck as an unspoken apology for his clumsiness. In less than a minute he fell asleep. She pulled his arms around her tighter, accepting his apology. There would be other nights. She remembered the good ones. They were worth waiting for . . .

The ringing telephone jarred his eyes open. He swung his feet to the carpeted floor and stood, feeling not at all fatigued despite the few short hours of sleep. He picked up the phone and began speaking to Gulaev.

'Yes. Yes, I see . . . Have the report ready for me. I'll be there immediately.'

Govorov's wife did not get out of bed, although she was wide awake as he dressed, getting into his dark grey flight suit. She did not want to see him hurrying off to Glowing Star. If for any reason he did not return, she wanted to remember him the way he had been the night before – strong but vulnerable, impatient but sensitive, a loving, caring husband, an imperfect man. Much more than a soldier, though she was careful not to let him know such thoughts. They would have embarrassed him . . .

General Govorov came into the Space Combat operations centre at Tyuratam at a pace that would have left most men short of breath. Gulaev had to rush to keep up with him as they hurried into the general's office. Govorov was already holding out his hand for the Operation Alpha report as his subordinate closed the door.

'It appears the Sary Shegan laser has been even more effective than we hoped, sir,' Gulaev said as he passed the space defence commander a sheet of computer print-outs bound in a notebook. 'The station's orbit is much more erratic than before, which suggests a guidance or

220

propulsion malfunction. Also, just a few hours ago we detected several objects near the station. Small in size, no propulsion, very hot.'

Govorov studied the printouts, looked up at Gulaev. 'Debris?'

'That's my guess, sir.'

Govorov looked down at the printout again, nodding in approval as his eyes scanned the columns of numbers. It seemed they'd managed to cripple the vaunted Armstrong Space Station, after all. It wasn't out of control yet – he would have received a report about a rescue mission – but it was damaged. Vulnerable.

A quick look at the rest of Gulaev's report brought no pleasure.

'Our attacks have stopped?'

'Temporarily, sir. For safety's sake, Colonel Sokilev at Sary Shegan has limited the laser firing schedule to a five-burst volley every eight hours – '

'But my orders were to fire continuously. Why were they countermanded?'

'The pulses generated by the facility are tremendously powerful. There was a problem with some of the computer circuits shorting. The circuits are reportedly fixed, but Sokilev feels continuous firing carries too great a risk – '

'I should have been consulted. Tell Sokilev that if he goes against my command again, he will be replaced. Also tell him that I expect Operation Beta to be put into effect within the hour. Armstrong is about to pass below the horizon. If we can destroy the Americans' only other eye on the region, NORAD's launch-detection satellite, we will be able to get very close to the space station without ever being detected.'

'But what about Armstrong's Thor missiles, sir? Even if the Americans only have minutes to react, they'll be able to target the missiles.'

221

'Yes, the Thors would be a problem . . . if we didn't have the means to get Armstrong to expend its arsenal.'

'You mean the Gorgons?'

'Why not? It doesn't matter if they are all destroyed. The point is, they will draw off Armstrong's fire and allow Voloshin and me to get within range of the station.'

Gulaev nodded. 'I'll see to the Gorgons immediately, sir.'

'Have a firing disposition report ready for me in half an hour.' Gulaev saluted and turned to leave the office. 'And Gulaev . . .'

The younger officer turned around. 'Sir?'

'I'll be leaving for the launch pad in fifteen minutes. See that I'm not disturbed until then.'

Gulaev nodded and left the room, closing the door behind him. As he did Govorov got up from his desk and stood by a large window overlooking the launch site. From there he could see the maintenance crews completing the final checks on the SL-16s. It was a beautiful day, the general thought to himself, a perfect day to ride a fireball into the sky. He couldn't wait to get started.

Armstrong Space Station

Jason Saint-Michael's warning to his crew not to get too cocky about the role the station had played in the invasion of Bandar-Abbas seemed prophetic now as he clicked his microphone to the off position and reflected on the message he had just received from Space Command. The Russians had apparently just used their laser to knock out an American geosynchronous TRW Black 750 infra-red launch-detection satellite, leaving Space Command and NORAD with no missile-launch detection for south-central Asia. It didn't take a genius to guess what would happen next. Odds were that at that very moment the

Gorgon missiles at Tyuratam were being readied for launch.

Which dictated he do . . . what? He had been about to order Jerrod Will to discontinue *Enterprise*'s orbit around the station and redock, so that Ann and Kevin Baker, who had also made the decision to leave, could be sent back to earth. But he wasn't so sure now that he shouldn't evacuate most of the personnel . . .

He mentally kicked himself for not getting Ann off the station earlier. Even though it bothered him to think of her gone, it bothered him much more to think she might be in serious danger. He just hoped Will could get the *Enterprise* docked and personnel aboard before he had to contend with those missiles headed their way. At least Will and Sontag had flown their most recent resupply mission to the station without Marty Shultz, so there would be that much more room in the cramped Shuttle. The hard part was going to be deciding who should go and who should stay.

Saint-Michael keyed his microphone. '*Enterprise*, what's your status.'

'Still orbiting the station, per your orders, General,' Will said. 'What's up?'

'More trouble, I'm afraid. I want you to redock immediately.'

'Will Airlines copies,' Jerrod said as he activated his forward thrusters. He turned to Sontag as if to say what now? but the co-pilot merely shook his head. They'd have their answers soon enough.

By the time *Enterprise* had docked with the station and Will had made his way to the command module, Saint-Michael had already received two more messages from Space Command. As Will stepped through the module hatch the general acknowledged him with a nod and continued talking to Ann, who had overheard the

223

exchange between Saint-Michael and the controller at Falcon Air Force Station in Colorado Springs.

'General,' she said, 'it looks like the station's going to be attacked. Skybolt could help. I'm sure I've just about solved – '

'No arguments, please.'

'But – '

'Damn it, Ann, report to *Enterprise now*.'

This time there was no argument. As she left the command-module hatch, Will moved next to Saint-Michael. 'General, we're ready to fly, if that's what you want. I've got Yemana rigging up for a token OMS and RCS refuelling – just a safety margin for us. Won't take long. Kelly is helping him in the docking adapter. What have we got?'

'Eight Soviet orbiting vehicles just entered orbits similar to ours,' Saint-Michael told him. 'We lost track of them, but ground tracking stations are keeping an eye on them.'

'Launched from Tyuratam?'

'Yes, two from the Glowing Star area, the rest from the antisatellite area at Baikenour.'

'Gorgons?'

Saint-Michael nodded. 'That's my guess.'

'Sounds like they popped the whole ASAT alert fleet. What about the two from Glowing Star? Do you think they're manned?'

'Don't know. They've had time to move two more Gorgons to Glowing Star, but I think our intelligence would've reported that.'

'What are our people doing in the gulf? Any major movement?'

'None. Matter of fact, most units on land and in our gulf appear frozen. The Russians haven't retreated, but they're not advancing either. They may be reassessing.'

'Or they may be waiting for Silver Tower to get blasted

out of the sky before finishing the job of overrunning Iran,' Will said. 'We'd better get loaded up . . .'

'I can't just abandon the station completely,' Saint-Michael said, checking the system status readouts. 'Not yet, not if the Russians are gearing up for a major offensive. We have to be there when they kick it off.'

'General, it might only take one more shot of that laser or one direct hit from a Gorgon to put you out of commission. One shot on a fuel tank or in your engineering module and whoever's left on board will be in deep – '

'We've got the lifeboat . . .'

'The *lifeboat?* Excuse me, but the term "lifeboat" applied to that hunk of tin out there was coined for the congressman and senators who yakked about having a rescue craft but who wouldn't put up the money for more shuttles or spaceplanes. You know that, sir. We both know it's not a lifeboat – it's more like a piece of waterlogged driftwood. It leaks like a bad condom and it probably wouldn't stand the stress of recovery in a shuttle. It's craziness to rely on it.'

'Some speech – and maybe all true. But it doesn't matter . . . It's what we've got to do the job. This is an emergency – '

'Don't create another one, then.'

'Jerrod, I hear you. That's it. Take care of your ship and your passengers. I'll cut the crew on the station down to two or three. You take the rest back to Vandenburg or Edwards. Now move it. We haven't got much time.'

As Will exited the module, Colonels Marks and Walker approached Saint-Michael. Marks handed the general a computer printout. 'Bad news, Skipper. My calculations show that we only have a day and a half's worth of fuel. Tops.'

Saint-Michael scanned the fuel figures. 'Even with a reduced crew. No experiments? Reduced power usage?'

'Those figures include all that, plus only a conservative

225

estimate on the necessary fuel consumption with the lost thruster – it could be worse than those numbers.'

'We'll need almost four-a-week refuellings at this rate,' Saint-Michael said, 'unless we get that thruster working – '

Walker cut in. 'General, there's another option . . .'

'I know, return to a standard polar circular orbit. Stop the retracking thruster course corrections. But then we'd have only a few minutes over the Persian Gulf every few hours. We'd be almost useless as a surveillance platform.'

'But we'd be secure, General. This station is a strategic defence laboratory, not really a surveillance satellite. We've proved our value in the first defence of Iran and the Persian Gulf region, but now the game has changed. *We're* the target, a major target. If the Russians shoot down this station, the United States has lost a lot more than just an SBR platform . . .'

Saint-Michael stayed silent, seemingly lost in thought.

Walker sensed the shift in the general's thinking and nodded to Marks, who said, 'At Jim's request, sir, I've worked up the fuel considerations involved in putting us back in polar orbit.' He handed Saint-Michael another printout. 'We *would* have enough fuel to reestablish the new orbit, and we wouldn't be dependent on so many refuellings – '

'Skipper, warning message from Space Command tracking,' Moyer broke in through the stationwide intercom. 'Orbiting vehicle within five miles vertically and one hundred miles laterally from the station.'

Saint-Michael quickly sat back in his commander's seat; Walker returned to his position beside Jefferson on the master SBR display.

Saint-Michael keyed the intercom. 'Jerrod, status of your refuelling.'

'Few more minutes.'

'You're out of time, Jerrod. Attention on the station.

226

Emergency. Discontinue all refuelling operations. All crewmen except command-module personnel report aboard *Enterprise* immediately. This station is on red alert. Jake, discontinue SBR earth surveillance. Launch commit all Thor interceptors for station defence.' He turned to Walker. 'Jim, can you handle the Space Command relays and back up Jake on the SBR board?'

'Sure thing.'

'Okay. Moyer, get into a space suit. You're our life insurance.' The young tech nodded and hurried off to where one of the space suits had temporarily been stowed in a corner of the command module. 'I want rescue balls within immediate reach.'

'Space Command tracking vehicle within two miles vertical, sixty miles horizontal,' Walker reported. 'Tracking reports vehicle is under power and manoeuvring.'

'Jerrod, get *Enterprise* the hell out of here.'

'Tracking reports three more vehicles manoeuvring within – '

'Ann isn't on board yet, Jason.'

Saint-Michael got both transmissions at the same time, pressed his earset closer to hear better. 'Say again, Jerrod.'

Will repeated the message. Before Saint-Michael could explode he heard, 'Fifty miles, now at our altitude. Collision course. Repeat, *collision course*.'

'What the hell . . .' Saint-Michael turned quickly to the stationwide speaker intercom. 'Ann Page, report to the command module immediately. Acknowledge.'

No reply. The general knew he had to force himself to put her out of his mind and concentrate on the attack. He turned back around towards the master SBR display. 'Jake . . .'

'SBR lock-on, Skipper. Laser target discrimination in progress.'

Tethered one hundred yards below Silver Tower, the

227

Thor space-based interceptor-missile garage had obeyed the steering commands sent to it by the station's powerful phased-array radar and had pointed the business end of the garage towards the oncoming antisatellite vehicle. When the SBR locked on, it also slaved a neutral particle-beam laser projector onto the Soviet space vehicle.

At that point the laser illuminated the three-ton Gorgon missile, and special sensors analysed the reflected laser energy. A solid object large enough to damage the station would reflect a different wavelength of energy than a less substantial, lightweight decoy. Once the decoys were discovered, Armstrong's weapons could be employed against only those objects that were a real threat to the station. The whole process, from lock-on to lethal target verification, had taken only seconds.

'Forty miles . . . thirty miles . . . target discrimination is lethal positive. Thor one auto launch . . .'

After launch commit was given, the missile's last check was target discrimination. Targets were checked as lethal, the SBR then automatically issued attack commands to the Thor missiles. The first Thor interceptor missile shot free of its garage, accelerating rapidly to its top speed of over four miles per second. The one-hundred-foot-diameter steel mesh net had hardly fully deployed when it hit the first Gorgon ASAT vehicle head-on.

'Direct hit.' But there were no victory cheers. This wasn't, after all, a planned exercise like their first operational test with friendly Trident D-5 missiles.

'Transmit warning message to Space Command, Mission Control, and JCS,' Saint-Michael said. 'Tell them we are engaging – '

A loud bang and a warning buzzer sounded from the environmental control panel. 'What the hell was that?'

'Rupture in the Skylab module,' Marks reported. 'Rapid pressure loss almost zero now . . .'

'Jason, this is Will on *Enterprise*. We were hit by

projectiles from that Gorgon just before it was destroyed. Minor damage to our right wing leading edge.'

'SBR has multiple inbound targets locked on,' Jefferson reported. 'Range eighty miles. Target discrimination in progress.'

'Cabin pressurization in rec section of Skylab module down to zero,' Marks updated. 'Skylab module sealed off. I think we took one of those Gorgon projectiles.'

Saint-Michael looked grim. 'Damn it, we've got to get *Enterprise* out of here.' He switched to stationwide intercom. 'Ann, where are you? *Report*, damn it.'

Silence.

'Target discrimination lethal positive for three inbounds – ' Jefferson had just finished his report when his computer monitors showed three automatic Thor missile launches.

'Thors two, three, and four away . . . straight track . . .'

'Space Command acknowledges our warning message.'

'Direct hit on number two . . . miss on four. Miss on number four – '

'Manual launch,' Saint-Michael called out. 'Jake, you got it.'

Jefferson's fingers manipulated his control board. 'Thor five away. Reacquire target four . . . Switching to auto track – '

'Target three direct hit.' Followed by dozens of bangs and scraping noises on the hull and throughout the station.

'More flak from those Gorgons,' Marks reported. He checked the environmental control panel. 'Leaks in the upper connecting tunnel. Cargo shovel defuelling system has a short-circuit. Major damage throughout the Skylab module.'

'SBR tracking four inbounds,' Walker said. 'Range of closest target eighty miles – '

'Snared target number four,' from Jefferson. His dark blue flight suit was already soaked with sweat.

'Only five more Thors,' Saint-Michael said. 'I don't like the way the math is working out here.'.

'We've got ten more Thors stored on the keel,' Walker reminded him.

'They might as well be on earth,' the general said. 'We've got no one to load them onto the garage.'

'*Enterprise* could do it . . .'

'It would take too long to load those missiles with the manipulator arm. If we only had – '

'I'll go,' Moyer said suddenly. 'Shouldn't take me too long . . .'

'It'll take you all day to load ten missiles by yourself,' Walker told him.

'At least I can load a few . . .'

'We can't spare you,' Saint-Michael said. 'If we run out of missiles and we're still under attack, we abandon the station. Period – '

'Target discriminating on four inbounds . . . showing two decoys. *Repeat*, tracking two decoys.'

'Decoys?' Marks said. 'They put decoys on an ASAT launcher?'

'A decoy can still do damage.'

'But we don't have the Thors to spare,' Saint-Michael told Walker. 'Target the other two.'

'Rog . . . Selective targeting option running . . . Thors six and seven away . . .'

'Warning message, Skipper,' Walker broke in. 'Recheck on that last target discrimination. Now showing *all four* as lethal positive.'

Saint-Michael looked dead ahead. 'Launch commit on all targets. Check the neutral-particle projector, find out what happened – '

'Thors eight and nine away. Straight track . . .'

'Direct hit on targets five and six . . .'

'Miss on target seven, clean miss on seven.'

'Manual launch Thor ten,' Saint-Michael ordered Jefferson. 'Make this one count, Jake.'

Didn't he always try, Jefferson thought, but said nothing as he ejected the last Thor interceptor missile and sent it towards its target. 'All Thors away.'

'Miss on target eight!'

All heads turned to Colonel Walker as he gave that last report. 'Clean miss, General. Targets seven and eight appear to be . . . to be following an evasive course. Still at seventy miles range but closing slowly.'

Jake Jefferson looked stunned as he watched his console. 'Skipper, I don't understand it. One second, Thor number ten was heading straight to target number seven, and the next, it was gone. I've lost contact with it.'

The realization was not long in coming. The fact that the targets were evading confirmed it. They were dealing with Elektrons . . . The Russians had launched *two* armed *Elektron* spaceplanes at them . . .

Elektron One Spaceplane

It was Colonel Ivan Voloshin who launched the first *Bavinash* Scimitar interceptor missile in space combat. Ironically, Silver Tower's crew would never realize the honour they did the Soviet pilot by launching a Thor missile at him.

Both Govorov and Voloshin had immediately detected all ten Thor missile launches. The Elektron's simple but highly effective infrared tracker and laser range finder had picked up the fast-moving devices easily and computed Scimitar launches against each Thor missile. But Govorov's orders had been to save as many of each Elektron's ten missiles as possible and not use them against a Thor missile unless attacked directly. Voloshin's single Scimitar missile followed the laser beam locked onto Thor number ten and destroyed it – Govorov guessed that the Scimitar hit the Thor missile directly, not just snagging on its large net.

But what especially counted was that Space Station Armstrong had just launched its last missile. It was now totally defenceless . . .

'Elektron One, this is Two,' Voloshin called over the discrete VHF frequency. 'I count ten Thors expended, General.'

'Affirmative, Two. Deploy as planned and be prepared to attack on my command.'

With the laser range finder locked on to the space station itself, Govorov began to manoeuvre his Elektron spaceplane above the station's keel, opposite from the free-flying Thor missile garage. Although he could not see him, he knew that Voloshin would be steering his spaceplane directly opposite, about a kilometre away from the station, keeping the Elektrons two kilometres apart.

In this position both he and Voloshin could target exactly one-half of the station with their laser target designators. They could pick and choose their targets with high precision, with special emphasis on the space-based radar, solar-array control boxes, sensors and communications antennae. They would be sure to destroy the station's fighting capabilities before administering the final blow: an attack on the pressurized modules themselves. Killing the crewmen of Space Station Armstrong was not Govorov's plan, but he was determined to eliminate the orbiting platform as a threat. If American lives were lost in the process, he couldn't be blamed. The station's crewmembers had forfeited any ordinary consideration when they had chosen to intervene in Operation Feather. Nobody had invited them. Now they would learn the price for their actions, and pay it . . .

'*Anything* we can do?' Moyer asked from behind his spacesuit helmet. The strain in his voice was evident.

'Whatever they're going to hit us with,' Saint-Michael said, 'we don't have to sit here and let ourselves get shot up.' He unstrapped himself and moved over to the station's attitude-control panel. 'Everyone, evacuate the station. Get aboard *Enterprise*. Now.'

'What's the plan, Skipper?' Marks asked him.

'I'm going to deorbit the station, use every last bit of fuel to slow us down so the station will reenter the atmosphere. They may try to destroy this station, or they might try to occupy it. Either way, they're not going to get it. I'll jettison the lifeboat just before the deorbit burn. Let's just hope they won't fire on a lifeboat . . .'

'There's got to be another way – '

'They're calling the tune now, Chief,' Saint-Michael said bitterly. 'We dance to it or pay the consequences.' He looked around the module, at Moyer, Walker, Marks and Jefferson. 'There'll be other times . . . Our job right now is to survive. And that means getting your butts on the shuttle in the next three minutes.'

A few minutes earlier Ann's chief worry had been what Saint-Michael would do when he found out she'd countermanded his orders and not gone over to the *Enterprise*. There just wasn't the time to explain why she thought she could get Skybolt running again, and she suspected that even if she'd had the time, even if the rush of events hadn't forced him into making a quick decision, she'd still have big trouble convincing him the laser was worth another try. She'd cried wolf too often, failing when it counted to get him to listen because too many of her earlier assessments of Skybolt's capabilities had proved overly optimistic.

Well, let the general get steamed. There were bigger

problems to worry about now. As she worked to thread the proper relays to the MHD reactor, her tracking indicator told her what was happening out in space . . . Two of the Gorgons – no, not really Gorgons but some sort of Russian spacecraft – had passed through Armstrong's Thor missile barrage untouched and were moving closer to the station. It became harder and harder to thread the wires and test the last of the circuits as fear caught hold of her.

She knew that the Skybolt laser now was the station's only defence against the two blips she saw moving ever closer on her tracking indicator. She knew it and yet she also knew that she was minutes away from having the laser ready. She started a prayer, stopped. Not fair, any last-minute invocation of the deity; it was up to her now. You asked for it, so get it done, she taunted herself, and once more she was able to focus all her concentration on the job at hand . . .

Elektron One Spaceplane

'Request permission to open fire, sir,' Voloshin radioed.

'Stand by, Elektron Two,' Govorov said. 'We'll begin in one minute. Do not attack the shuttle. Repeat, do *not* attack. They'll use the shuttle to evacuate.'

'An American space shuttle would be a nice prize, General.'

'There is only one prize here, Voloshin. Armstrong. Remember that.'

There was silence on the frequency for a few moments, then: 'General, do you think they'll try to scuttle the station?'

'It's what I would do. A remote-controlled or timed-thruster burn could be set up to do the job after they've

234

evacuated.' Govorov checked the digital chronometer on his instrument panel. 'Status check, Elektron Two.'

The reply came a few moments later, 'Status positive, Elektron Lead. Oxygen, twenty litres. Fuel, sixty per cent.'

'Lead has twenty-two litres oxygen and sixty-two per cent fuel. One hour until we need to begin deorbit or rendezvous with *Mir*.' *Mir* was the Soviet's orbiting module, a far cruder version of Silver Tower that had limited surveillance capabilities and no offensive or defensive weaponry. In recent years it had been used principally as a site for astronomical experiments and as a refuelling depot. 'We'll commence our attack in two minutes, whether or not the station has been evacuated.'

Armstrong Space Station

'*Enterprise* shows ready for crew transfer, General,' Jefferson reported.

'Very well. Signal JCS and Control that we'll transfer to *Enterprise* immediately.' Jefferson nodded and began switching his comm panel to the proper air-to-ground frequency when a new voice came over the intercom: 'General, this is Ann.'

Saint-Michael shifted towards his comm panel. 'Ann? Where the hell have you been?'

'In the Skybolt module. I – '

'Get out of there, *now*. We're evacuating the station.'

'I only need ten more minutes – '

'For *what?*'

Just then the loud hum of the interphone's CALL override blocked out Ann's reply. 'General, this is Will. Come up on interphone four.'

'What the hell – ? Ann, I want you in the command module on the double. Move out.' He switched his comm panel to the discrete closed-circuit interphone channel. 'All right, Jerrod, what is it?'

'A way out. Maybe . . .'

'Don't keep us in suspense – '

'Baker and Yemana are outside the shuttle, General. They're working their way down to the spare Thor missiles.'

'They're *what?*'

'Baker came up with a way to manually activate the missiles. He and Yemana are going to unstow two of the missiles, point them at those Russians, and cook 'em off.'

'Goddamn, Jerrod, I didn't authorize that. It's too risky. Once the Russians see – '

'General,' Will interrupted. 'It'll work. Those space-planes are right on top of you, but they're on the opposite side from the spare Thors on the underside of the keel. By the time they find out what's happening it'll be too late.'

Saint-Michael shook his head. Suddenly everyone in his command had turned into a damn space cowboy. He was losing control. He turned towards Moyer standing in his spacesuit near the hatch to the research module. 'Move down to the connecting tunnel between engineering and the storage module, on the double. See if you can signal Baker and Yemana. Try to tell them to get their butts back on board *Enterprise*.' On the discrete interphone channel he said, 'It's a damned stupid idea, Jerrod. Once those Russians see us fooling with the Thor missiles they'll blow us all away. Order Baker and Yemana back.'

'Sir, I think we should at least go out fighting – '

'*You* think? I'm still the commander of this station and I want those men ordered back. *Do it*.'

There was a short pause, then the reluctant reply: 'Yes, *sir*.'

But it was already too late. Moyer called over stationwide interphone. 'General, I can see one of them. He's made it to the spare Thor racks . . .'

Wearing large MMUs, the manned manoeuvring units, on their backs, Baker and Yemana unstowed two Thor missiles, refrigerator-sized cylinders with dozens of arms sticking out of each side. After the missiles were hauled out of their containers Baker opened an access panel on one side of each missile and activated a series of switches that bypassed the SBR controls and made the missiles autonomous. Next he removed a maintenance access-cover on each missile and manually activated the Thor's radar-seeker head. Finally he and Yemana helped each other to attach the missiles to brackets on their MMU cylinders, and together both men slowly, carefully edged their way underneath opposite sides of the central station keel and manoeuvred the seeker-heads of their missiles around the edge of the keel and up towards where they had last seen the Soviet spaceplanes.

Their only shared radio transmission came after they had manoeuvred their bulky missiles around the keel and aimed them at the point in the sky where the Soviet spaceplanes had been parked. Yemana put a finger on his MMU thruster, took a deep breath, and called, '*Now.*'

Yemana jetted forward six feet, stopped and swung his missile up. Ironically, since the SBR antenna on his side had been blasted away he had a perfectly unobstructed shot at one of the Soviet spaceplanes, which he could see as a dim oblong shape against the backdrop of stars. He waited a few moments until a tiny flashing green light on the removed maintenance access panel illuminated, then hit a button on the engine control panel, unclipped the missile and pulled back his right-hand MMU thruster controller. He had jetted only ten feet away from the Thor missile when it was engine-ignited . . .

Baker had to move forward a few extra feet to clear the

237

large SBR antennas on his side, but it took only a few extra seconds. Then he swung upward the front of the Thor missile, twisting the hand thruster controllers to counteract the huge inertia of the Thor missiles. It took a few moments longer for him than for Yemana, but Baker soon had his Thor missile pointing right where the Soviet spaceplane had been parked . . .

Except it was no longer there . . .

'General, missiles pointed right at us,' came the startled call from Colonel Voloshin. The Soviet pilot couldn't believe what he saw: an American astronaut manoeuvring a Thor missile around in open space. The sight would have been merely weird if it weren't such a clear warning of imminent attack.

Govorov reacted instantly, pulling his Elektron spaceplane straight up ninety degrees and applying full throttle. As an added measure he overpressurized one of the small tail-thrusters of his Elektron spaceplane, then cut the thruster off, sending a cloud of monomethyl hydrazine rocket fuel out behind the spaceplane. In seconds he had darted several hundred metres away from the huge American space station.

The Thor missile ran straight and true. Yemana fought the sudden back-blast of the Thor's main thruster and quickly regained control of his MMU. He watched, fascinated, as the missile's steel-mesh snare began to unfurl and quickly expand to nearly its full one-hundred-foot diameter. There was no way it was going to miss . . .

Except at that moment the Soviet spaceplane heeled sharply upward, and literally in the blink of an eye it was gone. The Thor missile ran straight towards the spot where the spaceplane had been, but it made no attempt to turn upward to pursue the fleeing Soviet intruder. Although Yemana had no way of knowing, the missile's radar-seeker head had locked onto the dense cloud of hydrazine fuel. When it reached the slowly dispersing cloud, the missile computed zero distance to its target and detonated its one-thousand-pound flak warhead.

Yemana saw the flash of the exploding warhead but saw or felt nothing else. The missile had exploded less than three hundred feet away, sending five hundred pounds of metal chips flying in all directions. Unimpeded by any obstruction or even the resistance of gravity, the chips easily found the astronaut and tore through his body, detonating the MMU's pressurized tanks and adding their explosive fury to the carnage. Yemana's ragged corpse was propelled by the explosion's shockwave out into space.

'General, the missile has exploded behind you. I'm beginning my attack.'

Govorov kept the throttle of his Elektron at full thrust until he heard Voloshin's message, then selected the roll thrusters and did a fast four-'g' dive back down towards the station. He heard a few pings of metal against the silica tiles of his Elektron but ignored it. He saw nothing now but his quarry in the sights of his Scimitar missile launcher . . .

Will and Sontag saw the flash of light and heard the rumbling of the first Thor missile.

'Yemana. Baker. Where are you?'

Sontag unstrapped and quickly propelled himself between the two flight deck seats and across to the aft crew station. He pressed his face to the windows facing into the cargo hold and scanned the sky behind *Enterprise* towards the centre keel and lower pressurized modules.

'I see one of them,' Sontag called out cross-cockpit. 'I don't know if it's Baker or Yemana . . .'

Baker saw the Soviet spaceplane almost on top of him, but there was no time to reacquire his target. He tried to manoeuvre his MMU down and over to aim the Thor missile's sensor at the spaceplane, but in his rush to steer

239

the missile he activated the MMU thruster controls too rapidly and sent himself into a violent forward spin. When he tried to apply opposite thrust to correct his spin, the Thor missile broke free from the attach point on his MMU, and he had to watch Silver Tower's last hope for defence spin away towards earth.

Colonel Voloshin saw the flash from the first exploding missile, and the sudden glare made him furious. He immediately activated his laser target designator and centred the aiming reticle on the first target in view: the white-suited body of Dr Kevin Baker just beginning to get his spinning MMU under control. He squeezed the trigger. A single Scimitar missile ejected itself from the rotary launcher in Elektron Two's cargo bay. Its tiny rocket engine ignited. The missile's seeker-head followed the reflected laser energy from Elektron Two straight to its target.

The laser seeker-head broke apart on Kevin Baker's MMU chest-mounted control pack, but the hypervelocity Scimitar missile kept on going. Right behind the seeker head was a nonexplosive arrow-pointed warhead made of an alloy of molybdenum and depleted uranium, designed to penetrate the thickest armour – Baker's chest offered no resistance to the missile, which was now travelling at well over a mile a second. The missile pierced Baker's body, his MMU, went completely through the storage module fifty yards behind Baker, and through the outer hull of Skybolt's MHD reactor before deflecting off one of the four-foot-thick MHD reactor walls and off into space.

'Oh . . . my . . . God . . .'

Will strained round and saw Sontag move back slowly from the cargo bay windows. 'What is it, Rich . . . ?'

'One of them . . . oh, God . . . they shot him point-blank with a missile.'

'Can we retrieve him? Can you see where he is?'

Sontag forced himself to look out the window once again. The space-suited figure was spread-eagled, in nearly the same position as before, but this time with a cloud of unrecognizable debris floating all around him. The body started to revolve, as though at the end of an invisible noose, and Sontag could see the softball-size hole in the corpse . . .

'*Enterprise*, this is Saint-Michael. Jerrod, what's happened?'

Will clicked open the ship-to-station interphone. 'General, Baker and Yemana . . . they're dead.'

A pause. 'You sure?'

Will didn't answer, instead put his head down on his chest and hammered on the front glare shield, realizing now what he had done . . .

Lieutenant General Govorov could identify only one possible source of the unexpected missile attack: the Thor missile garage tethered beneath the station. He quickly activated his laser designator and placed the aiming reticle on the neutral particle-beam projector mounted beneath the garage. He fired two missiles into the garage, creating a huge fireworks display of sparks and secondary explosions that finally caused the Thor garage to break free of its steel tether and spin away from the station.

He reestablished his original observation position above the space station and keyed his microphone. 'Elektron Two, report.'

'Status green, Lead,' Voloshin replied. 'Two American cosmonauts carrying what appeared to be Thor missiles . . .'

'*Cosmonauts?*'

'Affirmative. I can't see first one, he was close to the explosion of the Thor missile he launched at you. Second one has been . . . despatched. I'm manoeuvring to begin attack.'

'Acknowledged. Manoeuvre back to preplanned position and report when ready to attack. I am manoeuvring back into position.'

As Voloshin watched Govorov pull his fighter into a wide turn around the space station, the younger pilot thought about the wisdom of waiting to get back in position. No, the time to attack was now – before the Americans tried something else. He pulled his Elektron up twenty degrees, pointing it at the centre of the station, and activated his laser designator.

The aiming reticle rested on the first large object in view – the underside of the crew compartment of the space shuttle *Enterprise* . . .

Armstrong Space Station

'They're manoeuvring back to their original positions, General.'

Saint-Michael, already shocked by the report on Baker and Yemana, was motioning Jefferson, Marks and Walker towards the hatch to the main connecting tunnel. 'Get on board *Enterprise*. They're going to start tearing this station apart with those missiles. Moyer, report to – '

A sudden explosion threw all in the command module to the wall. A large red light began blinking over the hatch leading to the main connecting tunnel.

'Fire in the connecting tunnel . . .'

Saint-Michael helped Walker to his feet, then retrieved his earset. '*Enterprise*. Emergency. Fire in the connecting tunnel. Prepare for emergency disconnect.'

'*Jason*.' The voice belonged to Jerrod Will aboard the shuttle *Enterprise*. 'Under attack . . . rapid decompression . . .' But Will, Sontag and the other crewmen aboard *Enterprise* had no time left.

The Scimitar missile ploughed through the lower deck

of the pressurized crew compartment of *Enterprise*, tearing apart a fuel cell and creating a massive hydrogen-oxygen explosion. Within a hundredth of a second, the lower and middeck sections of *Enterprise* were aflame. Davis, Wallis and Montgomery died instantly.

The missile pierced the middeck, deflected off an aluminium spar, blew through the forward cabin bulkhead and went through the RCS engine pod on the nose of the shuttle. The exploding hydrazine and nitrogen tetroxide fuel tanks in the RCS pod dissipated the Scimitar missile's remaining energy, but the damage had already been done.

Without a space suit or pressurized cabin providing a protective layer of air pressure around their bodies, the temperature of the four remaining living crewmen's bodies bubbled the dissolved gases in their blood out of solution, exploding the blood vessels in their bodies. Within a few long, agonizing minutes, in the freezing-cold depths of space, Will, Sontag, Bayles, and Kelly boiled to death.

'*Will*.' Saint-Michael detached himself from the Velcro near the master SBR display and propelled himself over to the hatch leading to the main connecting tunnel. He hit the button to open the hatch: nothing. The special fire- and smoke-detection interlocks built into the hatch automatically closed and locked the hatch if fire or smoke was present.

Saint-Michael turned to Marks. 'Wayne, decompress the connecting tunnel down to the docking module. Moyer, can you hear me? What's your position?'

'I'm in engineering,' Moyer said, his laboured breathing obvious in the intercom transmission. 'I'm moving towards the connecting tunnel.'

'Copy.' Saint-Michael checked the status displays above the hatch. The FIRE warning light had gone out, and now a PRESS warning light had illuminated. 'I show the fire

243

out and the connecting tunnel depressurized to one-half atmosphere, Moyer. You're clear to activate the interlock bypass. Be sure to take a couple of POS packs with you in case they need them.'

'Roger. Opening the hatch now.' Moyer depressurized the engineering module, opened the hatch leading into the connecting tunnel, then closed and sealed the hatch behind him and moved towards the large airlock module.

It didn't take long for Moyer's report. 'Skipper?'

'Can you make it into *Enterprise?* How does it look?'

'I'm at the hatch to the airlock module. I've got a FIRE light on over the hatch – ' The transmission stopped.

'Moyer?' No reply. 'Moyer, report.'

'Skipper . . . my God . . . the whole airlock module is burned out. I can see two bodies in the airlock. They're both burned. I think it's Kelly and Bayles . . . I think they tried to get back to the station.'

'Moyer . . .' Saint-Michael paused, tried to calm himself, to think it through . . . A fire in the airlock, at least two dead . . . two dead outside . . . 'Moyer . . . Ted, we need you to inspect the *Enterprise*. It's our only chance to get out and be rescued. You've got to check out the shuttle.'

Moyer's voice was remarkably steady. 'Yes, sir. I understand. I'm ready.'

'Stand by. Depressurizing the airlock.' Saint-Michael turned to Marks, who activated the station's environmental control panel. Marks nodded back to the commander.

'Docking airlock module at five psi.'

'Roger,' Moyer replied, his voice hoarse but steady. He waited until the FIRE light over the entry hatch went out as the thinned atmosphere in the module extinguished any last remaining fires. 'Entering airlock.' In spite of all his efforts, Moyer could not avoid looking at the charred remnants of the men who had been his best friends for so many months. His stomach took over then . . .

Elektron One Spaceplane

From his vantage point high over Armstrong Space Station Alesander Govorov saw the bright flash and the explosion as the crew compartment of *Enterprise* was rent apart by Voloshin's missile. He saw the reflections of light in the cockpit windows and the rapidly spreading cloud of gases and debris around the shuttle.

'Elektron Two. Report.'

'Moving into position, Lead . . .'

'That explosion. What happened?'

A slight pause, then: 'Teaching the Americans a lesson, Lead. Before they can attempt another attack – '

Govorov pounded on an armrest in frustration, trying to vent his anger. Voloshin was a top-notch cosmonaut and atmospheric fighter pilot. He was also five years younger than Govorov, and like most young pilots displayed more than a little impetuousness. Govorov would have strong words with him later. For now . . . 'Follow your orders, Colonel. We have a job to do. I want it done as surgically as possible. We are not teachers or butchers.'

Govorov activated his laser designator and swept it across the centre beam of Armstrong Space Station. He had had only a few minutes to study the sketches of Armstrong Station before this flight, and those sketches had obviously been outdated. But some of the targets were obvious.

Such as space-based radar. One of the huge phased-array antennae had been sheared off, but its mate on the underside of the centre keel was still intact. Using the green-screen TV camera integral to the laser designator, he zoomed the picture in until the aiming reticle was centred on the huge control junction linking the radar antenna to the keel. Destroy this one junction box and the radar's steering, power and electronics went with it.

He activated the arming panel, placed one gloved finger around the stick-mounted trigger and gently squeezed.

Armstrong Space Station

'Cabin pressurization zero. Fire in middeck spread to upper deck. Big hole in forward bulkhead. Three . . . bodies in middeck . . . Davis, Wallis and Montgomery. Montgomery is still strapped into his chair. They . . . they didn't have a chance.'

Saint-Michael was leaning on an overhead handhold receiving Moyer's damage report of *Enterprise*. Seven dead on *Enterprise*. *Seven dead* . . .

'Can you find the damage, Ted?'

'Yes, sir. Huge explosion somewhere in the lower deck. Might be a fuel-cell rupture. There's a big hole in the forward bulkhead. Looks like it goes clear through.'

'Is it repairable?'

'I don't think so, not without a welder. Looks major.'

Enterprise was gone. 'Whatever the Russians shot at her, it was effective,' Saint-Michael said to no one in particular. 'Ted, report back here on the double.'

'What should I do with the *Enterprise* crew? Just leave them here – ?'

An ear-splitting sound like the crack of a whip echoed through the command module. The entire station began to vibrate. A warning message appeared on a screen surrounding the master SBR display.

'We've lost the entire number-two SBR array,' Jefferson said, scanning his instruments. 'No signal from that side at all.'

'They've started,' Walker said. 'They're not going to stop until they've sawed this station to pieces.'

'Moyer, get back here. All of you, report to the

246

lifeboat,' Saint-Michael ordered. 'I'll set the thrusters to deorbit the station; we'll time it so that – '

A voice broke in over stationwide intercom on the CALL position: 'Control, this is Skybolt. I think I have the laser operational again . . . I told you I was close to it . . .'

Saint-Michael was startled by Ann's voice. He paused half a second, then flipped a button on the communications panel. 'You *what*? Skybolt's working?'

'I need you to switch control of the SBR back to Skybolt from the Thor system. I can't do it back here. Switch the SBR over to – '

Ann was cut off by a loud bang and a warning horn blaring from the environmental control panel. 'Control junction on the starboard radiator system,' Jefferson said after checking the warning display. 'That's half our environmental system out.'

'We can't risk it,' Walker said. 'A few more shots like that and we've had it.' But Saint-Michael motioned him to be quiet.

'Ann, can Skybolt really be effective?'

'Baker error-trapped the system for me,' she said. 'I think the system will track targets now. I'm not sure if we trapped out the MHD ignition power problem, but – '

'We don't have the time, Jason,' Walker broke in, his voice tight. 'We've got to get to that lifeboat – '

Another loud bang; the station shuddered. The lights in the module dimmed for a moment and another environmental warning horn blared. The situation seemed too far gone to bother checking on the damage.

'Jason,' Ann said. 'You've got to do it now. It might already be too late . . .'

'All right, damn it. We'll try.' Walker was about to continue to protest but Saint-Michael rode over him: 'But not you five. I want *all* of you in the lifeboat. Immediately. I want you clear of the station when I fire the laser.'

'You can't do it alone,' Ann said. 'The laser has to be fired from the Skybolt module and I need someone to monitor the SBR from up there. We may also need to move the station. I've got to stay here in the Skybolt module . . .'

Saint-Michael hesitated again, but he knew there was no other option. This was her play. 'All right, Ann, stay in Skybolt. Walker, Marks, Jefferson, Moyer, report to the lifeboat.'

Several more loud bangs and a major fuel-cell explosion had occurred by the time Walker reported that all remaining crewmembers of the crippled space station were sealed aboard the lifeboat.

Saint-Michael received Walker's acknowledgement, wished the men luck, then lifted a large plastic cover on a yellow-and-black-striped button at his commander's station. Instantly a series of explosive activators and self-contained hydraulic thrusters pushed the lifeboat free of its moorings and propelled it away from the station. Well, maybe somebody would live to tell what had happened here. And why . . .

Elektron One Spaceplane

'Lead. Watch out. *Below you.*'

This time, Govorov easily spotted the object of Voloshin's warning. The long, silver, oblong vessel beneath the cargo-docking port jarred loose from its dock and moved quickly away from the station. In a few moments it was lost from view.

'The rescue craft,' Govorov radioed back to Voloshin. 'They've abandoned the station. It doesn't appear to have been jettisoned by accident.'

'Should we consider boarding Armstrong, Lead?'

'No, I still think they'll fire the station's thrusters by

remote control and deorbit the station. Stay in position and continue to pick off their station subsystems. If we have missiles left, we can target the pressurized modules.'

As he talked Govorov noticed the station start to slowly revolve and he expertly manoeuvred his Elektron to keep up with the station's slow rotation. It was not difficult to do, but the revolutions were a bit erratic – obviously the thrusters were no longer under computer control – and the station was revolving around the central keel, not along the pressurized module's axis.

Several pieces of the space-based radar array and other hunks of debris snapped off the keel and were sent crashing into the pressurized modules. It looked as if the station was tearing itself apart. They could save their Scimitar missiles for another sortie, Govorov decided.

Meanwhile, Voloshin had maintained his position in space and was watching the station revolve under him rather than trying to maintain his position in relation to it. The lowermost sections of the station were beginning to come into view now . . . He spotted the strange-looking device at the end of one of the lower pressurized modules – the Skybolt steerable mirror-housing. The mirror itself resembled a huge shiny bull's-eye.

As good a target as any, he thought as he activated his laser target designator . . .

Armstrong Space Station

'That's the best I can do, Ann,' Saint-Michael said over the intercom.

Talking was the least difficult thing to do with the POS mask on. The large curved glass faceplate distorted his vision and fogged up when he spoke or breathed hard. The hoses and interphone wires floating around his head obstructed his hands as well as his vision. Trying to

249

accomplish a task as delicate as steering an eight-hundred-ton space station was all but impossible.

'Can you hit the positive X axis just one shot?'

'It'll take me too long to fiddle with these controls,' Saint-Michael told her. 'If you can't do it, say so. We'll need time to get into spacesuits before the Russians blow this place.'

He was a prophet. A huge explosion rocked the station, sending him scrambling for another handhold. The impact felt as if it was only a few feet away. The lights flickered, steadied, flickered again, then blinked out. A few undamaged automatic power-failure lights snapped on. The station's spin seemed to accelerate, like a roller-coaster ride picking up speed at the crest of the incline . . .

'Ann . . .'

His call was drowned out by another explosion. His grip instinctively tightened on the ceiling handhold. But it was not another explosion on the keel. It was a loud, rhythmic drumming sound, reverberating through the entire station . . .

Elektron Two Spaceplane

The laser designator refused to lock on to the large round bull's-eye itself – some sort of mirror inside reflected the laser energy away instead of back to the spaceplane – so Voloshin had to target the housing of the bull's-eye instead. No problem there. The station was revolving at a perfect rate, not too fast, not too slow. In seconds the strange housing would be in range and he would send a Scimitar missile straight through –

Colonel Ivan Voloshin saw a flash of red light and felt suddenly hot, as though he'd been dunked in a tub of hot water. The feeling was so pleasant that he let the warmth wash over him like a gentle wave. He even had time to worry about something silly: that he had to urinate badly. Was it because his hand felt as if it had been stuck in a bucket of warm water? That was a favourite technique of his mother's, he remembered: before going to the store with him, she would always ask if he had to go to the bathroom, and he of course would always say no. Then she would tell him to wash his hands and make sure to use hot water, and all of a sudden he had to go . . .

Colonel Voloshin carried that pleasant childhood memory with him into oblivion as his Elektron spaceplane exploded into uncountable fiery pieces.

Elektron One Spaceplane

'Elektron Two. Report on that flash of light on your side.' Nothing, not even a hiss of static. 'Voloshin. Report.' Govorov had to jerk his lateral thrusters quickly to avoid a large piece of debris, probably from the crippled American space station, that had appeared out of nowhere.

He glanced at his spaceplane's fuel gauges. His wild escape manoeuvre and his present station-keeping pulses to maintain his position on the revolving space station were seriously depleting his supply. Wasting more precious fuel searching for Voloshin would probably push him right to the time-line. He no longer had the time to spend locating, identifying, targeting and shooting at individual station subsystems.

'Voloshin, fuel status.' No reply.

'Elektron Two, this is Elektron One. If you can hear me, break off your attack and join me one thousand metres above the station axis. Acknowledge.'

Still no reply. Things had just darkened for Govorov: low on fuel, lost wingman, only five Scimitar missiles remaining and their target not yet destroyed. He discontinued his station-keeping position and circled the wobbling space station. No sign of Voloshin. Instead of expending the energy to station-keep around Armstrong, Voloshin had probably stayed above the wreck and . . . been struck by a piece of debris . . .

Now only a few more minutes until the deorbit timeline limit. Govorov could not spend time targeting the station's subsystems. He manoeuvred to face the revolving station, activated his laser designator, and took aim on the station's pressurized modules . . .

Armstrong Space Station

'Ann? Can you hear me?'

The intercom had gone dead. The lights were completely out now except for one or two remaining emergency lights. He had no way of knowing if the SBR or Skybolt had worked. He didn't even know if she was still alive.

Suddenly Saint-Michael's huge sophisticated space station seemed like an orbiting mausoleum, and all he could think of was finding her and getting out of this dark, entombing crypt.

Ever since the command-module crewmembers had evacuated the station, Saint-Michael had been wearing the bottoms of his spacesuit. He now made his way over to where the upper half of his suit was floating, slipped into it and joined up the two halves. While breathing oxygen from his POS he connected his gloves, communications headset and helmet in place and activated his life-support backpack. He then moved towards the hatch leading to the connecting tunnel.

He passed through the connecting tunnel and had just entered the engineering module when the entire ceiling seemed to explode on top of him. He caught a glimpse of a projectile shooting straight through the module and crashing through the deck. The Velcro-covered floor seemed to erupt and buckle like hot tar. Sparks filled the cabin. A PRESS warning horn sounded, followed by a FIRE warning light that flickered on and off. In a few moments the only lights on in the module were the two warning lights, creating an eerie strobe-light effect. Saint-Michael had to overcome the sudden disorientation and will his legs to move. Carefully he climbed through the shards of metal, plastic, wiring and other debris now floating throughout the galley module and made his way to the hatch to the Skybolt module. Smoke began to billow through the galley as he peered through the thick Plexiglas window into the module . . .

Ann was suspended about a foot from the ceiling, her arms and legs dangling like a puppet's, her POS system hovering near her neck; Saint-Michael noted with relief that her mask was on. She was not moving. A few blobs of blood encircled her forehead.

He opened the hatch, closed it behind him and made sure the Skybolt module began to repressurize itself. When the pressure was nearly normal he slid down the narrow aisle between the massive electronics racks and pulled Ann to him. He quickly checked her POS connections and found them secure. Further examination revealed a large cut and a bump on her left temple.

He touched his helmet to her POS faceplate. 'Ann, can you hear me?'

After a long, tense wait he noticed her neck and face muscles jerk, and then her eyes opened.

'You all right?'

'I . . . I hit the instrument panel . . . big explosion . . .'

'We've got to get out of here. Can you move?' She nodded, reached out with a foot to find the floor was still several feet above the deck. 'I can move you, want to get you into a rescue ball.'

'Skybolt . . . it works, Jason. I fired . . . it fired . . .'

'Easy. Never mind Skybolt. Those spaceplanes are

shooting up the modules. This one could be next.' He unstowed a rescue ball from a yellow-painted container mounted on the module ceiling. 'Can you seal yourself up inside?'

She nodded weakly, her laboured breathing fogging the POS face mask.

Another explosion rocked the station, and with it the station's spin seemed drastically to change direction. Saint-Michael had to hold himself steady until his body caught up with the new wobble in the station, then he opened the rescue ball.

'Curl yourself up around the POS pack.' With his help she wrapped her arms and legs around the POS pack and lowered her chin on the top of it.

'Don't forget – seal up the ball when I cover you with it, and keep checking the pressure gauges. Keep the ball at seven psi with your POS if you need to.'

With Ann in a foetal curl a few feet from the deck, Saint-Michael enclosed her with the rescue ball and zipped it closed around her. He could feel her fumbling with the ziplock-style pressure seal inside as he steered her over to an oxygen panel in the Skybolt module, plugged an oxygen hose into a pressure fitting on the ball and began to inflate the rescue ball. He noted the ball's small pressure gauge steadily rise, pumped the ball up to one standard station atmosphere and checked the seal again. It looked like a big beach ball.

Leaving Ann connected to the oxygen fitting, he bypassed the safety interlocks and undogged the hatch leading to the engineering module. The galley had completely lost its pressurization, and judging from the occasional explosions he heard, the rest of the station was probably just as dead. Only one last possibility for survival. He disconnected Ann and her rescue ball from the oxygen supply and carried her through engineering and the connecting tunnel to the docking module –

Through the wireless intercom came a stronger, firmer voice: 'Jason . . . ?'

'How you doing?'

'I see stars every time I blink my eyes, and my head hurts like hell. Where are we going?'

'*Enterprise*.'

'Didn't the Russians attack it?'

'*Enterprise* won't get us home,' Saint-Michael said, opening the hatch to the docking module at the end of the main connecting tunnel, 'but maybe it can save us. My spacesuit has enough air and power for only seven hours. *Enterprise*, even damaged, has enough air and water for thirty days and it still has the thruster power to keep itself in orbit. It's our chance until – '

She wondered why Saint-Michael had suddenly stopped in midsentence. Then she understood . . . He had carried her into the docking module, where the burned-up bodies of Bayles and Kelly still lay. She almost imagined that she could see the crewmen trying to crawl back to Silver Tower for safety, chased by the wall of flame from *Enterprise*'s destroyed fuel cells . . .

Saint-Michael's eyes were drawn to the distorted faces, the sightless eye sockets, the scorched Space Command uniforms, the gnarled, bony hands. Gently lifting his precious cargo over the charred remains, he realized that the woman he carried in that plastic and canvas rescue ball could just as easily have been one of those bodies on the deck beneath him.

As he made his way down the docking tunnel into *Enterprise*'s air locks and into the shuttle itself he saw that the hungry fire had blackened everything.

'Are we in *Enterprise* yet?' Ann asked. He could not answer, and she did not press the question.

Montgomery, Wallis and Davis were still strapped in place, melted POS masks on their chests. The fuel-cell explosion in the lower deck storage area had torn apart

Enterprise's middeck. The air was filled with floating debris that would never settle, never fall.

'I'm going to leave you on the middeck,' Saint-Michael said. He let her float between the airlock hatch and the ladder leading to the upper deck, plugged the rescue ball into another oxygen supply hose and activated the oxygen supply. *Enterprise*'s oxygen supply, he noted with relief, still seemed operational. 'You can recharge your POS pack with the hose inside the ball. I've got to . . . to see if *Enterprise* is flyable.'

Ann did not acknowledge. She knew what he really had to do – move the bodies of Will and Sontag out of the charred cockpit.

Elektron One Spaceplane

One missile left.

General Alesander Govorov took every last second available to him before breaking off his systematic attack on the American space station. He had plunged Scimitar missiles into all but two of the station's eight pressurized modules, making sure that all within range were at least punctured. The two modules remaining were both on the outside of the revolving station and were therefore moving the fastest and were harder to hit, so he had targeted easier modules, the ones closest to the central keel, with his few remaining missiles.

Clouds of debris hovered everywhere around the torn-up space station. A sparking relay junction or fuel cell occasionally erupted somewhere on the keel, and pieces of the space-based radar, communications antennae and heat-exchange radiators fluttered in the weightlessness of space as if pushed by some strange, unearthly wind. The station's rotation was erratic. Originally centred directly along the central keel, now it was a wobbly, off-kilter eccentric spin. The space shuttle was still attached to the docking port, but the cockpit windows were dark and lifeless and the battered, ruptured nose ensured that the shuttle was useless.

Govorov had established contact with Soviet Space Defence Command shipborne tracking stations just after Voloshin had disappeared. The ground-tracking stations were not as sophisticated as the American Tracking and Data Relay Satellite system, TDRS, or WESTAR, so voice and data contact with small, low-powered craft such as the Elektrons was intermittent at best. They could not help with Voloshin's disappearance. They were also no help with a plan to dock with the Soviet Union's orbiting module. Besides, Govorov found he did not have the fuel to risk a long, protracted hunt for *Mir*, so his only option was to deorbit.

'Elektron One, this is Glowing Star Command Control.'

'Go ahead, Control.'

'Elektron One, we are recommending another orbit to align in the slot for deorbit.'

What? This was crazy . . . 'Control, I don't have the reserves for another two hours in orbit. I need to deorbit on this turn in the slot. What is your reason for the delay?'

'We are showing a possible obstruction within ten kilometres of your computed descent path, Elektron One.'

'An obstruction? Another spacecraft?'

'Affirmative. We predict that the object could be within five kilometres of you when you begin your deorbit burn. Please state your intentions.'

Govorov took a firm grip on his control stick. It seemed the fight was not over. 'Can you identify the object, Control? Its point of origin?'

'Negative. It is not a known orbiting spacecraft. It has

257

appeared in your vicinity within the hour, very close to your present flight path.'

'I want a vector towards the object, Control, immediately.'

'Say again, Elektron One.'

'I want a vector towards the object. I intend to engage the . . . obstruction.'

'Yes, sir. Stand by.' When Govorov received the range and vector coordinates to the subject, sweat broke out on his forehead. It had indeed moved very close to his flight path – dangerously close. It was less than thirty kilometres away, no more than five thousand metres from his own altitude.

He activated his laser designator and opened his cargo-weapons bay doors once again. He thought he knew what this oncoming spacecraft was. For several years the Americans had had a fighter-based antisatellite missile in operation. Fired from a high-performance F-15 fighter, the missile could seek out, track and destroy many kinds of Soviet satellites. Enhancements to the American ASAT weapon reportedly included a much higher altitude capability, a larger warhead and a more manoeuvrable design. It was supposed to be as long as a Thor space-based missile, perhaps ten to twelve metres long, but not as large in diameter and aerodynamically shaped for carriage under an F-15: like a flying torpedo.

It had to be an American retaliatory response. The Americans were mounting their ASAT attack at the one point in his mission when he was the most vulnerable: just before deorbit. Low on fuel, manoeuvring to enter the deorbit slot, busily inattentive to everything else – a perfect time to strike. Well, the Americans were going to get a surprise. He would be the hunter instead of the hunted . . .

'Elektron One, spacecraft is at your altitude, inside twenty kilometres, slow moving . . . now on collision

258

course. Repeat, collision course. You are on an intercept heading, twelve o'clock, now eighteen kilometres.'

Govorov put his laser viewfinder on widest possible arc . . . At the extreme magnification of the laser designator appeared a large, bright object moving across the stars at the very rim of the earth. As it came slowly into range he could make out its smooth, oblong shape and a circular device on one end – an active radar-homing device or infra-red seeker? At first he worried that he might be engaging someone's low-orbiting satellite, or perhaps even a reconnaissance 'ferret' satellite, but this thing was unlike any satellite he had ever seen. It was not pointed directly at him, but the laser rangefinder reported it was definitely moving closer. He placed the aiming reticle directly on the nose sensor of the weapon, received a READY beep in his headset, rechecked his weapons panel and at a range of fifteen kilometres fired his last Scimitar missile.

The hypervelocity missile tracked precisely on course, following the laser beam directly to its target. Govorov watched it all the way to impact. The missile plunged through the circular device at the nose of the spacecraft and sliced through it like it was paper. No explosion, only a puff of metal and some escaping gases. The spacecraft began to wobble a bit – obviously its directional control now destroyed – *but otherwise it continued on course*. Worried that the device wasn't yet dead – perhaps it had some sort of proximity detector or last-track-to-target capability – Govorov manoeuvred well above the space-craft, then rotated around so he could watch it. The device did not follow him. A few moments later it was safely underneath him, now noticeably wobbling. Its altitude had already decreased – it would not be long before it reentered the atmosphere.

There was no proximity explosion, no terminal or kamikaze detonation. Govorov reminded himself to inform Soviet intelligence of this new type of American spacecraft. He wanted more information on it, wanted to know what its capabilities were. Right now, though, he had to concentrate on the instructions the ground controllers were sending him in preparation for deorbit. As he manoeuvred to begin his deorbit burn, he thought that even with the unexplained loss of Voloshin and Elektron Two, the mission had been a success . . .

Space Shuttle *Enterprise*

Ann had been hanging in the same place on *Enterprise*'s charred middeck for an hour. Saint-Michael had passed by her several times during his grisly task, twice from the middeck level and a few times from the flight-deck level. A bad cramp had developed in her left thigh. She said nothing. Saint-Michael's job would be tough enough.

Finally she heard the more familiar whine of circulating pumps and electronic equipment, and through the vinyl and canvas surrounding her she could see a few lights wink on. Just the sound of *something* operating made her hope. . . . 'Jason?'

'Power is back on,' he said. 'We still have half our air supply left – two weeks' worth. Not as much as I'd hoped for but . . . plenty of thruster power, except for the nose RCS.'

'What about . . .'

'They're all in the docking module on the station.'

'I'm sorry, Jason.'

She could imagine the pain in his face. Armstrong Station, Skybolt, the Persian Gulf, Iran – even the earth seemed so very far away. What was left was a burned-out space shuttle. Seven charred bodies –

'I found something,' Saint-Michael said after a moment. 'There was an extra spacesuit on board that wasn't damaged in the fire. I can still pressurize *Enterprise*'s airlock. You'll be able to change in there.'

He carried her into the airlock and soon after that the airlock was pressurized enough so that she could unzip the rescue ball and climb out.

'Now I know what a butterfly feels like getting out of the cocoon.'

'I think you've set a record for sitting in a rescue ball.'

When he spoke she noticed that his breathing seemed to be a bit heavier, laboured. 'Matter of fact, I don't think a rescue ball has ever been used for real . . .'

'Jason, are you all right?'

He seemed not to have heard her. 'Hang on, I'm going to disconnect from Armstrong. The automatic system is out, I'll have to do a brute-force disconnect.' She felt a shudder and heard a loud metallic popping sound as *Enterprise* broke free of the docking clamps.

Five minutes later Ann emerged from the airlock in her spacesuit and made her way to the upper flight deck, where she found Saint-Michael strapped into the left-hand commander's seat punching instructions into the digital autopilot. He motioned for her to sit in the right-hand pilot's seat. As she passed the centre console and began strapping herself in, she looked out the front cockpit windows and caught a glimpse of Armstrong Station.

'My . . . God . . .'

'They did a job on her, that's for sure,' Saint-Michael said. 'They hit almost everything mounted on the keel – radiators, comm antennas, fuel cells, fuel storage . . . One of the SBR antennas seems okay. Good, they didn't get *everything*. But they put holes in all the modules except for the laser module and the MHD reactor. Looks like they got the Skybolt electronics module, too.'

'Well, there's a hole in it, but there may not be extensive damage – Jason, are you all right?'

Saint-Michael was shaking his head, blinking his eyes,

and licking moisture from his upper lip. 'I've got a headache, is all . . .'

'Check your oxygen.'

'I did,' but he rechecked it. 'On and one hundred per cent. Good blinker light.' He tried not to notice her worried look. 'I've got the lifeboat's rescue transponder tuned in but I'm not receiving it yet. We've got to try to contact someone on the ground to arrange a linkup with the lifeboat and send up a rescue craft.'

'Okay . . . just tell me what to do.'

'Switch over to air-to-ground frequency one and keep trying to raise someone. Try both air-to-ground channels. That Soviet missile ripped out most of the antennas on the bottom of the *Enterprise*, but the ones on top should work. I'll try the satellite network again.' The two worked apart for several minutes until a hiss of static and a faint, heavily accented voice made Ann jerk upright. 'Jason, I've got someone.'

'Which channel?'

'It's . . . air-to-ground two. I've got to set to UHF.' Saint-Michael quickly reset his comm switches to the same settings.

'Any station, any station. This is United States Space Shuttle *Enterprise*. Repeat, this is United States Space Shuttle *Enterprise*. Come in. Emergency. Over.'

Through waves of squeals and static they heard: 'Space Shuttle *Enterprise*, this is NASA Dakar. Repeat, this is NASA Dakar. We read you. Over.'

'Dakar, this is Lieutenant General Saint-Michael. Request a kilo-uniform-band satellite data link with any available network. This is an emergency. Over.'

'Copy, *Enterprise*,' came the heavy accent. 'Requesting Ku-band data link. Dakar is not Ku-band capable. Stand by.'

A few moments later a different controller came on,

this one with a definite American accent: 'General Saint-Michael, this is Kevin Roberts, GS-17, senior communications officer. Sorry, sir, but we weren't expecting a UHF call from any American spacecraft. We're triangulating your position. We should have a Ku-band link with TDRS East in a few minutes. Can you tell us the nature of your emergency?'

'Yeah . . . Armstrong Station has been attacked. Nine fatalities, repeat, nine fatalities. Shuttle *Enterprise* with two on board is damaged and unable to deorbit. Space-station lifeboat with four on board is in orbit. I want to join with the lifeboat and wait for rescue Shuttle sortie.'

'Copy, *Enterprise*.' The signal was getting stronger. '*Enterprise*, we have triangulated your position. TDRS link in progress. Stand by.'

'Have you heard anything from our lifeboat, Dakar?'

'Negative, *Enterprise*. We were pretty lucky to hear *you* in this backwater joint. I'll relay your query to Rota for immediate reply. Understand you want immediate linkup with the lifeboat.'

'Affirmative, Dakar. *Enterprise* standing by.'

The wait did not last long. '*Enterprise*, this is Falcon Control, Colorado Springs, on air-to-ground channel one. How do you hear?'

'Loud and clear, Control.' Saint-Michael switched his comm panel over from the direct line-of-sight UHF channel to the main TDRS system, which relayed voice and data through four geosynchronous satellites to a master ground station at White Sands, New Mexico. As if in reply, the computer monitor belonging to the shuttle's general navigation computer began to display several hundred lines of position and navigational update information. For the first time in hours Ann looked hopeful. 'Have you been informed of our situation?' Saint-Michael said.

'Affirmative, *Enterprise*. *Atlantis* will be airborne in twenty-four hours to retrieve you.'

'Copy.' Saint-Michael tried to sit back in his seat, appeared to be exercising his hands and arms inside his spacesuit. 'I'm receiving . . . receiving computer input.'

'Jason?' Ann said. He turned halfway towards her. 'I . . . I feel weak . . . my head . . . hurts bad.' And then he stopped moving.

'*Jason?*' She unstrapped and moved her helmet closer to his, staring into his face. Oh, God . . . it was twisted and contorted, obviously he was in great pain. 'Jason, can you hear me?'

'Get me . . . get me off the flight deck . . . *airlock* . . . max pressure, hurry.' One of his eyes rolled back up into his head, and he began to shiver, an oppressive, body-contorting shaking.

Ann moved free of the right seat and fumbled at his straps. 'Hurry, Ann . . . hurry for God's sake . . .'

'What is it, Jason? What's *wrong?*'

'Nitrogen . . . too much nitrogen . . . not enough prebreathing oxygen . . . oxygen . . .'

He began to fumble for his spacesuit's oxygen controls. 'Ann . . . suit pressure . . . increase my suit pressure . . .' She reached down to his spacesuit control panel on his chest and moved the suit pressurization selector to PRESS, increasing the suit's pressurization to maximum, nearly nine psi.

What had he said? Get him to the airlock. She lifted him up, an easy task in microgravity, brought him over to the ladder, then carried him down to the middeck level and into the airlock.

By this time he was unconscious. She sealed the airlock behind her and studied the airlock controls. She had received briefings on how to operate the shuttle airlock, but that was a long time ago . . . Finally she found the right switches and set the controls to maximum pressurization. While pure oxygen was being pumped into the chamber and the pressure slowly increased, she switched communication controls on her spacesuit chest panel from IC to A/G.

'Control, this is *Enterprise*. Emergency.'

'*Enterprise*, this is Falcon Control. Dr Page, is that you?'

'Yes. General Saint-Michael is unconscious. He passed out a few minutes ago complaining of extreme pain. We're in the shuttle's airlock with the controls set at emergency pressurization.'

'Copy, *Enterprise*. Stand by. We're calling the flight surgeon now.'

The wait was not long. '*Enterprise*, this is Doctor Haroki Matsui. Is General Saint-Michael wearing a spacesuit?'

'Yes.'

'Did he complete the proper prebreathing before wearing the suit?'

It was then she finally realized what was happening. Dysbarism, the bends, occurred when the body was moved from normal atmospheric pressure to an area of lower pressure. If the pressure was low enough – as it was when wearing a spacesuit – nitrogen in the bloodstream, which was denser than other dissolved gases, would bubble out of solution. Tiny bubbles of nitrogen would then float through the bloodstream, lodge in blood vessels or joints, grow larger and cause tremendous pain. In many cases nitrogen bubbles in the brain caused nitrogen narcosis, which made the victim feel angry or depressed or schizophrenic. Prebreathing pure oxygen before putting on a spacesuit was critical to flush nitrogen out of the bloodstream. The normal prebreathing time was two hours before exposure to a low-pressure regime. Ann had been spared the effects of dysbarism because the rescue ball had been inflated to one standard atmosphere with pure oxygen, which she had been breathing for hours. But Saint-Michael had been wearing a POS off and on before putting on his spacesuit, which did not provide enough time to flush the deadly nitrogen from his bloodstream. So he had had absolutely no protection. The physical labour he had done on Armstrong Station and on *Enterprise* only made things worse . . .

'No, I don't think he prebreathed properly,' Ann said, having sorted it out.

'Then it's dysbarism. You've done the only thing you can do for him now. Listen carefully. When the pressure in the chamber exceeds ten psi, the pressure in the airlock will be greater than his suit's pressure. Remove his helmet and yours. Monitor the airlock pressure to make sure it climbs to at least twenty psi in the emergency setting. If it falls below ten psi for any reason, seal him back up in his spacesuit and set his suit controls to EMER again. Understand?'

'Yes.'

'Keep him quiet and immobilized as much as possible. You'll be in there for at least twenty-four hours until the rescue craft reaches you. How do *you* feel?'

'I feel like I wish you guys were here now . . .'

'No pain in your joints? Lightheadedness? Nausea?'

'No, no . . .'

'You should be okay if you follow the same regime as prescribed for the general. We'll fly a hyperbaric chamber up with *Atlantis* in case he hasn't recovered by then.'

'Thanks,' Ann said. Then had a sudden thought: 'Can you retrieve the lifeboat with a hyperbaric chamber in the cargo bay? Will there be enough room?'

No reply.

'Control? Do you copy?'

'Falcon here, *Enterprise*.'

The controller had come back on the channel, and his

voice was muted, a monotone. Ann felt a shiver, antici-pating what was coming next.

'Dr Page, we lost contact with the lifeboat some hours ago. We were in radio contact with them shortly after separation from Armstrong Station. About a half-hour later they said they . . . sustained some damage. We lost control soon afterwards . . .'

'I see.' Her body went limp. 'Control, what sort of damage? What . . . happened?'

There was a moment's pause, then, 'The last survivor, Airman Moyer, said they were under attack from a Soviet spaceplane. It apparently fired a single missile into the lifeboat. They didn't have time to get into spacesuits before their air ran out. There were no survivors . . .'

8

Govorov entered the Stavka conference chambers, accepting congratulations as he made his way to his place at the conference table. He gave a polite bow, then sat down, giving the other Stavka members their cue to follow. The Soviet general secretary remained standing, saying, after the room had quieted, 'Welcome home, General Lieutenant Govorov. I'd like to ask you at this time to please step forward.'

Govorov got up, walked to the front of the room beside the general secretary, and stood to attention.

'Attention to orders,' Minister of Defence Czilikov said in a properly ringing voice. The members of the Stavka got to their feet. Czilikov held up an ornately lettered document and read: 'By order of the commander in chief of the military forces of the Union of Soviet Socialist Republics, Alesander Govorov is hereby promoted to the rank of *Marshal Aviatsii*, Soviet Space Defence Command, Troops of Air Defence, effective this date. The Politburo joins with the Kollegiya and the people of the Soviet Union in honouring the accomplishments of Comrade Marshal Alesander Govorov this day.'

The general secretary moved forward, unclipped Govorov's gold and black three-star shoulder boards and replaced them with shoulder boards carrying one large five-pointed star underneath a gold four-blade propeller. Govorov saluted the general secretary and turned again to face the members of the Stavka.

Czilikov called out, 'Present *arms*.' Govorov and the members of the Stavka saluted the hammer and sickle over the general secretary's right shoulder, then saluted Govorov, who returned their salute.

'Ready, *front*.' The Stavka members returned to attention and were motioned back to their seats. When the group was settled it was all the general secretary could do to keep to himself the Politburo's wanting to award Govorov the Order of Lenin for his exploits in space the previous month, but he couldn't reveal it – at least publicly – because of Govorov's accidental destruction of the American space station rescue craft, mistaking it for a missile. It was damned unfair but there it was: he could just imagine the international press screaming about the Russian barbarians. True, it was against policy to shoot down a rescue craft, but it hadn't been intentional . . . Well, perhaps later, after things had calmed down . . .

The general secretary nodded to Czilikov, who now took the podium beside him. 'I extend my personal congratulations to Marshal Govorov, to his staff, and to every member of his command. I also extend to him the condolences of a nation for the loss of his comrade and wingman, Colonel Ivan Voloshin, who will receive the Order of Lenin for his role in the attack on the American space station. His actions are worthy of praise in any world forum.' Followed by a short, polite round of applause. A few astute people understood that this was also a way of honouring Govorov . . . once removed.

As for the new Soviet hero, so far he had managed to keep his own feelings in check – about shooting down the American escape craft, mistaking it for a new weapon. But the honours and celebrations of his so-called great exploits by the general secretary – reflecting, of course, on the general secretary – were beginning to get to him. Yes, he was proud of what he *and* his men had accomplished. He believed in their mission, had fought for it, in

269

fact. But it wasn't so easy to shut out of his mind what those men in that helpless craft had suffered . . . Had death been instantaneous? Who knew? He had to hope so. If it had happened to him, he knew he would have wanted it swiftly. There was no special honour or nobility in suffering. That was for martyrs and sick would-be heroes. He hoped he was neither of these. Ever since it had happened – or rather, ever since he had found out what he had done – he had thought about a simpler time when air war was plane against plane . . . He had read avidly as a boy the accounts of wartime 'dog fights', as they were called, between airmen in World War I and in World War II. He had always preferred that one-on-one confrontation, between fighting men who depended on their own skill and managed to have some respect for each other. The notion might be romantic – heaven forbid that he should reveal that side of his character except to his wife in bed – but he still secretly longed for that kind of combat . . . All right, he chided himself, enough of this. You are also a patriot, and it's undermining your usefulness to go about wringing your hands . . .

'Now to the situation in the Persian Gulf region and the status of Operation Feather,' the general secretary said, breaking through Govorov's thoughts.

Czilikov recognized his cue. 'Yes sir, there is much to report. In the weeks since the destruction of the space station Armstrong, we have consolidated our forces in the region, strengthening not only the battlefield units in each tactical location but moving to unify the entire triple theatre forces – the Persian Gulf flotilla, the Iraqi unified command in the west, and the Iran-Afghanistan command in the east. Complete unification is still weeks away. Our movement has been delayed by American naval troops in the southern Persian Gulf whose efforts have been helped by seagoing and aviation forces.'

The general secretary cut in. 'I am beginning to believe,

270

Admiral Chercherovin, that our forces will never take control of the Persian Gulf. Your plan to attempt to move your flotilla southward to reinforce air strikes against Bandar-Abbas and the other southern Iran airfields seems to be stalled once again.'

'Both sides are at an impasse, sir,' the admiral said. 'The advantage is with the ground-based defenders. They can move air-to-air missile batteries into the area faster than we can move carrier-based fighter-bombers to the *Brezhnev*.'

'Supersonic low-altitude bombers from the Southern TVD have had success attacking Iranian forward enemy positions,' Chief Marshal Rhomerdunov said. 'Enemy advances to positions of tactical advantage have all been stopped or neutralized by small-scale Tu-26 bomber attacks. The Tupolev-26s are virtually invulnerable in the central mountains of Iran – '

'Yet the strikes are strategically useless,' the general secretary said. 'They are not offensive moves, they gain absolutely no ground nor do they advance the objectives of Operation Feather. They are mere *reactions* to American offensives. If this war of attrition goes on, sooner or later the side on the offensive will take control. That should be us. Must be. At present it clearly is not.'

The general secretary turned to Czilikov. 'The solution is obvious to *me*. Of the three tactical theatres of operation, the weakest is obviously the Persian Gulf flotilla. We have a limited number of vessels in the gulf with almost no hope of replenishment or reinforcement. We have only two sources of refuelling these vessels, and we are under constant danger from attack by Iranian guerrillas on the Kharg Island and Abadan petroleum shipping ports. The carrier *Brezhnev* must use so much of its own resources for fleet self-protection that it is all but useless as a support vessel for other land-based strikes . . . Admiral Chercherovin, what can you say to this? Your

271

efforts in securing the coastal ports in the initial phases of Feather were laudable, but now that big, expensive, vulnerable fleet stuck in the northern Persian Gulf is impotent. I just read a report that four Iranian madmen carrying bazookas in an inflatable rubber speedboat inflicted extensive damage on the cruiser *Dzerzhinsky* before being destroyed. Is that how the great Soviet navy is going to go down in defeat? By crazed Muslims in toy rafts?'

'No, sir – '

'The time has come, gentlemen, to make another decision on the direction of this conflict. There has been considerable pressure from the West to withdraw from Iran. The economic embargoes against our country are beginning to be felt. We are drawing off valuable resources to maintain an uneasy stalemate that threatens to blow up in our faces, while imports of needed raw materials and food are being halted.' He sat, slowly folded his hands, and let his eyes wander across the highly polished table surface. 'Perhaps we should withdraw from the region . . .'

No reaction from any of the civilian or military members of the Stavka – except for Govorov. He put both palms down on the table as if to push himself up to his feet in anger.

The general secretary was looking directly at Govorov when he made his quiet announcement, and a knowing smile creased his face.

'Or perhaps I should dismiss all of you – all except Marshal Govorov, of course – and replace you with a military council that will show some leadership, some initiative, some damned *backbone*.'

Czilikov's face turned crimson. The general secretary ignored it. 'I pledged to this council once that I will not become the first general secretary of the Soviet Union to retreat in the face of inferior forces and I will keep that promise. In fact, I will never retreat.'

He stood and pointed a finger at Govorov while addressing the other Stavka members. 'How can you sit here after we have just honoured such a soldier as Marshal Govorov, a man who risked his life to give this nation the advantage we so badly needed and wanted, and then, with your silence, acquiesce in a plan for surrender and withdrawal?'

'What would you have us suggest, sir?' Czilikov said. 'A nuclear strike against the *Nimitz* carrier group? An atomic cruise-missile strike against Bandar-Abbas? Perhaps a flight of SS-20 missiles targeted against the American fleet? We can blow the United Arab Emirates off the map and create a whole new Strait of Hormuz . . .'

The general secretary seemed to ignore the outburst. 'I want a plan for breaking this stalemate and accomplishing the goals of Operation Feather.' He turned to Govorov. 'Marshal Govorov, put yourself in the shoes of the minister of defence. What would you suggest?'

Govorov understood he was being wedged between the minister of defence and the general secretary. Some unfriendly space. Well, he'd made a career out of speaking his mind . . . 'I must agree with you, sir, it was important for our forces to halt their advances while the space station Armstrong was being neutralized. A stalemate-breaking offensive such as the one we were talking about could have triggered a larger response, perhaps even a theatre nuclear response from the Americans. Now Armstrong Station is no longer a threat. So I believe it is necessary to secure a strong foothold in the region, act quickly and decisively.' He paused for a breath – and to have his head handed to him – and when he saw they were waiting for more substance and less speech, pressed on . . . 'I would suggest that two major operations begin as soon as possible. The first would be designed to

273

break down the land-based emplacements of the American rapid deployment forces by overwhelming them, then attacking and occupying their positions; the second would be to command and hold the region from the Arabian Sea to the Strait of Hormuz and control the access to the gulf . . .' The silence was a vacuum to be filled, though he couldn't be sure it was because of approval or the opposite . . .

'I also propose a cruise-missile attack on Bandar-Abbas and the forces along the Persian Gulf. This type of attack was successful on the *Nimitz* fleet in the past. The Americans must engage the cruise missiles with their surface-to-air and air-to-air assets. The attack should be followed immediately by heavy bomber attacks, progressively moving to lighter fighter-bomber attacks until the targets can be occupied by paratroopers. In two days, if the strike is swift and devastating enough, we should be able to reoccupy Bandar-Abbas.'

Finally a reaction: a murmur of voices. Then Chief Marshal Yesimov of the air force said, 'It *can* be done. Our older Tupolev-95 turboprop bombers, which could not survive over the heavily defended coastal areas around Bandar-Abbas itself, can be armed with cruise missiles instead of gravity bombs. The bombers can launch their missiles from well inside occupied Iranian territory, far from the American surface-to-air missile emplacements. Each Tu-95 can carry four AS-6 missiles, which have twelve-hundred-kilogram high-explosive warheads.'

'How many Tu-95s could be made available?' Czilikov asked.

Yesimov shrugged. 'We can immediately send ten bombers to Tashkent, the largest available staging base in the region. Within a week I can dispatch our entire fleet of H-model bombers to Tashkent: forty planes, one hundred sixty cruise missiles.'

'Forty Tu-95 bombers in Tashkent would also be immediately noticed,' Chief Marshal Rhomerdunov, commander of the troops of Soviet air defence, noted. 'However, Zhukovsky Military Airfield at Tashkent can easily conceal the initial ten Tu-95 bombers.'

'I can have the bombers at Tashkent in less than a week,' Yesimov said. 'I will draft an operation plan for the bomber deployment right away.'

The general secretary was visibly pleased. 'Now you're beginning to sound like the men I thought I knew.' He turned to Govorov. 'Comrade Marshal, what is your second operation?'

The space defence commander looked around the conference table. 'The second operation is more crucial . . . It involves moving the *Arkhangel* battle group into the Gulf of Oman to oppose the American *Nimitz* battle group directly.'

This time a loud murmur of voices, clearly not approving.

'It's out of the question.' Admiral Chercherovin was first with the nay-saying. 'The *Arkhangel* is not just an aircraft carrier. It is our newest and best. It is more than just a vessel. It is our future . . .'

Czilikov took over. 'Marshal Govorov refers to the new class aircraft carrier in its final year of sea trials, sir. It is now on a shakedown patrol of the South China Sea, but has been based at Cam Ranh Bay Naval Base in Vietnam for the past month. The *Arkhangel* is the largest naval vessel ever built, much larger than the *Nimitz*. She carries eighty-five aircraft, all of them Sukhoi-27 air superiority and antimissile fighters. Even more, the *Arkhangel* comprises her own battle group. She uses two Kiev-class short-takeoff-and-landing aircraft carriers, the *Iev* and *Novorossiysk*, to carry the battle group's land-and-ship attack aircraft and a number of antisubmarine warfare helicopters. All together, the *Arkhangel* battle group contains one hundred thirty combat aircraft and helicopters.'

Czilikov watched the general secretary's eyes as he listened to the description of the *Arkhangel* and her battle group. He stopped abruptly. 'We cannot send the *Arkhangel*, sir. It is out of the question.'

'Back that up, Czilikov.'

'Sir, sending the *Arkhangel* battle group to the Persian Gulf area would be like . . . like the Americans landing a squadron of B-1 bombers in Berlin or London or Norway, or sailing the *Nimitz* into the Black Sea. It would be an overconcentration, and it would be a major escalation – '

'But the Americans have the *Nimitz* group in the Gulf of Oman,' the general secretary broke in, 'and that is a major force.'

'But, sir, the *Nimitz* balances the *Brezhnev* carrier force,' Czilikov said. 'Besides, the Americans have always had a major carrier group in that area. They are, frankly, the only nation that can afford to maintain such a force to just cruise around thousands of kilometres from home.'

'The *Arkhangel* would be as vulnerable as the *Brezhnev* is in the Persian Gulf,' Chercherovin now added.

'With *two carriers* as escorts?' the general secretary asked. 'If the world's largest carrier, protected by two other carriers and twenty surface combatants, is still vulnerable to attack in the open ocean we have no business building such vessels. No, I don't believe this *Arkhangel* force would be so vulnerable. This is no time for caution, Admiral. If we have the power, we should *act*. Immediately. I want this option explored. I want a briefing in three days, outlining all possible contingencies involved in moving the *Arkhangel* to the Gulf of Oman to oppose the *Nimitz*.' He paused, reconsidered, obviously caught up in the spectacle of what they were likely to achieve, or were trying to achieve . . . 'No, I want that report in forty-eight hours. And I want the *Arkhangel* group ready to sail one week after the plan is approved by the Politburo.'

Admiral Chercherovin, still the voice of can't-do, said: 'It is impossible to prepare an entire twenty-three-ship fleet for an extended deployment in – '

'Then put that in your report. But yours will not be the only opinion I rely on. You have a habit, Admiral, of telling me what is impossible. I am tired of military commanders telling me what is impossible.'

The general secretary turned to Govorov, who had returned to his seat. He motioned at him. 'Here is a young, innovative commander who *does* the impossible. You older officers would do well to take him as a model.'

The general secretary glanced at Czilikov, who was usually expected to come to the aid of his senior Stavka officers at moments like this. This time he did not. Unlike the admiral, he knew when to shut up. He did, though, look at Govorov, as much as to say, 'It's all yours, hero. And welcome to it . . .'

Bethesda Naval Hospital, Washington, DC

Jason Saint-Michael woke up to find a warm hand entwined in his. He tried to speak but all he could manage was a rasping croak. He squeezed the hand tight as he could, and after a moment felt a rustling near him.

'Jason?' The sound of her voice was life itself to him. He squeezed her hand again.

'Thank God . . .'

He opened his eyes but found his vision blurry, his eyelids heavy and oily feeling.

'What is it?' Another female voice.

'He's awake. He squeezed my hand.'

'Are you sure?' He felt a movement near him, then a

277

cold hand in place of the warm one. 'General Saint-Michael? Can you hear me?'

He still couldn't see anything but could feel her near him. He moved a hand up and out slowly across a warm metal railing and rested it back onto the warm hand that had been pushed out of the way.

'I'll get the doctor.' The cold hand went away. He was determined not to let go of the warm one again. 'Don't go.'

'I won't. I'm right here.'

'My . . . eyes . . . ?'

'Wait.' A moment later a dry towel was being wiped across his eyelids and forehead. He blinked a few more times, and the focus began to come back . . . He was in a small white . . . what else? . . . hospital room. Ann was standing over him, his hand in hers. Her small, angular face was surrounded by long, thick hair, the ponytail now wrapped back and looped over her right shoulder. He tried to squeeze her hand again but his strength had seemed to drain away. He did manage a sort of smile.

'You look good,' he said.

'I wish I could say the same of you,' she said, smiling too brightly. He ran a dry tongue across his lips. 'Get me some water, will you?'

She poured a cup of water and held it for him as he drank. The water backed up slightly in his throat, but he forced some more down and felt much better.

'God,' she said, 'now I know what it feels like to – ' Ann had lost her smile and was looking past him. He studied her face, realizing it was thinner than before. The tighter she held his hand, the softer her voice sounded, and the more worried he became.

Who knew how many things she was keeping from him, so he picked the easiest, he thought. 'How long have I been out?'

Her eyes came back to his. 'What do you mean . . . ?'

As soon as she said it, she realized how evasive it sounded.

He held up one of his hands, touching the palm with the index finger of his other. 'Smooth. I had callouses before.' He forced a bit of the old steel into his voice, which took more effort than he expected. 'Ann, *how long*?'

'Jason, you've been in a coma for three weeks. Almost four.'

It registered in his head, but he found he could dismiss it. It didn't matter how long he had been out – the important thing was, he was awake. He experimented with moving various muscle groups in his legs, arms and shoulders and found them all responsive but weak. 'All parts seem to be working. Hey, come on, I'm okay.' He put his left hand down on the bed and found he had enough strength to push himself upright a few inches. Even that slight movement cheered him. 'Damn, I feel like I've just wakened up from a long nap. I feel good, really. Four weeks racked out, huh? What else?'

She didn't get a chance to reply. A white-robed physician had come into the room and put himself between them.

'Welcome back, General. I'm Captain Matsui. You're at Bethesda Naval Hospital. How do you feel?'

'A little weak, thirsty, and hungry as hell.'

'Good, good and good. All good signs. No stiffness, headaches, chest pains?'

'No. Should there be?'

Matsui hesitated.

'Have a seat, doc. Let's have the gory details.'

Matsui sat down, the cheerful smile fading a bit.

'Give it to me straight. I can take it.'

'It's not quite that dramatic, General, although you did give us a few scares. You were suffering from dysbarism on board the *Enterprise*.'

'I suspected it.'

'You got hit with the worst form of it,' Matsui said. 'Cerebral dysbarism. Big bubbles of nitrogen lodged in your cerebral cortex. Lucky for you, Dr Page here got you into *Enterprise*'s airlock and back to normal atmospheric pressure so fast. You were probably only a few minutes from complete cerebral dysfunction.'

Saint-Michael looked at Ann. 'How about her, doc? Is she all right?'

'She was in no danger. She used her POS longer, she was in the properly inflated rescue ball long enough and stayed with you in the airlock for nearly thirty hours. She's in good condition. You, however, are not out of the woods. As a matter of fact, it's been touch-and-go until today. You never woke up, and you had seizures, possibly even a heart attack, as your body continued to throw off the nitrogen. You – '

'I think that's about all the gory details I care to hear right now, doc. Thing is I'm alive, I'm up and I'm ready to get out of here. I suppose you're going to say that's impossible.'

'On the contrary, General, let's run a few blood tests, an EKG and EEG. You may need some physical therapy – you were in space for several months and in a coma for four weeks, after all. I'd say your heart and other muscles at least need some toning up. If they all check out you'll be clear of here in a few days. Meantime, get some rest.' Matsui looked directly at Ann, then left with the nurse.

'Rest, hell,' Saint-Michael said after Matsui was out of earshot. 'That's their answer for everything. I've been in a damned coma for four weeks, what do I need more rest for?' He took Ann's hands in his again. 'I'm glad you're here. When I heard your voice I . . .' He stopped, looked at her uneasily.

She pretended not to notice. 'I've been here every day since we got back, Jason. I – '

He pulled her closer. 'This is no sudden conversion or

confession, Ann. It's just a chance to say what I've felt and covered up too long. It's as unprofessional as all get-out, but the fact is . . .'

'Same here, Jason.' And she leaned down and kissed him. 'Action speaks louder than words for the likes of us. Right?'

'Damn right . . . but I've got to know about the station. They didn't take it out altogether, did they?'

'. . . It's still up there. But – '

'Good. After Matsui and his buddies finish poking at me I'll get together with Jim Walker and the others and we'll draft a plan to get the station going again. We'll – ' He stopped short, she was looking away from him. 'What is it, Ann? Come on, level with me.'

She thought she'd never get it out . . . 'Walker and Jefferson and – '

'What about them?'

No reply.

'We got them into the lifeboat, Ann. I ejected them myself. They were all right before the attack . . .'

'There was an accident . . . At least they said it was an accident – '

'What the hell kind of accident? A malfunction? Did the lifeboat – ?'

'They're *dead*, Jason. One of the Russian spaceplanes shot it down, destroyed it.'

He said nothing.

'The Russian pilot has claimed he thought it was one of our antisatellite missiles. He said it came out of nowhere, no identification signals, no visible markings. He said it followed him just before he was going to deorbit, so he fired a missile at it . . . Walker, Marks and Jefferson died right away. Moyer was hurt during the depressurization. He lived long enough to report the attack and try to make repairs, but he couldn't, the damage was too bad and he couldn't get the others into rescue balls fast enough and . . . oh, God, Jason, they're all dead, everyone, *dead*.'

He took hold of her by the shoulders and held her close, feeling her body shake as the tears came. A nurse entered the room, left quickly. He just held her while she cried. And this was the woman he'd once thought was so cold and unemotional. Wrong again. Hell, he felt himself close to tears, thinking of those men in the lifeboat, dying in the frigid, airless void of space.

'When were they retrieved?'

She shook her head.

'They're *still* up there?'

'Shuttle flights have been suspended except for evacuation trips to the industrial space stations. The Soviets keep saying that the attack on the lifeboat was an accident, but their general secretary has also said that attacks on US military manned and unmanned spacecraft will continue – '

Anger was burning inside him, giving him strength to come to a sitting position in bed. 'They're just shooting at anything we launch? We can't let them get away with it – '

'You're not going to do anyone any good if you can hardly move, let alone get up and walk out of the hospital. Let the doctors examine you. I'll help with your therapy. Before you know it you'll be – '

'We've got to get organized – ' He was ignoring her now – 'Start holding planning sessions right here. I'll need you to set things up for me. By the time I get out of here – '

'*Whoa*. . .' a voice said behind Ann. 'I've just arrived, and you're leaving already?'

She turned, and Saint-Michael looked over her shoulder to find US Space Command head Martin Stuart coming through the door. Stuart had been appointed administrative head of Space Command after Saint-Michael had declared a preference for a duty assignment aboard Armstrong Space Station.

'How you feeling, General? I just got the word that you're back with us.'

'I'm feeling fine. Looks like I'll be checking out of here pretty quickly. Sir, I'd like to meet with you soon as possible about reactivating Armstrong.'

'Jason, easy,' Stuart said. He looked at Ann without really recognizing her. 'What about this man . . . Just woke up from three weeks in a coma and he's ready to blast off again – '

'I feel this is urgent, I think we – '

'Hold *on*, stop a minute. The doctors tell me you've got at least two weeks of rehabilitation here before you'll be able to get around the way you used to. After that the procedure is at least a month of convalescent leave. We can't even begin your medical reevaluation for duty until you come back from convalescent leave.'

'That can be moved up, sir. With the situation in the Persian Gulf, I know these things can be signed off in no time. I also know I'll be able to pass a flight physical after I get out of here. I guarantee it.'

'We can't afford to just "sign you off", Jason. You're an astronaut, not in undergraduate pilot training. We'll go through all the channels to make sure there's no doubt in anyone's mind about your fitness for duty. Then we'll see about getting you cleared for flight duty. It may take a few weeks to convene a flight evaluation board, maybe more. Then we – '

'So there's doubt in people's minds about my fitness for duty?'

'I didn't say that.' He looked again at Ann standing in the corner and finally recognized her. 'Did you tell him about the lifeboat, Page?'

'Yes, sir.'

283

'That should have waited for the debriefing. You – '

'I think it's a disgrace that it hasn't been retrieved yet,' Saint-Michael interrupted. 'I'd like to know the reason.'

Stuart's face tightened. 'All manned space flights have been postponed until the Russians' intentions are made clear. We – '

'I know a dozen shuttle and spaceplane pilots who'll volunteer to bring those men home.'

'That's really not relevant – '

'What the hell are we waiting for, General?' Saint-Michael was half-rising out of his bed. 'Are we waiting for the Russians to retrieve the lifeboat for us?'

'God*damn* it, Jason . . .' General Stuart looked over his shoulder at the closed door, at Ann, then back at Saint-Michael. 'You've been through a lot, General. Do yourself a favour and get some rest.' He fidgeted uneasily with his flight cap, nodded to Ann, and left the room.

When the door closed behind Stuart, Saint-Michael let his head fall back on to his pillow. 'Nice going, Jas,' he muttered to himself.

Ann sat at the edge of the bed. 'This has been tough for everyone, Jason. Most people feel like you do – that it's outrageous to have the bodies of thirteen scientists and technicians stranded in space. They're calling for a rescue mission and retaliation if the Russians try to stop them. The Russians are saying that we won't rescue anybody but will put nuclear weapons in orbit to force them to withdraw from the Persian Gulf. They're threatening to escalate the war in the Middle East if we try sending anything up to the space station.'

Saint-Michael rubbed his temples. 'I never felt so damn powerless before. What are the Russians doing in the Gulf? Have they occupied Iran yet?'

'Things are still pretty much the same. Iran is divided in two. The Russians control the northern two-thirds of the Persian Gulf. Our rapid deployment force and the navy control the Strait of Hormuz. Each side makes several raids a week trying to get a toehold in the region but they're always pushed back. A stalemate . . .'

He shook his head. 'Something's bound to crack pretty soon.' He reached to pour himself another cup of water. 'Either we both move to neutral corners pretty damn quick or someone's going to come out swinging. I just hope we can control the escalation when it happens . . .'

'I haven't been given a full intelligence briefing,' Ann said, 'but we hear on the news it's getting harder and harder for the Russian naval forces to get fuel from their gulf suppliers. They must be getting pretty desperate for fuel if they. . .'

She stopped and turned back towards Saint-Michael. He was holding trembling hands tightly over his face, and he was jerking up from the waist as if he was doing short situps. His breath came out in low, guttural grunts.

'Jason? *Jason*.'

'Ann . . . oh, God, I'm starting to feel it again . . .'

She sat down on the bed beside him, reached out to him and held his trembling body against hers. He shivered again, she could feel tears on her neck. The last barrier had been broken. She reached for the nurse's call button, pressed it, then wrapped her arms around him as convulsions shook his body.

The US Defense Intelligence Agency, Five Days Later

Jackson Collins, as the new director of the KH-14 Block Three digital photo imagery division of the Defense Intelligence Agency, did not need to schedule an appointment in advance to see the director, but he had never taken advantage of his new position or his new privileges – until now. He came into George Sahl's office first thing Monday morning with a locked carrying case. Sahl was dictating a letter into his computer terminal when Collins appeared, set his case down on the director's desk and began to fumble with the combination lock's thumbwheels.

'C'mon, Jackson,' Sahl said, hitting the PAUSE button on his voice-recognition computer's microphone. 'I haven't even finished my first cup of coffee.'

Collins stopped. With him, even a lack of movement was significant. 'Mr Sahl, you told me that if I had anything significant from my section to bring it to you immediately.'

Sahl sighed. 'Yes.'

'No matter what.'

'Yes.'

'Did you mean it, or was that just to make me feel important?'

Sahl rolled his eyes. 'Well, dammit, let's see what you got. Move it.'

'Yes sir.' Collins had the locks on the chart case open in a few moments and took out several digital satellite photos.

'Aha. We're back to interpreting scrub photos again, Jackson?'

'Marginally scrub. I've applied the new set of guidelines to these photos and – '

'Those new guidelines – *your* new set of guidelines, the ones you forced on my section – haven't been approved yet.'

'They will be. Never mind that, sir,' Collins went on. 'Recognize this location?'

'Sure. What else would Jackson Collins, boy genius, bring me? Scrub photos of Nikolai Zhukovsky Airfield. The same big Condor hangars.'

'Except there are now twelve hangars there. And ten are occupied.'

'By . . . ?'

Collins displayed another photo, an enlargement of a thermal imagery photo of the tarmac just outside one of the hangars. 'Tyre tracks. Aircraft tyre tracks.'

'I know *you* know why this isn't conclusive evidence . . .' Sahl began.

'All right, tyre tracks can be too easily faked. But if you're moving aircraft, men and supplies in and out of Tashkent all day, every day, in support of a major offensive in the Persian Gulf, I'm betting you don't have time to doctor ten major hangars for a satellite overflight.'

'Still . . .'

'Sir, I've been watching these hangars since before Feather started. I've seen all sorts of aircraft go in and out of these hangars. I've measured the tracks on every one, and in every case my identification has been confirmed by some other source.'

Sahl looked at Collins. 'With any other interpreter I'd say get out of my office until you have something concrete. But I know better now. I suppose you've measured these tracks, measured the tyres and fit them to a particular aircraft?'

'Yes.'

'And that was . . . ?'

'H-model Bear bombers.'

Sahl took a closer look at the photo. 'Well, that *is* interesting. They're a long way from home.'

'I haven't found exactly where they're from – I think Vinnica Airbase southwest of Kiev is missing a half-dozen at least – but I've been checking on something even more interesting.' Collins pulled up a chair in front of Sahl's desk. 'Tashkent has been the major staging area for most of the strategic aircraft – bombers and large transports – involved with Operation Feather, right?'

'Go ahead.'

'I think the Russians are putting AS-6 cruise missiles on those Bears parked at Tashkent.'

Sahl frowned as he picked up the digital photographs of the large 'satellite bluff' hangars. 'Now how the hell can you tell that from these photos?'

'By this.' Collins retrieved another photo from his carrying case. This one was a more conventional optical satellite photograph taken several months earlier of a completely different, much larger military airbase. 'While I was checking on things, trying to score a few points with the boss, I did some note taking on strategic cruise missiles. I wrote down every detail I could find on AS-6 and AS-4 cruise-missile operations. Of course, one of the biggest Bear bomber bases is Murmansk, so I concentrated my search there, took a lot of notes on the cruise missiles based with the Bear Gs and Hs, with particular emphasis on the support vehicles.'

'This story, I know, must have a point. Please get to it.'

'I'm getting there, sir. Here's the scoop. The AS-6 missile uses kerosene liquid-fuelled rocket engines, with nitric acid as the catalyst. Dangerous stuff. What's more, the stuff has got to be pumped into the missile's tanks under pressure to facilitate airborne ignition. They've built a special truck to do this. Here's a picture of one of those trucks.'

Sahl, looking at it under a pair of stereo magnifiers, thought it resembled a huge square-nosed firetruck with a distinctive set of silverized tanks on either side. The photo even showed a crew of four men in silver-coloured fire suits working around the truck. Sahl checked the date-time stamp on the photo – it was recent. 'Now if you could only find one of those trucks in Tashkent . . .'

'Ask and ye shall receive.' Collins pulled the last photo out of his case. 'Taken yesterday.'

It was one of the most unusual photos Sahl had ever seen. It showed, quite clearly, one of the cruise-missile fuel trucks being towed by a large tractor-trailer truck after it had apparently struck an aircraft tow-bar on a flight-line access road. Sahl thought of the luck element that was required in this business of reconnaissance photography: a few seconds more or less and the accident never would have occurred or the KH-14 satellite never would have spotted the truck. A few more minutes and the wreck would have been towed away without a trace and they might never have known for sure about the cruise missiles.

'Impressive, Collins. They've got AS-6 or AS-4 cruise missiles in Tashkent.'

'Probably AS-6s. They stopped production on AS-4s back in 1989 in favour of the AS-6.'

'Those things could be real trouble – correct me if I'm wrong. The AS-6 has both a ground and ship attack version. Either a three-thousand-pound high-explosive warhead – '

'Or a two-hundred-kiloton nuclear warhead,' Collins said. 'Fairly long range on a normal launch profile – they could probably launch at high altitude as far north as Shiraz in central Iran, well out of range of our Patriot, Hawk and RAM surface-to-air missile sites, and hit the strait. If they overwhelm our perimeter defence they could launch attacks against the fleet in the Gulf of Oman.'

Sahl did not have to think very long to reach a decision. 'I need an analysis brief by one o'clock for the afternoon meeting . . .' But Collins was already opening his photo case again, and a red-covered folder with a security strip-seal dropped on to Sahl's desk.

'Jesus, Collins, am I going to have to spend the rest of my four years to retirement looking over my shoulder to see when you're going to bury me, like you did Barnes?'

'Nah,' Collins said. 'I got faith, sir . . . I figure a smart man like you is going to *help* me move on up.'

Sahl smiled, opening the intelligence brief. 'If you can't beat 'em, help 'em beat up on someone else.'

It was a sight Ann Page had never wanted to see.

A whole section of the hospital's intensive-care ward had been occupied by a portable hyperbaric 'altitude' chamber. Jason Saint-Michael lay inside the chamber on a hard plastic table. Ann winced as she looked at his inert form – he looked even more emaciated, more drawn. Electrocardiogram and electroencephalogram leads were attached to his body, running to terminals outside the chamber, where technicians and doctors studied the sensor readouts.

'His heart seems normal,' Doctor Matsui said as he rechecked the EKG paper strip. 'Strong as a horse, as a matter of fact. He's in excellent condition.' He shook his head. 'Except for the . . . other thing.'

'What happened?' Ann asked.

'The same thing he's been experiencing during his comatose state. His body is still throwing off the nitrogen. Nitrogen is absorbed easily in the soft tissues of the body – that's why it accumulates in the joints, causing the bends. The general's case is more serious. The nitrogen accumulated in his brain, causing his blackouts, seizures and the pain. He probably absorbed a lot into his brain tissue, and in normal atmospheric pressure the nitrogen bubbles slowly work their way out of the tissue and into his bloodstream, in his nerve centres.'

'But all this happened a month ago,' Ann said. 'He came out of the coma. Why is he still having these seizures?'

'I don't know . . . Obviously his body is still being affected by the nitrogen bubbles in his system, or perhaps there was some sort of neural, vascular or chemical damage. I'm afraid we don't know very much about cerebral dysbarism – fact is, we don't know much about anything when it comes to the brain or the nervous system. But there are a few things I do know. First, General Saint-Michael is no longer on flight status. His condition is obviously disqualifying. I'll also have to recommend that he be relieved of duties as commander of Armstrong Space Station or what's left of it.'

Ann had to turn away. What she was hearing, whether Matsui knew it or not, was in effect a death sentence. *No*, damn it. That wasn't going to happen. To hell with the doctors. Matsui said he didn't know much. Good, that put them all even – starting from scratch. She'd take those odds.

9

Topography and climatology tactical situation briefings
said it was a region dry with a subtropical climate, but no
one could convince First Lieutenant Jeremy Ledbetter of
that. The twenty-two-year-old army officer, fresh out of
ROTC at Penn State University and speciality training at
Fort Devins, Massachusetts, was packed in a layer of
'Chinese underwater' thermal-quilted underclothes
beneath his desert grey fatigues, which themselves were
covered by a reinforced plastic poncho. In the predawn
hours in central Iran, even in mid-August, he was freezing
his butt off. On top of that, Iran, which rarely got any
rain during the summer, was experiencing a real Kansas-
style gully-washer.

As Ledbetter surveyed his encampment he felt as if he
was in charge of the entire defence of Iran. In fact he was
in command of a combined air defence battery, a CAB: a
MIM-104 Patriot and a MIM-23 I-Hawk missile battery
just outside the sleepy little peat-farming town of Robat
in the Meydan Valley of Iran. He commanded an eighty-
man detachment of US Rapid Deployment Force soldiers
and at least ten million dollars' worth of high-tech surface-
to-air missiles. His three Patriot high-altitude missiles and
eighteen I-Hawk low-to-medium-altitude missiles virtually sealed off the entire Meydan Valley to unidentified
aircraft for one hundred miles in any direction.

Ledbetter's CAB was also the 'snare,' the choke-point
between two other Patriot sites on either side of the

Meydan Valley. Enemy aircraft would circumnavigate the Patriot missile batteries at Anar and Arsenjan. That would force them down the Meydan Valley and right into Ledbetter's all-altitude-capable missiles. Once enemy aircraft were caught in the narrow valley, there was no escape for them except to try to outrun or outmanoeuvre the oncoming missiles – both hugely difficult feats.

The proof was there for all to see: a Soviet Backfire-B supersonic bomber had been caught in the 'snare' and had tried to use its speed to outrun one of the I-Hawk missiles. Unfortunately for the Backfire's pilot, in his hurry to escape attack he had been diverted from his job as a pilot. His Backfire had splattered all up and across the western wall of the Jebval Barez Mountains to the east of Robat, travelling at least at Mach one at three hundred feet off the valley floor. Ledbetter's Patriot and Hawk missile radars could still pick up the wreckage of the crash on the mountainside. No doubt other Soviet bombers' radar could detect it too.

Well, let it be a warning, Ledbetter thought, as he sipped coffee from a metal cup. The message: don't mess with the Three-Thirty-Fifth.

He had got up early this morning to check on his perimeter security units. His rapid deployment force unit had been supplemented with Iranian Revolutionary Guard regulars, some of the toughest and meanest men he had ever met up with. The problem was that the Iranians had no idea how to fire a Patriot or Hawk missile, even though Iran had had Hawk missiles for years, so Ledbetter used the Iranians as security guards. But being a mere watchdog was way beneath a Muslim revolutionary guard – in centuries past guard duties had always been left to slaves, peasants, conquered heathens or eunuchs – and so arguments would often break out between Ledbetter's people and Iranians. Ledbetter's surprise inspections would usually help keep conflicts down and morale and watchfulness high, but he couldn't really blame the eager Iranian soldiers for grabbing an American rifle and charging Soviet-occupied Shiraz or Tehran. Even so, he tried to convince them that their responsibility was here.

Ledbetter cruised by the first sergeant's tent just as his unit's senior NCO, Sergeant Plutarsky, was emerging from his tent. 'Good timing, Sergeant.'

'Heard you coming, sir.' Plutarsky threw his young commander a salute. The two men, the veteran NCO and the green officer, had somehow become friends after arriving at one of the hottest hot-spots in the Iran conflict. They complemented each other well: Ledbetter knew surface-to-air missiles and electronics; Plutarsky knew his men. Seldom did the two cross, which seemed to make the unit hum along. Ledbetter didn't mess with the men; Plutarsky didn't mess with the missiles.

Ledbetter nodded in return at Plutarsky; neither stood for much formality. 'I want to take a look at Whiskey Three first.' Whiskey Three, or West Three, was one of the posts guarding the main long-range search radar.

'You mean you want to take a look at Shurab,' Plutarsky said. 'Me too. Mister Shurab has had a stick up his rear ever since he's been here. He's got all the rest of the Iranians kowtowing to him.'

'He says he's from the family of one of the religious members of Alientar's government, or something like that,' Ledbetter said. 'But you're right. He acts as if this whole war is being fought for his benefit.'

Along the way, they stopped and inspected several of the other components of the CAB. To reduce the risk of one bomb taking out the entire missile system, the individual units of each missile system were widely separated. The control centre for the whole CAB was in a trailer that had been buried underground to protect it from attack; that was where Ledbetter slept. To help secure the site, most of the men slept at their posts. The main

Patriot phased-array radar was on a hill overlooking the valley about five miles away.

In the centre of the encampment Ledbetter's CAB had a standard search-radar system that provided long-range surveillance of the area. Although the search radar was not tied into any of the surface-to-air missiles, the radar could detect aircraft approaching the area up to two hundred miles away, from ground level to well above fifty thousand feet, and the search radar could 'slave' the other acquisition, tracking and uplink radars with it to help the smaller radars find targets for their missiles.

The search radar had been hoisted on top of an old rusted oil derrick about thirty feet above ground, along with a satellite communications dish and other shorter-range radio antennae. Nearby was a circular sandbag bunker with another set of acquisition radars inside, and a hundred feet beyond was the first of eight four-missile Patriot missile launchers, also in a sandbag bunker. Ledbetter could just barely make out the outline of the derrick on the horizon as he blew warm air onto his hands while they approached the derrick.

'Cold, Sarge?'

'I'm from Florida, sir,' Plutarsky said. 'Anything below sixty degrees is the next Ice Age to me.'

At the derrick a few minutes later, they heard a rustle of footsteps and the unmistakable sound of an M-16 rifle on its web sling. 'Stop,' a voice called out, except the heavy Maine accent sounded more like, 'Stawp. Who gowahs theah?'

Plutarsky was chuckling. 'These Iranians speak better English than you do, Cooper.'

They heard the rifle clattering back on to the technician's shoulder. 'Good moawnin', First Sahgeant. Up early, ayuh?'

'Me and the lieutenant are touring the grounds. We're thinking of building a Hilton here.'

295

'A Hilton. That's a *good* one.'

'Where's the ragheads?' Plutarsky got a disapproving look from Ledbetter.

'Around heah somewheahs, Sahge,' Cooper replied. 'They's quiet like mice, don't ya know.'

'Shurab too?'

'King Shurab says he switched shifts with some of his pals.'

'Again?' Ledbetter said. 'I don't think he pulls any guard duty.'

'I know damned well he don't,' Plutarsky agreed. 'When I find him I'm going to straighten his ass out.'

'Better take it easy, Sarge,' Ledbetter said. 'The Iranians are at least technically our allies, and Shurab is an allied officer. Let them run their detachment the way they want it. If he's doing something that affects security, then *I* will put the hammer down. Emphasis on the "I".'

'Yes, sir.'

They left Cooper to guard the oil derrick and continued on. After a few moments they came across a circle of five Iranian guards armed with M-16 rifles. All five came to attention, and one saluted Ledbetter.

'Good morning to you, Commander,' he said. Ledbetter returned his salute.

'Where's First Captain Shurab?' Ledbetter asked.

'He is at the guard house, Commander.'

'He's supposed to be on patrol.'

The Iranians looked puzzled, as if they didn't understand. Plutarsky then stepped forward. 'Shurab, dammit. Patrol. He has patrol.'

'No patrol,' one of the other revolutionary guards said. 'I take patrol. I patrol.'

'You're Khaleir, aren't you? Khaleir?' The soldier nodded.

'You had the morning patrol. Shurab has the night patrol.'

'No. I take.' He bent to listen to one of his comrades, then said in carefully accented English, 'I switch.'

'Get Shurab. Bring him here,' Plutarsky said. The soldiers stood around, only superficially trying to act as if they didn't understand but obviously trying to decide what to do.

'*I* want Shurab here,' Ledbetter said.

'Yes, sir,' a voice said. Out of the darkness walked a tall, mustachioed man, unshaven, dressed in a clean desert grey combat jacket and immaculately spit-shined boots, and smoking a cigarette. He was easily the best-groomed man in camp – even the mud seemed to refuse to stick to his boots. His well-tended veneer only served to increase Plutarsky's foul mood.

'First Captain Shurab, sir, you are supposed to be leading the northern guard patrol,' Plutarsky said. 'Why aren't you at your post?'

'I switch with Abdul, sir,' Shurab said to Ledbetter, pointedly ignoring Plutarsky.

'You can't switch with a man who has already pulled one twelve-hour patrol,' Ledbetter told him. 'I won't have tired guards on duty, especially at night. We're only a few miles from Soviet-held territory – '

'I spit on the Soviets, sir . . .'

'Good for you.' Ledbetter turned to Plutarsky. 'First Captain Shurab will lead the remainder of the night patrol and the whole morning patrol. He is not authorized a replacement under any circumstances. If he is not at his post as ordered he will be reported to the revolutionary guard commandant at Bandar-Abbas for dereliction of duty. See to it, Sergeant.'

'Yes, sir.' Ledbetter walked off towards the oil derrick. Plutarsky moved forward towards Shurab. 'Do you understand your orders, sir?'

'I will not be addressed by a subordinate – '

'I don't give a flying – ' But Shurab had turned his back

on Plutarsky and was walking towards the guard house. At which point Plutarsky blew a fuse. He reached out, grabbed Shurab by the collar from behind and yanked him up and back so that he landed on his rear end. This time the mud was sticking – all over Shurab's starched fatigues.

Shurab, appropriately enough, swore loudly in Farsi and shouted an order. All five of the Iranian guards moved towards Plutarsky, but before they could take two steps towards him Plutarsky's nine-millimetre Beretta service pistol appeared in his hand.

'One more step and fancypants gets a hole in his starched shirt.' Everyone then froze . . . until abruptly Shurab laughed, stood up and brushed himself off.

'My apology, Sergeant,' Shurab said, smiling. 'I will go.' He ordered his men to back away, and Shurab headed towards the northern guard post. With Plutarsky still watching him, pistol drawn, Shurab suddenly stopped and turned. 'Touching a superior is a capital offence in my country, Sergeant. And you are in my country.'

'I'm not impressed by you or your damned country . . .'

Shurab waved gaily at Plutarsky, turned and left. Plutarsky held the pistol in his direction until he was well out of sight, then holstered it and trotted back to the oil derrick, feeling he had lost for winning.

'I heard some shouts back there,' Ledbetter told Plutarsky when they met a few minutes later. The lieutenant was absently staring up at the revolving antenna belonging to the main search radar. 'Problems?'

'Nothing I can't handle, sir.' Plutarsky followed his young commander's gaze up to the top of the derrick then to L-band radar bunker nearby, but all he noted was a slight squeak in the massive bearings supporting the search antenna every time the green mesh dish swung towards the north. 'I'll get someone on those bearings, too . . .'

But Ledbetter wasn't listening. Suddenly, without a word, he took off at a fast trot towards the underground command trailer.

'Sir . . .?' Plutarsky had to run to catch up to the lieutenant's long-legged lope. 'Something wrong, sir?'

'Didn't you hear it, Sergeant?'

'Hear what? The bearings . . .?'

'The L-band pulse-acquisition radar,' Ledbetter said. 'They turned the L-band radar on.'

'I didn't hear anything,' Plutarsky said. Ledbetter was speeding up, and Plutarsky had to hustle to keep pace with him. 'How can you hear a radar?'

'The L-band radar in the bunker is slaved to the search radar,' Ledbetter told him. 'Every time the bearing in the search radar squeaked at the ten o'clock position I could hear the L-band radar move. I-Hawk's been activated.'

'Well, shouldn't we have got a – ?'

Just then Ledbetter's walkie-talkie beeped. Ledbetter already had it in his hand and didn't wait for the message.

'Ledbetter here. Sound air-attack warning. I'm on my way.' Both he and Plutarsky were back to the underground trailer by the time the first air raid warning horns began blaring.

'I'll make the rounds of the launchers,' Plutarsky called out as Ledbetter hurried for the dirt stairs leading down to the trailer.

'Better clear the Patriot launchers first,' was the last thing he heard Ledbetter say as he disappeared underground.

The trailer smelled musty. Three radar operators sat on the right side of the trailer at bare control consoles, and a long row of power transformers, electronics racks and circuit breakers lined the left side. The only light in the trailer came from the radar screens and the control panels.

Just as Ledbetter entered he heard one of the operators on the combined UHF-VHF radio calling: 'Unidentified aircraft one hundred miles north of Robat, heading one-six-zero, altitude two-zero thousand, authenticate Delta Sierra. Over.' The operator had a finger on a switch that would broadcast a computer-synthesized warning message in Russian and in Farsi, but Ledbetter put a hand on his shoulder.

'No need to give them more than one chance to identify themselves, Sergeant. If they don't have an IFF transponder or didn't call ahead of time it's a bad guy.'

'Yes, sir.'

'Tracking six, repeat six inbounds,' the search-radar operator said. 'They look like they're almost line abreast. Slightly staggered altitudes . . . now showing eight aircraft, sir, eight inbounds.'

'Range?'

'Approaching max Patriot range in about one minute.'

'Patriot has the inbounds, sir,' one of the other radar controllers reported.

'I-Hawk has the bogeys,' the third put in.

'All batteries clear to launch at optimum range,' Ledbetter said. 'I need a report on – '

'Inbounds turning, sir,' from the search-radar operator. 'All inbounds turning right towards . . . Now I have several high-speed inbounds, altitude three-zero thousand and climbing, speed . . . speed well over the Mach and accelerating. Heading towards us . . .'

Ledbetter went over to the search-radar scope. The picture showed the whole scene in sharp relief. The classic Kingfish Soviet cruise-missile launch and flight profile was being represented just like a training simulation: the big heavy launch platform, probably Tr-95 Bear or Tu-16 Badger strategic bombers; the launch just before the bombers reached the engagement circle for the long-range Patriot missiles and the escape turn; the missiles in their high-speed climb to supersonic cruise altitude. In less than a minute they'd be bearing down on their target: the Americans' SAM emplacements.

'Radio warning message in the blind on all tactical and emergency frequencies and on FLTSATCOM,' Ledbetter ordered. 'Three-thirty-fifth CAB under attack; attack profile shows Soviet missile attack. Send it.'

'Yes, sir.' There was a one-minute pause, with the search-radar operators calling off the range to the nearest missile.

'Message acknowledged on FLTSATCOM. I'm receiving warning messages from the other sites.'

'Missiles now climbing above five-zero thousand feet, speed approximately Mach two, range fifteen miles . . . Altitude decreasing now . . . Missiles dropping rapidly . . . Range ten miles . . . nine . . . eight . . . seven . . .'

Sergeant Plutarsky had just received a ready-for-action report from the second Patriot missile launcher bunker he visited when the first of the high-altitude Patriot missiles cooked off, the sudden glare and awful ear-shattering sound of the Thiokol solid-fuel motor almost knocking Plutarsky off his feet. Two more missiles launched in rapid succession, along with missiles at other bunkers. Most of the missiles were headed almost straight up. The air was quickly filled with hot, acrid-tasting smoke.

Plutarsky had just stopped to wipe sweat from his face and decide where to go when an explosion erupted ahead of him. This time he was not merely knocked off his feet – he was picked up by a red-hot hand and thrown ten yards backward. The air seemed to be sucked right out of his lungs and replaced by superheated gas that choked him as if he were drowning in lava.

Somehow he found himself alive and whole when he dared to open his eyes. There were fires all around him. The ground for dozens of yards around looked as though it had all been run through a huge grater. There was nothing taller than a clump of dirt standing anywhere. He tried to stand but found his right ankle twisted or broken.

There was one barely recognizable object nearby, and he crawled on his hands and knees, down where the air was a bit cooler, towards it. He didn't have to crawl far to realize what it was. The explosion had been so great that it had excavated the command trailer completely out of the ground and then crumpled it like a sheet of paper. The ten-foot-tall trailer had been squashed down to no more than a few feet high.

Plutarsky couldn't believe the carnage around him. Only a few seconds before it had been a peaceful, quiet, rainy morning in Iran. Now, after one explosion, it was a burning nightmare. Had he been unconscious? He rested for a minute on his hands and knees until he heard footsteps nearby.

He raised his head and saw five men running towards the town of Robat, their arms full of M-16 rifles, ammo boxes, cases of rations and desert combat jackets. Plutarsky got to his feet and pulled his Beretta.

'Halt. Stop.' His voice barely sounded over the background noises of out-of-control fires and men calling and yelling, but all five of the running men stopped and turned towards him. They were Iranian revolutionary guards.

'Where the hell do you think you're going with – ?'

Plutarsky stopped, felt a piece of metal touch his left temple and turned to find First Captain Shurab holding the muzzle of an M-16 rifle in his face.

'Hello, Sergeant Polack.'

There was a brief show of fear in Plutarsky's eyes, which pleased Shurab; then the fear was replaced with anger.

'Going somewhere?' Plutarsky said.

'It is an insult for elite Muslim heroes to work like dogs for Polack inferiors. I am taking weapons and supplies to

mountains. I will fight Soviets without American missiles.'
He started to back away from Plutarsky.

'You'd better pull the trigger, raghead,' Plutarsky said,
now looking directly into Shurab's eyes, ''cause otherwise
I'm going to track you down, skin your deserter hide and
feed your carcass to the dogs.'

Shurab stopped and shrugged. 'All right, Sergeant.'

Plutarsky saw a flash of white light, felt a red-hot
tongue of flame strike his face. Then nothing.

Marshal Govorov had predicted the fall of Bandar-
Abbas would take two days. It took six. But the fall of
the principal Iranian military stronghold guarding the
Strait of Hormuz was now a certainty.

Only ten of the forty AS-6 Kingfish cruise missiles that
had launched against the twelve outer American rapid
deployment force SAM emplacements north of Bandar-
Abbas reached their targets, but the ten that had hit had
devastated the area defences. The whole Meydan Valley
lay open as two of the three CAB missile sites protecting
the valley were destroyed, and Soviet Backfire bombers
rushed through the new opening. Carrying AS-6 cruise
missiles themselves, as well as gravity bombs, the faster
ground-hugging turbojet bombers quickly destroyed the
fourteen I-Hawk missile batteries surrounding Bandar-
Abbas. In two days Bandar-Abbas and the Strait of
Hormuz lay completely unprotected.

Transport aircraft filled with elite Soviet army shock
troops then flew unmolested down the Meydan Valley
and landed on the outskirts of Bandar-Abbas. After four
days of fierce combat, with a full division of Soviet troops
massing around them, the rapid deployment force troops
evacuated Bandar-Abbas. With no land-based support
left to them, the few American naval vessels in the
southern Persian Gulf and in the Strait of Hormuz
retreated to the protection of the *Nimitz* battle group,
which in turn, because of a lack of shore support and

increased AS-6 cruise-missile attacks, pulled back to the Gulf of Oman, nearly two hundred miles southeast of Bandar-Abbas. The *Nimitz* still controlled the Strait of Hormuz through the Gulf of Oman, but it was a shaky grip.

With unprecedented speed the drive to occupy Iran moved to completion. Armed opposition was sporadic: as in Afghanistan, opposition forces were run mostly by rival families or religious sects that fought with each other more than they fought the Soviet invaders. A few chemical weapon attacks against the natives in the mountains and central highlands were reported, but for the most part the Iranian people in the urban areas simply decided to follow the new government rather than risk being wiped out by the Soviets. To the Iranian people there was little difference between the rival factions: both retained their fundamental Islamic foundations; one was supported by the Soviet Union, the other by the United States. For now the Soviets had the upper hand, so the people lined up with the winning side.

The result was that a new government quickly installed itself in Tehran. To no one's surprise the new nation of Allah-al-Kastan, the Islamic Nation of God, was immediately recognized by the Soviet Union, but to everyone's surprise Syria and Iraq formally recognized the new government and suggested entering into negotiations to unify their countries under the laws of Islam. The long Iran–Iraq war came to an end, and representatives of the two governments signed a peace treaty soon afterwards. Many other nations, not wanting a continuation of hostilities, also recognized the new government . . .

The Soviet invasion and takeover of Iran was complete, but the conflict was not over. The world watched as slowly, inexorably, the huge *Arkhangel* carrier battle group departed Cam Rhan Bay, Vietnam, bound for the Persian Gulf. The *Brezhnev* carrier group dominated the

Persian Gulf, but it could not safely dock at any port in the gulf for fear of guerrilla or commando attack, nor, thanks to the *Nimitz*, could any replacement ships pass through the American blockade of the Strait of Hormuz and the Gulf of Oman.

The world knew that the *Arkhangel* was coming to break the blockade, once and for all.

Headquarters, Falcon Space Command Base, Colorado

The meeting of Space Command officers and crewmen was called to attention as General Martin Stuart, commander of the Space Command, entered the small conference room. Under more normal circumstances, Stuart would have told everyone to be seated immediately, but this time he was silent. He took his seat at the head of the oval conference table, and motioned for the others to do likewise, remaining silent as the room quieted down.

Jason Saint-Michael sat alone, on the left side of the table from Stuart, as if he represented some sort of contagion. Dr Matsui, his flight surgeon, sat behind him, almost as if disassociating himself from his patient.

Across from Saint-Michael sat a small group of Space Command officers. Ann Page was among them, seated alongside shuttle mission specialist Captain Marty Schultz. Schultz's customary youthful grin was gone. Ann looked uneasily, almost furtively, from General Stuart and back to Saint-Michael.

'All right,' Stuart began, 'we're here to select a crew to return to Armstrong Station on the spaceplane *America*, recover the bodies of the dead crewmen, then detach the Skybolt module from the station and attach a PAM payload booster to it and send it to a higher storage orbit until it can be retrieved via shuttle. This sortie must be accomplished within the next eight days, before Armstrong reenters earth's atmosphere. Let's get started.' Stuart opened four folders on the desk in front of him, scanned them, but returned his attention to Jason Saint-Michael. 'You're recommending these crewmen for the rescue sortie, General?'

'Yes, sir.' Saint-Michael nodded to the most senior officer across the table from him. 'Colonel Jonathan Hampton is the only choice as pilot. He's the senior hypersonic transportation system pilot in the command besides myself.' He even spelled out HTS for them. 'Only two sorties aboard *America* and one station docking, but one year as operations officer of the HTS cadre and one year as a simulator instructor at Little Rock . . . Major Ken Horvath as first officer was a choice among many qualified people. He topped out best in examination and simulator scores of all recent HTS-school graduates . . . Captain Schultz was again the only real choice of all volunteers for this trip. He's qualified both as an HTS and shuttle-flight engineer and payload specialist. He also had a special claim for being included on this flight; he crewed with Colonels Will and Sontag aboard *Enterprise* for most of his career . . .'

'Can you give me your assurance, Captain Schultz,' General Stuart said, 'that the . . . personal nature of this duty won't affect your performance?'

'I'll tell you what I told General Saint-Michael, sir. I feel like I have a duty to Colonel Will and Colonel Sontag to fly this mission. I demand the opportunity to do it.'

Stuart nodded, looked again to Saint-Michael.

'Of course, General, Dr Ann Page here is the best qualified for the . . . other task on this sortie.'

Stuart folded his hands on Ann's personnel file and shook his head. 'I disagree, Jason. Dr Page has gone through enough already. I don't see any need to put her through – '

306

'Excuse me, *sir*,' Ann said, 'you're talking about me as if I weren't here. The fact is, you have no alternative. I happen to be the best qualified to handle Skybolt, and I'm the *only* person familiar with the laser who is qualified for space flight. I'm also a volunteer – '

'I question *that* more than anything else,' Stuart broke in. 'Do you think it's wise to cause your family more worry after what they went through two months ago? The Armstrong attack, your father's death . . .'

'General, I don't want to be a bore, and I think you know I'm no radical feminist or whatever, but such considerations really are no more relevant for me than any of the men. But I should tell you, my only family is my mother, and she's in full agreement with me.' Feeling warmed up, Ann kept going. 'The thing both of us have a hard time accepting is the way this country is being affected by threats from the Soviets. How can *they* tell *us* when to retrieve our own dead? How can they tell us we can only use an HTS spaceplane instead of a shuttle to approach Armstrong Station?'

'They have the capability to intercept any spacecraft they feel is hostile,' Stuart said. 'That's a fact. A shuttle sortie to Armstrong could be seen as an attempt by us to rearm the station, for all they know with offensive nuclear weapons. A spaceplane doesn't have the cargo capacity to – '

'So why don't we tell them that if they shoot down any more unarmed American spacecraft we'll . . . retaliate? . . . Why are we being pushed around by – '

'*Ann*,' Saint-Michael said, giving her a look. She turned to him, asking with her eyes why he was silencing her. He tried to signal back that the argument was going to be made, and soon.

'The decision has already been made,' Stuart said, stifling his irritation and surprise. Dr Page was obviously more than a lady scientist. 'Our government has decided it is not going to risk a nuclear confrontation over Armstrong Space Station. I'm sorry. There are three other private commercial and government research space stations in orbit that need servicing. If we challenge the Soviets on Armstrong, which as you know is badly damaged, and only a few days from reentering the atmosphere, they could shut off *all* sorties to the other stations.'

Ann was about to respond by pointing out that it never paid to give in to blackmailers but thought better of it. The real issue here was her involvement in the flight. 'All right, General. So we use the HTS. We play the game by the Russians' rules. But please . . . no one touches Skybolt but me. It may sound arrogant to say so, but there's no other mission payload specialist qualified to detach Skybolt from the station and attach the payload assist module to it. Remember, Skybolt is a free-electron laser. It uses a controlled nuclear reaction to create the electron-particle stream necessary for lasing. There's just too much to know about fissionable materials and triggering devices to make it safe for anyone but me to do it.'

Stuart looked steadily at her, finally nodded, more in grudging acceptance than approval. 'All right, the crew list is approved as presented. The sortie is scheduled to depart in four days. That will give you three days to recover the crewmen, detach the skybolt module, attach the PAM, and boost it into its storage orbit. Any difficulties with that rough itinerary?'

'I have a problem with the setup, sir,' Saint-Michael said.

General Stuart had been steeling himself for this. 'I told you that I'd listen to your arguments during this meeting, Jason. I don't know what good it will do, but I'll take your recommendations to the Pentagon and even see to it that they get to the president. But I don't think – '

'Ann was right, sir,' Saint-Michael began in a rush, trying to provoke Stuart into listening. 'We are giving in to blackmail – or, more accurately, to terrorism. We can't let Silver Tower be destroyed. We have got to reactivate the station, put it back into its earth-surveillance orbit and repair its systems as soon as possible – '

'You're suggesting putting it back into orbit over the Persian Gulf?' Stuart asked. He shook his head as if he hadn't heard Saint-Michael correctly. 'You want to put Armstrong over that laser again? Put it in an orbit where the Soviets can accurately track it and send killer satellites to engage it? That's crazy, Jason. Why?' Privately Stuart thought he knew why: Jason was still far from a well man. His doctor was with him and obviously didn't approve his getting involved . . .

'Because the station's SBR and sensors will be needed in a few days. It will take the *Arkhangel* carrier battle group ten days to reach the Arabian Sea within striking distance of the *Nimitz*. The SBR has to be up and running before that.'

'But the Soviets' laser – '

'The laser at Sary Shegan was hardly effective against the station,' Saint-Michael interrupted. 'True, we suffered some damage, but the station was still operational. If the laser had been any more powerful we would have been out of business long before the spaceplane attack . . . Sir, the SBR has proved its value. It will be needed more than ever if the *Nimitz* carrier group is cornered in the Gulf of Oman. They'll have their hands full watching the *Arkhangel* and her escorts, and if they get driven closer and closer to land the Soviets can engage with land-based missiles. They'll need our SBR to protect them.' He paused for a moment. 'And Skybolt as well.'

'Skybolt?' Stuart asked. 'What has Skybolt got to do with it?'

'Skybolt is operational, General,' Ann put in quickly. As Stuart's face went from surprised to sceptical, she hurried on: 'It's working again, sir. I managed to repair it just as the Gorgon missile attack was beginning.' She paused for a moment, then added, 'And I shot down the second Soviet spaceplane with the laser.'

'*What*?' Stuart turned on Saint-Michael, who was studying Ann before meeting his commander's surprised expression.

'I can't verify that, sir. I was in the command module during the attack, and all power had been lost. We were getting nailed by those spaceplanes – I couldn't tell if the sounds were from the MHD reactor or from the Soviet missiles.'

'Well, damn it, I showed a solid lock-on to one of the spaceplanes attacking us, and a solid data link between Skybolt and SBR,' Ann said. 'The Soviets reported losing one of their spaceplanes during the attack – doesn't that prove it works?'

'Not necessarily,' Stuart said. 'The Soviets claim we shot one of the Thor missiles at the spaceplane . . . That was the provocation for their attack. They said nothing about the laser.'

'*That* definitely is not true,' Saint-Michael said. 'All of the garaged Thor missiles were expended during the Gorgon missile attacks. Baker and Yemana detached only two Thors from the ten spares; one missed, the other was never fired. There are eight Thors still on board.'

'And I tell you, sir, with respect, Skybolt works,' Ann said. 'It destroyed that spaceplane. I believe that the laser can protect Armstrong Station from spaceplane attack, and it can protect the *Nimitz* from any more of those AS-6 cruise-missile attacks too.'

'Impossible. Shoot hundreds of miles through the atmosphere and destroy a cruise missile? You've only had one operational test of Skybolt, and until shown otherwise, it failed. Now you're saying it can protect a fleet of ships hundreds of miles away?' Stuart shook his head. 'I know how committed you are to your project, Dr Page, but all this sounds too far-fetched – '

'If the SBR can track it, Skybolt can hit it,' Ann pressed. 'With the laser guided by the SBR and the MHD running at full power, it has the power to shoot through a thousand miles of atmosphere and destroy its target. I don't believe an AS-6 is armoured well enough to take a laser burst, even attenuated by the atmosphere.'

General Stuart stared at a coffee mug ring on his otherwise polished oak conference table without really noticing it.

'Armstrong Station *can* survive,' Saint-Michael said. 'We don't *have* to burn thirty billion dollars' worth of hardware up in the atmosphere. If the Russians decide to go all out, Silver Tower's SBR could be critical.'

Stuart finally looked up. 'All right, Jason, I'll take your recommendation to the Joint Chiefs tonight and ask that it be presented to the president tomorrow. That'll leave him three days to make his decision.'

'Thank you, sir.' Saint-Michael knew he couldn't count on Stuart to state his case as strongly as he would want. He just hoped the president would see the logic of reactivating the station. Well, one thing was sure: If the plan was approved, he was going to be part of it. Better start pitching now . . . 'General, if we get the green light I want to pilot *America*.'

Stuart immediately shook his head. 'No way, Jason. You're grounded. Hampton is still the pilot, no matter what the man decides.'

'Sir, you don't have any choice on this one. If the plan is authorized you'll need a station commander on Armstrong – someone who's checked out on SBR and all of the station's subsystems. Hampton's the best HTS jockey we have, but he's not a station commander.'

'*Jason*' – Stuart's patience was wearing thin – 'all we

311

need is someone to keep things together until the station gets reoriented – '

'That *someone* would have to take the first officer's place aboard *America*, leaving Hampton with the job of putting the HTS into orbit by himself. He's good, but he's not that good.'

'If it came to that, Jason, I'm sure we could rig up a makeshift seat for the extra crewmember. I'm still not convinced you're essential.'

'Sir, nobody knows that station better than I do.'

'What about your dysbarism, sir?' Horvath asked, fearing he might lose his chance at his first real ride in the hypersonic spaceplane *America*. 'What if your episodes recur in space?'

'*America* is a spacesuit-environment craft. As long as I prebreathe oxygen and stay in a spacesuit I'll be just fine.'

'Jason, you don't *know* that,' Dr Matsui said from behind him. Saint-Michael didn't bother turning around. 'The lower pressure in the suit could trigger a seizure. The excitement, the adrenaline – even the noise could set you off. And if there was an emergency – rapid decompression, a suit puncture – '

'Then we're out both an HTS pilot and a station commander,' Stuart finished for him, 'and we bring you back in *America*'s cargo hold, along with all your crew.'

That last hit Saint-Michael hard. His *crew*. Would he be endangering them by heading up the mission? It was one thing to take chances with his own life, but with the lives of the crew . . . He scanned the faces of the others in the room. What he saw renewed his determination.

'Look, General,' Saint-Michael said, 'there's no denying I'll be risking my hide by going up there. We all will. It goes, as they say, with the territory. But I think the chances are better than even we'll put that station back in business. Right now, all things considered, "better than even" seems like pretty good odds.'

Stuart said nothing for a long moment. Then: 'Like I said, Jas, I'll take your proposal to the Pentagon. I'll tell them you want in – let them decide.'

Good old Martin Stuart, Saint-Michael thought. Always an expert at passing the buck. Well, nothing to do now but wait . . . and hope. His thoughts drifted . . . then fixed on an image of Jim Walker stepping into the lifeboat. That look on his face. What was it? A parting look . . . a final farewell . . .?

Saint-Michael's own face hardened as he stood in the Space Command conference room. Somehow, some way, he had to get back on board that station.

The Chevy Blazer turned off the main highway, down a graded dirt road with a large sign that read 'Calhan Municipal Airport Welcomes You.'

Ann looked at Saint-Michael. 'An airport? You live on an airport?'

'I get that reaction all the time. I guess I'm one of the few people who've got the chance to fulfil a childhood fantasy. When I was a kid, I used to wash airplanes, pump gas and sweep out hangars to pay for flying lessons. I got my pilot's licence before I got a driving licence. I was always at the airport. Years later, when I was reassigned to Colorado Springs, I began hunting around for a place and ran across this abandoned county airport. Thirty acres, a hangar, fuel storage, a house, a terminal building and a paved runway. Plus I've got fresh air – sweetened once in a while from the stockyards up the road – the open sky, and the Rocky Mountains. And all it cost me was the back taxes. Paradise.'

They pulled up in front of an old but imposing ranch-style house surrounded by trees several hundred yards from the terminal building. Ann was surprised to see a beacon light revolving on a tower near the terminal.

313

'The airport's active now,' he explained. 'Another deal I made with the county.'

'Doesn't the noise ever bother you? It would drive me crazy.'

'It's not *that* active. Besides, I'm hardly ever here.'

'You have your own plane?'

'Yes. A beauty.' They got out of the car and made their way through the darkness to the house. 'Of course, if the docs at Space Command don't give me a clean bill of health I'll have trouble flying even my Piper Malibu.'

He punched a code into a keyless door lock and swung the door open. To her surprise, lights immediately went on in the foyer and front two rooms.

'I'm also into gadgets,' he said. 'If houses can be described as "high tech", then this one is.' He helped her take off her coat and hung it in the front closet just off the white tiled foyer.

'It's warm in here,' Ann said. 'You keep the heat on all the time when you're gone?'

'Another gadget. Before I leave headquarters I call home. When the computer answers, I punch a code into the phone that tells the computer to turn on the heat or air-conditioning, outside lights, everything – it even makes a pot of coffee.'

Ann smiled back, pleased to be seeing a new side of him.

He led her into the great room, an oak-panelled palace dominated by a cathedral ceiling and a massive stone fireplace. She sat on a leather sofa in front of the fireplace, and he poured a snifter of Grand Marnier for both of them. When he returned with the liqueur he was pleased to see her curled up against one of the big arm pillows.

'You look right at home,' he said. She smiled, accepted the snifter.

He went to the fireplace and within a few minutes had a roaring fire built, then returned to the sofa and sat beside her, watching the logs being consumed by the blaze. After a while she moved towards him – Ann Page was neither coy nor a tease – and put her head on his shoulder. He reached over and brushed her hair from her forehead.

'It's peaceful here,' she said. She looked up at him, watched the reflections of fire in his eyes. 'What do you think they'll say? I mean, about reactivating the station? About your going along?'

'I'm counting on a yea to both points.'

'But what if – '

'I can't think about that now,' he said. 'I think my desire to get back to the station, the feeling I've *got* to and will, is what's helped me fight off this damned sickness. And you've been an important part of it. I hope you realize that.'

'Jason . . .'

He would have been a fool or worse not to understand that the time was now. He kissed her. She pressed against him, holding the kiss for as long as possible. When they parted, they looked into each other's eyes, reading thoughts and desires – the same for them both.

'Make love to me, Jason. *Now.*'

And General Saint-Michael, for once in his life, did precisely as he was told.

Afterwards they shared the unspoken feeling that their loving time together was unlikely to be repeated soon. The dark void of space lay ahead, a place with no promises, and a future unknown.

The Pentagon

The computer-synthesized voice that came through the Pentagon's 'safe-line' sounded like Jason Saint-Michael, but General Stuart could tell immediately that a machine had answered. No matter. It was five o'clock in the morning in Colorado, seven A.M. in Washington. Give the man a rest.

When the voice was replaced by a beep, Stuart said, 'Jason, Stuart here. I just left a meeting with the Joint Chiefs. The president and his cabinet were listening in on a video teleconference. Not the news you'd hoped for, I'm afraid. The secretary of defence is dead set against the station and he convinced the president to deny your request.

'I'm real sorry, Jason, but the decision is to give you a medical retirement. *America* will be piloted by Hampton. The crew will be responsible for salvaging bodies and boosting Skybolt into storage. That's it, Jason. Sorry . . .'

As he returned the receiver to its cradle, Martin Stuart admitted to himself that he had been hoping to get Saint-Michael's machine. He and Jason had knocked heads a fair amount over the years, but he'd always respected the young general, considered him a brilliant field commander. It would have given him no pleasure to tell Saint-Michael directly that Space Command no longer had use for his services. So he was a coward. In this case, he had no apologies. He just hoped Jason would come to accept it. But did he really believe there was a chance of that?

10

This was no longer the world's most extraordinary flying vehicle, Ann thought, and they were no longer a crew of highly skilled astronauts and engineers: this magnificent spacecraft called *America* was nothing more than a glorified hearse, and they were the pallbearers. They were being sent to do a dirty job, with the whole world looking on.

Ann and Marty Schultz were observing the loading of *America*'s cargo bay two days prior to launch. They stood on a steel arch over the massive spaceplane watching huge cranes and scores of workers manoeuvre supplies into the cargo bay. Ann's first glimpse of *America* had been so striking that, for a moment, she'd forgotten the reason for their voyage, forgotten the pain of knowing that Jason would not be joining her. 'She's beautiful. Really beautiful,' she had said when they'd climbed on top of the observation arch for the first time.

Schultz had first taken her on a walk-around inspection of the huge space vehicle. Unlike the husky, boxlike STS space shuttles, *America* was a sleek, rather ominous-looking craft. It was twice as large as the shuttles, closely resembling an oversized version of the Mach Three-plus US Air Force SR-17 Blackbird military reconnaissance plane (the fastest aircraft in the world until *America* had come along), with its pointed hawknose bow sweeping gracefully out towards its broad, flat fuselage and impossibly thin edges.

The craft was built primarily of an exotic metal called rhenium, which was stronger and lighter than titanium and more heat resistant than reinforced carbon-carbon. The cockpit, crew cabin and cargo bay rose out of the top of the smooth black-and-grey rhenium body in a graceful hump, blending smoothly into the broad, flat tail. The sides of the fuselage flared out into short, thin wings that, a few minutes after launch, would swing into the body when their lift was no longer needed. Two short, rounded vertical stabilizers jutted out of the top of the fuselage near the tail, pointing in towards the spine. But most impressive about *America* was her three large engines: long, boxy devices slung under the fuselage with rows of dividers and chambers throughout. Ann had walked around to the front part of the engine and, out of habit and curiosity, looked into the engine inlet. To her surprise she could see right *through* the engines. She asked the obvious question:

'Where the hell are the engines?'

'*Those* are the engines,' Marty explained, welcoming the chance to lecture her on something *he* knew a good deal about. She understood and kept quiet. 'Those are the scramjet engines – supersonic ramjets. Instead of using fan blades to compress air like ordinary aircraft jet engines, the scramjet uses what's called a Venturi – the internal shape of the engine itself – to compress air for ignition. The underside of the fuselage is an integral part of the engine, slowing and cooling the air before it enters the Venturi.

'A conventional turbofan or turboramjet engine is limited to around Mach three-point-five; it just can't suck more air. A simple ramjet engine is far more fuel efficient and can go as fast as Mach five or six – a lot of early military anti-aircraft missiles were rocket-boosted ramjets. Ramjets are limited by the metals used in their construction, which burn up or disintegrate at high speeds. But a scramjet is designed to use its hydrogen fuel as well as its composite construction to cook the inlets. That helps the internal parts withstand the hypersonic speeds over Mach five.

'Once the heat and disintegration problems were solved we were ready to race. There theoretically is no upper limit to the scramjet's speed, but Mach twenty-five is enough for our purposes; that's orbital speed.' Marty pointed to the rail rack below the spaceplane. 'Since a scramjet engine can't suck in air by itself, the spaceplane is shot down this track on a rocket sled to get enough air going through the engine for ignition. At about two hundred miles an hour the Venturi in the scramjets begin to work, and *America* lifts herself off the sled.'

'But how do the engines work in space?' Ann asked. 'There's no air up there.'

'These engines are hybrids; they're true scramjets in the atmosphere but they convert to liquid-fuelled rocket engines once there's no more air passing through the engine. *America*'s primary fuel is hydrogen, with oxygen to burn it. As you know, oxygen is supplied in the atmosphere at lower altitudes. As *America* climbs and the air thins out, the front of the scramjet engine gradually louvres closed and oxygen is fed gradually into the engine from the ship's fuel tanks as needed. The scramjet becomes a true rocket engine at about seventy miles altitude. The spaceplane is really a big fuel tank; everything except the crew cabin, cargo bay and avionics bay is fuel storage.

'On return it's just the opposite: hydrogen and oxygen fuel are mixed in the engines until there's enough oxygen flowing through the Venturi from the atmosphere to sustain ignition. The scramjets can be used almost all the way to landing, so *America* can land at almost any long runway. Los Angeles International and San Francisco International are our designated alternative landing sites, but if necessary we can fly all the way across the country in one hour to find a more suitable one.'

As Marty talked Ann couldn't help thinking about Saint-Michael. He had not been with her these past two days while she trained for hypersonic spaceplane duty at the Space Command HTS flight simulator at Little Rock, then went to Southern California for the launch. Although he didn't say so, she guessed that after seeing her off in Colorado Springs he'd flown to Washington to appeal the ruling that had grounded him. She doubted, though, that he'd be able to convince the Joint Chiefs to reactivate the station, and as each new hour passed and she failed to hear from him, the possibility of his getting his way seemed less likely.

She looked up to see *America*'s cargo bay doors fully open, the silver radiator lining reflecting the blaze of hundreds of spotlights surrounding the craft. Even though the spaceplane was twice as large as her older, less sophisticated cousins, her cargo bay was the same small size. Indeed, dwarfed by the sheer size of the spaceplane, the cargo bay seemed to have been installed as an afterthought. One glance at its payload, though, brought the mission's grim reality into sharp focus.

Most of the cargo bay was occupied by the two PAMs, payload assist modules – large liquid-fuelled rocket engines with remote-controlled guidance units and mounting adapter. It would be Ann's job, with help from Marty Shultz, to attach the Skybolt laser module to the PAM, align it pointing away from earth and activate it. Using steering signals from Falcon Mission Control on earth relayed through the NASA TDRS satellite relay system, the PAM would boost the laser module into a six-hundred-mile storage orbit, giving Space Command another few months to assemble a shuttle sortie to retrieve the modules. Even though *America*'s cargo bay was the same size as a shuttle's, the spaceplane was not designed to bring large objects like Skybolt back from space. A second PAM was being carried as a spare or, if the first was successful and if there was time, to boost Armstrong Space Station's command module itself into a storage orbit.

A huge crane was lowering a large cylindrical object, eight feet in diameter and ten feet long, into the forward part of the cargo bay. For some reason its stark simplicity made it even more painful to look at. This was a space-borne crypt, a huge coffin, the device that would be used to bring back the bodies of the crew of the Armstrong space station and the space shuttle *Enterprise*.

Ann looked at it, then turned away. 'It looks like an old fuel tank,' she said to Marty.

'It is,' he said. 'The kind brought up on shuttle flights to refuel satellites. It's been heavily insulated to protect the . . .' he paused, swallowed hard, 'the crew during reentry. The cargo bay can get as high as a thousand degrees Fahrenheit during reentry.'

She touched him lightly on the shoulder. 'I don't like what we're doing here,' she said. 'We're being pushed around by the Russians, even told when and how to claim our own dead. Damn, I really wish Jason . . . General Saint-Michael were going with us. Somehow right up until now I thought he'd manage it . . .' (As, she thought, he'd managed to make love to her after a sickness that would have kept most men in a hospital for weeks.)

The American and Soviet carrier battle groups were still separated by over two thousand miles of ocean, but even one-eighth of a world apart they had already started the first few tentative steps towards a conflict both knew was all but inevitable.

The *Nimitz* carrier group had moved out into the Arabian Sea to allow its escort ships room to spread out more and manoeuvre at higher speeds. The group had been augmented by three frigates, two cruisers and two

321

armed reserve supply ships from Diego Garcia, the tiny island naval base south of India. It was still enforcing a strict blockade of Soviet-bloc ships trying to enter the Persian Gulf, which prevented the weakened *Brezhnev* from refuelling from Iran, and airlifted fuel and supplies were not sufficient to allow the Soviet carrier battle group to operate at peak efficiency.

The Americans had sent several flight B-52 bombers with F-15 fighter escorts from Diego Garcia to shadow and test the response pattern of the huge *Arkhangel* carrier group, which had just crossed the Eight Degree Channel west of Sri Lanka and was now in the Indian Ocean. The B-52s, the assault aircraft of choice because of their fuel capacity, were armed with twenty-four Harpoon medium-range antiship missiles apiece, making them formidable threats against the carrier fleet.

But the *Arkhangel* was not about to let the B-52s anywhere near the fleet. The Soviets first engaged the B-52s as far as three hundred miles away from the carrier, using their Sukhoi-27 Flanker carrier-based fighters in seemingly never-ending streams. The Soviets knew that at high altitude the B-52s' improved Harpoon missiles had a range of one hundred miles; they simply doubled that figure and set up a stiff air cordon. The Su-27s were docile at three hundred miles, shadows at two hundred and fifty miles and aggressive in warning off the B-52s and their escorts at two hundred and twenty miles. Warning shots were fired at two hundred miles, with more emphatic verbal warnings given.

The F-15s were at a huge disadvantage. They had to leave their vulnerable KC-135R and KC-10C aerial refuelling tankers far behind, out of range of the Su-27s, so their combat range was severely limited. The B-52s could count on enough fighter protection only to break through the first wave of Su-27s from the *Arkhangel*; then they were on their own for the last dangerous one hundred miles to their launch points.

The B-52s obeyed the very last verbal warnings received and turned around right at the two-hundred-mile point. Even so, they were able to accomplish their primary mission, which was to collect valuable data on the shipborne tracking and acquisition radars that had been sweeping them, as well as radar data from the Su-27s that had pursued them. But the scraps of information the B-52s collected did not alter the basic fact: it was going to be a nightmare, if not an impossibility, trying to get close to the Soviet fleet.

Like the *Arkhangel*'s carrier group, the *Nimitz*'s had to contend with airborne threats of its own. The *Nimitz* was only a thousand miles south of Tashkent, the Southern Military District headquarters, where ten Tu-95 Bear bombers were now based. The Bears carried the naval-attack version of the AS-6 cruise missile, which could be launched against the *Nimitz* well within the protection of Soviet land-based surface-to-air missile sites in occupied Iran. The Soviets also had a new weapon, the AS-15 cruise missile, a long-range, nuclear-tipped supersonic cruise missile. The AS-15 could be launched from well within the Soviet Union, or its shipborne version could be launched from one of the *Arkhangel*'s escorts at extreme range. Supersonic land-based bombers from the Soviet Union were also a major threat against the American fleet.

Another series of strategic manoeuvres were being accomplished in an entirely different realm: under the sea. A small fleet of American attack submarines had moved into the Indian Ocean and were edging closer and closer to their adversaries. But unlike the sky-spanning manoeuvres of a high-altitude B-52, this precombat dance was measured in single miles or even in yards. It might take days for a Los Angeles-class attack submarine to move two miles closer to the escort ships surrounding the *Arkhangel*; then, in a chance encounter, it would be discovered by a lucky helicopter sonar dip or a tiny tell-tale sound from within the submarine, and then the sub would be forced to run off and start all over again. Four subs were involved in this tension-filled chase, manoeuvring bit by bit towards their huge target.

The *Nimitz* was a bit more fortunate: the four Soviet attack submarines from Vladivostok remained with the *Arkhangel* battle group in a defensive posture, prowling the seas close to their battle group. Other subs were being reassigned from Havana and from the Mediterranean towards the Persian Gulf, but they could be tracked as they made their way through the Suez Canal or Strait of Gibraltar or around Cape Horn. If hostilities erupted they at least could be intercepted before they reached the *Nimitz* battle group. What the outcome would be was, of course, uncertain.

The battle lines were already drawn. Even though the combatants were still several hundred miles apart, the chief players in the final battle of the Persian Gulf had already been chosen. The confrontation would soon be at hand.

There was no jovial prelaunch breakfast with family members and politicians, no press conference, no words of congratulations or encouragement. The crew of *America* had the traditional steak-and-eggs breakfast, but it was served in strict privacy in the HTS Launch Control Facility mess hall. A few words passed between the crew members, but they were hushed and confined strictly to the flight or the launch.

After breakfast the crew filed towards the life-support shop for their prelaunch suiting-up. Each of the four crewmembers pulled an anti-'g' suit over his coveralls, which would protect him against the sustained five to six 'g's he might experience in the first ten minutes of flight. Because breathing might be difficult in the high 'g' environment, each would also wear a POS facemask, with oxygen fed into the masks under pressure.

After their last-minute physical and suiting-up the crew walked to the loading dock on top of the spaceplane. *America* was still in her loading hangar, sitting on top of the huge sled, with the sled's hydrogen-oxygen rocket engines on either side. They took a long escalator ride to the top of the loading dock, walked across a catwalk to the top entry-docking entry hatch and then rode a moving ladder down to *America*'s airlock on the flight deck.

In spite of *America*'s huge size, the flight deck was no larger than a shuttle upper deck. They moved through the large airlock chamber and into the flight deck area. The galley, waste-control-system facilities and storage lockers were on the left. The right side of the cabin held numerous storage lockers for space suits and EVA equipment.

Forward of the airlock were two permanently mounted seats with space beside each seat for another temporary jump seat. The HTS seats were hydraulically dampened, heavily padded seats that would help the occupant to better withstand the high 'g' forces.

Forward of the passenger seats was a small area with auxiliary controls and circuit-breaker panels, and forward of that was the cockpit. The entire flight deck forward of the airlock was a huge life-support capsule. In an emergency the flight deck would explosively cut itself free of the spaceplane, rocket away from the stricken craft and parachute to earth under a two-hundred-foot-wingspan delta-wing parasail.

Under strict Master Mission Computer ('Mimic') control, preflight preparations in the cockpit were already well under way by the time the crew had boarded, so Ann and her fellow crewmembers had little else to do but strap in and monitor the computer's progress. A wall of four large computer monitors on the front instrument panel explained each preflight step being performed. As a sort of token gesture to the humans, the computer would pause after each step and ask if the humans wanted to proceed. The reply was always 'yes'; the computer would proceed anyway if no reply had been given within five seconds. After only thirty minutes of computer-actuated switching and lightning-fast electronic commands and replies, *America* was ready for launch.

'Falcon Control, this is *America*,' Colonel Hampton radioed. 'Mimic reports prelaunch checklist complete. Acknowledge.'

'*America*, we confirm. Checklist complete. Be advised, launch sled fuel-pressurization complete.'

'Roger. Awaiting final clearance.'

'Stand by, *America*.'

The last radio exchange puzzled Ann: it was an unusual amount of human intervention for a normal hypersonic spaceplane launch. Usually any clearances required for launch were obtained by Mimic enquiries to various other computers around the facility. Humans were not ordinarily consulted.

Ann turned to Marty and keyed her interphone switch. 'Is there something wrong? I don't recall this step in the simulator rides.'

Marty hesitated before replying: 'I'm sure with all the brass observing this flight, someone just hit the pause button somewhere to give the brass time to get caught up. Mimic can move pretty fast.'

The wait lasted for some five minutes, then a sudden voice on the radio announced: '*America*. This is Falcon Launch Control. Ignition sequence interrupt. Launch abort. Launch abort.'

Ann had her harness buckles, oxygen hoses, 'g'-suit hoses and communication cords off in five seconds. Marty followed suit and immediately got to his feet.

'Remember, get a good tight grip on that safety belt on the rescue tower,' Marty was saying. 'It'll jerk you pretty hard when it pulls you away from the – '

They heard the sound of the upper airlock hatch being wrenched open. 'Someone's out there,' Marty said, not quite believing. 'How? They just called the abort . . .'

They both hurried across to see who could possibly have made it on top of the spaceplane only five seconds after the abort was called.

In reply the huge curved airlock door swung open and a tall figure stepped through. Ann's eyes showed stunned recognition, but before either Ann or Marty could speak, the figure addressed them.

'No time for explanations now,' Jason Saint-Michael said straight-faced and moved quickly past them towards the cockpit.

Ann merely stared at the back of the cockpit seats for several moments, then turned around to see two launch technicians dropping through the open hatch. She moved to the cockpit as Horvath slid past her and Hampton began strapping into the right seat.

'Jason . . . you're all right : . .? You're going to fly . . .?'

'Looks like it.'

'But you told me your plan was disapproved . . .'

'It comes down to good old-fashioned arm-twisting. More later,' he said as he strapped into the left-side commander's seat. 'Get ready for launch; we can't delay too long or we'll lose the optimal launch window. We've only got ninety minutes to pull that damned casket thing out of the cargo bay and put a fuel tank onboard – a *full* fuel tank this time.'

She squelched her questions and went back to her seat. Schultz and Horvath were helping the technicians assemble a spare crew seat beside the two permanent ones.

Marty motioned Horvath into his permanent seat. Horvath accepted and began strapping himself into the seat beside Ann while Marty began securing himself on to the flimsy-looking tubular seat they had just assembled.

'You're going to fly in *that*?' Ann asked.

'You bet,' Marty said. He gave his best swashbuckling grin. 'Only rookies need anti-'g' seats.'

'But what about the mission to retrieve the bodies . . .'

'Looks like it's a different mission now,' Marty said. 'They sure cut it close, though. It's dangerous as hell to interrupt a launch countdown after the rocket fuel tanks have been pressurized. A few more minutes and it would've been too late without a week-long abort.'

He jabbed a thumb aft. 'If I know General Saint-Michael, he's organized the world's fastest cargo switch in history. One of those fuel tanks can hold five thousand pounds of liquid oxygen and ten thousand pounds of liquid hydrogen – more than enough to refuel Silver Tower's depleted fuel cells. The PAM boosters? They'll make great boosters for Armstrong Station.'

'So we're really going to do it. . . *we're reactivating Armstrong Station* . . .'

Tyuratam, USSR

Marshal Alesander Govorov was on a late afternoon tour of Glowing Star, the Soviet spaceflight centre in south-central Russia. He had shunned his military escort, although his staff car with armed driver was following along a few dozen metres behind. In the growing dusk, wandering around his Elektron launch facility – now, by Stavka decree, unquestionably *his* – he preferred solitude as he observed his workers scurrying around the launch pads.

He looked ahead and saw his dream standing before

him, illuminated by banks of spotlights on tall towers: three SL-16 Krypkei rockets, service gantrys and umbilicals in place, ready for launch. On top of each booster was an Elektron spaceplane, gleaming in the Space Defence Command colours of silver and red.

Each spaceplane, he knew, was armed with ten Scimitar hypervelocity missiles, now for the first time being mass-produced in the Leningrad Malitanskaya-Krovya exotic weapons factories. They had proved their worth in combat with stunning results. He also had three top Soviet cosmonauts, hand-picked and personally trained, on twenty-four-hour alert at the Space Defence launch centre.

His newly formed combat unit, the first of its kind, was the talk of the Soviet military, but despite – or perhaps because of – the unit's success much effort was being expended in instituting refinements and improvements. Changes had already been proposed, for example, in Govorov's simple but effective hypervelocity missile-weapon design. Undoubtedly the changes would end up complicating things, requiring more cosmonaut intervention before launch, but that, Govorov thought, would be considered a reasonable price to pay.

One change already made was an added explosive warhead to the Scimitar missile, needed because some midlevel engineer had noted that fifteen Scimitar missile hits on the space station Armstrong did not produce the devastation everyone had expected. With new explosive Scimitars in the Elektron's cargo bay, it was that much more dangerous to fly, but that was always the way. The better, the more dangerous.

Govorov also knew that careers were made by those eager to make such refinements, and sometimes those men would steamroll over those in their way. He was on the lookout for such men, but at the same time he was careful not to hold on too tightly to his precious *Bavinash* missiles. Progress, for better or worse, was inevitable.

More important, his big gamble had paid off. Even in the Soviet military hierarchy those with the guts to stand for what they believed in could have some success. High rank usually meant heavy inertia, and the members of the Kollegiya had more in common than they would ever want to admit.

But leaders could reward as well as strike down – when they perceived their own self-interest. Govorov, once commander of a small tenant unit at Tyuratam, now was commander of half of the entire base – over two thousand square kilometres, a dozen launch pads with support equipment and two thousand men and women – and he could summon as much hardware as he required from any corner of the Soviet Union to fill those launch pads. On his own authority, he could launch a half-billion kilograms of men and machines into earth orbit. He could do everything and anything except attack a foreign space-craft, and then he needed only the word of one man, the general secretary of the Soviet Union himself, to attack any spaceborne target he felt was a threat to the nation.

It was a level of responsibility unprecedented in the Soviet Union – and, with very few exceptions, anywhere else. American nuclear submarine commanders, under extreme circumstances, could launch an attack in time of war; the commander of the American strategic bomber forces could launch his planes at his own discretion to improve their survivability in case of attack or natural disaster; the three Israeli fighter-bomber theatre commanders could assemble their stockpiled nuclear weapons and launch an attack if provoked or in danger of being overrun. But not one of them had the power to take command of outer space. Only Marshal Alesander Govorov of the Soviet Union had that.

Take command of outer space. Govorov reflected on

the implications of that as he moved down the main concourse towards the launch control centre. He had been in the control centre only a few minutes later when Colonel Gulaev approached him.

'Sir, launch-detection report has been relayed to us by our reconnaissance satellites. The spaceplane *America* has launched from southern California . . .'

Govorov glanced at the chronometer over the command centre consoles. 'Ninety minutes later than their announced schedule. Has the launch been confirmed by any other means?'

Gulaev checked his watch. 'Yes, sir. Agents in place near Edwards Air Force Base reported it to intelligence, and the news reports of several countries were filled with detailed descriptions of the launch.' He paused. 'Trouble, sir?'

Govorov's earlier mood quickly melted away. 'Do you think the late takeoff is significant?'

Gulaev shrugged. 'The most important, the most widely publicized space flight by the outraged Americans, and it takes off ninety minutes late . . . It could be, sir.'

Govorov nodded, went quickly to a computer-monitor at the extreme right end of the master command console, moving a technician aside as he scrolled through the display.

'These tracking data are hours old,' Govorov said. Gulaev moved to his side and noticed that his superior was checking the orbital status readouts of the space station Armstrong.

'We can update the data in three hours,' Gulaev told him, checking the chronometer again. 'But the station's orbit is erratic and its altitude is decreasing rapidly. It's becoming harder and harder to track.'

Govorov studied the information. Armstrong was, miraculously, still in one piece, judging by the signal strength of the radars tracking the station. It seemed they would need to redefine what they considered the upper limits of the atmosphere. One hundred thirty kilometres was the usual altitude where atmospheric heating due to friction should cause damage to a spacecraft, but it was also generally acknowledged that the upper atmosphere was not flat like a desert but as craggy as the Himalayas: in some spots it only extended to eighty kilometres, in others perhaps a hundred fifty. Earth's atmosphere, as Govorov had observed many times from space, was like a boiling cauldron. Clouds revealed only a small fraction of the real turbulence in the sky. Surely the American space station should have impacted with enough of the higher peaks of the atmosphere to cause *some* damage. Apparently, it had not . . .?

A vague sense of unease began to grip Govorov as he recalled his words to Colonel Voloshin – something about the space station Armstrong remaining a threat as long as it was in orbit. For the past few weeks he had allowed himself the luxury of thinking the station was doomed, that his two-ship attack force had inflicted a mortal blow. But the station was still aloft. Was it also still a danger?

Logic said no. The station was mere hours from reentering the atmosphere. The crew of the spaceplane *America* had little time to retrieve the bodies of their dead crewmembers, let alone boost the station into higher orbit. Their late takeoff was like a death sentence for the station. No, he had accomplished his mission . . . The station was just taking a little longer to expire.

He took a deep breath, nodded to Gulaev. 'Be sure careful records are made of the spaceplane's progress. I will be in quarters.'

A few more hours, Govorov thought as he left the command centre for his waiting vehicle. Just a few more hours . . .

It was long, long after *America* had reached orbit that
Ann was able to recover fully from the sheer excitement
of the launch. Marty Schultz almost had to shake her to
get her attention.

'We're in orbit,' Marty said. 'Sorry to startle you but I
haven't seen you move in a few minutes.'

'I feel drained, like I just ran a marathon.'

'Well, it's not your usual shuttle launch, for sure.'

That, Ann decided, was a rank understatement. Unlike
the shuttle, which gradually climbed into orbit, the spaceplane *America* sprinted into orbit. From the moment the
rocket engines were ignited on the sled that propelled the
spaceplane down the long launch track in the high southern Californian desert, she had felt the crushing 'g'-forces
pin her body to her seat. *America* had been boosted from
zero to two hundred miles per hour in less than fifteen
seconds . . . It was nearly impossible to believe that seven
hundred thousand pounds of machine could be accelerated at such a rate.

She'd thought the 'g's would diminish after they'd lifted
off the rocket sled, but they hadn't even begun to slacken.
The first indication of a force even greater than the
rockets on the sled came when the centre scramjet engine
ignited. The three-hundred-fifty-ton spaceplane bucked
like a living thing, lurching so hard that the hydraulic 'g'-
dampeners in Ann's seat could hardly absorb the shock.
One hundred miles an hour of airspeed was added to the
forward momentum of the spaceplane in the blink of an
eye. Her 'g'-suit had immediately inflated to keep her
from blacking out, and if her face mask had not shot
oxygen under pressure into her lungs she would have
suffocated. As it was, her rib cage felt heavy as lead and
breathing was suddenly impossible. When the other two

scramjet engines ignited shortly afterwards, her 'g'-dampening seat had hit its limit and her body was forced to endure the ever-building, crushing pressure. She had had to perform an 'H-manoeuvre', whereby blood was forced to the upper body and head by partially closing off the trachea, and then grunting against the pressure. She glanced sideways during the ascent and saw Horvath's chest heave and flutter as he performed the manoeuvre too.

By the time all three scramjet engines were running *America* was travelling at well over three hundred miles per hour and had already streaked down three of the five miles of launch track. The restraining clamps were then released, and the spaceplane lifted off the sled and shot skyward. If the three engines hadn't ignited, high-pressure steam jets on the last mile of the track would have automatically activated and begun slowing the spaceplane down below two hundred miles an hour, where arresting cables and hydraulic brakes could be applied.

As it was, *America* broke the sound barrier twenty seconds after lifting off from the take-off sled. She was then pulled up into a forty-five-degree climb at six 'g's, racing skywards at over fifty thousand feet per minute. The craft went hypersonic – past the Mach five mark – fifty seconds later as it passed forty thousand feet altitude, the ear-shattering sonic boom rattling across the Sierra Nevada mountains far below. By the time *America* reached the Canadian border five minutes later it was at Mach fifteen, still climbing on top of a column of hydrogen fire nearly a mile long. Her wings were retracted at that point because at two hundred thousand feet altitude there was not enough air to generate lift.

The louvres at the front of the scramjet engines automatically closed as the spaceplane climbed, so five minutes into the flight the aircraft had transformed itself into a liquid-fuelled rocket. As the engine began to burn more pure internal liquid oxygen, the speed increased. Finally, ten minutes into the flight the crushing 'g' forces began to subside as *America* completed its acceleration to orbital velocity.

Now several banks of orbital manoeuvring jets were activated to begin matching *America*'s orbit with that of the stricken space station. The climb to Silver Tower's altitude didn't take long: on the lowest part of its orbit the station was now down to only five hundred thousand feet – eighty-three miles – altitude, low enough to be clearly visible to observers on earth. Following tracking and steering signals provided by ground-based tracking stations – Armstrong had stopped transmitting a position and docking beacon weeks earlier – Saint-Michael and Hampton began to chase down the stricken space station.

'Digital autopilot slaved to Ku-band tracking signals,' Hampton reported. 'Mimic is estimating thirty minutes to rendezvous.'

Saint-Michael was studying *America*'s flight-profile readouts and environmental displays. 'Eighty miles,' he muttered. 'We're barely above entry interface altitude' – where the spacecraft began to enter earth's atmosphere and decelerate on account of friction. 'Check the radiator and coolant cross-flow. It's already midway in the caution range.'

'Coolant flow is maximum,' Hampton said, checking another screen. 'We can try partially closing the radiators to cut down on the friction. Or we can go to EMER on the cross-flow system to bring the temperature down to the normal range.'

'How about that fuel back there?' Saint-Michael said. 'We can't play around so close to the atmosphere like this. We may have to jettison the fuel in the tank when coolant temperature reaches the danger level. There's no sense holding on to it longer and endangering the ship.'

'Can you power up the station or reposition it without a refuelling?'

'I don't know. I don't remember how bad the solar panels on the station were hit.'

Like Ann, Horvath and Schultz, Saint-Michael had kept his POS facemask on to continue prebreathing pure oxygen in preparation for their spacewalk into the station. As he spoke, he began massaging his temples.

'You all right, General?' Hampton asked.

Saint-Michael quickly lowered his hands from his head. 'Sorry, bad habit. Just thinking, believe it or not . . . That Russian spaceplane attack knocked out power in the command module, but I think the SBR and Skybolt were still running when I found Ann unconscious in the Skybolt control module. That may mean that the station is still functioning, at least partially.'

'But Falcon Control lost the station's ID and TDRS tracking signal weeks ago. They've assumed all power is out.'

'We'll assume the same.' Saint-Michael pressed the button on his comm link. 'Listen up, crew. We won't have much time, and we've got to assume that the station is completely dead. Our priority will be to boost the station to a safe altitude. After that we'll try to power her up, reposition her, set up SBR surveillance of the Indian Ocean and the *Nimitz* carrier group in the Arabian Sea and begin to make some structural repairs. In between we'll probably have to fight off another attack . . . Ann, you'll be in charge of setting up the PAM boosters on the keel. I know Marty's explained how and where they go. Any questions?'

'No,' Ann said, still finding it hard to believe they were going to reactivate the station after all. 'It's a lot simpler than disconnecting Skybolt would have been.'

'Good. Marty, you'll be in charge of refuelling the cells on the keel so we can get electric power back on. The cargo shovel appeared damaged so you'll have to do it the hard way: drag the fuel tank around to the cells with the MMU manoeuvring unit and use the remote fuel-transfer system. Any problems with that?'

'I used to pump gas in Ohio when I was nine years old.'

'Just be ready in case Ann needs help.'

'Rog.'

'Ken, you'll follow me into the station,' he told Horvath. 'The environmental and electrical controls are easier to work than a shuttle is, so you shouldn't have too much problem figuring them out. We'll try to get solar power on, followed by fuel-cell power. If you can find and patch up any holes in the command module, it'll make our work easier. Otherwise we'll just try to reactivate the station's attitude and environmental system . . . Jon, you take care of *America* and try to help anyone out that needs help. The PAM installation has priority. After that, refuelling and repairs. Keep us advised of any messages from Falcon Control until we get communications going on Silver Tower.'

'Right.'

Thirty minutes later, they had moved to within a few hundred yards of Silver Tower.

For a few long moments the sight of the station in the distance dampened everyone's enthusiasm . . . The damage was worse than any of them had imagined.

The station's spin had decreased in velocity but it was gyrating on at least three or four different axes at once, like some sort of unearthly multilegged monster with dozens of different appendages reaching out to grab the spaceplane and devour it. Ionization from frequent scrapes with earth's upper atmosphere had created a multicoloured, undulating aura of energy around the station. Parts of the central open-lattice keel glowed like hot embers, and clouds of debris and frozen water, gases and fuel hovered everywhere. Several large panels from

337

the SBR arrays and solar collectors were missing or damaged.

Hampton looked uneasily at Saint-Michael. 'Do you think it's safe to approach the station with all that junk and sparking out there?'

'No. But we've got to do it.'

'Sir, wait.' Hampton turned in his seat to face Saint-Michael. 'The "ifs" are really starting to pile up here. We'll be driving right into the middle of all that debris and heat ionization. Then we've got to try to match the moves the station is making . . . One mistake and we've got another dead ship.'

'You knew the risk, Jon. We all did . . .'

Hampton paused, considered. Finally he shrugged and said, 'Okay, General. We'll do it your way. Let's stick our noses into the beehive.'

Saint-Michael nodded, wrapped a hand around the manual control stick.

'Here we go . . .'

He had applied forward thrust for exactly two-point-one seconds when a terrific *bang* shook *America* from bow to stern. He glanced towards Hampton as they checked the computer monitors for damage indications.

'Pretty big bees,' Hampton said.

Saint-Michael, ignoring him, took a tighter grip on the control stick and nudged it forward into the swirling mass ahead.

America provided no visibility out the cockpit windows except for the commander and pilot, so the others were spared seeing the source of the explosions, rumbles and flashes of light and heat that threatened to tear their ship apart during the final docking with Silver Tower.

The cargo bay temperature had risen to the danger zone when they moved only two hundred yards closer to the crippled station. 'Cargo bay overtemp warning,' Hampton reported.

Saint-Michael promptly overrode the preprogrammed command – which had been to jettison the fuel tank – and chose 'EMERGENCY COOLANT SHUNT' instead, opening a manifold from the scramjet intake coolant system that allowed supercooled hydrogen to flow from *America*'s fuel tanks through to the radiators. It was a risky choice – the tiniest leak in the radiators would have allowed the hydrogen to be ignited by the superheated ionized particles streaming past the spaceplane from the station – but there was no explosion and the temperature moved away from the danger zone.

Saint-Michael's fingers moved over the control buttons on the stick, switching between translate – straight-line – and rotate thrusts. Because it took less time to rotate in one direction than it did to reverse directions, *America* literally corkscrewed its way towards the docking port. They had been forced to hit smaller pieces of debris to avoid impact with larger ones. Debris breaking off or exploding from the station didn't always 'fall' or disappear: it seemed to hang around the station in a dangerous orbit of its own.

After nearly thirty minutes *America* was hovering a mere ten feet from the docking adapter, held in place by the spaceplane's intricate station-keeping computers. But ten feet was still ten feet too much. 'We can't go any further, General,' Colonel Hampton said. 'We've got the station-keeping routine running as precise as the system allows.'

Horvath spoke up. 'I'll go to the docking module and – '

'No. I'll go,' Saint-Michael said.

'I'd advise against it, General,' Hampton said. 'Your dysbarism . . .'

'I've got to do it sooner or later, Jon, and I'm the best

qualified to check out the station. I've been prebreathing oxygen for the whole flight so I should be okay. You've got the ship.' Saint-Michael waited until Hampton had adjusted his manual controls and situated himself, then unstrapped and floated back towards the airlock.

Ann reached out and stopped him. 'If you feel . . . if you get in any trouble, get back.'

He nodded, moved past her.

It took him five minutes to get into a spacesuit and backpack. Ann prepared to suit up after he exited the airlock, was watching him through the observation port on the chamber door as he began to depressurize the airlock. Suddenly, just as he moved the AIRLOCK DEPRESS switch from position five to zero, he quickly punched it back to five.

'Jason?'

He held up a hand towards her but seemed to be shaking his head trying to clear his vision.

'Switch back to PRESSURIZE,' she called to him.

'I'm all right.' Saint-Michael slowly stood erect, shaking his head as if recovering from a fall. 'It's gone . . .' He reached for the depressurization control again – .

'No,' Marty said quickly. 'You can't do it, General – '

'I'm all right.' He waited a few moments, then switched the depressurization knob to zero. A few minutes later he gave Ann and Marty a thumbs-up and undogged the upper airlock hatch. Ann was repressurizing the airlock as soon as the general had locked the hatch after exiting.

'Bad news,' Saint-Michael said over his comm link. 'The docking tunnel is unusable – the whole docking module is about ready to break off the station. Everyone has to EVA.'

Saint-Michael scanned the spaceplane. The view of *America* against the chaos around the station was quite a sight . . . The grey-black spaceplane seemed to add a sense of power and strength to the damaged station it hovered near. He could see tiny puffs of gas escaping from the manoeuvring jets on *America*'s nose and tail as the spaceplane maintained its tenuous position beside the station.

The scene looked normal if he concentrated on just the station and the spaceplane, but when he tried to look at earth the view became chaos again.

With *America* in near-perfect synchronization with the station, there was no apparent movement between them – but *earth* appeared to be spinning all around them, making one revolution over Saint-Michael's head every minute. At first it was disorienting and he had to fight off the 'leans' – his eyes telling him he was standing still, his head and body spinning and oscillating in reference to earth. It was like being on a crazy roller coaster with one's eyes closed.

'Be careful when you step outside – the ride out here is a wild one. I don't see any major damage to *America*. Ann, I'm going to start unstowing the PAM boosters. I'll attach one, you get the other.'

'Roger. I'm a minute from EVA.'

Saint-Michael made his way carefully along *America*'s spine towards the open cargo bay, his attention continually drawn to the damage on the station. The most serious was on the keel, especially the SBR antennas.

'The Russians did a job on the SBR control-junction boxes,' he said. 'It looks like we'll have to splice all of them but I can't be sure at this distance. One or two of the arrays might be intact.'

He continued down to the cargo bay and manoeuvring beside one of the PAM booster engines, removed restraining pins on the cargo bay attach-points.

'Both PAMs are unpinned.'

'Copy, General,' Marty Schultz said. Saint-Michael looked up as *America*'s remote manipulator arm rose out

341

of its launch stowage cradle and the tiny closed-circuit TV camera aimed itself at him. 'Ready to eject the aft PAM.'

The general manoeuvred back a few feet away from the booster. 'Go.' With a puff of gas the large booster slid out of its attachment sleeve and lifted slowly out of the cargo bay. As it rose up before him Saint-Michael manoeuvred himself up and across to the reinforced mounting bracket on the side of the booster, then jetted forward until he could grasp the booster. He pulled himself into the booster and latched the front of his MMU to the bracket. His head was just above the top of the booster.

'I've got the first PAM,' he said. 'Ann, I'm heading along the keel towards the spaceplane's nose to attach the booster. You take yours towards the *America*'s tail to the keel. Mount your PAM perpendicular to *America*'s alignment to the keel; I'll mount mine parallel to *America*. Maybe we can stop the spinning at the same time we boost the station away.'

'Copy.'

'General, this is Hampton. We're at seventy-five miles altitude. Cargo bay temperature is back in the danger zone.'

'Go to EMER on the radiator cooling system again.'

'I did. It came down but it's heading back up again. We've run out of time. I suggest we jettison the fuel cell and pull out.'

'Forget it . . . Ann, where are you?'

He saw her emerge from the upper airlock hatch before she could answer. 'On my way.' He passed her a few moments later as he headed out past *America*'s steeply angled cockpit windows, over the pointed flat nose around the manoeuvring jets, and down and along the open-lattice keel.

'We've got to hurry. Marty, we're going to need you and Horvath out here. Now.'

'We're both in the airlock suiting up,' Marty told him. 'Should be out in four minutes.'

It took Ann and Saint-Michael ten minutes more to attach the boosters to the keel. Meanwhile Schultz and Horvath had exited the airlock. Marty took the last MMU – America carried only three – and helped Ann attach her booster to the keel. Horvath without an MMU but using tethers and safety clips, made his way through the damaged docking tunnel and into Silver Tower's docking module.

'My booster is secured,' Saint-Michael reported. 'Ann?'

'Just one minute more and – '

A gasp from Horvath. He had come across the grisly scene inside the docking module where seven of the dead Space Command crewmen lay. He tried to blot it out, knew he never would. A few moments later he announced, 'General, I'm in the connecting tunnel. It's depressurized, but the Skybolt module is showing pressurized. And I can see lights on in the galley module and in Skybolt. I see some damage, but it looks minor – '

Thank God, Ann said to herself.

'General,' Hampton said again, 'it's now or never . . .'

'We're ready,' Marty called out.

'Ann, Marty, secure yourselves to the keel. Ken, grab hold of something in there. Jon, you'll have to manoeuvre clear of the station before we set off the boosters.'

'Moving away now.' Ann watched with fascination as the huge dark form of the spaceplane seemed to fall away from her, the tiny manoeuvring jets on the broad tail flashing on and off like spotlights. In a few moments America was a hundred feet away from its original position, looking like a large, finely detailed toy hovering against the revolving backdrops of stars and the hazy upper atmosphere of earth.

'Commit both PAM boosters,' Saint-Michael ordered.

'PAM boosters armed,' Hampton replied. 'Ku-band

earth station data link good. Data transfer . . . here it comes . . .'

Ann felt her body strain against the clips holding her to a mounting bracket on Silver Tower's keel as the PAM booster fired. She could feel an intense vibration ripple through the keel; then the booster abruptly cut off, but the spinning went on.

'Why did it stop?' she asked. 'Is there – '

She didn't have a chance to finish the question as Saint-Michael's PAM booster fired in sequence. It was followed by another longer burst of thrust from her PAM booster, followed again by a shorter pulse from the opposite booster. The effect was to move the station and its tethered crewmembers upward towards outer space at a rate of ten miles per hour. For Ann and the others it was like being dragged along by a slow-moving car. *America* seemed to slide forward and sideways, then tip on edge. Even the scattered debris seemed to swirl and drop away like a cloud bank being pushed back out to sea by a fresh breeze.

Following guidance commands from the ground tracking stations, the two PAM boosters alternated each of their pulses of thrust until, after several minutes, the station's wild multiaxis spinning slowed nearly to a stop. As the rotation decreased, the booster thrusts became longer as the station fought for altitude. A couple of minutes later the roar of the engines was constant. Earth was now firmly beneath them, slowly but surely dropping away. Ann was no longer pinned to the keel, but found instead that she could move freely.

Saint-Michael spoke first. 'Jon, how do you copy?'

'Loud and clear, General,' Hampton said. 'Ken's got the station emitting a tracking beacon now. *America*'s back on digital autopilot. I'll bring her back beside the cargo bay so we can start refuelling the energy cells.'

'Horvath here. I've got auxiliary power on in the

344

command module. It's depressurized. I don't think we can fix it: it's got two or three monster holes in it – '

'How about environmental and SBR controls?'

'I think I can reset the environmental controls, sir. I have no idea if that SBR stuff is operational, but there's backup power going to every console.'

More than they'd hoped for, Ann thought. Silver Tower was alive. Now if the Russians would just give them the time they needed . . .

Tyuratam, USSR

Marshal Govorov came into the Space Defence Command control centre, joined up with Colonel Gulaev, then kept stride with his subordinate as both hurried to the main tracking computer monitor to scan the information that was scrolling across the screen.

'We didn't notice the change until the station was at two hundred fifteen kilometres . . .' Gulaev said. 'We thought it was an error, an anomaly – '

'It's impossible,' Govorov said, realizing as he said it how much that sounded like the Kremlin bureaucrats he'd gone up against all these years. He'd deceived himself. Well, let's go from there . . . But wasn't more time needed to boost the station into higher orbit?

'Sir, shall I alert the – '

'Alert *no one*. I want this tracking *confirmed*.'

Gulaev took off for the communication centre to call Sary Shegan for a confirmation. The answer did not take long. The young officer returned to the control console only sixty seconds later to find the Space Defence commander alone at the console – no one else wanted any part of him – including himself.

'Sir, the Shirov-25 space surveillance site at Sary Shegan has just issued an advisory to Space Defence Command headquarters. The tracking is . . . confirmed. Armstrong appears to be under power and being directed to a standard circular orbit, inclined less than five degrees from the equator . . . Is it possible that the Americans could reestablish surveillance over the Persian Gulf or Arabian Sea . . .?'

Govorov came close to giving him a murder-the-messenger look, then shook his head, trying his best to control himself. 'The station's pressurized modules are uninhabitable. Our Scimitar missiles had to penetrate the radar array and solar cells. It would take a full workcrew months to bring Armstrong back on line.' Or at least it should . . . He clapped his hands together, as though to jog himself out of his unaccustomed funk. 'All right, I want a secure videophone connection established among Rhomerdunov, Khromeyev and myself, the conference to be set up in tactical situation briefing room three. And I want General Kulovsky of intelligence on hand. Get him here.'

Gulaev hurried off to give the orders, relieved that Govorov seemed his old self, back in control, in command, at least a step ahead of the Americans . . .

But why did it feel like they were one step behind?

The videophone terminal had been set up on a pedestal at the front of the large conference room near Govorov's office at the Glowing Star Manned Launch Facility. Govorov and General Kulovsky, the Space Defence Command's chief of intelligence, stood in front of the terminal waiting for the two senior Stavka members to make contact.

They did not have to wait long. The videophone buzzed once, long and insisting, and the screen suddenly flared to life, revealing Deputy Minister of Defence Khromeyev and Commander in Chief of Aerospace Forces Rhomerdunov seated at the main battle staff conference table at Supreme Headquarters in Moscow.

Khromeyev spoke first. 'We already know about the American space station, Govorov. I assume you have an explanation . . .'

Govorov did not feel better, hearing he'd apparently been scooped by the space warning and tracking facility at Sary Shegan. Make the best of it, he told himself, and try to tell it as you see it . . . 'Comrade Deputy Minister, it's not as we hoped, and believed. True. But I believe it likely that the station has been destroyed beyond the point of *near-term* usefulness – '

'Then how is it being moved at all?' Rhomerdunov interrupted.

'I believe the Americans may have brought aloft the rocket boosters needed to send the station to higher orbit – '

'Isn't it more likely,' Khromeyev put it, 'that you overestimated the damage done to the station?'

'Yes, sir, that's possible, but I point out that *America*'s cargo bay, from what we've learned of it, is more than large enough to carry a fuel tank and several small rocket boosters to attach to the station's central keel.'

Govorov hit a button on a small wireless control unit, and the pedestal that the videophone monitor was mounted on swivelled up so that the camera faced a large plastic and balsa wood model of Armstrong hanging from the ceiling. The model, carefully constructed and precise in every detail, had been just as precisely broken in several places.

'The model you're looking at, sir, represents the last full image of the station as seen through my Elektron spaceplane's Scimitar missile laser designator.' With a long pointer he then motioned to each of the station's damaged systems.

'Yes, yes, General. And your opinion, Colonel Kulovsky?'

'That the station does not have the capacity to counter

347

earth's gravity,' Kulovsky said. 'Even with full-thruster capacity, the station can't change altitude more than a hundred kilometres without a refuelling. So, as Govorov says, the spaceplane must have brought rocket thrusters to move the station.'

'The most important target for myself and Colonel Voloshin,' Govorov said, 'was the station's space-based radar array attach points. As you can see – ' – he used the pointer for emphasis – 'three of the four attach points have been hit and two destroyed.'

'So that leaves two SBR arrays,' Khromeyev said.

'Yes, though not enough to let the Americans duplicate the extent of earlier surveillance, sir,' Kulovsky said.

'The other strikes against the station,' Govorov said, 'took out or damaged the solar arrays, which are necessary to recharge the station batteries and convert water to fuel . . . the fuel-storage vessels on the keel . . . and the pressurized modules themselves. It's possible these punctures in the modules are repairable in orbit, but they will leak so badly that the modules can't be safely inhabited unless the crew wear space suits the whole time. *However*, sir, I grant that the seemingly impossible may be possible. We are not infallible, and I do not underestimate the Americans. I have warned against that myself over the years, and I don't intend to change now. And so . . .'

'And so . . .?' Rhomerdunov said. 'Finish the thought, General.'

Govorov took the leap, the one he'd been moving towards, if in a roundabout fashion, since this little lecture had begun. 'And so, sir, I believe we should not take the chance, however remote, that Armstrong will not regain its surveillance capabilities and be a substantial threat. I recommend that I attempt another attack against the space station . . .'

Khromeyev clearly wasn't so sure. 'The first attack on the space station was easily justified,' he said. 'The

Americans moved their station directly over the Soviet Union and used it to direct an attack against our defensive forces. But if we mount another offensive against a crippled station, one that is not, at least at the moment, orbiting over Soviet territory, world opinion may very well turn against us. We have already received much criticism for the deaths aboard the American rescue craft; if we attack America's only hypersonic spaceplane, one ostensibly launched to retrieve the bodies of the other crewmembers that died in Govorov's first attack, we could be subject to the kind of international condemnation that could expand the conflict beyond the present boundaries – something we must avoid.'

'I agree, sir.'

Khromeyev and Rhomerdunov conferred briefly; then Khromeyev turned to the camera:

'Marshal Govorov, continue to monitor the space station Armstrong's orbit and advise us immediately if there are any significant changes, or if any other space-craft dock with the station. The responsibility for deter-mining whether or not the station becomes a threat to Operation Feather is, of course, yours.'

It was not what Govorov wanted to hear, though he wasn't surprised. It seemed he'd done too good a job of making a 'balanced' presentation. But if he knew the Americans, and he was beginning to know them too well, they would soon give him a good reason to resume the attack he believed necessary . . .

11

It certainly wasn't pretty.

The command module, connecting tunnel, engineering and Skybolt control module all leaked like wet paper bags. Environmental alarms went off constantly, sending the already exhausted and nervous crew scrambling for POS masks. But to Jason Saint-Michael it marked a major step in the reactivation of Armstrong Space Station, and as such he had to admit that, all things considered, it looked beautiful. Not pretty, but beautiful.

Saint-Michael had volunteered to be the first to take watch while the rest of the crew stayed aboard the spaceplane and got their first sleep in forty-eight hours. He didn't completely trust the 'bubble-gum and baling wire' repair jobs they'd made on the modules, so he'd ordered everyone except one person to sleep in *America*. The spaceplane was now docked with the station, using yet another jury-rigged device made from the undamaged parts of the docking module so the crew could transfer between *America* and the station without prebreathing or wearing a spacesuit.

The general was keeping himself awake with shots of pure oxygen from his POS mask and by checking and rechecking the systems, all in various states of repair, in the command module. He took pride in the patch job they'd done. Luckily they had the supplies on board to fix pressurized module penetrations. Those supplies and a

350

generous amount of elbow grease had got the job done so far.

Fixing the modules to allow for working without space-suits was minor compared to repowering and repositioning the station itself. It had taken Marty Schultz three hours of exhausting hard work to refuel the two undamaged fuel cells from the large fuel tank they had brought from earth. But it had paid off: direct system power had been applied an hour later, and enough systems were restored to allow the station's built-in self-test equipment to analyse and point out other malfunctions and damage. Once the equipment began looking after itself and telling its human keepers what was wrong, things began to ease up a little.

Now they had to try to position the station in a usable orbit. One main attitude thruster and both main station thruster fuel tanks had been destroyed in the Soviet spaceplane attack. After refuelling the fuel cells to provide electrical power Marty had attached the fuel tank, still with three-quarters of the fuel left, into the station's attitude and positioning thruster system. By the end of the first twenty-four hours they had restored enough inertial navigation systems and satellite tracking and positioning data links to activate the station thrusters, and with far more human intervention than normal they managed to kick Silver Tower into a low equatorial orbit. Now at two hundred miles altitude, orbiting almost directly over the equator, Silver Tower passed approximately six hundred miles south of the *Nimitz* carrier group in the Arabian Sea. At seventeen thousand miles per hour they could theoretically scan the fleet for twenty minutes on every orbit, or twenty minutes out of every ninety – almost one-fourth of the time. *Providing* they could get the space-based radar system working. They hadn't brought along an SBR engineer on the flight, but as long as the master system processor was working it could direct the SBR operator to system faults – the system would fix itself.

They had been following the SBR computer's direction for nearly twenty hours when Saint-Michael called a halt. Now he was there alone, monitoring the systems and watching in case the Russians staged another attack – although if they did there was no way he could detect it beforehand and not a damn thing he could do even if he *did* know they were coming. Silver Tower wasn't yet ready to fight. Not yet.

He looked over to the master SBR console. The huge master SBR monitor wasn't broken, as far as anyone could tell, but for some reason it wasn't coming on. After taking it down off its mounting spot on the bulkhead to try to fix it someone had used a couple of strips of tape to secure the huge screen back to the wall. He went over to the console and checked the two screens, one of them cannibalized from a TV set found in the recreation area in the Skylab module. If the SBR screen had been working properly a political map of the earth would be scrolling across the screen with the SBR's scan pattern superimposed on it. Without the mapping display the only readout of where they were was a series of complicated digits zipping across the TV set, representing azimuth, declination, latitude, longitude, inertial velocity and planetary motion corrections of the station relative to earth. It might as well have been written in ancient Egyptian hieroglyphics.

He went back to what was left of his seat (one of the Russian missiles had blown off the backrest), strapped himself in, thinking that in the days before the attack he would have automatically picked up his earset and electret microphone and set it in place. Not so now. There wasn't any point – even though the station's tracking beacon had been activated, the tracking and data relay satellite system was smashed to hell. They could only talk with someone on the ground using the ultrahigh frequency radios that were limited to line-of-sight. With TDRS you could talk or exchange data with someone on the other side of the planet – with UHF, *if* you could cut through the static, *if* you talked at night, you *might* be able to talk to an earth station you could see out of the window. Maybe.

He wished he could have the same problem seeing or thinking about *Enterprise* . . .

The thought of the wrecked shuttle and her dead crew back in the docking module suddenly deflated him, left him with a deep sense of frustration and anger. Nothing he nor anyone else did would make a difference as far as they were concerned. And by forcing this mission to reactivate the station he'd exposed other crewmen . . . including Ann . . . to the same risk . . . But *no*, he had to remember this mission was about much more than revenge. It was about *saving* lives. American lives out there in the Persian Gulf . . .

That was what he'd told the Joint Chiefs and the president when he'd met with them to argue the case. He'd had a tough time at first . . . Stuart had done a good job convincing people that Armstrong's station commander was a casualty who, for his own good and the country's, ought to be put out to pasture. What he was after would needlessly provoke the Russians. Saint-Michael had countered with the very likely scenario if they *didn't* reactivate the station, and when he'd finished even Secretary of Defense Linus Edwards seemed to comprehend the seriousness of the situation. Saint-Michael had gotten authorization only just in time, though, to put a hold on the launch so he could arrange a cargo switch . . .

Alone now in the command module, he was not so all-fired sure he was right. And with that thought came another: that he'd better be, or the folks back home might invent a Yankee Siberia for him if his plan backfired.

The USS *Nimitz* in the Arabian Sea

'The most sophisticated radar ships in the world,' Admiral Clancy grumbled, 'and I still feel naked as a jaybird out here.'

The commander of *Nimitz* carrier fleet was talking to Captain Edgewater, captain of the *Nimitz*, in the carrier's combat information centre. He was talking about the USS *Ticonderoga*, *Shiloh*, *Valley Forge* and *Hue City*, the Aegis battle management cruisers operating alongside *Nimitz* as the battle group steamed slowly eastward in the Arabian Sea.

Ticonderoga and her sisters, although over a decade old, were indeed some of the most sophisticated vessels in the world. Their four large phased-array radar antennas could scan the skies for hundreds of miles in all directions, electronically link dozens of ships together and direct gun, aircraft or missile attacks against hundreds of targets all at once. They carried nearly a half-billion dollars' worth of nuclear-hardened twenty-first-century equipment. Yet here in the middle of the Arabian Sea they were made virtually impotent by the sophistication of weaponry and the preponderance of enemy forces surrounding them.

Clancy pointed to a five-foot-by-five-foot liquid-crystal display in the centre of *Nimitz*'s CIC. 'I need more eyes up there, Captain,' Clancy was saying, jabbing his finger towards the centre of the Arabian Sea. '*Ticonderoga*'s detection range for high-flying aircraft is only about three hundred miles; for surface vessels and low-flying aircraft it's about two hundred miles, and for fast-moving, sea-skimming missiles or aircraft the detection range could be as little as eighty miles.' Edgewater agreed with the commander of the Persian Gulf flotilla. Clancy continued: 'It's just not enough. With Soviet cruise missiles having Mach five speed and supersonic bombers that could carry fifty-thousand-pound payloads at Mach two and fifty feet above the water, *Ticonderoga* can barely keep up. An AS-6 cruise missile diving down on us at nearly Mach speed would only give our escorts five minutes to destroy the missile. A Soviet Blackjack or Backfire bomber at extreme low altitude, detected at maximum range, would be right on top of us in seconds, giving us barely enough time to react.'

'They have to get past the fleet defences first, Admiral,' Edgewater said. 'We've got nearly a hundred missile launchers on-line, plus fifty fighters aboard *Nimitz* ready to fly – '

'But we're already stretched to the limit,' Clancy said, pointing around the periphery of his fleet's escorts. 'We've got Soviet ships from the Red Sea and Yemen, Soviet aircraft and cruise missiles from Iran, and the *Arkhangel* carrier group from the south and east.' He shook his head, trying but failing to manage a rueful smile. 'Some old sea dog I turned out to be . . . A carrier's main defensive weapon is not getting itself into indefensible tactical situations in the first place. Here's a perfect example of what *not* to do: getting yourself surrounded on all sides by the bad guys . . . We need a good five hundred miles of reliable surveillance before we can safely secure this group. Right now we don't have it. We need some important help if we're going to pull this off.'

'The best we can get out here,' Edgewater said, 'are our own carrier-based EF-18s and Hawkeye AWACS radar planes.'

'Which will be prime targets when the shooting starts. And we just don't have the assets to assign one fighter to one Hawkeye for protection.'

'We can try another Himlord recon drone sortie . . .'

Clancy shook his head. 'Those drones are worth their weight in gold, but they're sitting ducks against shipborne surface-to-air concentrations. We sent four of them up two days ago and the Soviets used them for target practice.' He paused for a minute, staring at the screen; then: 'What about Diego Garcia? Any help from the air force available?'

'Same deal with air force E-3C AWACS,' Edgewater said. 'The Russian Su-27s will pick them off right away. Command won't risk them so far out without fighter escort.'

'*They're* trying to tell *me* about risk.' Clancy had no trouble getting up a sarcastic smile. 'I'm up to my eyeballs in risk.' He studied the huge SPY-2 Aegis repeater display in front of him. 'Y'know what we need, Joe?'

Joe knew: they needed their space-based eyes back.

The Kremlin, USSR

For the last ten minutes the general secretary had listened with scarcely disguised impatience as Khromeyev and Rhomerdunov briefed him on their conversation with Govorov about the recent movement of the space station.

'Stop right there,' the Soviet commander in chief said, holding up his hand. 'I've heard enough to worry me. Thank you very much, but in spite of your emphasis on Marshal Govorov's assessment of the damage done to the station, you cannot dismiss that he did recommend a second attack.'

'Nor would we wish to, sir,' Khromeyev said quickly. 'But I have already pointed out why an attack would be unwise at this time. Further intelligence has come up with the very credible explanation that the Americans may be simply retrieving components.'

'I can't believe that. The Americans would not have gone to the trouble of boosting Armstrong into a higher orbit if their only objective was to salvage scrap . . . Govorov should have finished off the station while he had the chance.'

356

'Oh, I agree, sir,' Rhomerdunov said. 'But logic tells us there is no possible way Armstrong can be repaired and reactivated in time to contribute to the American fleet's operation in the Middle East. Their rescue of a nonoperational Armstrong is of no consequence to our operation.'

'I would like to believe these assurances of yours . . .' The general secretary moved back to the seat behind his desk, leaving the two men standing ill at ease. He stared directly at them. 'So your recommendation is to do nothing?'

'No, sir,' Rhomerdunov said. 'Not at all. I have ordered Space Defence Command on full alert. Armstrong's new orbit will be carefully monitored, and any other spacecraft that attempt to dock or service the station will be tracked and reported to the Stavka. We will also monitor the station for radar emissions in case the Americans somehow manage to partially activate their space-based radar – '

'So your absolute assurances are not so absolute, after all.' The general secretary shook his head. 'You know as well as I the consequences of the Americans being able to use their space-based radar. Any advantage we hoped to gain by moving the *Arkhangel* into the area will be largely minimized; the balance of power will be restored.'

'Sir,' Khromeyev said quickly, trying to rebut but not too strongly, 'the advantage of having a crippled space station with a partially active radar cannot be compared with having the world's most destructive war vessel.'

'But we've seen what Armstrong's radar can do. And we have yet to see what the *Arkhangel* can do.' He paused a moment, considering. 'You're right, though, about the effect of an attack on the station now, without verification that the Americans are reactivating it and right after that unfortunate incident with the Americans' rescue craft. It would no doubt turn world opinion against us, possibly even upset relations with some of our allies. It appears then that we only have one option . . .'

'And that, sir?' Khromeyev didn't like where this was heading. He wished Minister of Defence Czilikov had been at the meeting, but Czilikov had allowed him and Rhomerdunov to report to the Soviet commander in chief directly, assuming no action would be taken. It now appeared that was a mistake.

'It should be obvious that we cannot wait any longer to give *Arkhangel* the order to strike. I will *not* allow the advantage we now hold to slip away.'

Khromeyev tried to keep his composure. 'Sir, the fleets are still days apart. We can't mount a large enough strike force from such long range – '

'Then, damn it, augment the *Arkhangel*'s forces with land-based bombers or cruise missiles. The heavy Tupolev bombers and cruise missiles were most effective – '

'Against targets in Iran,' Rhomerdunov put in. 'The bombers were able to launch their missiles while still over their territory. If we were to strike at the *Nimitz* carrier group, the bombers would have to fly over the Gulf of Oman. They would be within range of the *Nimitz*'s own fighters.'

'Then use *faster* bombers. Use those supersonic Tupolev-22 bombers instead of the turboprop Tupolev-95s – I don't know why the damn things are still in our inventory anyway.'

'Sir . . .' Khromeyev reached for the right words to tell his commander in chief that he should leave the battle plans to his generals, 'I would like to suggest we involve Minister Czilikov. He no doubt will want a meeting of Stavka; there are factors involved – '

'I am *tired* of meetings, Khromeyev. Every hour we delay is a wasted one, allowing the Americans to prepare defensive measures. We have the upper hand – *now* is the time to act.'

He sat back in his chair, looked at them, rapped his knuckles on the desk. 'All right, brief Czilikov. Call your meeting. But by four o'cock . . . no, three o'clock, I want a complete strike plan ready for execution. Clear?'

Armstrong Space Station

A barely heard crackle in his earset told Saint-Michael someone on board *America* was calling him. He picked up the earphone, put it on his head. 'Saint-Michael here.'

'Jason, it's Ann. Coming aboard.'

The general was surprised. It had only been three hours since the crew had transferred over to the spaceplane.

'All right,' he said, putting on his POS mask, 'come on through.'

An environmental alarm immediately sounded in the connecting tunnel. The airlock they had built leaked connecting-tunnel air rapidly when opened, setting off the alarm. With a spacesuit Ann would have had about sixty seconds to get into the connecting tunnel, seal the door and repressurize the connecting tunnel before the atmospheric pressure reached the danger level. The repressurization always took away a bit of air pressure from the command module, which was why Saint-Michael had to wear a mask during a transfer. A few moments later, with the general monitoring the transfer and repressurization, Ann entered the command module.

Saint-Michael pulled off his mask. 'You came alone?'

'I couldn't sleep any longer,' she said, removing her mask. 'I thought it would be nice to spend at least a few minutes with you alone . . .'

'Sounds like a good idea to me. We haven't had a chance to talk since Colorado Springs.'

'And then you were so upset about Space Command's decision . . . You didn't say it but I knew it. I'm just glad all that arm twisting of yours worked. I have to admit that right before the launch, well, I'd pretty much given up hope.'

'Well, luck had something to do with it . . . something we'll need more of in the next few days . . .'

'They'll be coming, won't they?'

Saint-Michael reached out, pulled her against him, felt her body tight against his. 'Yes,' he said. 'They have to . . . I'm sure they've realized that Silver Tower hasn't crashed into the atmosphere. They're probably asking Govorov, their Elektron pilot, how bad he thinks the station's been damaged. If they send him up again it'll be an act of aggression, and they'll want to be damn sure it's necessary. They're not fools or idiots, despite what some of our armchair heroes back in DC might think. Still, I've got to bet that Govorov will try his best to convince them he should attack again. There was too much celebrating over how effective the first attack was. He'll feel that he has to finish the job . . . Ann, you said that Skybolt was operational. *Is* it?'

'I don't know,' she said, obviously frustrated she couldn't answer with a flat yes. 'I haven't had a chance to check all the systems yet, but judging by the condition of the SBR, I don't think so . . .'

'We've got to know. Skybolt is our only defence against those Elektron spaceplanes. As of right now I'm putting you on Skybolt exclusively; I'll work on the SBR as much as I can. Marty and Ken can finish the repositioning and look after the station. There may be another way we can protect the station until Skybolt can be repaired. I can check on the – '

'Not now, Jason. Look, you need some rest. You'll be no use to anyone if you're – '

'Right, but we just don't have time . . .' He turned to his comm panel. 'I think Marty's had enough sleep.' He pressed his earset closer to his head and keyed the microphone.

'*America*, this is Alpha.'

'Good mornin', General,' said Colonel Hampton. 'Go ahead.'

'I need Marty Schultz over here.'

'Yes, sir.'

'And Jon, have Marty bring some chow and coffee.'

Saint-Michael turned back to Ann, who gave him a sour look. 'I know, I know,' he said. 'There'll be time for sacking out later. I want you on Skybolt as soon as you've had something to eat. Get that gizmo of yours working, *whatever it takes*. Meantime, I've got me an air force to assemble.'

'Air force? You're going to use *America* for – ?'

'Not *America*. If the shooting starts I want *America* as far away from it as possible – back on earth if necessary.'

'Then what?'

But before he could answer Marty Schultz came in and Ann was left to speculate. Which she suspected Saint-Michael intended anyway for the time being.

For Marty Schultz this new job was nearly as painful as seeing the burned and disfigured corpses of his fellow crewmen stacked in the docking module. *Enterprise* was something special to him; he was the expert on its operation. He had flown on every shuttle in the fleet, old and new, but *Enterprise* was uniquely his.

He was a child during the early shuttle free-flight tests, and it was *Enterprise* being dropped from the back of a modified Boeing 747 that had ignited his desire to be an astronaut. He had imagined himself at the controls, retrieving satellites, rescuing stranded cosmonauts, building a city in the sky.

When *Enterprise* had been refurbished and activated as an interim replacement for the shuttle *Challenger*, Marty

361

had set a new challenge for himself. Every waking moment had been spent preparing to fly aboard her, and since then he had flown *Enterprise* more than any other person.

Now he saw . . . *Enterprise* a few hundred yards away through his bubble space helmet, and the sight tore at his guts. He saw the initial impact point of the Russian hypervelocity missile, saw the remains of the terrible explosion and fire in the lower decks, saw the devastation in the RCS, the nose reaction-control system pod. The shuttle's docking adapter and airlock were wide open, like the open spout of a dead pilot whale washed up on the beach. Her remote manipulator arm was sloppily sticking out of the open cargo bay, its grappler claws extended like fingers of a hand reaching for help.

Well, he was here to help. 'Beginning translation,' he said.

'Roger,' Colonel Hampton said from *America*. Marty nudged his MMU thruster-control and slid towards the shuttle.

'Damn it, damage is worse than I thought,' Marty said as he approached the shuttle.

Hampton glanced nervously at the inertial altimeter. 'Maybe we're only a few miles above the atmosphere entry point. There won't be much time. Can you fly that thing without a forward RCS pod?'

'She'll fly just *fine*. It'll be hard to dock her – maybe impossible – but if she's got power and fuel she'll be all right.' He had to sound as though he believed it. For his own sake as well as the others'.

He glided over to the cargo bay, unclipped the MMU and stowed it in a restraining harness on the forward bulkhead, then glided over to the docking adapter on the airlock and slipped inside. The sight of the middeck made him recoil. 'I . . . I'm in the middeck, *America*. Everything's wiped out. There may be nothing salvageable.' He paused for a minute longer, then, looking away from the unidentifiable hunks of debris remaining on the crew seats, announced, 'Moving to the flight deck.'

'Roger.'

A few moments later Marty was in the commander's seat and surveying the instruments. 'It looks good, *America*. Still have battery power on. I'm going to try to repower the fuel cells.'

He examined the electrical distribution panel on the pilot's side of the cockpit. The switches were arranged on the panel with lines and arrows to show the relationship between the various circuits and power controls, but he knew them all by heart. As long as the cells weren't damaged, Marty told himself, they should be working . . .

'Oxygen and hydrogen manifolds one, two and three open,' he recited as he flipped switches. 'DC battery power tied to essential bus. Tank heaters on . . .'

He continued his litany of system checks, identifying faulty connections and making the necessary repairs. Finally the main instrument panel lights came on.

'We've got it, *America*,' Marty said excitedly. '*Enterprise* is alive.' His enthusiasm peaking, he finished reactivating *Enterprise*'s fuel cells, then moved back to the left-side commander's seat.

'C'mon, lady,' Marty said, patting the digital autopilot panel. 'I know you're alive. Now we need to get back into the game.'

The computer-monitor in front of him was blank except for a tiny blinking rectangle no bigger than the size of a kernel of corn – but that tiny dot was the ballgame. *Enterprise*'s brain, the GPC, was alive and awake – the problem was it had forgotten it was a General Purpose Computer. He had to perform an IPL, an initial program load, the series of commands that would tell the computer that it *was* a computer.

He did it quickly, entering a series of digital commands

that told the computer where in its permanent memory it could find a program that would initiate the computer's speedy education. After each lesson the computer would perform a final exam, writing another program for itself in volatile memory that it would use to move to the next lesson. Marty coaxed each step into the progress with commands that would periodically quiz the GPC on its progress. On the ground prior to launch these complicated steps were usually performed by ground personnel so that when the crew arrived on the shuttle they found a perfectly running fully educated GPC. Marty was one of the few who had taken the time to watch this procedure from the beginning.

'How's it going, Marty?'

'We're up to high school.'

'Say again . . .?'

'We're doing fine, just fine.'

Thirty minutes later the computer screen was filled with messages telling of malfunctions, environmental problems, shortages of supplies. But to Marty it all meant *Enterprise* was thinking once again. He entered one final code into the GPC and grabbed the flight-control stick.

'*America. Enterprise* is ready to manoeuvre.'

'Roger. Moving clear.' Hampton commanded *America*'s computer to move away from *Enterprise* on a heading back towards the station. 'Well clear.'

'Here we go.' Marty double-checked his switch positions and nudged the stick forward.

Nothing.

'*C'mon*, baby.' He nudged the stick a bit more. Still no reaction.

'*Enterprise*, any luck?'

'Stand by.' Marty cleared the in-flight manoeuvring code from the GPC and reentered it. This time the GPC refused to accept the code. He sat back in his seat, scanned the panel.

'Last chance,' he said to the instrument panel. He checked the RCS fuel-pressure gauges, power supplies, circuit breakers, bypass circuits – all nominal.

'We don't have much time, *Enterprise*. Get her started or abandon her.'

'One more minute.' He cleared the GPC flight code once again. 'This is it, you contrary s.o.b. If you don't go, I leave you to fry on your way down.' He reentered flight code two-oh-two and the computer screen blanked.

'The GPC's not accepting the manoeuvring code,' Marty radioed to Hampton.

'Then let's get the hell out of here. Hull temperatures are increasing. If you wait much longer . . .'

'On my way,' Marty said. He was about to leave the commander's seat when a sudden thought stopped him. He sat down and cleared the in-flight manoeuvring code, punched in the code to erase the IPL and the mass memory areas. He was eliminating all the shuttle's schooling.

Suddenly the code came back as '202', the in-flight manoeuvring code.

'A perverse lady . . . Reverse psychology, works every time – '

'Say again, *Enterprise*?'

Marty sat back in the commander's seat and took a firm grip on the control stick.

'I say, lead on, *America*. *Enterprise* is right and ready to go.'

Marty Schultz, along with Ken Horvath, hovered over yet another piece of free-floating SBR console, grabbed it and secured it back in place with another piece of tape.

'Attention on the station,' Saint-Michael announced over the interphone. 'Target-area horizon crossing in one minute. Stand by. This station is on red alert.'

Horvath nudged Schultz, looking around the command module. Almost every panel and console in the entire module – ceiling as well as wall mounted – had been removed during the past five days and only about half of them had been put back in their original places. The rest were either floating, attached or semi-attached to some other piece of equipment somewhere else in the module. Bundles of wiring of all descriptions crisscrossed the module in all directions: it was easier for the crew-members to float around the wires than to try to route the wiring behind the ever-changing landscape of electronic components. Pieces of equipment borrowed from other modules – computers and monitors from the recreation module, wiring from *Enterprise*, tubing and insulation from the cargo module, test components and, in many spots, entire console sections from the scientific module – added to the seemingly random piles of equipment scattered throughout the command module. But the mountains of gadgets only partially concealed the huge silicone patches on the module walls, the areas of scorching where fires had broken out, and the occasionally flashing environmental warning lights (the warning horns had been deactivated long ago; they went off all the time but everyone watched the warning lights anyway).

One of the silicone patches had recently been removed, and a large data-transmission cable had been strung through the hole before a new silicone patch was applied. The cable ran from the command module out across space and connected to a port in *America*'s cargo bay; the spaceplane had been secured beside Silver Tower by having *America*'s manipulator arm grasp and hold the station's central keel. A few consoles had been removed on *America*'s flight deck and a hasty rewiring job had also been managed there.

'Jon, we'll be ready to transmit in a few minutes,' Saint-Michael radioed to Hampton aboard *America*.

'Roger,' Hampton replied. 'TDRS set to fleet tactical, and TDRS link for *America* to Armstrong shows active and ready. Standing by.'

Saint-Michael turned back to the master space-based radar console – actually, the one that was acting as the master display. Parts of the master console were spread throughout the module, but they had managed to cluster most of the important controls together to make it easier for one person to operate it. Ken Horvath took his place beside Saint-Michael and studied the displays, shaking his head.

'I'm having trouble deciphering all this.'

'I'll explain,' Saint-Michael told him. 'You may have to relay this information to *Nimitz* or *Ticonderoga* like an air-traffic controller if the TDRS relay doesn't work. Okay, our SBR display computer is all gone, so it can't draw the informational maps and target symbols for us. But we still get the raw data that could have been fed into the SBR display computer – range, bearing, altitude, heading and velocity of the object being tracked. All of that is displayed on these two screens. The SBR can also analyse the target – tell us if it's an aircraft, a ship, its origin and even possible destinations – and that's displayed on the left-hand screen. You match up target designation codes to find which is which.'

Horvath was feeling more confident. 'Sounds easy enough.'

'It isn't. The SBR can pick up objects weighing as little as a few hundred pounds, so we'll be getting a flood of information. We'll probably need to squelch some of the SBR data – delete stuff we don't want to look at. We have a monitor that records what's being squelched but we can't see it from here. So be careful . . . If we link up with the *Nimitz* via TDRS, the third monitor here will

367

show his position as well. I'm hoping that *Ticonderoga*'s computers can digest these raw data into their information-centre's digital display.'

Saint-Michael checked the right-hand display. 'Attention on the station. Target-area crossing.' Then to Hampton aboard *America*, 'Activate the TDRS link, Jon.'

USS *Nimitz*

'Admiral, urgent message from the *Ticonderoga*.'

Edgewater quickly read the message form. 'Admiral, it's from Armstrong Space Station. *They're back transmitting . . .*'

Clancy was already staring in surprise at the liquid-crystal repeater display. It began to shimmer and undulate as if streams of phosphorescent water were pouring down its face. The numbers and scales of the display itself began to change at first, then came the symbols of the ships belonging to the *Nimitz* carrier group. After a few moments land and political boundaries were drawing themselves at the upper edge of the screen.

And at the right-hand side of the screen was the *Arkhangel* carrier group, its escort spread out into the 'Russian Star' formation. Soon even finer elements were being added: the display identified aircraft, helicopters, even types of radar emissions from each vessel. The side of the display showed codes belonging to each ship and its course and speed.

Clancy hurried over to the master CIC console and picked up a headset. 'Patch me into *Ticonderoga*. I want to talk with the space station.'

The relay took a few minutes, but Clancy soon heard the familiar crackle of the scrambled satellite transmission and another familiar sound . . . '*Nimitz*, this is Armstrong Station. How copy? Over.'

'Jason, I'm damned. I heard someone in Space Command might get off their duffs and fix that station but I didn't dare believe it. Very glad to hear your voice.'

'Likewise, Admiral,' Saint-Michael said. 'We don't have much time. I've passed the essentials to *Ticonderoga* but here's our situation: we're on an equatorial orbit this time. That means we have coverage of you for only twenty minutes every ninety minutes. That's twenty on, seventy off, twenty on, seventy off. Best we can do.'

'I understand, Jas. That's fine. Hell, even twenty minutes of SBR data is valuable. Listen, what's your level of damage up there? Do you have any defence?'

Saint-Michael gave a sideways glance at Marty Schultz as he exited the command-module hatch. 'We're working on that, Admiral. We might even have a surprise for anybody who happens to drop in on us. Anyhow, we're hanging tight here. Out.'

Ruzlan Attack Formation

The attack plan had been coordinated down to the very second.

The six Soviet Tupolev-26 Backfire bombers attacking from Iran each carried one AS-6 Kingfish antiship cruise missile semirecessed along its centreline weapons hardpoint, plus two AS-12 Kegler antiradar missiles on the intake-weapons stations. At three hundred miles distance from the northernmost escorts of the American aircraft carrier *Nimitz*, the six Backfire bombers would launch their missiles from eleven thousand metres. Then as the six cruise missiles climbed and accelerated to their cruising altitude the bombers would drop low for the long overwater supersonic dash towards the fleet. Once within ninety kilometres of any American vessel, the Backfire bombers would launch their antiradar missiles at any acquisition of tracking radars they met up with.

At the same time as the AS-6 missile launches, the first wave of Sukhoi-27 Flanker fighters would launch from the *Arkhangel* towards the Nimitz. Along with the fighters, two waves of five supersonic swing-wing Sukhoi-24 Fencer bombers would launch from the escort attack-carriers *Kiev* and *Novorossiysk* and begin attacks on the *Nimitz*'s escorts from the south and west. Each bomber carried two AS-12 antiradar missiles, four AS-16 advanced long-range armour-piercing missiles and one thirty-millimetre Gatling-type strafing gun with armour-piercing shells.

The two-pronged attack, involving twenty-four heavily armed supersonic aircraft, was timed to near-perfection. The copilot aboard the lead Backfire bomber, First Lieutenant Ivan Tretyak, was responsible for force-timing for the six Backfire bombers from the Caspian Sea aviation base at Baku.

'Checkpoint coming up, copilot,' the navigator-bombardier called up to Tretyak. 'Ready, ready . . . now.'

'Seven seconds late,' Tretyak said, checking his flight plan and chronometer. 'New groundspeed, navigator?'

'Stand by . . . New groundspeed to next checkpoint – one-one-nine-five kilometres per hour.'

'Copy,' the pilot, Major Andrei Budanova, replied. Carefully watching his Doppler groundspeed readout, he nudged the throttle of his twin Kuznetsov NK-144 turbofans up until the groundspeed read the proper value, then reset the Backfire's wings until the proper launch angle of attack was reestablished. 'Groundspeed set.' He switched his radio to the air-to-air command frequency. '*Ruzlan* flight, new throttle setting ninety-four per cent. Wingsweep setting forty degrees.' His five wingmen acknowledged the call.

Perfect, the attack-formation commander told himself.

Dead on time, six good bombers and not one hint of detection or threats anywhere. Perfect . . .

USS *Nimitz*

'Sir, SBR is reporting six large high-speed aircraft approaching on an intercept heading from the northwest. Armstrong Station's SBR is calling them Backfire bombers.'

'Range?'

'Aircraft are still over Iran, sir,' the seaman aboard the *Nimitz* said. 'Six hundred sixty nautical miles and closing at Mach one. All still at high altitude.'

'Sound general quarters,' Edgewater ordered, then looked to Clancy, waiting for a countermand or change. Instead he got: 'Launch alert flight Romeo to intercept and get Whiskey One on the catapults. Send the cruiser *Mississippi* northwest to follow the Tomcats to assist. Broadcast messages on all frequencies warning all aircraft within four hundred miles to identify themselves or we will fire without further warning.'

'Aye, sir.'

Clancy slapped his hands together as his aide handed him a life jacket and helmet.

'*Nimitz*, this is Armstrong. We're showing aircraft heading your way. Do you copy?'

'We got 'em, Jason,' Clancy radioed back. A happy warrior now. 'You guys spotted 'em a full three hundred miles before Aegis would have even known they were there. You may have just saved this battle group. *Well done*.'

Saint-Michael took a deep breath. 'Thanks, Admiral. We'll be maintaining surveillance for another one-five minutes. Let's hope the Russians don't get too feisty while we're on the back side of our orbit.'

'That's up to us. Thanks again on this end. *Nimitz* clear.'

'Luck, Admiral. Armstrong out.'

Ruzlan Attack Formation

'I am showing ninety seconds to launch point,' Tretyak announced.

'Acknowledged, copilot,' the bombardier replied, inside the dark bombardier cubicle a few metres behind Tretyak. Khabarovsk glanced across the narrow aisle to the defensive-system operator, pulled a flask from his boot and took a long pull.

But he wasn't quick enough about it: the electronic warfare officer, First Lieutenant Artemskiy, spotted him. Khabarovsk thought he'd be in big trouble. To his surprise, Artemskiy nodded towards his own electronics countermeasure cubicle behind the pilot and opened his two gloved hands. Khabarovsk expertly tossed the flask into them.

Artemskiy unscrewed the flask and sniffed the contents. Not vodka? He swirled it around, glanced at Khabarovsk. The bombardier rolled his palm over his stomach.

'Coming up to missile-launch point.'

'Acknowledged.' Khabarovsk gave Artemskiy a thumbs-up and carefully rechecked his switch positions for missile launch. 'Checklist complete. Ready for launch commit and ten-second alignment countdown.'

'*Ruzlan* flight, *Ruzlan* flight,' Budanova, the pilot, called over the air-to-air radio, 'launch commit. Repeat, launch commit.' Bombardier Khabarovsk moved the LAUNCH COMMIT button to the COMMIT position.

Artemskiy returned Khabarovsk's salute, then nodded at the flask. One sip couldn't hurt. They were still miles away from the extreme range of the Americans' radar. He tipped the flask to his lips –

A threat-warning buzzer sounded on his panel. Startled, Artemskiy dumped a mouthful of home-made distilled grain alcohol straight down his trachea and into his lungs.

'Defence section. Threat warning. Bearing and type *immediately*.'

Artemskiy upchucked onto his tiny workshelf beneath his electronics console, but it did little good – he couldn't breathe, couldn't speak. The flask clattered down his flightsuit, drenching his pants leg and deck with alcohol.

'*Defence. Report.* Bearing and type of threat . . .'

Still no reply.

'*Ruzlan* flight, evasive manoeuvre Echo-five-echo. *Execute*.'

'Negative,' Khabarovsk called out. 'Still five seconds to go to missile countdown . . .'

'Disregard missile countdown, bombardier. Place your missile in countdown hold and get ready to launch after we roll out. Defence, give me a bearing on the threat.'

But it was already too late. The lead pilot's only evasive manoeuvre in a line-abreast cruise-missile launch formation was a hard pushover to a three-'g' dive for the safety of the sea, and because he would be on the same heading during the manoeuvre the push had to occur immediately after threat detection. He did not have time to ask for bearings or give orders. Just at the point he decided to execute the evasive manoeuvre a US Navy AIM-54 Phoenix missile struck the Backfire bomber's right-wing root and sent the one-hundred-fifty-ton bomber to a fiery crash in the Arabian Sea.

Attacking from one hundred miles away with long-range Phoenix missiles, six F-14E Tomcat Plus fighters from the USS *Nimitz* screamed towards the scattering Backfire bombers. The Phoenix missiles were relatively less reliable launched at their extreme range limit, but even though only one Phoenix missile found its target the attack achieved its effect. The AS-6 cruise missile required a steady launch platform within narrowly defined acceleration limits ten seconds before launch, and all six of the Backfire bombers had immediately exceeded those limits.

The devastation continued after the Tomcats closed in. With no internal bomb bay and the AS-12 antiradar missiles installed on the underside intake weapon stations, the Backfire's limiting speed was Mach 1.5, but the bombers were already at Mach one before they began their evasive manoeuvres. As soon as they started their emergency descents for the safety of the radar clutter of the sea, they reached and then exceeded the normal weapons limits. The fortunate ones jettisoned the AS-12 and the AS-6 missiles before reaching the emergency carriage speed limit of Mach 1.8; the rest found their supersonic bombers shaking themselves to pieces and their AS-12 missiles ripping free of their weakened pylons.

Of the original six-bomber attack force, three survived the initial F-14 Tomcat attack that had seemed to come out of nowhere. Of these three, one was chased down and destroyed by a medium-range Sidewinder heat-seeking missile. A second failed to jettison its AS-12 missiles, one of which ripped free of its pylon and struck the horizontal stabilizer, making the aircraft spin out of control.

The remaining Backfire bomber ended its evasive manoeuvre immediately after beginning it, realigned its AS-6 cruise missile and launched it seconds before two Tomcats hit it with three air-to-air missiles. The AS-6 missile, riding a long, bright yellow column of fire, sped skyward, levelled off at fifty thousand feet and went south-east at Mach three. The American Tomcats had no hope of chasing it down.

But the AS-6 missile tracked directly over the guided missile cruiser USS *Mississippi*, which had been trailing the Tomcats from the *Nimitz* and had been tracking the AS-6 almost since launch. It brought both of its fore-and-aft Mark 26 dual-rail vertical launchers to bear and fired a salvo of four SM2-E Standard missiles at the speeding AS-6 cruise missile. The AS-6, in spite of its advanced design, accuracy and awesome destructive power, was still not capable of any evasive manoeuvres; flying at high altitude and in a straight line towards its target, it also made itself an inviting target. The US defence missiles intercepted the Soviet cruise missile several seconds later.

USS *Nimitz*

'Bridge, CIC. Aegis reporting radar-contact aircraft bearing one-five-zero true, range three-one-five, closing fast. Multiple inbounds.'

Well, the fleet wouldn't have Silver Tower to help them out on this one, Admiral Clancy thought as he and Captain Edgewater paced the bridge of the USS *Nimitz*, dividing their attention between flight-deck operations and the Aegis battle-management radar-repeater scope.

Edgewater studied the scope. 'We've got Tango flight on patrol to the southeast, Admiral. Four Tomcats.' He picked up the phone to CIC. 'Combat, this is Edgewater. Got a count on those inbounds?'

'Negative, sir. So far only three targets, high altitude, fast moving, within two hundred miles of our cruiser *South Carolina*'s position.'

'Better get another flight airborne to back up Tango against those inbounds,' Clancy told Edgewater. 'I don't believe the *Arkhangel*'s only sending up three planes. It's more than likely three *formations* – two attack and one fighter escort . . .'

'Aye, sir.' Edgewater replaced the phone to CIC and picked up the phone to flight operations. 'Air ops, this is the bridge. Get Whiskey One airborne and Sierra on deck. Send Whiskey One to back up Tango.'

He turned back to Clancy, who was staring at the buzz of activity surrounding the two F-14 Tomcats on the catapults. Behind the retractable blast-fence two more Tomcats waited for their turn on the catapults, and eight more were lined up waiting to taxi behind them. The number-three elevator was bringing still another Tomcat up out of the hangar deck to take its place in line. The flight deck was noisy and smelly, and cold rain began to pelt the lookout deck surrounding the bridge of the *Nimitz* – but Clancy was in his element as he watched his sailors do their stuff.

A messenger ran up to Edgewater and handed him a sheet of computer paper. 'Message from the *Mississippi*, Admiral,' Edgewater called out. When Clancy did not reply, Edgewater went out to him on the catwalk. 'The *Mississippi* intercepted a Soviet AS-6 cruise missile launched from the north Arabian Sea.'

'What about the Backfires? Did the Tomcats . . .?'

'All six down,' Edgewater said, allowing a smile. 'The Tomcats took out five of them. A sixth went out of control.'

Clancy raised his eyes skyward, letting pellets of cold rain hit his face.

Thank you, Silver Tower . . .

Tyuratam, USSR

The night of the abortive Backfire bomber attack in the Arabian Sea a uniformed man appeared at Govorov's home at the Space Defence base at Tyuratam. The banging on the apartment door startled Govorov's wife

376

and caused their five-year-old daughter to wake up, asking if the apartment was on fire. Govorov opened the door and found an aide of the Minister of Defence with a sealed letter in his hand. The letter told him there was a MiG-33 waiting for him at Tyuratam Aerodrome; he was to report to the Kremlin immediately. The letter stated the exact time of his appointment with the Stavka.

Govorov was irritated but hid it from Czilikov's aide. There was no way he could arrive at the designated time, even aboard one of the world's fastest jet fighters. But that was intended, an obvious ploy to show how displeased the Stavka was with him.

Telling the aide to give him a few minutes, he went back to the tiny bathroom in his master bedroom and without a light began to run hot water to shave. His wife propped herself up on one elbow in their bed. 'Who was it, Alesander?'

'A messenger from Moscow. They want me there.'

'And you were going to shave in the dark?' She got up from bed and snapped on the bathroom light. 'I'd better check on Katrina. The messenger scared her.'

He could hear his wife's soothing voice trying to calm their daughter and had to steady his razor hand to keep from nicking himself. If one of the august members of the Stavka were roused out of bed as he had been, heads would roll. He didn't really stand much on ceremony or rank, but they were still treating him like a squadron commander.

He knew why, of course . . . It was because of the American space station Armstrong's *not* being destroyed as he'd thought at first . . .

He shaved, quickly washed, dressed in a space defence command flight suit and a pair of boots. His wife was waiting at the door with his flying jacket, an insulated bottle of coffee and an egg-and-sausage sandwich wrapped in a napkin.

He took her face in both his hands and kissed her on the lips. 'I do not deserve you,' he said.

'Oh, I think you do,' she said, helping him on with his jacket, 'but I deserve *you* as well.' She zipped up his jacket for him and returned his kiss with a long, warm one of her own. 'Will you call me before you launch?'

Her question had been unexpected. 'I won't ask how you knew that I might be flying today. If I could conquer the mysteries of a woman, I could conquer outer space, maybe even the Stavka members.' She smiled, but it was strained. 'Yes,' he said quickly, 'I will try to call.'

'I love you, Alesander.'

Her tone held him. He searched her round eyes – looked away. What he saw bothered him . . .

'I'll call you,' he said, and hurried out. He nearly stumbled over the aide in his rush towards the stairway. The man ran ahead to open the door for him as they emerged into the cold darkness. Govorov snatched up the telephone in the rear of the car as the driver hustled behind the wheel and sped off.

Govorov punched four digits into the dialling keypad. 'Marshal Govorov here. Duty officer. Gulaev? Put him on. Nikolai, I've been ordered to Moscow. Call dispatch at the aerodrome and take whoever is the pilot of the MiG-33 off the flight orders. I'll fly myself to Moscow. Have life-support put my gear on the plane, then put me on the flight orders for Elektron One effective upon my return to Glowing Star. Shift Colonel Kozhedub to Elektron Two and Litvyak to Three. Put Vorozheykin on the flight orders of Elektron One until I get back. He will drop back to standby with Pokryshkin when I take command of Elektron One.'

Govorov dropped the phone back onto its cradle and leaned towards the front seat. 'Drive faster.' A vivid image of his wife and daughter came to him and he forced it away. He had seen something in his wife's eyes back in the apartment that he badly wanted to change. She was scared, too scared for her own good . . . or his.

'*Faster*.'

12

It was the first time in months that any member of the
Stavka VGK, the Armed Forces Supreme High Command, had been in the Soviet military's alternative command post located one hundred and sixty kilometres south
of Moscow. This particular post was never involved in any
preparedness exercises or drills, was manned by only a
small staff of hand-picked technicians and soldiers and did
not have a major military airfield associated with it –
Stavka members from Moscow were flown in to Novomoskovsk by helicopter. The other well-known 'high-
value' alternative command posts under the Kremlin and
in Pushkino received all the attention and publicity and,
it was assumed, were the ones targeted by the West in the
event of a thermonuclear exchange. Novomoskovsk, well
away from military targets, factories, rail depots and –
most important – publicity, was designed to escape all but
a direct hit. Unless an attack had already been launched
against the Soviet Union and time was running out, the
eleven men of the Stavka and their aides and assistants
knew that the Novomoskovsk command post was far safer
and more secure than any in Moscow.

In fact, the Novomoskovsk command post was probably
the most secure place in eastern Europe. When the Soviet
Union perfected the technique of welding ultrathick
pieces of metal they had immediately applied that technology to the walls of the three-thousand-square-foot

underground facility. The main construction of the bunker consisted of four-foot-thick walls of steel welded by small nuclear detonations in industrial reactors. The steel chamber rode on huge shock absorbers that would cushion the chamber from the terrific overpressures of a nearby nuclear explosion. Two dozen men and women could live and work there in reasonable comfort for at least a month. No question, Novomoskovsk was the place to be if there were ever a nuclear war.

But at the moment the command post was not the place to be if one wanted to be safe from the stinging disapproval of the general secretary of the Soviet Union. The Soviet leader sat at the apex of a large triangular table, listening with growing irritation to First Deputy Minister Khromeyev as he stood before an electronic briefing board, reviewing the progress of Operation Feather. The Stavka members were arranged on either side of the general secretary, each with a communications terminal and a telephone at his side.

Yesterday, when the first of the massive air attacks on the *Nimitz* carrier group had begun, the general secretary had postponed all his appearances and appointments to take personal command of the Arabian Sea conflict. The breaking of the American blockade around the mouth of the Persian Gulf was now the major focus of his attention, and he was growing progressively angrier as he realized nothing was working as planned. And who could blame him? He also had a rather complex domestic economy to run. His military people were supposed to handle their end once the goals and strategies had been spelled out.

'The *Arkhangel* task force will soon open the high-speed air-attack lane around the *Nimitz* carrier force,' Khromeyev went on. 'This lane will provide a relatively clear path for our Mikoyan-Gureyvich-23 carrier-based fighter bombers to transit the American fleet and reinforce the *Brezhnev* carrier group in the Persian Gulf. We are expecting – '

'*Stop,*' the general secretary broke in. 'What is all this about a "relatively clear" air attack lane? I want to know about the damned *Nimitz*. It's still blocking the Strait of Hormuz, isn't it? Why aren't we launching another attack on the *Nimitz*? Why don't we have control of the Arabian Sea? Why can't we bring the *Arkhangel* carrier group through to the Gulf of Oman? *Why?*'

'We have not sufficiently reduced the American forces to allow our vessels to pass,' Admiral Chercherovin said. 'Sir, it will take time – '

'How much have we reduced the American forces? How many ships have we sunk?'

Chercherovin's silence said it all.

'None? We've sunk *none*?'

'The conflict has not progressed far enough where the surface combatants are in direct conflict,' Minister of Defence Czilikov put in. 'That is a phase of battle still a few days away. The battle is being fought in the air, with our aircraft winning the ships' right to move forward . . .'

'And we have inflicted heavy damage on some American vessels,' Chercherovin added. 'Our AS-12 missiles are very effective against the older American search-and-tracking radars. Once their guided-missile cruisers are made ineffective our bombers can clear a path for the *Arkhangel* group to pass – '

'You seem fixed on this idea that we are conducting this latest offensive merely to let the *Arkhangel* pass into the Persian Gulf, Admiral,' the general secretary said. 'That is not our goal. Our goal is to remove the *Nimitz* carrier group as a presence in the Persian Gulf area. If necessary I want the *Nimitz* and all her escorts blown out of the water . . . I believe that's the phrase you people use. Well, is that *clear*, Admiral?'

'Yes, sir,' Chercherovin said, literally feeling the heat. The Soviet commander in chief turned to the other Stavka members. 'All right,' he said, 'let's get the rest of the bad news out in the open. What about our losses?'

'Principal surface combatant losses are still zero,' Khromeyev quickly put in. 'Damage has been reported aboard five vessels, all due to antiradiation missile attacks. The Krivak-class frigate *Karamarov* was seriously damaged but is still under way. Aircraft losses reported from *Arkhangel* are twenty Sukhoi-27 fighters, three Kamov-27 anti-submarine warfare – '

'*Twenty fighters*,' the general secretary said. 'In two days we have lost twenty fighters from the *Arkhangel*? How many were on it to begin with?'

'Seventy-four – '

'We have lost nearly *one-fourth* of our carrier-based fighters? How?' He turned to Chercherovin. 'The *Arkhangel* was supposed to be the ultimate weapon, Chercherovin. So far it has been damn near worthless.'

'That is not true, sir,' the Admiral said quickly. 'Our losses have been higher than anticipated because the Americans apparently aren't concerned about the dangers of escalating this conflict into a major confrontation. The *Nimitz* group should have pulled back from the Persian Gulf area – instead, it has not only blocked the sea lane but has used force to repel any overflight of the area – '

'*Admiral*, what is the problem here? . . . *We* should be the ones willing to engage the enemy whatever the cost. *We* should be taking the battle to *them*. Instead we're being pushed around the Arabian Sea by a much inferior force.' He glanced at Czilikov, anticipating a response. When none came he added, 'I think it's time a younger, more aggressive admiral take charge of the Arabian Sea flotilla.'

Admiral Chercherovin quickly scanned the room, searching for supporters. No one said a word. Not even Czilikov. Then the Admiral looked to Alesander Govorov.

'I think, Comrade General Secretary, that you should first ask Marshal Govorov the status of the American military space station. That station he supposedly crippled has obviously increased the Americans' ability to repel our attacks these past two days.'

The general secretary understood Chercherovin was trying to shift the blame, though the admiral did have a point. He gave Chercherovin a look that told him he wouldn't get off this easily, then turned to Govorov. 'Marshal, military intelligence *has* reported that the Armstrong space-based radar is operational again. Satellite relay signals suggest that the station is warning American vessels of attack and directing attacks against our forces. Is it possible?'

'Yes, sir, it is. I was mistaken in my damage estimates. We carried only twenty nonexplosive missiles on our first attack, and Colonel Voloshin was lost before exploding all his missiles. In my rush to search for Voloshin I depleted my fuel reserves and had to withdraw from attack before all missiles were directed on the station. The damage estimates on each station subsystem were accurate – '

'Marshal Govorov, I respect you. At least you aren't making stupid excuses, although it seems you made some stupid, or at least unwise, decisions. Concern for a comrade is admirable, but there are times when difficult decisions need to be made. You left the job half finished. And more than one man has suffered for it. Well, Marshal, do you have any thoughts about what you can do to make some amends?'

At that moment Govorov was easily the most resented man in that room. And he understood the general secretary's indulgence was a double-edged sword. He was being given a second chance – partly at least because he was still the most qualified man to do what had to be done. But he also understood if he should fail again, it would be better for him if he didn't come back.

'Sir, I propose to lead another attack on the space station – to complete what I should have finished the first time.' He turned to include the other Stavka members. 'The way I see it, the attack will be preceded by a chemical-laser barrage from Sary Shegan Research Facility against the new American Air Force geosynchronous surveillance satellite over the Indian Ocean. The laser will keep firing at the satellite while the space station Armstrong is on the opposite side of the earth, until we can be sure that the satellite has been neutralized or knocked out of its orbit. This will ensure that our launch from Tyuratam will go undetected. Ground-tracking stations will find it difficult to track us without first knowing our launch point or orbital insertion point, so the space station Armstrong can receive no advance warning of our attack . . .

'The attack will again be made by armed Elektron spaceplanes launched from Glowing Star Launch Facility at Tyuratam, but *this* time there will be three Elektron spaceplanes instead of two. My two wingmen will each carry ten *Bavinash* missiles aboard each spaceplane, which have been modified with forty-kilogram high-explosive warheads instead of depleted uranium and molybdenum armour-piercing nosecaps. The objective of my two wingmen will be to disable the Armstrong's space-based radar system, station propulsion and any defensive armaments. My Elektron will carry a far more important cargo, sir. The Scimitar missiles cannot destroy such a large station as Armstrong, and our spaceplanes cannot drag the station into the atmosphere. Therefore I will carry a two-thousand-kilogram space-reactive bomb into orbit. The bomb uses a chemical reaction to provide the heat and the power to mix a large volume of hydrogen and oxygen gas together in a compressed chamber that

385

will produce the power of over two tons of TNT in the vacuum of space. When Armstrong's defences have been neutralized I will fly to the station, plant the explosive on it, then detonate it once my wingmen and I are away . . . On my first mission I took it on myself to slow my attack to allow the station's crew to evacuate the station. I don't apologize for my intent. But I also understand that it gave the Americans time to build a defence that ended in the death of Colonel Voloshin. By returning to their station and reactivating their offensive surveillance and warning systems, the Americans have shown that they don't consider our spaceplane force a threat. So this time my attack will begin immediately. And this time I *will* destroy that station.'

The general secretary didn't show it, but he was pleased. At least this young officer came up with options. He wished the others in the room could be as creative. 'It sounds like a workable plan. Do you agree, Czilikov?' He did. 'Comments?' There were none. 'Then it is authorized.'

'Thank you, sir,' Govorov said. 'I'll be requesting final launch approval in eight hours. The attack will begin approximately three hours later.'

'Very well, Marshal. You are dismissed.' Govorov stood, saluted the general secretary and left.

After he had gone the general secretary turned once again to Chercherovin. 'Any other scapegoats, Admiral?' Chercherovin kept his mouth shut.

'If, as I believe, Marshal Govorov makes good on his promise to destroy the American space station,' the general secretary said, 'will this mean that the *Arkhangel* group can force the *Nimitz* carrier group to withdraw, or is there some other small bit of information that has not been revealed, some other excuse that you will tell me only after we have had another defeat?'

'The aircraft lost on the *Arkhangel* must be replaced,'

Chercherovin said. 'We have no accurate figures as to how many the Americans have lost – '

'Which to me sounds like they have not lost any,' the general secretary broke in. 'I sense the worst. If I can't get the truth, the whole truth, out of you, I will assume the worst has happened . . . so we will assume the Americans lost no fighter aircraft, and we have lost twenty fighters from the *Arkhangel*. How soon can we send twenty fighters out to the *Arkhangel*?'

'It may be difficult,' the admiral said slowly, expecting another outburst. 'Sukhoi-27 aircraft modified for carrier duty aboard the *Arkhangel* are only stationed at Vladivostok, the *Arkhangel*'s home port. An operation to move twenty Su-27s from there will take at least a day of planning and a half-day of flying.'

'A day and a half,' the general secretary said. 'And that, I assume, is a very optimistic figure. *And* that only places us at the same force level that we were at when the first twenty aircraft were destroyed. When the space station is finally knocked out, what do we have to take advantage of that?' He stood and walked around the triangular table. 'Hear me now, I will *not* be forced to use thermonuclear weapons to secure the Persian Gulf. I will *not* go down in history as the first Soviet leader to use nuclear weapons, *especially* on an inferior enemy force. Well, let me hear some alternatives.'

'A suggestion, Comrade General Secretary,' Ilanovsky, the commander in chief of the army, said. 'Sir, the objective is to destroy or cripple the *Nimitz* and her escorts. I still believe a massive cruise missile attack is the best way to attack the American fleet, but not with air-launched missiles. The flight profiles of the AS-6 and AS-4 missiles are too vulnerable to engagement by the *Nimitz*'s guided missile cruiser escorts, and the other air-to-ground cruise missiles currently deployed, such as the AS-15, are nuclear.'

'Then what *else* is available?'

'We have in early deployment a ground-launched cruise missile, a variant of the SS-N-24 naval cruise missile currently deployed on some of our older attack submarines. It's called the GL-25 Distant Death. It has transsonic speed, inertial and terrain-comparison guidance with active terminal-radar homing, and it can carry an eleven hundred kilogram conventional high-explosive warhead or a five hundred kiloton thermonuclear warhead over three thousand kilometres to its target with high accuracy. Only a hundred or so have been deployed, but most were sent to the Southern Military Headquarters region during the readiness exercise Rocky Sweep. From Tashkent and the mountains north of Afghanistan it would be possible to strike at the American fleet in the Arabian Sea.'

'But the *Nimitz*'s escorts have already proved that they can protect themselves from cruise-missile attack,' Chercherovin put in.

'Not from the GL-25,' Illanovsky told him quickly. 'This cruise missile does not stay at high altitude as it gets closer to its target like the AS-4 or AS-6, but is preprogrammed to travel at low altitude when in areas of high-threat concentration, and it can make a supersonic dash for the last hundred kilometres to the target. By the time the *Nimitz* or her escorts spot it, it will be too late to intercept.'

'But the time required to plan a strike sortie – '

'The missiles can be reprogrammed in a few hours,' Ilanovsky said. 'The missiles have been stored in surveyed launch positions since Operation Feather began, targeted on suspected areas of resistance in Iran and Afghanistan. They can be ready to launch well before Marshal Govorov's strike against the space station Armstrong is finished.'

The Stavka was silent. 'Any other objections?' the general secretary asked. There were none. 'Then I'm in favour of the operation.' He turned to Ilanovsky. 'How many missiles can be fielded against the American fleet?'

Ilanovsky paused, then: 'Sir, I believe seventy-five missiles were delivered to the southern TVD in support of Rocky Sweep. I must allow for a certain number to be out of commission due to normal maintenance difficulties, but I believe I can field at least fifty GL-25 cruise missiles for launch against the fleet.'

'Fifty missiles against twenty American ships. Can a definite number be targeted for the *Nimitz*?'

'The GL-25s can't be targeted that accurately, sir. Once within a certain distance from their preplanned target points, their homing radar is activated and the missile flies directly to the largest radar reflector in the area. But the American carrier fleet is spread out enough in the Arabian Sea to make it very likely that each missile will seek out its own target rather than join with others to attack one vessel. I think the GL-25s will have a devastating effect on the American fleet.'

The general secretary actually looked pleased. 'The GL-25 attack, using conventional high-explosive warheads, will immediately be implemented. I want a briefing on the missiles' exact flight path before launch.'

Ilanovsky, relieved and excited, nodded and issued orders to his aide, charging him with alerting the missile brigades in the south-central Soviet Union.

Armstrong Space Station

Saint-Michael switched his comm panel to the TDRS channel and adjusted his earset. '*Nimitz*, this is Armstrong. Horizon crossing in one minute. Over.'

'Copy, Jason,' from Admiral Clancy. 'Standing by for data transmission test.'

They had performed this routine several times in the

past two days, and each time the difference between having the station's eyes and not having them was startling. While Armstrong was on the other side of the globe the *Nimitz* had to rely on FR-18 Hornet maritime reconnaissance jets, E-27 Hawkeye turboprop early-warning-and-control planes, and Himlord drones to know what the Russians were up to. The *Nimitz* would launch two Hawkeyes and one Hornet, and the USS *Kidd* would launch four Himlords all at once. Eventually they all became targets for the escorts and fighters of the Soviet battle group to practise on. So far, two Hornets, one Hawkeye and an entire squadron of Himlords had been lost to Soviet attack.

By contrast, Silver Tower's SBR provided a much wider scale and more detailed look at the region; in fact, Admiral Clancy had begun to talk about the navy acquiring its own space-based radar platforms to be deployed with all its front-line carrier battle groups. It was no wonder he warmly greeted Silver Tower's reappearance every seventy minutes.

Saint-Michael monitored the system self-tests and status reports as they scrolled across the monitors. Ken Horvath pointed to a blinking line on the status monitor. 'There's that relay-circuit fault again.'

In the Skybolt control module Ann shooed away sweat blobs, pulled her POS mask to her face and took several deep breaths of oxygen. She was lying on her back placing the securing camlocks back into a relay circuit. The top of the module had been caved in by the force of one missile during the first Soviet spaceplane attack, so the monitors and console that used to be overhead were now squashed almost to the deck. The module was frigid, the air so thin on account of leaks that she got dizzy if she forgot to take a few deep breaths of oxygen every few minutes.

She had an unsecured ten-thousand-volt wire hanging a few inches from her head, pieces of computer components taped and Velcroed everywhere. Relays, memory chips and power supplies designed for one circuit now had to handle three or four. But it was worth it . . . maybe. At least Skybolt was put back together. But would it work?

'Just finished. I'm ready for a test.'

'Sorry, we're about to cross the horizon again.' A few moments later the fault indication cleared and reported itself normal. Ann, who had spent most of her time in the Skybolt control module since the station had been repaired could only work on the relay circuitry between Skybolt and the SBR, when the SBR was not being used to scan the Arabian Sea.

A few minutes later she entered the command module bringing three cups of coffee and a few pieces of hard candy, the only uncontaminated food still on the station. Saint-Michael and Horvath reached for the coffee.

'How's it going back there?'

'Bad to maybe better. The Russians put a missile right through one of the SBR relays that controls the slaving system to the laser mirror. I'm patching the circuits through to another relay, but it's sort of like reinventing the wheel. I'm beginning to discover how much I don't know about all that electronic stuff back there. I'll need a system test when we go below the target horizon.'

'You got it.' Saint-Michael rechecked the system read-outs. 'System self-test completed,' he announced, clicking the ACKNOWLEDGE key on his computer terminal. He switched his comm link to TDRS. '*Nimitz*, this is Armstrong. Data transmission link-check good. How copy?'

'*Ticonderoga* acknowledges data self-test good,' said the chief sensor technician aboard the Aegis command-and-control cruiser *Ticonderoga*. 'Trying to get acknowledgement from *Nimitz*. Standby.'

A few moments passed. By matching longitudinal coordinates Saint-Michael was able to announce when they'd crossed the target horizon, and they watched with quiet satisfaction as *Ticonderoga* and *Nimitz* began hungrily feeding on SBR transmissions relayed to them from Silver Tower.

'Armstrong, this is *Nimitz*. Come in.' Admiral Clancy's serious voice erased the smiles on the faces of Silver Tower's crew.

'Saint-Michael here, sir. Go ahead.'

'Jason, Aerospace Defense Command has just relayed a message to us from defence intelligence. While you were on the back of that last orbit the laser at Sary Shegan attacked our replacement satellite over the Indian Ocean. It's been destroyed. Kaput. No missile-launch-detection capability exists in this region.'

Horvath looked to Saint-Michael. 'What's it mean, skipper?'

'It means it's their opening volley, just like last time,' Saint-Michael said. 'Their spaceplanes can now launch without being detected. We can expect them to show any time.' Over the TDRS comm link he said, 'I copy, Admiral. Can you provide even limited launch warning over Asia?'

'Negative. We're stuck with either tactical reconnaissance or SBR. No deep-space capability. SPACETRACK or Pacific Radar Barrier in Diego Garcia may be able to pick them up, but the only reliable detection and tracking station close enough to help is either Pulmosan in South Korea or San Miguel in the Philippines.' An ominous pause, then: 'We can try to get you a link with San Miguel or Diego Garcia, but that won't do you any good. Face it, Jas. Time's run out. You're going to have to get your butts off that station.'

Saint-Michael turned to Ann. 'What do you say? Can Skybolt work? Is there a chance?'

'It's the SBR that's the sticking point, Jason. The error-trapping functions of the SBR weren't made for the

392

Skybolt interface – I have to backtrack and find all those error points myself. I think I can do it but – '

'Don't hedge on me, Ann. Can it work or not?'

She hesitated, trying to separate reality from wishful thinking. 'I don't *know*. I think I can trap all the error, but it'll take time – '

He'd already pulled the microphone to his lips, and his words had the force of a missile all on their own: 'Roger, *Nimitz*. We will begin evacuation immediately. Advise us of any problems with the SBR relay. Armstrong out.' And he clicked off the comm link.

'We're *evacuating*?' Ann said.

'We've got no other choice.'

'But all our work . . . We made this station *operational* again . . .'

'Ann, I can't forget those bodies back in the docking module. Those men died because I made the decision to stay after the first laser attack – '

'But you had a damned good reason – '

'Good, bad . . . they're dead. We've got the same situation happening all over again, only worse. This station is hanging on by putty and prayers. I'm risking lives every time we open the goddamned hatch . . .' He paused, touched her lightly on the shoulder. 'Listen to me. Skybolt was our last hope, our big ace in the hole – and now . . . now you can't assure me we have that. We've got no choice . . . We probably have a few hours until their spaceplanes make it back up here. It'll give us some time to prepare . . . And we can still salvage Skybolt if you and Ken can disconnect it from the station. We can put the laser module in *Enterprise*'s cargo bay and the control module in *America*'s and boost them both up into a storage orbit.'

Ann, miserable, nodded.

'I'll try to set up the SBR computers for automatic or remote-controlled operation,' Saint-Michael said. 'At least we'll be able to get a few more hours' work out of her before . . . before they completely destroy her.'

As they turned to make final preparations none of them had any doubt that, this time, the destruction of Silver Tower was going to be final.

They did not have long.

Timing, flawless; execution, perfect. A nineteen-second, full-power, sustained chemical laser-barrage over the Indian Ocean, first electronically blinding the satellite and then piercing a thruster fuel line, causing an explosion. The satellite's now errant death-spin had been easily detected by space-scanning radars at Tyuratam, and the message was relayed to Glowing Star that the satellite had been rendered inoperative.

Govorov and his two wingmen, Colonel Andrei Kozhedub in Elektron Two and Colonel Yuri Litvyak in Elektron Three, were all aboard their spaceplanes during the laser attack, at the last planned countdown hold only ten minutes from launch. When they got word of the satellite's destruction the countdown was quickly resumed.

Once again Govorov was the first to launch, riding a column of kerosene and nitro-acid fire on top of his two-million-pound-thrust SL-16 Krypkei booster. Separated by only thirty seconds, just long enough for Govorov's two-hundred-thirty-foot-tall, five-hundred-fifty-ton Krypkei rocket to clear the launch tower, the other two SL-16s successfully lifted off, gaining on Govorov's rocket in a matter of seconds.

The triple rocket launches were first detected by seismic sensors at NATO intelligence sites in Pirinclik, Turkey, but without satellite-launch detection the seismic reading told the US Space Command nothing except that there had been a series of powerful explosions. The west-to-east flight path of the Soviet boosters, however, allowed the air force SPACETRACK long-range FPS-17 detection and FPS-79 tracking radars on the tiny island of Diego Garcia, over three thousand miles south of the launch site, to spot the boosters rising through the atmosphere. It was the SPACETRACK site that detected the boosters' first-stage impact in Mongolia and the second-stage impact in the Pacific Ocean north of Japan. The boosters' launch progress and orbital positions were updated from the Pacific Radar Barrier radars at San Miguel in the Philippines and then by the air force's south-facing sea-launched ballistic-missile tracking radars in Texas and Georgia.

Although it did not take long for the three spaceplanes to reach Armstrong station's orbit altitude, the tail chase to intercept the station would take two complete orbits, over three hours, to move within a few hundred miles of the station.

With the third-stage booster still attached to each spaceplane, Govorov ordered the thrust-power setting and carefully monitored the intercept using tracking signals from ground- and satellite-based space tracking systems. He needed to strike a balance between using up fuel in a fast tail chase and wasting precious time and oxygen on a lengthy chase.

He made up his mind to be patient this time. Everything – his life, his career, the success of Operation Feather – depended on his not making another mistake. The time to hurry would be when the intercept was made and the final attack on the Americans' space station began . . .

Govorov was ending his first orbit of the earth, closing the gap between himself and Armstrong when another spectacular multiple launch took place in south-central Russia.

Once every ten seconds a tongue of flame would erupt from a rugged mountain valley south of Tashkent. Boosted by a solid rocket motor, a GL-25 Distant Death ground-launched cruise missile would leap off its railcar-mounted launcher into the dark skies. Resembling a small jet fighter, with a long cylindrical fuselage, swept wings and cruciform tail section, each GL-25 launched amid a peal of thunder that echoed off the steep granite walls of the surrounding mountains.

The rocket motors accelerated the missile to five hundred kilometres per hour, then detached from the fuselage and fell away into the desolate Zeravanskij Mountains north of Afghanistan. Air inlets along the sides of the fuselage popped open and the missile's ramjet engine automatically started. With the ramjets at full power the GL-25 missiles quickly accelerated, and using their inertial navigation system and taking position update terrain-comparison snapshots of the terrain below, they sped southward, hugging the earth less than three hundred metres over ground. Travelling eight hundred kilometres per hour, the missiles crossed into Afghanistan and streaked towards their preprogrammed target-acquisition initial points over twenty-eight hundred kilometres away. After reaching their initial points three-and-a-half hours later they would activate their terminal radar-homing sensors, then for the last two hundred kilometres of their flight seek their individual targets, the nineteen auxiliary vessels and escorts surrounding the *Nimitz*.

In the rugged mountains there were no radars powerful enough to spot the fast-moving, ground-hugging missiles. The shepherds and farmers and the scattering of people living in the wild middle-eastern coastal mountains were accustomed to the ear-shattering sounds of Soviet military aircraft passing overhead and ignored the almost continual rocket booms. Now, unheeded, the roar of the GL-25's ramjet engines echoed up and down the lonely mountain walls as the deadly missiles sped towards their targets.

Two hours later Ann's breathing had become shallow and slow as her prebreathing stint was nearing completion. She was in the command module helping to monitor the progress of the SBR computer reprogramming. The few remaining computers had to be taught to steer the space station to achieve the best SBR presentation, so that in turn the comm link between Silver Tower and various military and civilian experts on the ground could provide help for the crewmen.

But her duty would be much more difficult. While prebreathing in preparation for putting on her spacesuit she had studied diagrams of the attachment points of her Skybolt module, tracing the mechanical, electrical and pyrotechnic separation mechanisms. She'd also studied the status readouts in the Skybolt control modules to be sure she had the right indications. The last thing she wanted was to damage the laser or its control module, trying to detach it. What she'd told General Stuart about the dangers of handling the nuclear particle-generating components of Skybolt was a bit overstated, but not by very much. Her job was to preserve Skybolt by parking it in orbit without damaging it so badly it had no potential at sometime in the future.

Saint-Michael had been expecting a briefing from her before she began the EVA, so she waited now until he turned from the computer terminal.

'Ready to detach?' he asked. She nodded glumly. 'Okay, one thing. We save Skybolt only if there's time. If Govorov's spaceplanes launched within minutes of that laser firing we may not have time to load the module into *Enterprise*. You'll have to move fast . . .'

She got the message – no time for any last nostalgic tours of the module. She detached herself from the strip of Velcro she'd anchored herself to, moved up to the control board mounted on the ceiling and –

Suddenly she found herself propelled to the far end of the command module as a terrific explosion rocked the station.

'What the hell was *that*?' She pushed herself away from the bulkhead, reattached her sneakers to the Velcro deck, wiped a trickle of blood from her nose.

Saint-Michael had no time to answer as another explosion tore through Silver Tower, and a warning light illuminated over the hatch leading to the connecting tunnel.

'Low pressure in the connecting tunnel,' Saint-Michael read out. The station now seemed to be sliding sideways, skidding like a truck out of control on an icy highway. Fighting acute vertigo, he made his way to his communications console, attached his microphone to the clip inside his POS mask, pulled the facemask over his head and keyed the intercom button:

'All personnel. Evacuate the station. Now.' He unplugged his POS walk-around pack from the station's oxygen supply. 'Ann, let's go . . .'

Another explosion — it felt as though it was right over their heads – sent both of them to the deck.

She manoeuvred her way back towards the main hatch, passed the ceiling-mounted module jettison control, reached up and closed and locked its safety cover, then hurried through the hatch and into the connecting tunnel.

Saint-Michael saw her go through the hatch and keyed his microphone. '*America*. Jon. Ann's coming through. Help her . . .'

A fourth sharp explosion sounded through the station, followed by the screech of tearing and twisting metal. Now both pressurization and fire-warning lights were blinking in the connecting tunnel. Saint-Michael was thrown head-over-heels half the length of the command module, finally entangled on some jury-rigged consoles and bundles of wiring that had broken free of their temporary mountings. He managed to pull himself upright and start for the hatch when he glanced out through the observation port midway along the outward-facing side of the command module.

What he saw made his heart sink.

America was drifting aimlessly hundreds of yards from the station, its fuselage ripped open as if a huge scaling knife had sliced into it. Waves of fire gushed out of the gaping wound as the spaceplane's hydrogen and oxygen fuels ignited and hungrily fed on each other.

'Oh, God . . .' Saint-Michael was less awed by the fire and demise of the spaceplane than the thought that there were *people* inside, including Ann, if she'd made it to the plane before it separated from the docking adapter . . .

Then he heard it, the sound of her voice coming over the microphone: 'Jason . . . you *okay*?'

'Where are you?' he managed to get out.

'In Skybolt. You seen Marty?'

'No.' Over interphone: 'Marty, come in . . .'

No reply.

'He was in *Enterprise* . . .'

Saint-Michael switched to the air-to-air UHF frequency. 'Marty, this is Jason. Report. *Report*, damn it . . .'

But when he looked out the observation port again he saw where Marty had disappeared to. The shuttle *Enterprise* was speeding away from Silver Tower, and Saint-Michael just caught a glimpse of it before it disappeared.

'Marty, on board *Enterprise* . . . come in . . .'

Space Shuttle *Enterprise*

Marty Schultz was sitting in the left-hand commander's seat on *Enterprise*'s flight deck, nudging her thrusters forward in an atttempt to fly the shuttle away from the space station and the attackers bearing down on it. He'd already made up his mind. He wasn't going to be the hunted; he was going to be the hunter. Not to be vainglorious, but, well, better to go doing some good in the space shuttle that had been his inspiration than wait around for the Russians to shred the patchwork shuttle with their missiles.

He keyed the microphone button on the control stick. 'Sorry to be late reporting, General. As I guess you've noticed, I've been sort of busy here on *Enterprise* – '

'What the *hell* do you think you're doing? Where do you think you're *going*?'

'One at a time, General. What I was doing was getting ready to load Skybolt . . . saw the Russian plane's missiles hit *America* . . . Hampton and Horvath bought it . . . where I'm going is away from Silver Tower. Figure those planes will be on my tail pretty quick now. Well, I've always wanted to see what this baby can do. Now I'm going to find out . . .'

Saint-Michael wanted to kill him . . . He was so upset the irony of that thought went right by him . . . First it had been Jerrod Will. Now it was Marty Schultz. What was it with these shuttle jocks? Did they all have to be heroes . . .?

'Marty, listen . . .'

But Marty wasn't listening. Leaving *Enterprise*'s thrusters on full power he unstrapped himself from the commander's seat and moved across the flight deck to the payload specialist's station. The cargo bay doors were open and he could see out through the twin aft-facing observation windows into the cargo bay and behind *Enterprise*.

He activated the reaction-control-system thruster controls at the payload station, checked them, then unstowed the manipulator arm. Swinging the arm out of the cargo bay he pointed the TV camera aft, set it to wide-angle view and swept it behind the shuttle.

Almost instantly he had a picture-perfect view of two Soviet Elektron spaceplanes giving chase.

'I got two Elektrons on my tail,' he radioed back to the station. 'These gumballs are in for a surprise . . .'

Elektron One Spaceplane

'Damn it,' Govorov said over the command radio, 'don't let that shuttle get away – '

Kozhedub and Litvyak had fired two *Bavinash* missiles each at Armstrong, when Govorov saw the shuttle suddenly bolt from the vicinity of the lower pressurized modules. He had no way of knowing if it was a bluff or not, but the shuttle did seem to be piloted by a space-suited astronaut, so he ordered both his wingmen to give chase.

For a moment he hoped Litvyak would leave the job to Kozhedub because, from his vantage point about a kilometre behind and above his wingmen, Govorov had seen Litvyak's second Scimitar missile, a *single* missile, obliterate the spaceplane *America* docked at the station, creating an instant ball of flames. Flames in outer space were a rare sight. The blast must have had the force of at least a kiloton of TNT.

Deciding it was not necessary to wait for his wingmen to return, Govorov pressed a switch on a newly installed panel near his right knee. Behind him, a hydraulically powered pallet lifted the spacereactive bomb out of Elektron One's cargo bay. The side of the weapon opposite the pallet was uncovered, revealing a series of mechanical grapples all along the outer surface of the bomb.

He was going to manoeuvre Elektron One underneath

the station's central keel, as close as possible to the pressurized modules without running the risk of hitting an antenna or a piece of the debris that seemed to cluster everywhere around the crippled station. When he was positioned properly he would gently nudge the bomb up onto the central open-lattice keel until the grapples caught, then release the bomb and pallet from his cargo bay. Once away from the station – five to ten kilometres was safe in this case – he would detonate the bomb. It would be fast and sure. No more mistakes . . .

He began his slow, careful approach to the station, manoeuvring well above the central pressurized modules to begin a visual scan of the station. Not the time to charge ahead blindly. Logic said the station's crew should have abandoned the station in the shuttle or spaceplane, but it was such an incorrect assumption that got Voloshin killed on the first mission. There was time. He would wait and watch the explosion, watch as the huge American space station folded and tore apart. As for the men who might still crew the station, well, he would try not to feel for them. At least they would die quickly . . .

He nudged his control stick forward and watched as his laser rangefinder counted down the distance to the station: three thousand metres, twenty-eight hundred, twenty-six . . .

Space Shuttle *Enterprise*

They were close enough now . . .

From the magnification setting on the arm camera Marty Schultz estimated that the two Elektron spaceplanes chasing him were no more than four or five miles behind. The *Enterprise*, powered by its two monomethyl-hydrazine engines, had accelerated another thousand

402

miles an hour since the chase had begun, but the Russians were slowly but surely catching up.

Just as he wanted.

He shut down the engines and using only the aft thrusters spun *Enterprise* head-over-tail until she had turned a full hundred eighty degrees back towards her pursuers. He then grasped the arm controls and studying the TV monitor that gave the best view of the cargo bay and the manipulator's claw, reached into the cargo bay with the arm and extracted a large cylindrical drum device from an attach-point in the centre of the bay.

He had conceived his plan shortly after making *Enterprise* flyable. Realizing that a Soviet spaceplane attack might come with very little warning, making it impossible for them to abandon the station, he'd suggested loading up *Enterprise*'s cargo bay with Thor interceptor missiles and launching them by shuttle-directed remote-control.

In spite of the disaster after the first time they'd tried to launch Thor missiles for station defence, Saint-Michael had agreed to the plan, at least the idea, and told Marty and Hampton to load the missiles. But by the time the Soviets had announced their assault by firing their chemical laser, he'd changed his mind. *Enterprise* would only be used to carry the Skybolt laser module to a high-storage orbit.

That had been it – until Marty had got back aboard *Enterprise* to get ready to accept the Skybolt laser module Ann would be detaching. From his docking point beneath the central keel near the Skybolt module, the eight remaining Thor missiles he'd taken off the shuttle only hours before had been well within reach of his remote manipulator arm. When the Soviet spaceplane attack had begun it had not been difficult to detach two missiles, activate the mechanical ejector-arming mechanism, stow the missiles in *Enterprise*'s cargo bay, and jet away from the station. He had deliberately circled Armstrong once to get the Russian's attention, then flown away with as much speed as possible . . .

It took thirty seconds for Marty to extract the two missiles from the cargo bay, then click on the air-to-air comm channel. 'Armstrong, this is *Enterprise*. Come in.'

'Marty.' Saint-Michael's voice again. 'Where are you?'

'Where I should be, General. Listen, you have to launch-commit the Thor missiles now.'

'You got some of the Thors on board?' Saint-Michael didn't wait for a reply, instead immediately threw himself towards the far side of the master SBR control console hunting for the Thor missile controls. Almost every control panel had been moved or replaced, and during the first spaceplane attack the impact explosions had thrown any unsecured panels all across the module. But after a few frenetic moments of searching he found the Thor arming controls and ordered an automatic launch-commit on all Thor missiles.

The six missiles under the central keel were not affected by the command; only the two missiles that Marty had manually armed responded. The Elektron spaceplanes were less than three miles away when the Thor missiles' rocket engines ignited. Marty stayed long enough to watch both Thors shoot into space towards the Russian spaceplanes, then made his way back to the cockpit and strapped into the commander's seat.

Time to take off, babe. He reactivated the digital autopilot and RCS thruster controls. If those missiles didn't hit their targets, he knew there were two Russians who were going to come at him with everything they had.

They had indeed agreed between themselves who would take the first shot on the American shuttle *Enterprise*: Colonel Kozhedub in Elektron Two had the honours. Colonel Litvyak, who had put the Scimitar missile into *America*'s fuel tanks, kept his laser seeker-range finder activated but caged it to scan directly ahead of

Elektron Three. If he had illuminated *Enterprise* with his laser, Kozhedub's missile might try to slide across to the second beam and miss the target, or the two lasers could interphase and cancel each other out.

'It's moving away,' Kozhedub called out as the shuttle slowly rotated on its longitudinal axis and sped away at right angles to the Elektron's line of flight.

'Can you follow him?' Litvyak said. 'I can – '

Kozhedub told him no thanks, he could get this one just fine.

Litvyak started to say something but a glance at his front instrument panel stopped the words in his throat. Directly centred in his laser spotting-scope was a Thor missile unfurling its steel mesh snare!

'*Watch out*. The shuttle has just launched missiles . . .' Litvyak yanked on his control column, trying to translate directly to the right and dodge the missile. It tracked towards him. He switched thrusters again and moved downward at full power, changing direction so hard that his helmet cracked against the cockpit canopy. No change. The Thor missile was still following him, looming larger and larger . . .

The missile was less than a mile away when Litvyak, in a last-ditch effort, fired three Scimitar missiles at the large cylindrical interceptor. The first two missiles exploded harmlessly on the mesh, but the third impacted directly on to the sensor nose of the missile and detonated the Thor's high-explosive warhead.

No sound, but the wall of heat and energy that washed over Elektron Three pounded on the small spacecraft. It went out of control, and Litvyak had no choice but to release his thruster controls and ride out the turbulence, hoping it didn't tear his ship apart. It took a few minutes, but soon the awful vibration and pounding on his spacecraft's hull began to subside.

Kozhedub was not so fortunate. With his laser designator locked on to the *Enterprise* and watching as intently as he was for the perfect firing aspect, he never saw the second Thor missile. Just as Litvyak shouted out his warning the missile hit Elektron Two's right wingtip and detonated right on top of the canopy. Kozhedub died instantly, and a moment later his Elektron exploded, spinning off into earth's atmosphere.

Litvyak, hearing his comrade's dying noises echo in his helmet, knew he could plunge into earth's atmosphere as well if he failed to bring his spaceplane under control. Using short thruster bursts and concentrating on the gyroscopic inertial horizon, he finally managed to reduce the violent multiaxis spin down to one recognizable spin axis, then gradually applied more powerful bursts until his plane was under control.

He scanned the dark grey skies around him until he spotted the shuttle beginning to accelerate back in the direction of the space station. Stabbing the thruster controls, he applied full power and took up the chase, this time drawn by a need for revenge . . .

USS *Nimitz*

'Jason, this is Clancy. Come in. We've lost the SBR signals.'

No reply.

'Get them back, Sparks,' Clancy said to the communications officer. 'Whatever it takes.'

The CPO tried hard but there was no change. 'It's dead silent, sir. No carrier, no data, nothing. It's as if they – '

Clancy looked at the CPO. 'Don't say it, Sparks. Don't even think it.'

But the unthinkable was unavoidable, for the admiral

as well as the chief petty officer: another disaster had just happened on Silver Tower.

Armstrong Space Station

'Ann? How's it – ?'

'It's ready, Jason. Ready to switch SBR to Skybolt control . . .'

Saint-Michael took a deep breath, put a finger on the SBR switchover controls. He pressed the button.

The SBR immediately issued a solid TRACK indication on Ann's console. 'SBR is tracking targets,' Ann announced. 'Now showing two hostiles. Friendly identification complete . . . Target discrimination in progress . . . Neutral particle-beam laser projector showing faulted.' The neutral particle beam used to discriminate between decoys and real targets had been shot off long ago. 'Override.'

He searched the SBR command menu, found the command and entered it. 'Done.'

'Override accepted.'

Now what?

Space Shuttle *Enterprise*

Marty Schultz could feel the presence of an enemy behind him even before he visually confirmed it.

'One got away,' he said out loud, to himself, to his shuttle. 'We're in deep shit now, babe.' Think multi-dimensional, he told himself, then selected ROTATE and PULSE on the digital autopilot and jammed the control stick forward. Without the forward RCS pod the motion was a tail-over-heels flip, done by the aft RCS thruster so that the cargo bay was now facing in the direction of

flight. He ignited the engines once again, which put
Enterprise in a dive straight for Earth . . .

At that instant a flash of glaring light washed out his
vision. The control stick felt warm, then hot, then rubbery
in his hand, even through the thick nylon gloves. Warning
tones, like confused cries for help, from *Enterprise* beeped
over his headset.

Elektron Three Spaceplane

Colonel Litvyak aboard Elektron Three felt the blast of
heat as well, but for him it was not just a slight glare – it
was a throbbing, blinding sheet of light that seemed to
illuminate each crevice of his spaceplane's cockpit. His
eyelids, then his solar visor when he could finally command his muscles to lower it, had no effect.

When his eyes cleared a few moments later he stopped
all thrusters and did a quick systems check. A few minor
ones had faulted but they all reset. His lips were dry as
sand, as though he hadn't taken a drink in days. The skin
on his face seemed dry and cracked as if from a bad
windburn. No use flying around half-blind . . . He used a
few short bursts of power to stop his forward momentum
and keyed his microphone.

'Elektron One, this is Three. Do you copy?'

Elektron One Spaceplane

Govorov was only a few hundred metres away from the
Skybolt module when his skin seemed to crawl and feel
dusty. He did not feel any of the soaring heat felt by the
other two spacecraft near the path of the free-electron
laser beam, but the side lobes of energy that coiled out of
the muzzle of the nuclear-powered laser stream did seem

to turn his Elektron One into a huge transistor. The pulse of energy coursing through his body made stars appear before his eyes, and his fingertips tingled and burned as if about to catch fire.

As the unearthly sensation subsided and he began to think more clearly, he realized what had happened. Someone aboard the station had just fired a powerful laser. *Armstrong hadn't been abandoned after all . . .*

'Elektron One. Come in.'

Govorov keyed his microphone. 'Litvyak? Where are you?'

'In pursuit of the American shuttle . . . There was some sort of energy burst. I'm checking for damage.'

'*Disregard the shuttle*. The space station is still manned and they've got some sort of laser. I want you manoeuvring as backup while I plant the space-reactive bomb.'

'But Andrei was killed by a missile from that shuttle – '

'Do as I say. There'll be plenty of time to chase down the shuttle later.'

Govorov stopped suddenly and stared at the command module, the centre-pressurized module facing him. He was now less than fifty metres from the station, close enough to see the patches over the holes his missiles had made, close enough to see the data-transmission cables . . .

And, as he moved closer he could see a figure peering out through the observation port in the command module. He applied gentle reverse thrust and manoeuvred a few metres away.

Yes, it *was* the General Saint-Michael he'd heard and read so much about, whose picture he'd seen. A shock to see him now, like this. He had always wondered what it would be like to face his enemy. He had thought he would prefer it . . . fight man to man without the influence of a technology that made killing impersonal. Now he was not so sure –

'Moving out to a five-kilometre orbit, Elektron One.'

Litvyak's words brought him back. 'Cruise further out, Three. I'm going in to plant the bomb now.'

Govorov selected minus-Y translation and moved away from the station. 'Good-bye, General,' he said, nodding towards the command module's observation port. Strangely he felt no elation. Indeed, more a sadness. . . .

Armstrong Space Station

The laser burst had not dimmed the lights in the command module, as it had the other times it had fired. Even so, Saint-Michael could not see if it had hit anything.

'Ann, what happened?'

'I can't tell anything. I'm resetting the SBR relay circuit – it overloaded. The laser fired but I can't tell if it – '

'Armstrong, this is *Enterprise*. Come in.'

Saint-Michael almost jumped at the communications controls. '*Marty*, we thought – '

'General, there's a plane right by the command module. *Look out*.'

And then Saint-Michael saw it. The Elektron space-plane, an engineering thing of beauty with its flowing lines, compact and trim, was also a deadly creature. The general took it in, but his eyes were drawn to the sleek cockpit windows. He couldn't clearly see the face behind the space helmet, but he had a very strong feeling – a premonition almost – that he was looking at Alesander Govorov.

The sight momentarily rooted Saint-Michael to the spot, but then just as quickly as the spaceplane appeared, it dropped out of sight. He couldn't help but be impressed by the audacity of the pilot, manoeuvring so close to the module. It had to be Govorov . . .

'He's moving away,' Marty reported excitedly. 'He

didn't shoot anything; he's moving down to the keel – hey, his cargo bay is open . . .'

'Ann . . . any other planes nearby?'

'Yes. There's a fast-moving one three miles out and pulling away . . . Yes, he's definitely moving away. I'm picking up *Enterprise* . . . too. He's less than a mile. Two spaceplanes – must mean Skybolt missed . . .'

'*General*.' Marty's voice boomed over the air-to-air channel. 'That Russian spaceplane by the keel . . . he's attaching something to it, right beside Skybolt . . . Oh, God . . . looks like a bomb, a big one . . . He's attached a bomb to the space station . . .'

Saint-Michael watched, frozen, as the spaceplane accelerated back and away from the station. *That* was why the second spaceplane was retreating so fast . . .

'Marty, stay clear. Get away from the station – '

'I can reach it, General; I can reach it. Stand by . . .'

'Negative. There may not be time. Get *away* from here.'

Marty, ignoring him, selected autopilot controls and jetted towards the station. He unstrapped from the commander's seat and moved back to the payload specialist's console. Schultz, he told himself, you'd better pray this doesn't take too long. Pray anyway . . .

Saint-Michael watched as Govorov's spaceplane became small, then smaller, then a tiny speck – and then he unfroze . . . 'Ann, target the closer plane, the one that just moved away from the station. Govorov's . . .'

'But Skybolt's not locking on – '

'Fire anyway. Widest possible pattern. Maybe we can get him before he sets off the bomb by remote control.'

The wait was excruciatingly long. Govorov had all but disappeared, intermingling with the stars and the bluish haze surrounding earth. By now he had to be far enough away to detonate his bomb . . .

Elektron One Spaceplane

Govorov, his laser range finder locked on to Armstrong, decided to wait until ten kilometres before detonating the bomb. If the laser was operating, the resulting secondary explosion of the laser module might be far more violent than a mere hydrogen-oxygen explosion.

He let the laser range finder click up to ten kilometres, then moved his finger across the special-weapon control panel near his right knee, and pressed . . .

The first free-electron laser pulse had missed Govorov by over a hundred feet, but even at that distance the two-megawatt burst of nuclear-fired energy was still hot enough to melt steel. In a fraction of a second Govorov's heat-resistant quartz glass windscreen, which could easily withstand reentry temperatures of three thousand degrees Fahrenheit, softened, melted, vaporized. The pressure of the atmosphere in the cockpit blew the liquid glass out into space, creating a huge glass bubble just moments before bursting and flying off in all directions. Alesander Govorov was cremated in the atomic heat of the beam.

A second laser burst from Skybolt knifed through the spaceplane itself, creating another huge bubble – this time of titanium, not glass. The heat was so intense that the plane's fuel had no time to detonate. In the blink of an eye – both pulses had lasted less than one-tenth of a second – the spaceplane Elektron One and the commander of the Soviet Space Defence Command had simply vanished in a puff of plasma.

Elektron Three Spaceplane

'Elektron One. Do you read? Over.'

Litvyak got no reply. Ever since the last energy surge –

the laser, Govorov had said? – the tactical air-to-air frequency had been silent.

Lost communications procedures for this mission were different than for other space flights with more than one manned spacecraft. The standard procedure was to proceed immediately to the nearest hundredth altitude – one hundred kilometres, two hundred, three hundred – establish a circular orbit and await reentry or station-docking instructions. For this mission the instructions were simpler:

If weapons are aboard, continue the attack on the space station Armstrong. The space-based radar, rescue spacecraft, pressurized modules and fuel cells have priority. Withdraw only if all weapons are expended.

Litvyak turned his Elektron around, guided it a few kilometres closer to the station and locked his laser range finder on Armstrong's starboard space-based radar array. He fired one of his five remaining Scimitar missiles at the station. The missile, running hot and true, slammed into the face of the upper starboard array. The explosion from its warhead blew a ten-metre-diameter hole in the antenna, which wobbled and weaved for a moment, then wrenched itself in two and toppled over, slamming into the keel.

Armstrong Space Station

'The bomb didn't go off,' Saint-Michael called out. 'Ann, you did it. Skybolt worked – '

His congratulations were sharply interrupted by a loud *bang* and rumbling vibration that shook the command module. The one usable attitude-adjustment thruster could be heard trying to move the station upright again, but the station began to tip slowly backwards. Streams of SBR fault messages raced across Saint-Michael's monitors, but he didn't need to read the screen to know that there was at least one more Russian plane out there.

'Jason, reset the SBR. *Fast.*'

He moved back to the SBR control terminal, entered the command to reset the radar's circuitry. But the computer refused the input.

'It won't take.'

'You have to find out what component is out and power it down,' Ann told him, 'or else the SBR will keep short-circuiting.'

Saint-Michael scrolled through the error messages that had zipped across the screen. It seemed every single part of the SBR had been hit by a Russian missile. He switched his comm link to A/A.

'Marty, can you see the station? What did he hit?'

'Stand by.' Marty, who had stopped trying to detach the Russian bomb when the laser fired, boosted himself away from the keel, flipped upside down to get a better view and manoeuvred over the station.

'Try the number one SBR array.'

Saint-Michael erased the error log and had just entered the code to deactivate the damaged SBR array when a thunderous explosion rocked the command module.

'Fire on the keel,' Marty shouted over the air-to-air frequency. 'The master fuel cell's been hit.'

Fire-warning lights blinked on all the surviving panels. Saint-Michael ignored them. 'SBR's reset, Ann. Hurry up, we're going to run out of power any – '

As he said those words the main lights in the command module flickered out. A few battery-powered emergency lights snapped on, but they lit a corpse. Silver Tower was dead once again.

414

Litvyak's second Scimitar missile hit finally produced a spectacular result, even better than the collapsed radar antenna. The secondary explosions, fire and sparking on the keel from the missile hit on the fuel cell created a multicoloured fireworks display for dozens of metres from the impact point, then began to creep along the keel towards the pressurized modules. The explosions fizzled out just a few metres away from the double column of modules in the centre of the keel, but the end result was still satisfying to Colonel Litvyak: the few visible lights remaining on the station had all gone out. That last hit had finally killed the station.

It was dead, but not destroyed. Govorov had ordered the station destroyed. The Americans had already reactivated a 'dead' hulk once; they might do it again. Litvyak swept his laser range-finder designator around the station and finally rested the red beam on the best and most obvious target of them all: Govorov's unexploded bomb.

It was all about to end, right now. Litvyak selected his three remaining *Bavinash* missiles, locked the laser designator on the bomb. He squeezed the trigger. The three missiles fired straight and true with a solid lock-on –

And all three were caught in the intense free-electron laser beam that shot from the station. Skybolt had needed only a millisecond of the station's warning power to energize the laser's ignition circuitry, and once delivered – Skybolt's internal battery did the rest. Skybolt's beam vaporized the Scimitar missiles, and three one-millionths of a second later the beam travelled the remaining five miles to Elektron Three and turned the two-hundred-fifty-thousand-pound spacecraft and its pilot into a few milligrams of cosmic dust.

As Saint-Michael and Ann Page struggled into space suits, the first of the Soviet GL-25 cruise missiles were just a few dozen miles from the sea. Running undetected, they had navigated through the western rim of the Selseleh Ye Safid Mountains in Western Afghanistan, down into the Margow Desert Valley and along the Chagal Hills down the border between Iran and Pakistan. Now they were well within the Central Makran Range in southwest Pakistan, only minutes from the Gulf of Oman. Their inertially guided course had been well chosen by Soviet army planners to conceal the missiles in the most rugged terrain available and to keep them away from known surveillance sites or large population centres.

Each of the fifty GL-25 missiles had expended three-quarters of its fuel on only two-thirds of its journey, but the easier part of the flight was ahead of them. Once over the ocean the missiles would gradually step-climb to twenty thousand feet, where their ramjet engines would be more efficient. They would cruise at high altitude until within three hundred miles of the outermost escort ship of the *Nimitz*, then gradually descend back to fifty feet above the water. At approximately one hundred miles from the last known position of the *Nimitz*, their homing radars would activate . . .

And the devastation of the American fleet would begin . . .

13

Without power, Silver Tower was little more than a fifty-billion-dollar orbiting mausoleum. Air could not circulate, module pressurization could not be maintained because of the leaks in the hull. Electronic carbon dioxide scrubbers were inoperable, and old-style lithium hydroxide carbon dioxide scrubber canisters were much less effective without air being circulated through them. The attitude thrusters that kept the station on a proper orbit were useless without computer control.

The station was suddenly deaf, dumb and blind.

But days before, right after arriving back on Armstrong, Saint-Michael and his crew had prepared for another attack, and safeguarding backup power sources had been their first priority. They'd labelled their make-shift control panel the 'planter box' because it had been constructed using one of the command module's green plant boxes – Saint-Michael didn't know whatever happened to the dirt. Even now it resembled a planter box, sprouting a dozen thick bundles of wires, some ending in round twist-lock junction caps or ribbon-cable snap connectors, and others looping back around through the box and out along cable conduits to other parts of the command module.

This was no computer terminal or sophisticated electronic relay centre; the circuits were the wire bundles themselves. As for the switches, if a wire junction was plugged into another, the switch was 'on'. If it was unplugged, it was 'off'. They had labelled each wire bundle with descriptions of where the wires led and what they did. Saint-Michael anchored himself now to the Velcro deck and began unplugging, watching for the last connector to snap into place and the lights to flicker on in the command module.

He reached down to his spacesuit control panel and clicked on the stationwide interphone. 'Ann, how do you copy?'

'I can hear you, Jason.'

'Switch to air-to-air with me.' He switched to A/A on the comm control. 'Marty? How do you read?'

'Loud and clear, General. You missed a Fourth of July barnburner out here. Those Russian spaceplanes sparkle when you hit 'em with the laser. You all done with your fireworks? Can I come back in to pick up my fares?'

'You can come back in but we're not leaving. It may be crazy, but we're going to try to reactivate the station again.'

'One problem, General. That last Russian missile took out your master fuel cell. Where are you going to get the power? I'm pretty good but I can't figure out how to jump-start Silver Tower from *Enterprise*.'

'What about the solar arrays? Can you see them out there? What's their status?'

'Stand by.' A few moments later Marty came back on channel. 'Looks bad, General. I can't even find half of the arrays. Three and four are still attached but they're collapsed against the keel. It would take an army of techs and a shuttle a week to repair them – *if* it's possible.'

Silence, then Ann clicked on channel. 'Jason, I might have an answer . . . We still have a power source on this station bigger than all the fuel cells and solar arrays put together. I'm talking about the MHD reactor.'

'You mean you can hook the reactor into the station power circuits?'

'Why not? Until Kevin Baker and I fixed it that's what it was doing all by itself. I can undo some of the fixes we did, reverse the power relays and send MHD power from Skybolt back through the ignition circuits to the station batteries. The battery transformers and overload protectors should be able to protect the batteries from overvoltage damage. All you have to do is route battery power from the emergency bus to the station main bus and we should be able to use the MHD reactor to charge the batteries.'

'Sounds too simple,' Saint-Michael said, his irony lost on Ann for the moment. 'Well, let's do it.'

Marty said, 'And I can tether *Enterprise* to the keel and transfer to – '

'Negative,' Saint-Michael said as he began to pull apart the consoles in the command module. 'I want you to get in contact with someone on earth, tell them our situation and request a rescue sortie soon as possible.'

'That'll be a trick,' Marty said. 'I never did fix *Enterprise*'s TDRS.'

'So use UHF standby radio. The Dakar-Ascension earth stations will be your best chance, or Yarra Yarra in Australia and Manila. Keep trying. I don't know how much longer our air is going to last . . . You copy that, Marty?'

USS *Mississippi*

The GL-25 cruise missiles sped south of the Tropic of Cancer, still without being detected – any ships larger than small fishing vessels had long since abandoned the Gulf of Oman and the Arabian Sea, like townfolk in the Old West scattering off the main street as the sheriff and the outlaws began squaring off. Two of the cruise missiles had guidance-system malfunctions and automatically crashed themselves into the sea, but the rest were precisely on course, speeding towards the twenty American naval vessels now only five hundred miles away. Three hundred miles from the outermost escort vessel the missiles began their preprogrammed descent back to low-altitude cruise modem, a manoeuvre designed to duck under the extreme farthest range of any maritime radar.

The inertially guided missiles had been programmed as if all of the *Nimitz*'s escorts were still arranged in a protective circle around the carrier. If the fleet had remained in the same defensive formation as when the missiles were programmed some twelve hours earlier, the missiles might never have been detected until it was too late. The target-run point, at which the missile's homing radar would be activated, was designed to allow for movement of the fleet; but the planners had to work under the assumption that the fleet would stay together and not change course by more than a hundred miles after launch. Secrecy meant everything to the success of the Soviet missile strike.

But one ship, the USS *Mississippi*, was no longer with the *Nimitz* group. After the Backfire bomber attack, the *Mississippi* had been ordered to the arca of the Backfire–Tomcat dogfight to search for Russian survivors. It had taken several hours to steam north to where the battle had taken place, and they stayed in the area for some eight hours rescuing a handful of survivors and retrieving bodies. When they started back towards the *Nimitz* to retake their place in the cordon they were a hundred miles out of position. Which put them three hundred miles south and west of the first of the GL-25 cruise missiles . . .

Commander Jeffrey Fulbright, captain of the *Mississippi*, was on the bridge trying to warm his insides with a fresh mug of coffee.

'Those Russians were really scared of us,' Fulbright was

saying to Lieutenant George Collene, the deck officer. 'I guess they thought we were going to put fire on their fleet. Credit doses of negative propaganda.'

'Or good old-fashioned fear of retaliation, sir,' Lieutenant Collene said. 'If I had just tried to bomb an enemy vessel I'd sure as hell think twice about getting on their ship afterwards.'

Fulbright glanced at the young officer, closed his right hand into a fist. 'Wouldn't you just love to go down there and properly welcome those sonsofbitches to the USS *Mississippi*?'

Collene looked at his captain over the top of his glasses. 'That, sir, is what their political officers *tell* them we do.'

'So let's not disappoint them – '

'Bridge, CIC. Radar contact aircraft bearing zero-four-zero true, range two-eight-seven nautical miles. Fast-moving, heading south.'

Fulbright picked up the phone. 'CIC, this is Fulbright. Got an ID on 'em?'

'Negative, sir.'

'Feed me the numbers.' He lowered the phone and called to the deck officer. 'Lieutenant, steer heading zero-four-zero true. Make it zero-six-zero. We'll try to cut them off, whatever they are. Make flank speed. Let's go take a look.'

'Zero-six-zero true, flank speed, aye, sir.' Collene repeated the command to the helmsman, who repeated it to Collene, steered the ship to that heading, made the speed change to engineering and then read off his instruments to Collene when the course and speed were set.

'On course zero-six-zero. We are at flank speed, showing two-seven knots, sir.'

'Very well.'

'Bridge, contact one now two-six-five miles, bearing zero-four-five. We have a rough altitude estimate of angels ten and descending. Speed estimated six-zero-zero knots.'

'Any identification beacons? IFF?'

'No codes, sir.'

'Lieutenant, steer zero-nine-zero, maintain flank speed. I want – '

'Bridge, CIC. Radar contact aircraft two, range two-six-zero nautical miles, bearing zero-three-eight, fast-moving, same heading south as contact one. Speed and altitude the same as contact one.'

Fulbright swore and picked up a second phone. 'Communications, this is the bridge. Get *Nimitz* on FLEET-SATCOM. Advise him of our contacts. Broadcast warning messages on all emergency frequencies to all aircraft on those contacts' course and speed. Tell them to change course and stay clear of all vessels in this area or they will be fired on without further warning – '

'Bridge, CIC. Radar contact aircraft three, range two-four-zero, bearing zero-three-zero, moving below angel's five. Same course and speed as the . . . Now radar contact four, same course and speed . . . looks like a stream of them, sir. Now contact five . . .'

'Discontinue reports, radar, I get the picture,' Fulbright said. 'Lieutenant, sound general quarters.'

Armstrong Space Station

There was irony in the station's near destruction: if the command module had not been as torn up as it was by the previous Soviet attack it would have taken hours, perhaps days, to trace all the wiring and circuitry leading from Skybolt and the MHD reactor to the station's banks of batteries. As it was, the main, emergency and essential power buses, and the connecting point between the power supply and the circuits powered by it, were all now readily accessible.

Saint-Michael's job was to connect the backup power system to the main bus. Finally he stood up from the planter box, clicked on his interphone, and told Ann that he was ready. She reported finishing the rewiring in the Skybolt control module, so he switched the channel to air-to-air and raised Marty.

'We're going to fire up the reactor, Marty. Stand by.'

'Roger, General . . . hey, wait a sec, I'm picking up UHF broadcasts from . . . the Seychelles, or someplace like that. It sounds like the navy. Something's up . . .'

'Okay, listen in and give me a report later. We're going to fire her up and see what happens.'

Ann manoeuvred herself to the one control panel in the entire module that was illuminated. It was a simple switch that would allow power from the backup batteries to flow to the ignition circuits. 'Jason, when I start up the reactor it'll go full bore until I get power to my main reactor controls. I only hope the batteries can handle it . . .'

'Look at it this way: if something goes wrong we can't be in any worse shape than we are now. Any explosion will be out on the keel where the batteries are. Plug 'er in.'

Ann touched the switch and closed her eyes. 'Here goes everything . . .'

The Soviet attack on the *Nimitz* carrier group was going as planned.

Five minutes after the last GL-25 cruise missile hit its initial point, the *Kiev* and *Novorossiysk* attack carriers began launching the first of a dozen Sukhoi-24 Fencer supersonic bomber aircraft off their ski-ramp launch platforms towards the American vessels. Each swing-wing bomber, a synthesis of technology borrowed from the American F-111 and British Tornado strike bombers and modified for carrier operations, was armed with four 'launch and leave' AS-N-16 laser-guided antiship missiles, a thirty-millimetre cannon and an undercarriage pod with twelve laser-guided missiles. The missiles would be used to attack random targets as the fighters left the target area.

The bombers' task was to penetrate the *Nimitz*'s outer fleet protection immediately after the GL-25 cruise missile attack, when the fleet would be at its weakest, and attack the *Nimitz* itself with its high-explosive antiship missiles. Using their advanced jammers and flying only a few metres off the water, the Fencers would be hard if not impossible to spot after the havoc of the cruise-missile strike. On withdrawal the fighters had the weapons to pick off any targets of opportunity.

USS *Nimitz*

In the opening activity after the *Mississippi* sounded the alarm, the Fencer launches from the *Kiev* and *Novorossiysk* went almost unnoticed.

The missile-frigate FFG-48 USS *Vandergrift* was the first naval vessel to feel the impact of the Soviet GL-25 missile. She was the northernmost antisubmarine ship protecting the *Nimitz*, and because she was primarily an antisubmarine vessel her anti-air capabilities were limited: she carried only one Mark 13 anti-aircraft missile launcher on her forward deck. Although the *Nimitz* rebroadcast the *Mississippi*'s warning for all her escorts it was impossible for the *Vandergrift* to defend itself against the attack. Once the oncoming missile had acquired and locked onto the frigate with its homing radar, it accelerated to nearly Mach two for the last thirty miles of its flight and hit the *Vandergrift* square in the centre of her helicopter hangar before she could fire a shot. The frigate was nearly sawed in half . . .

Some escorts fared better, but one by one a path was being cleared by the GL-25s that led straight to the *Nimitz* herself. The Aegis-class cruisers were set to confront the *Arkhangel* carrier group to the west and were not positioned for such a massive assault from the north. Though the newer, faster Standard-ER and the new NATO Valkyrie vertical-launch missiles did a credible job against the oncoming swarm, the older Standard missiles could barely keep up.

The GL-25s were winning. Although only one ship was killed for every three GL-25s, the northern escorts were giving way to the Soviet attackers.

'Get as many Tomcats airborne as you can, Captain,' Admiral Clancy said over the phone to Air Ops. 'I want two air patrols to counter the *Arkhangel* to the east. The rest head north with the Hawkeye radar planes and find those damned cruise missiles. Keep four Tomcats and two Hornets on alert . . . Yes, that's right, only four. If we don't chase down those cruise missiles it won't matter how many we keep in reserve.'

'Aye . . .'

The sound of staccato thunder penetrated the noise of the flight deck below *Nimitz*'s bridge. Edgewater and Clancy hurried over to the port observation deck, and saw one of the northern escort vessels lighting up the night with a spectacular rocket display, rapid-firing missiles.

'Bridge, CIC. *Shiloh* engaging hostile targets.' *Shiloh* was one of the four Aegis-class anti-aircraft vessels, operating with the *Nimitz*, assigned to protect the carrier's northern flank.

As the message was transmitted to the bridge an explosion lit the horizon, silhouetting the entire five-hundred-thirty-two-foot cruiser. There was no fire, no magazine explosion, and the sudden glare subsided.

'Got 'em,' Edgewater said. '*Shiloh* must've tagged the cruise missile – '

Edgewater was cut off by a boom that erupted just across the flight deck from their observation position. At the same time a loudspeaker blared, 'Collision warning, all hands, collision warning . . .'

The direct phone to CIC rang, but Clancy had no chance to answer it before a blinding flash and a wall of fire washed over the flight deck of the *Nimitz*, thick clouds of oily smoke obscuring everything, even the enclosed bridge.

'Damage report, all decks,' Edgewater shouted but from behind the heavy steel wall of the bridge. 'All decks – '

Another explosion, this time on the flight deck itself. One of the F-14s ready to launch had caught fire, the loudspeaker was calling for fire crews and crash crews on deck. . . .

The phone rang again. This time Clancy snatched it up.

'Bridge.'

'Bridge, this is Crash One. We had a cruise missile explode right off the port side. One elevator, one catapult, one CIWS and one Sea Sparrow launcher out. One F-14 caught by collateral damage, two casualties. No casualty reports from below decks yet.'

'Get me word soon as you do.' Clancy phoned to CIC as Edgewater picked himself off the deck. 'CIC, what's the story down there?'

'Soviet missiles all round us, Admiral,' Commander Jacobs, senior CIC officer, told him. 'Our close-in weapons systems got that last one just before it hit. *Shiloh* was blind after the missile that almost got *them* . . . No way they could knock it down . . . Stand by, sir . . ' And a moment later: 'Message from the *Bronstein*.'

The *Bronstein* was a thirty-year-old antisubmarine frigate positioned as the innermost antisubmarine warfare vessel astern of the *Nimitz* and carrying only a three-inch gun and a close-in Gatling gun for self-defence. 'She's still underway but listing badly and calling for help.'

'Better dispatch three HH-65 Dolphin helicopters with engineers and rescue gear to help,' Clancy said, glancing at the surface radar to assess the position of the rest of his escorts. 'We'll use all the Dolphins for rescue if necessary; if there are subs around, we're really in a world of hurt.'

'Aye, sir.'

'That was too close,' Edgewater said. 'With *Shiloh* out of commission we're going to be playing tag with more of those missiles pretty damn soon. Should we place *Hue City* up to the north to replace *Shiloh*?' The USS *Hue City*, the first US vessel to be named after a battle from the Vietnam War, was *Nimitz*'s westernmost Aegis-class ship.

'We've got no choice,' Clancy said. 'A blind Aegis cruiser is no help to us – '

'Admiral, message from CIC. Our Tomcats are reporting enemy aircraft one hundred fifty miles east of the *Ticonderoga*.' *Ticonderoga*, the most heavily armed vessel in the support group, was cruising the 'point' between the *Nimitz* and the *Arkhangel*. 'No report yet from *Ticonderoga*. The Tomcats are – '

'*Collision warning. All hands, collision warning.*'

Armstrong Space Station

Saint-Michael had just given the order for Ann to hit the switch that would send power from the backup batteries to the Skybolt ignition circuits when a huge explosion hit like a wrecking ball against the outer hull of the command module. Smoke billowed from a half-dozen spots in the debris-clogged module, quickly becoming so thick that the general could no longer see.

As Ann called to him, trying to find out if he was okay, he half-floated, half-crawled to the jury-rigged control panel and activated a switch that depressurized the command module into the connecting tunnel. Almost immediately the smoke was gone as the last bit of air left on the station rushed into space.

'I'm okay,' he said, moving back to the SBR control console. 'I had to depressurize the – '

Ann heard a barely audible intake of breath. 'Jason?'

'My . . . head. . .' He reached down to his chest-mounted spacesuit control panel and checked to be sure the pressurization switch was still on EMER.

'*Jason* . . . I'm coming across.'

'N-no.' The pain was a knife, but he thought he could fight it off without feeling as if he would lose consciousness. 'Stay there . . .' He refocused his eyes on the planter-box power junction. 'It looks like the SBR dropped off line. It's not tracking. I'll try to reset the auto-track circuit . . . Marty, what do you see out there?'

'One of the batteries on the keel exploded,' Schultz replied. 'Blew right off and hit the command module.'

Saint-Michael wedged a small flashlight against his helmet to steady its beam into the planter box. He fought to concentrate against the surge of pain. 'Damage?'

'Negative.'

He finally managed to find the wire bundle from the auto-track circuit to the main bus and unplugged it. He had no way of monitoring the circuit, no way of knowing if just unplugging the thing would reset it or if it had suffered any damage or was permanently burned open.

With unsteady fingers he plugged the wire bundle

connectors back in. 'All right, Ann,' he said. 'We'll give it one more try . . .'

USS *Nimitz*

Another blinding flash of light off the port side of the *Nimitz*, but this one was accompanied by a ball of flame that rolled up from the deck of the *Shiloh*. The heat and the concussion even from miles away could be felt by the whole *Nimitz* crew.

Edgewater, feeling the intense heat, understood it meant the death of *Shiloh*.

'Bring *Callaghan* north alongside her,' Clancy ordered, wiped the sweat from his forehead and stared for a moment at his smoke-blackened hand. 'Have the destroyer help transfer the wounded. Have them take over the anti-air duties until *Hue City* moves into position. Air Ops, bring Bravo flight north to help find those Soviet aircraft. Looks like *Arkhangel*'s getting into the act.' As Edgewater turned to issue the orders, Clancy picked up the phone to CIC, at the same time looking out through hazy oily smoke at the burning Aegis-class cruiser on the horizon. Another secondary explosion sent a mushroom of flames skyward. He waited until the sound of the explosion rolled across the *Nimitz* a few seconds later before speaking. 'What's the tally, Commander?' He almost didn't want to know.

'*Valley Forge*, *Vandergrift*, *Arkansas* and your old Persian Gulf flagship *Lasalle*,' Jacobs said, his voice flat. 'All badly damaged or destroyed. *Vandergrift* . . . was lost with all hands. Sorry, sir.'

Sorry . . . just *sorry* as hell . . . Would it have happened if the armchair boys hadn't held the tight leash on him for so long . . .?

Two Aegis cruisers dead . . . it was worse than Clancy

had thought. Without the anti-air coverage provided by the two cruisers, they were almost sure to suffer even heavier losses. In another hour – maybe minutes – the whole fleet could be destroyed . . .

'We've got casualties ourselves,' Jacobs forced himself to go on. 'There's a hundred injured and we've lost both waist catapults, one elevator and all our port-side guns and rockets. May have problems recovering planes on the landing strip: the first set of arresting cables is fouled up.' He paused. Then: 'Orders, sir?'

Orders? Any orders he gave at this point would be too little too late. But orders were what admirals gave. Good, bad, too late . . . okay, at least he would not make it easy for the Russians. He'd give them the fight they wanted . . . 'Call battle staff to the bridge,' Clancy said. 'We've got to get the wagons in a circle – '

The loudspeaker blared: 'Collision warning, all hands, collision warning.'

'Port side, Admiral,' Jacob's voice was blaring at him but seemed strangely remote, like a surreal movie dream sequence . . . *'Port side, heading right for us . . .'*

Clancy stared out the bridge through broken window panes. His rational head told him that he wouldn't be able to see the missile, travelling low and fast and just skimming the waves, but he stood there anyway, as though mesmerized.

'Hard port, flank speed,' Edgewater was shouting now. 'Signal the fleet that *Nimitz* is manoeuvring to port . . .'

But the missile kept coming, splitting the air at supersonic speed, seeking its target, and an end to its long, lethal journey.

Armstrong Space Station

Skybolt fired. Saint-Michael's body felt as though it had burst into flame. The pain was a weight, crushing him.

430

A flash of light in the command module changed to a yellow glow, as if the module were a piece of burning phosphorus. A high-pitched whine blared, louder and louder, undiminished by helmet or earphones. The module, exposed to open space now, should have felt icy cold, but instead it felt as if it were a boiling cauldron.

Through it all he thought he heard a pounding from somewhere beneath him, growing more insistent as he fought to stay conscious. Then a piece of some long-destroyed console broke free and slammed into the side of his helmet, deciding the fight for him. Everything – the pain, the heat, the sound – mercifully snapped off.

USS *Nimitz*

Back on *Nimitz* there was a flash of light, a split-second of pure whiteness like a powerful flashbulb going off. Clancy blinked. *Was that what death was like? A quick flash? Poof and out?*

A magnum explosion now roiled the sea into foam not a half mile from *Nimitz*'s scarred port side. The concussion from the blast hit the *Nimitz*, rattling the ninety-one-thousand-ton vessel like a rick of straw in the wind, but . . .

But that was all. Noise, rolling thunder, then dead silence.

'What the *hell* . . .?' The admiral picked up the phone again. 'Clancy here. What the hell happened out there? Did the missile self-destruct?'

'Damned if I know, Admiral,' Jacobs said. 'We got hit with a powerful energy surge just before that last explosion. Knocked a lot of our stuff into standby. Radars, comm, sonar – everything was bumped off the line . . . We just now got it back. Could someone have popped a nuke off up there?'

'Well, if it were a nuke I think we'd be on our way to the bottom or to the moon. Get a poll of the other ships – '

Off the bow about ten miles in the distance, he saw what appeared to be a perfectly straight arc of lightning slice across the dark sky. Its flash was like lightning, except Clancy had never seen a *straight* lightning bolt before . . .

This one terminated in a huge fireball with tongues of flames shooting out in all directions. The fireball flared to an enormous size, lighting the ocean like a second sun, then disappeared.

'There it goes again, Admiral,' Jacobs said from down below. 'Another glitch, we're resetting now – '

'Wait a minute . . . *wait* a minute . . .'

'There's another one, sir.' This from a damage-control seaman on the bridge, pointing back towards the north-west. 'They're all around us, like some damn crazy lightning storm.'

'That's not lightning,' Clancy said, beginning to understand. He stared up into the night sky, shaking his head slowly at the thin clouds and hazy stars. 'That, gentlemen, is our guardian angel . . .'

For the next few minutes the scene around the *Nimitz* was eerie, unearthly, near-supernatural. A straight light-ning bolt would flash, followed by a fireball near the sea. A few times the lightning would strike the sea, sending a geyser of steamy water a hundred or so feet into the air; then another bolt would strike and a fireball would erupt again.

As spectacular as the sight looked to the men aboard the *Nimitz* and her support vessels, it was even more impressive to the pilot of the lead Soviet Sukhoi-24 bomber, who was viewing it out of his windscreen. While trying to concentrate on radar indications, threat-warning receivers and strike-radar returns, his attention was being diverted outside to the strange flashes of light that kept dancing out of the sky. Several times a minute the clouds would erupt in a circle of light and then a streak of fire would lance down and hit the ocean. Almost each time there was an answering explosion – but apparently the explosions were not happening on any of the American ships. The whole phenomenon reminded him of a meteor shower, the most dazzling meteor shower he or anybody else had ever seen . . .

As the Soviet strike force approached the outermost American escorts, the flashes of light began to form eerie pillars of fire that seemed to block their path like a shimmering curtain pulled towards them. At the same time the intermittent threat-warnings from the American carrier-based fighters began to diminish. Had they managed to run under the F-14 Tomcats?

Suddenly the lead Sukhoi pilot's cockpit was filled with a flash of fire and light. He struggled for control of his bomber, watching with disbelieving eyes as the radar altimeter, which measured the distance between the belly of the bomber and the deadly waves below, dipped almost to zero.

The formation was in abrupt disarray. The curtain of flashing light was now surrounding them, and one of the twelve Sukhoi bombers had simply blown itself apart. The other bombers had broken ranks to recover from the shock of the explosion, and now, less than a hundred kilometres from the first escort ship and less than two hundred kilometres from the *Nimitz*, the strike package had virtually come apart: the precisely coordinated strike formation had suddenly turned into a gaggle of uncoordinated solo attackers. A few of them even climbed out and headed back the opposite way towards the *Arkhangel*, appearing to their fellow attackers like enemy aircraft and heightening the confusion.

* * *

The *Ticonderoga* got off a few shots at the bombers, but the strikers had been dispersed before they reached the Aegis ship's lethal range. The crew of *Ticonderoga* could only look on in awe as the mysterious curtain of light moved eastward into the night.

When the lightning bolts subsided, the air felt cleaner, colder, quieter. Even the smoke from the fires and exploding missiles seemed to dissipate. A few of the *Nimitz*'s escorts blew their horns in celebration – of what, they couldn't possibly be sure. Even Admiral Clancy felt like tooting a horn.

'Launch the Intruder tankers to refuel the fighters we sent after those cruise missiles,' Clancy told Air Ops. He spoke slowly, as if afraid to disturb the mystical air that seemed to surround the fleet and the bridge. 'We'll need to keep them airborne until we get the deck cleared off. As soon as possible get Kilo flight on deck to change over with the eastern patrols.' He turned to Edgewater. 'I want a battle-staff meeting and a full report on the status of the group in thirty minutes.'

He put a hand on the captain's shoulder and clasped it tightly. 'And get me a damned radio. I want to make a call to a certain damned space station that's been looking over us.'

The Kremlin, USSR

The sealed chamber in which the Stavka VKG, the Soviet Supreme High Command, was meeting was deadly quiet. The general secretary sat at the head of the triangular table, staring blankly.

'Strike,' he said. 'Destroy the *Nimitz*. Launch the nuclear AS-15 cruise missiles from Tashkent, or the SS-N-24 missiles from the attack submarines. Destroy the *Nimitz*.'

434

Then the whispers and muted voices began:

'The American laser could intercept anything . . .'

'What if the laser strikes the *Arkhangel* . . .?'

'The space station Armstrong can vector in American B-52s and can steer cruise missiles . . .'

'We must have time to evaluate this . . . this new development, sir,' Czilikov said, abruptly riding over the *sotto voce* murmurs of disbelief and dismay. 'We've no available ground-launch satellite interceptors, no space-planes . . . so we can't destroy the space station, not yet. And it holds the high ground' – in more ways than one, he thought – 'against the *Arkhangel* carrier group. We can't send a strike force without risking the *Arkhangel*.'

'I will *not* accept it,' the general secretary said, glaring at Czilikov. 'I will not retreat. I will not have this nation denied access of the seas – '

'Sir, we control Iran and the Persian Gulf – '

'Oh? Control it with *what*? And for how long? It is only a matter of time before the Americans move in again . . .'

'If we withdraw, the situation remains as it is. If we advance against the *Nimitz* without further dealing with the space station Armstrong, we risk everything.'

The general secretary sat back, stared at the shaken generals ranged about him. Once, he thought, there *had* been a man sitting at this table who'd not been afraid to take on a challenge. A man who, like himself, would not even consider accepting defeat. Was another like him out there somewhere? He had to hope and believe so.

Otherwise the Americans would have scored a victory far more important than the military one. They would have stolen the future . . .

Epilogue

'He wanted to be where he could see the bay,' Ann said. 'That's what he said in his will: "I want to rest where I can see the bay and touch the sky where my daughter lives."'

She bent down and placed the bouquet of flowers on the mound of earth near the low headstone that bore the name of Captain Matthew E. Page, United States Navy. She and Jason Saint-Michael stood on a low hill on the edge of the cemetery northeast of the Alameda Naval Station. The low clouds and mists obscured San Francisco and Oakland Bay Bridge far below them in the distance, but the clouds had seemed to part just before they reached the top of the Berkeley Hills, and the sun now shone brightly on the summit.

Saint-Michael gripped Ann's hand, released it, then moved off towards the edge of the hill and stared out into the vista below. She watched him as he moved away.

It was obvious that the mists rolling up from San Francisco Bay had invaded his nitrogen-tortured joints: he walked with a cane now in the cool, damp air. It was an old, gnarled shillelagh given to him in a private ceremony by the president. He had accepted it with a smile and a handshake, but he'd been quiet and moody ever since.

It had turned out to be his retirement ceremony as well, since the doctors had decided that it would be too risky for him to go into space again. With no field to command

and no interest in sitting behind a desk, he'd reluctantly agreed to the medical retirement that Space Command offered him. Come next month, he'd be a civilian again. Could he accept that?

Ann had hoped that getting him to California for Thanksgiving would somehow improve his mood, but it seemed to have the opposite effect. Her mother, Amanda, was supportive, but even her upmood didn't really help. He was about to leave her home when the unexpected call from Admiral Clancy came, requesting his presence at the Oakland-Alameda Naval Base, headquarters of the *Nimitz* carrier group, the next day.

They had stopped at her father's gravesite to lay a small bouquet on his headstone, but now she thought that it hadn't been a good idea at all. The reminder of Matthew Page's death only seemed to resurrect other painful memories of the past few months, driving, it seemed, a wedge deeper between them.

She moved close to him, linked her arm in his as they looked out at the swirling mists of San Francisco Bay.

'Strange in a way,' he said, 'but I miss that station. I mean, what is it anyway? Computers, instrument panel – nuts and bolts, really. But I miss the damn thing. You wouldn't believe how I miss it.' He looked at her, thinking of her life-saving skill and the fierce dedication she'd shown towards Skybolt. 'I take that back . . . Of course, you would know.'

There was no good answer to that. What she said was, 'Jason, why did you agree to come here?'

'I thought I should say goodbye to your father . . . When will you be going back?'

'Back?'

'To the station.'

'Never,' she said.

'*Never?* Why?'

437

'Because that part of my life . . .' She didn't add, *his life*, 'is over. I would never do anything to hurt you.'

'But what about your career? That's your laser device up there. That's *yours*. You can't just – '

'I seem to remember this guy, a cocky sonofabitch Space Command general who said it wasn't *my* laser. You know something? He was right. You want to know something else? I don't want it anymore. Don't look at me that way. I just don't want anything more to do with it. I built that laser as a defensive device, Jason. Not an offensive one.'

'So what were we supposed to do? Let those Elektron spaceplanes use us for target practice?'

'No, of course not. We had no choice – it was them or us. But Space Command's already rebuilt most of Armstrong and placed it in the same orbit over the Arabian Sea that you put it in. They're using it to shadow the *Arkhangel* group – '

'I still don't see – '

'If Skybolt is supposed to be a defensive weapon, protecting us against strategic nuclear weapons, what's Silver Tower still doing over the Arabian Sea?'

He paused for a moment – 'Surveillance. It's still by far the best surveillance platform we've got. And it can help protect the fleet from a sneak cruise-missile attack . . .'

'Or fighter attack? Bomber attack?'

'Sure . . .'

'How about hitting the *Arkhangel* direct? I wonder what Skybolt would do against a carrier? Blow up a few planes on its decks? Set off a weapons magazine? Do some serious damage to its electronics? Maybe even kill a few sailors on deck? Why not go one better? You don't have to be a think-tank guru to come up with the idea. Just a sincere dedicated chief of staff, secretary of defence – or president? The Russians are going to have the *Brezhnev* leave the Persian Gulf and sail to South Yemen for resupply. They say that it will rejoin with the *Arkhangel* and form a new, stronger battle group to hit the *Nimitz* again. So why isn't it logical we attack the *Brezhnev*? Attack it when it gets to port? But better still, why don't we run our laser over the *Arkhangel*'s home port of Vladivostok? Or Murmansk? Or Leningrad? Or Moscow?'

'That's going pretty far, Ann . . .'

'Maybe, but are you so sure? You used to work on Space Command planning staffs. What if you now had the weapons with the destructive capability of Silver Tower and Skybolt? Can you really say you'd never consider using them to stop a war before it starts? Preemptive strike? Surgical strike? Or just good old sabre-rattling from seven hundred miles in space?'

'I don't believe we'd ever do that . . .'

'I wish you would convince me. But you know as well as I, too much success, like Skybolt has had now, can breed a need for more and more . . . I wanted to develop it for defensive reasons only. But now . . .'

He didn't argue with her, but turned away and stared at the huge ridgelines of fog rolling across the bay. They stood together quietly for a long time, until she noticed him shifting his weight from one leg to the other.

'We should leave,' she said. He followed her back to the car.

Rush-hour traffic had thinned as they made their way down Mount Diablo Boulevard to the Minitz Freeway and on into the Oakland-Alameda Naval Base. When they reached the gate and showed their IDs, the shore patrolman pointed towards a waiting staff car parked at the reception area.

'Admiral Clancy is waiting for you, General. His driver will take you and Dr Page.'

Puzzled, Saint-Michael returned the SP's salute, turned

across traffic into the parking lot and parked beside the large navy-grey sedan. The driver saluted and held the doors open for them.

'All this for a simple debriefing?' Ann said, peering out the darkened windows. She could see very little in the fog and haze surrounding the base. 'We're not heading for carrier group headquarters, either. Driver, where are we going?'

'Slip seventeen, ma'am.'

'But we *are* going to meet Admiral Clancy . . .?' Saint-Michael said.

'Yes sir. He's waiting.'

Ann shrugged. 'The boonies. We may as well sit back; it'll be a long ride.'

The base was not very large, but the warehouses, docks, and buildings that they were forced to weave among made the trip seem endless. After ten minutes they pulled alongside a long, dark drydock area in front of a maintenance enclosure. The drydock was filled with oil-clogged water and a bit of debris, but it was still relatively fresh-looking water; the drydock basin had only recently been filled with seawater. The enclosure was contained on all sides, but by the looks of the four-inch-diameter hawsers leading to the diesel, ship-moving 'mules' on the pier, the vessel inside was huge.

The driver stopped at the foot of a security tower located a hundred yards from the maintenance enclosure, opened the door for his two passengers, saluted, then quickly departed.

'This is getting *very* strange,' Saint-Michael said. 'I wonder what – '

Suddenly, a horn began to sound from loudspeakers on the maintenance enclosure. The two rail-mounted mules outside the enclosure were started, and the front doors of the enclosure began to slide open.

'I think we're about to find out.'

When the doors were fully opened the mules took up the slack on the hawsers, and with clouds of diesel exhaust billowing skyward, the tractors began to pull on the vessel hidden inside. It had only been pulled a few feet out of the building when Ann suddenly grabbed his arm.

'It's the *California*,' she said. 'Number thirty-six. They brought the *California* back to Oakland.' But as it was gently pulled out of its enclosure it was obvious it was not the same *California*.

'I hardly recognize her. Look – I'm not sure but I think those are twin missile-launch rails on the nose.'

'And two RAM missile-launchers on the forecastle,' he said. 'Also cannons everywhere . . . but what the hell is *that*?'

The *California* was a bit more than halfway outside when they both gaped at a huge new structure just behind the midships masts. Four massive legs dozens of feet high and several feet wide sprawled across the entire aft section of the ship; it appeared the battleship had had to be lengthened a few feet in the stern just to accommodate the huge legs.

Two RAM missile launchers were mounted between the legs to provide defensive cover for the rear quadrant of the ship, but the most impressive new feature was the device on top of the pedestal: a huge elongated dish at least forty feet wide and fifty feet long, arranged so that the long part of the dish was parallel to the ship's beam. The dish had two sections of steel folded down on top of it, hinged on the sides and supported by hydraulic pistons.

'What the hell . . . I've never seen anything like that,' Saint-Michael said. 'It looks like some kind of wing, but on a navy warship . . .?'

The *California* was towed clear of the enclosure and the maintenance and security towers surrounding it, then pulled to a halt by two mules in the rear. A gangway was set in place with the familiar 'USS CALIFORNIA' on the canvas sides, but its vessel designation no longer read 'CGN-36'; it now read 'DWRS-36.'

'Well, stop gawking and get up here,' they heard from the ship. They looked up the newly painted side of the *California* and saw Admiral Clancy waving them towards the gangway. According to naval etiquette, they saluted the colours aft, then the officer of the deck, and then hurried up the gangplank and were met by the admiral.

'Permission to come aboard, Admiral,' Saint-Michael said, saluting him. Clancy returned the salute.

'Get your butts up here. I've been waiting all day to show you this.'

They had to step lively to keep up with Clancy, who rushed up to the bridge and then around the catwalk facing aft across the huge device sprawled over the *California*'s fantail.

'All right, all right, Admiral,' Saint-Michael said as they finally stopped and stared out over the top of the curved stack of dishlike plates mounted on the ship. 'What is all this?'

'The future, Jason.' Clancy turned to a lieutenant commander waiting behind them. 'Hit it, Commander.'

'Aye, sir.' A few moments later a loudspeaker blared, 'Attention on deck. Stand by to deploy array panels.'

A deep-throated rumbling began on the pedestal below them, and suddenly the curved panels on top of the pedestal began to move, unfolding like giant flower petals. In less than a minute they had dropped into place. The device was now an oblong dish one hundred feet long and forty feet wide at its broadest point, deeply curved in the centre. At the precise centre was a receiver horn. On the face of the dish was painted 'USS CALIFORNIA'. Then the dish began slowly to incline and swivel until it was pointing almost directly south, its rim almost touching the two pedestal legs supporting it.

'Not a bad piece of work, right, Jas?'

'Not bad, Admiral, but what *is* it?'

'You haven't figured it out?' He gestured at the dish with a sweeping wave of his hand. 'This, sir, is my new California-class SBR fleet command and control ship. And *that* is my space-based radar data transreceiver.'

'That's an SBR receiver? Amazing . . .'

'Dedicated one hundred per cent to sending and receiving SBR data signals,' Clancy said. 'Eleven thousand square feet of antenna, over one hundred ten tons – the largest antenna afloat. Shielded and hardened against electromagnetic pulses and designed to operate even in a nuclear environment. But that's not the best part.'

Again Ann and Saint-Michael had to scramble to follow Clancy as he led them down through a series of hatches, past crewmen standing at attention along the bulkheads, and into a circular room labelled 'CIC'.

'The *California*'s new combat information centre.' The admiral motioned towards the centre of the circle, where a raised platform, fifteen feet in diameter and curved like a shallow bowl, was under construction. 'It's not quite finished but you'll get the idea. We call it the "DANCE floor" – but you don't dance on it.'

He led them over to the platform so they could examine it. '"DANCE" stands for Digital Advanced Near-space Communications Equipment. A mouthful, I grant you. It's a twenty-first-century version of the old craps-table situation-boards they used to have on command ships, the ones with the operators with long croupier sticks moving little ship models around. DANCE floor is actually a horizontal screen that displays SBR data in three dimensions. With it a fleet commander can get an instant three-dimensional map of the area around his fleet for thousands of miles. Images are put on the screen by laser projectors, so ships and their datablocks appear to be hovering in midair in perfect relationship to the fleet. When SBR data aren't available the images can be frozen or the computer can predict where the ships or aircraft would be and update the board accordingly. We can also integrate shipborne radar and other satellite sensor data into the DANCE floor for real-time mapping . . . I think that station of yours, and its gear, got to me. You and Ann saved thousands of lives out there. When I realized none of my ships had the capability to fully utilize SBR signals, well, I decided to build one. The navy and even the Joint Chiefs were very supportive. What the hell choice did they have? The *California*'s new combat information centre should be finished in a month,' Clancy said, moving out of CIC and back up on deck. 'One month after that she'll be ready for her first shakedown cruise.' They reached the port rail near the gangway and stopped to watch as the huge SBR receiver-antenna was being folded up again.

'I wish you luck, Admiral,' Saint-Michael said. 'She's a beauty. Silver Tower should be operational in two months and as long as the *Arkhangel* and the *Brezhnev* stay in the Middle East, the station will be there – '

'Not so fast, Jas. You still don't get it. I'm going to need someone special aboard *California*. Someone who has command experience and knows Armstrong's SBR system. I can think of only one man who fits the bill.'

'You want *me*?'

'Hell, yes, I want you. As commander of the new SBR section you'll oversee all operations, fleet integration and training for the new system. We'll knock the stuffy old US Navy kicking and screaming into the twenty-first century, Jas.'

Just then the loudspeaker clicked on. 'Attention on deck. Admiral Clancy to the bridge. Admiral Clancy to the bridge.'

'Got to go, Jas. I need your answer. Soonest. You've got to look over your new command and get ready for your new trainees in one month. Ann, you're a wonder

'. . . Please give my love to your mother.' He turned and trotted down the deck.

'He's a little bit crazy,' Ann said, smiling. 'Well, do you think you could spend a few months at sea with a fifty-year-old kid?'

'Depends.'

'On?'

'Us.' He took her hand in his. 'I'd love to go, you know that. But I want you, I want us to be together on this. We deserve it. You could go back to the station and – '

'No.'

'Ann, listen. Leaving Space Command won't change anything. If they have plans to turn that station into an armed fort and Skybolt into an offensive as well as defensive weapon, just leaving won't change that. It's a cliché, okay, but you've got to work within the system, not outside it if you're going to accomplish anything . . .'

'What could I do? I wouldn't have any effect on the big brass's decisions – '

'Maybe not right away, but you could sure as hell speak up. And they'd have to give some weight to your opinions . . . After all, not all the bugs in the laser have been worked out yet. You're still probably the only one around who really knows how Skybolt works . . . Besides, we could keep an eye on each other if you went back to the station. And I'd know Silver Tower was being well taken care of.'

She moved closer to him. 'I'd like to take care of *you*.'

'No problem from me. You figure Clancy could spare me for a few days? We could take off, Acapulco maybe, the Bahamas, Lake Tahoe – '

'Hey, General . . . I've been in space. Can't we just – '

'We can,' he said, took hold of her arm and signalled to their driver.

Dr Ann Page was not coy. 'Wherever we're going, hurry up.'

Saint-Michael leaned forward, instructed the driver, and settled back into her waiting arms.

Storming Heaven

Dale Brown

The USA is under siege. With chilling ruthlessness terrorist Henri Cazaux has demonstrated the vulnerability of the USA's air defences by using large commercial aircraft to drop bombs on unsuspecting major airports. When he hits San Francisco Airport the destruction of life and property is enormous. The national panic that ensues reaches all the way to the White House.

Only one man can end the chaos: Rear Admiral Ian Hardcastle. Charged by the President with re-establishing security in the skies, Hardcastle must take drastic action to control the emergency – and quickly. But then Cazaux sets his sights on the biggest target of all – the nation's capital . . .

Storming Heaven is ex-pilot Dale Brown's most relentlessly action-packed novel yet, filled with the spectacular flying scenes, technological detail and astonishing realism that have won him his place at the leading edge of modern military thriller writing.

'Aviation ace Dale Brown has firmly established his high-tech credentials in seven bestselling aviation thrillers – *Storming Heaven*, his new, edge-of-the-cockpit novel, should rocket him out to the Van Allen belt.'
New York Daily News

'Suspenseful flying scenes – high drama in the skies.'
Today

'Cazaux is a fascinating monster; *Storming Heaven* is an explosive success.'
Booklist

ISBN 0 00 649357 2